KING JOHN
&
HENRY VIII

The RSC Shakespeare

Edited by Jonathan Bate and Eric Rasmussen

Chief Associate Editors: Jan Sewell and Will Sharpe

Associate Editors: Trey Jansen, Eleanor Lowe, Lucy Munro,
Dee Anna Phares, Héloïse Sénéchal

King John & Henry VIII

Textual editing: Eleanor Lowe and Eric Rasmussen

Introduction and "Shakespeare's Career in the Theater": Jonathan Bate

Commentary: Eleanor Lowe and Héloïse Sénéchal

Scene-by-Scene Analyses: Jan Sewell

In Performance: Mark Taylor (*King John*), Jan Sewell (*Henry VIII*)

The Director's Cut (interviews by Jan Sewell and Kevin Wright):
Gregory Doran, Josie Rourke, and Gregory Thompson

The RSC Shakespeare

William Shakespeare

KING JOHN & HENRY VIII

Edited by Jonathan Bate and Eric Rasmussen

Introduction by Jonathan Bate

Modern Library
New York

CONTENTS

Introduction   **vii**
    King John   vii
    Henry VIII   xiii

About the Text   **xx**

The Life and Death of King John   **1**

Key Facts: *King John*   **3**

Textual Notes   **101**

Scene-by-Scene Analysis   **103**

***King John* in Performance: The RSC and Beyond**   **119**
    Four Centuries of *King John:* An Overview   119
    At the RSC   130
    The Director's Cut: Interviews with Gregory Doran
        and Josie Rourke   142

The Famous History of the Life of King Henry the Eighth   **157**

Key Facts: *Henry VIII*   **159**

Textual Notes   **276**

Scene-by-Scene Analysis   **278**

***Henry VIII* in Performance: The RSC and Beyond**   **294**
    Four Centuries of *Henry VIII:* An Overview   294
    At the RSC   306
    The Director's Cut: Interviews with Gregory Doran
        and Gregory Thompson   320

Shakespeare's Career in the Theater   **340**
    Beginnings   340
    Playhouses   342

The Ensemble at Work   346
The King's Man   351

Shakespeare's Works: A Chronology   **354**

**Kings and Queens of England: From the History Plays
  to Shakespeare's Lifetime**   **357**

King John Family Tree   **359**

The History Behind the Histories: A Chronology   **360**

**Further Reading and Viewing: *King John*
  and *Henry VIII***   **365**

References: *King John* and *Henry VIII*   **370**

Acknowledgments and Picture Credits   **377**

INTRODUCTION TO TWO HISTORY PLAYS: *KING JOHN* AND *HENRY VIII*

Shakespeare dramatized the history of pre-Tudor England in two epic tetralogies, sweeping from the reign of King Richard II in the last years of the 1300s to the defeat of Richard III by the future Henry VII, first of the Tudor monarchs, at the battle of Bosworth Field in 1485. But he also wrote (or in one case cowrote) two stand-alone English histories: *The Life and Death of King John* and *The Famous History of the Life of King Henry the Eighth*, otherwise known as *All Is True*. Though the former is a solo-authored Elizabethan play and the latter a collaborative Jacobean one—it was cowritten with John Fletcher in 1613, at the very end of Shakespeare's career—they make an exceptionally interesting pair, since both are deeply concerned with courtly political maneuvering in the context of the heated religious debates about Catholicism and Protestantism, which constituted the great fissure within early modern English and European society and statecraft.

KING JOHN

During April 1811 Jane Austen was staying in London with her brother Henry. In a letter home to her sister Cassandra, she complained of "a very unlucky change of the Play for this very night—Hamlet instead of King John—and we are to go on Monday to Macbeth instead, but it is a disappointment to us both." Two centuries on, we are likely to be astonished that so discerning a woman as Jane Austen would rather have seen *King John* than *Hamlet* or *Macbeth*. There is, however, a simple explanation: Austen was a seasoned admirer of Sarah Siddons, the greatest actress of the age, one of whose most celebrated roles was that of the impassioned Lady

Constance, as rewarding a female role as any in the whole corpus of Shakespeare's English history plays.

It was not for the wronged mother Constance alone that *King John* was held in high regard in the nineteenth century. The Victorians, with their penchant for sentiment, delighted in the pathos of the boy Arthur persuading Hubert not to burn out his eyes with hot irons. But the largest role, bigger than that of the vacillating king who gives the play its title, is that of the Bastard, Philip Falconbridge. The German Romantic critic A. W. Schlegel was compelled by this figure: "He ridicules the secret springs of politics, without disapproving of them, for he owns that he is endeavouring to make his fortune by similar means, and wishes rather to belong to the deceivers than the deceived, for in his view of the world there is no other choice." The Bastard—a dramatic invention, not a real historical figure—is a key character in Shakespeare's development of the self-serving type that reaches its apogee with Iago in *Othello* and Edmund in *King Lear*. Yet he is the most sympathetic male adult in the drama. He has wit and wisdom as well as the desire for advancement. The rest are mere politicians. In its anatomy of the mechanisms of their intrigue, *King John* is one of Shakespeare's most modern plays. Set in a feudal world where monarchs were supposed to be God's representatives on earth, it exposes power as a "commodity" for which men are in hungry competition.

The Bastard is the only character in whom the audience have confidence because he has confidence in us. Soliloquies offer access to his thought processes and self-conscious theatricality allows the spectators to share his space. "Your royal presences be ruled by me," he says to two kings at once, and we enjoy his presumption because he makes us part of the story: his lines about the citizens of Angiers, watching from the "battlements" of the stage gallery are equally applicable to the paying crowd "in a theatre, whence they gape and point / At your industrious scenes and acts of death."

"Speak, citizens, for England," says the King of France to the townsmen of Angiers as it is besieged by rival armies from opposite sides of the English Channel. Of all Shakespeare's history plays, *King John* is the one that most explicitly asks what it might mean to speak for England. It explores questions about legitimacy and inheritance that were of concern to all propertied families in Tudor England, but of monumental significance to the monarchy—especially at a time when an aged childless queen was sitting on the throne. In the much better known play of *King Lear*, the legitimate son Edgar is the virtuous one and the illegitimate Edmund is the villain. *King John* imagines a more challenging possibility: suppose that a great king dies and that his bravest, most honest and most intelligent son is an illegitimate one. In such a circumstance, inheritance on the basis of merit is not possible: if a bastard were to ascend the throne, the legitimacy of the entire monarchical system would be called into question. The seamless interdependence of patrilineal state, law, church, and family would begin to unravel.

Richard I, the Lionheart, the exemplary king, has died without a legitimate son; the next brother in line (Geoffrey) is also dead. Who should succeed: the next brother down (John) or the son of the first brother (Arthur)? As if this were not difficult enough, the question of who speaks for England is intertwined with other debates about legitimacy. What is the geographic limit of England's domain—does England retain the right to rule parts of France? And who should speak for England's religion? This thorny issue is focused on the appointment of a new Archbishop of Canterbury to head the English church. Does the Pope have the right to impose his candidate or should the English retain a voice in their own ecclesiastical affairs? Is there a point at which the monarchy may legitimately reject the will of the papacy? For a Tudor audience, a confrontation of this sort was bound to reverberate with Henry VIII's disputed divorce and the break from Rome in the 1530s.

In Protestant ideology, King John was a hero because he stood up against papal tyranny. He was seen as a kind of Henry VIII before his time. In the mid-sixteenth century, the Protestant zealot John Bale wrote a court drama on these lines, while the text of Shakespeare's probable primary source, the anonymous two-part play *The Troublesome Reign of King John* (published in 1591), is awash with raw anti-Catholic propaganda. Shakespeare's own play has often been read as testimony of his Protestant allegiance: in the 1730s, at a time of anxieties about a potential Jacobite uprising, an adaptation of it was performed in London with the unambiguous title *Papal Tyranny in the Reign of King John.* Yet the authentic Shakespeare is profoundly ambiguous. There is a clear vein of anti-Catholicism in John's "no Italian priest / Shall tithe or toll in our dominions," together with the way in which the papal legate Cardinal Pandulph is a scheming politician who speaks by indirections and equivocation ("But thou dost swear only to be forsworn, / And most forsworn, to keep what thou dost swear"). At the same time John is accusingly addressed as "The borrowed majesty of England" and his tergiversation hardly makes him a model ruler.

Back in the first scene, before there is any resolution to all the difficult questions of succession and faith, power and proprietorship, a sheriff enters. His presence signals the jurisdiction of the shires, the "country" as opposed to the "court" interest. The question of which of two brothers will inherit a parcel of land in the shires parallels that of which of Richard Coeur-de-lion's brothers, John or Geoffrey (through Arthur), will inherit the nation as a whole. Again, for the original audience in the 1590s, an encounter set in the distant thirteenth century would have echoed with debates in their own time, where it was not unknown for a Member of Parliament to give voice in the House of Commons to words that one might have expected to belong to the queen alone: "I speak for all England." In many quarters, there was a strongly held view that "England" was not synonymous with the English queen and her court based in and around London. Though the Tudor monarchs had tried to unify the nation by establishing a network of legal representatives across the shires, the "country" gentry as well as the great barons of the north and west guarded their autonomy fiercely.

The Bastard announces himself as a gentleman born in Northamptonshire; he is "A good blunt fellow," that is to say a plain-speaking English countryman; later, he appeals to St. George, the patron saint of England. His, then, is the voice of Shakespeare's own place of origin, the Midlands, deep England. He is given a choice: to inherit the Falconbridge estates or take his "chance" and assume the name, though not the patrimony, of the royal father who sired him out of wedlock.

The norm in the English gentry was for the older son to inherit the land and the younger to become mobile, to go to London and find a career in the law, the clergy, the army, the diplomatic corps, or possibly even the entertainment business. Settled legitimacy was pitched against the life of the adventurer. By accepting his illegitimacy and renouncing the land he is actually entitled to (because it was the mother's adultery, not the father's, he is not forcibly disinherited in the manner of Edmund in *King Lear*), the Bastard takes the route that was usually that of the younger brother. Shakespeare did the same when he left Stratford-upon-Avon.

The Bastard's origin in middle England is further stressed by the arrival of Lady Falconbridge and James Gurney, wearing riding-robes that signify the journey from country to court. The Bastard then describes his half-brother as "Colbrand the Giant, that same mighty man." Colbrand was a Danish invader who was defeated in single combat by Guy of Warwick—a legendary figure who was immensely popular in chapbook, ballad, and drama. If Robert Falconbridge is symbolically Colbrand, then Philip the Bastard is symbolically Guy, a Warwickshire folk hero. Perhaps he is even a version of Robin Hood, with the Sheriff of Northampton standing in for his colleague from Nottingham. Robin Hood himself, the most famous folk hero from the reign of John, cannot be mentioned because his name would immediately turn the king into a villain, which Shakespeare did not want to do at the beginning of the play, both because he wanted to keep open the question of the relative legitimacy of the claims of John and Arthur and because he was working in that tradition of chronicle and drama in which King John was a proto-Protestant hero because of his refusal to allow the Pope's nominee, Stephen Langton, to become Archbishop of Canterbury.

When the Pope excommunicates the English king and gives permission—indeed promise of canonization—to anyone who conspires to kill him, the parallels with contemporary England, where the Pope had delivered the same sentence upon Queen Elizabeth, are impossible to ignore. So too with the way in which the fickle French swing one way and then the other ("O, foul revolt of French inconstancy!" exclaims Queen Elinor): in the sixteenth century, France was racked by religiously motivated civil wars and it was well nigh impossible to guess whether the state would end up with a Catholic or a Protestant on the throne. "The grappling vigour and rough frown of war" dominates the action of this play, just as wars of religion and dominion in the Netherlands, Ireland and elsewhere impinged upon the lives of Shakespeare's audience. Like Thersites in *Troilus and Cressida*, though without the vicious streak, the Bastard anatomizes the resulting chaos of alliances and divisions: "Mad world, mad kings, mad composition!"

The Bastard stands in for Guy of Warwick, who stands in for Robin Hood of old England. It was Robin who maintained the values of good King Richard at home, while the latter was fighting his crusade in the Middle East ("Richard that robbed the lion of his heart / And fought the holy wars in Palestine"). As the play progresses, the Bastard's role shifts to that of stand-in for the dead Coeur-de-lion himself. He ends up fighting the war on John's behalf and at one point comes within a whisker of ascending the throne. He speaks for England in the closing lines:

> This England never did, nor never shall,
> Lie at the proud foot of a conqueror,
> But when it first did help to wound itself.
> . . .
> . . . Nought shall make us rue,
> If England to itself do rest but true.

The world-weary voice is that of a dramatist who in his *Henry VI* plays has shown the bloody consequences of England turning against itself.

Tragedies and history plays had a convention that the final lines were spoken by the person left in charge of the nation, so we may assume that the Bastard effectively takes on the role of regent during Prince Henry's minority. Historically, Henry III was ten years old when he came to the throne; in the play, he calls himself a cygnet and is clearly a boy actor (the part could neatly be doubled with that of the dead Arthur).

The Bastard is the conscience of the nation, the symbolic heir of Lionheart, the voice of the shires. But he is also an adventurer, the embodiment of illegitimacy, a new man, an individualist who foreshadows the more sinister figure of Edmund in *Lear*: "I am I, howe'er

I was begot." Improviser, player, speaker of soliloquies, both inside and outside history, could he be the voice not only of Guy but also of William of Warwickshire? Who speaks for deep England? A bastard. An entrepreneur. A player. A man who idealizes the shires even as he leaves them to enter the theater, the market, the emergent empire. Who speaks? A Shakespeare.

HENRY VIII

Henry VIII, coauthored with John Fletcher, is the only English history play of the second half of Shakespeare's career, when his men were under the patronage of King James I. Written at a time of nostalgia for the age of Queen Elizabeth, the action comes to a climax when a doll representing the newborn future queen is brought on stage, her reign as a "maiden phoenix" is predicted, and her chosen successor, King James, is praised:

> This royal infant—heaven still move about her—
> Though in her cradle, yet now promises
> Upon this land a thousand thousand blessings,
> Which time shall bring to ripeness: she shall be—
> But few now living can behold that goodness—
> A pattern to all princes living with her,
> And all that shall succeed . . .

"A pattern to all princes," she is later described as one who "shall make it holiday": such language suggests how the English Protestant cult of the Virgin Queen derived some of its power from the way in which it reworked the Roman Catholic cult of the Virgin Mary.

The speech is spoken by the princess's godfather, Thomas Cranmer, famous as the architect of the English Reformation and a martyr burnt to death in the reign of bloody Queen Mary: the linking of the infant Elizabeth to Protestant ideology could not be more strongly expressed. Though the final scene was written by Fletcher, Cranmer's subsequent image of a "cedar" tree as a representation of the royal genealogical line replicates a prophecy spoken by the god Jupiter in Shakespeare's *Cymbeline*. Events in *Henry VIII* do not, however, seem to have been driven by that sense of destiny, of a providential design leading to the establishment of a new dynasty, which shaped Shakespeare's earlier chronicle plays. The emphasis is rather on the vicissitudes of court life. The play's structure is built on an apparently arbitrary pattern of rises and falls: Buckingham falls, Anne Bullen rises, Wolsey rises, Katherine falls, Wolsey falls, Cranmer rises. Again, as Wolsey goes down, Thomas Cromwell comes up: Anne Bullen is "the weight" on this pulley of fortune. There is some skilled compression of history for the sake of dramatic effect: in the play, the fall of Cardinal Wolsey and the triple elevation of Thomas More, Thomas Cranmer, and Anne Bullen effectively work as a single event, whereas in reality these three came to eminence in, respectively, 1529, 1532, and 1533. Wolsey actually died in 1530, three years before the coronation of Anne as Henry's second queen.

Though grounded in history, the pattern of ascent and descent is analogous to that of romance, with its highs and lows, its voyages and reunions, things lost and found. It was originally staged under the title *All Is True*, a wittily ironic pointer to its romance-matter, such as Queen Katherine's divine vision, which can hardly be literally true. Shakespeare and Fletcher may have chosen to infuse their play with the spirit of romance, so far from the tough world of the Richard and the other Henry plays, in order to create a safety zone that was necessary because *Henry VIII* dramatizes the still contentious issue over which England broke from the Church of Rome, the replacement of Queen Katherine with Anne Bullen. The crux of the action is the fall of Wolsey, mediator between the king and the Pope. It becomes the occasion not to pass judgment on the rights and wrongs of the Reformation, but for a generalized reflection on the fickleness of fortune and the fruitlessness of hanging "on princes' favours." *Henry VIII* was a great favorite on the eighteenth- and nineteenth-century stage. That was partly because of the opportunity for spectacle provided by the coronation and the play's other scenes of procession and court business. But it was also because of the opportunity given to actors by Wolsey's great set piece:

> Farewell? A long farewell to all my greatness.
> This is the state of man: today he puts forth

The tender leaves of hopes: tomorrow blossoms,
And bears his blushing honours thick upon him:
The third day comes a frost, a killing frost,
And when he thinks, good easy man, full surely
His greatness is a-ripening, nips his root,
And then he falls, as I do.

Shakespeare's Elizabethan history plays were dominated by wars, either civil or on French soil, and battles for succession to the crown. They were written in times of war when the question of the succession to Elizabeth was deeply troubling to the nation. *Henry VIII*, by contrast, was written after several years of peace. Indeed, King James regarded himself as an international peacemaker. Furthermore, he was a married king, so there was no anxiety about the succession, despite the nation's sorrow at the premature death of his eldest son, Prince Henry, in November 1612. The wedding of the king's daughter, Princess Elizabeth, to Frederick the Elector Palatine, the most prominent Protestant ruler in continental Europe, was postponed until February 1613 so as not to be overshadowed by the funeral. *Henry VIII*, a play with both a royal death and a royal wedding, was written in the next few months.

Despite the Protestant match for the princess, there were anxieties about a possible revival of Roman Catholicism: the religious allegiance of James's queen was a matter of public interest about which rumors circulated. And there was considerable concern over court favorites, as different factions jostled for power. Ever since the spectacular entrance procession of King James into London at the beginning of his reign, the new court had displayed its power through pageantry. The theater played a key role here. The king, his family, and his courtiers participated actively in masques, and, in their new capacity as the King's Men, Shakespeare and his fellows were frequently called upon to play at court. All these concerns are woven into the fabric of *Henry VIII*, making it a distinctively Jacobean drama.

Kingly authority is asserted by pageantry, but also by the ruthless axing of counselors who have served their purpose. Buckingham says of York that "No man's pie is freed / From his ambitious finger," a sentiment that could apply to any one of the play's thrusting courtiers as they jostle for the top seat at the table of power. A stage direction in the third act is typical of both the world of the drama and the environment that Shakespeare would have experienced when he took his men to play at court: "*Exit King, frowning upon the Cardinal, the nobles throng after him, smiling and whispering.*"

The question inevitably raised is whether or not the personal authority of the monarch is absolute. In order to please the courtly audience it was necessary for Shakespeare and Fletcher to follow a broadly pro-Henry line, but there do seem to be moments when a critique of the conscience of the king is built into the action. Specifically, a series of puns on words such as "prick" and "rule" imply that his policy is being determined by his sex drive as much as his desire to serve and shape his nation. The king clearly suffers a failure of "temperance," a key Protestant virtue, in relation to Anne. And at the most elementary structural level, there is a tension between the representation of the two queens and the state ideology of Protestantism. Katherine of Aragon is the Catholic queen who becomes a near-saint granted a divine vision, while Anne, the trigger for the Reformation, is given a very small part and serves primarily as an object of sexual desire. Equally, although the chancellorship of Sir Thomas More only figures briefly in the play, there is a clear allusion to his subsequent martyrdom for the Catholic cause:

That's somewhat sudden,
But he's a learnèd man. May he continue
Long in his highness' favour, and do justice
For truth's sake and his conscience, that his bones,
When he has run his course and sleeps in blessings,
May have a tomb of orphans' tears wept on him.

Shakespeare's late plays share a fascination with the very different directions in which poetic language may lead. Elaborate rhetoric and honeyed words reveal how the verbal arts are tools for preferment and power. Words are both baits for advancement and means of getting off the hook: "may it like your grace / To let my tongue excuse all." On other occasions, there is a plangent poetry of withdrawal, of retirement from the courtly fray. How is one to achieve inner peace in this world of political turmoil? The courtiers have varying degrees of success in their attempts to learn the Senecan art of patience, of using soliloquy and self-examination as a means of coming to terms with the buffets of political fortune. For Queen Katherine, uniquely, there is a moment of transcendence and divine vision. But it is only a moment, ending with a dissolution analogous to that of Prospero's masque in *The Tempest:* "Spirits of peace, where are ye? Are ye all gone, / And leave me here in wretchedness behind ye?"

The voice that is absent from *Henry VIII* is the one that was so forceful in *Henry IV* and *Henry V:* the commoners, whose plain prose pricks the bubble of pretentious courtly language. As in *The Winter's Tale*, gentlemen are brought on stage in the role of witnesses. But there are no equivalents to *The Winter's Tale*'s lower-class characters of shepherd and clown. The only prose intervention belongs to a porter in the final act, who hears the hubbub of young gallants outside the closed door of the council chambers. "These are the youths that thunder at a playhouse, and fight for bitten apples," he remarks, perhaps implying that of the three audiences for whom Shakespeare was writing—the court, the select company of the indoor Blackfriars theater, and the mass public who paid a penny to stand in the yard of the Globe—it is the first two who now interest him more. Insofar as the play does explore the consciousness of the low born, it is when a commoner such as Cromwell and above all Wolsey—son of a provincial butcher—becomes a "great" man, provoking the enmity of the dukes and earls born to ermine. At some level, Shakespeare— son of a provincial glover who had close links with butcher's business—is reflecting upon his own extraordinary rise. Fletcher, by contrast, was born into a higher social echelon; he and Beaumont did write for the public stage, but always with a particular eye to the court audience.

There was, perhaps, a particular frisson when the play was performed at the Blackfriars, since this was the very location of the trial of Queen Katherine. But there is no doubt that *Henry VIII* was also played at the Globe soon after it was written. At a performance in June 1613, there was an accident when "chambers" (small cannon) were discharged in the fourth scene, resulting in the burning down of the theater. One of the several surviving accounts of the fire, by the diplomat Sir Henry Wotton, combines reportage with a perceptive reading of the play:

> Now, to let matters of state sleep, I will entertain you at the present with what has happened this week at the Bank's side. The King's players had a new play, called *All is True*, representing some principal pieces of the reign of Henry VIII, which was set forth with many extraordinary circumstances of pomp and majesty, even to the matting of the stage; the Knights of the Order with their Georges and garters, the Guards with their embroidered coats, and the like: sufficient in truth within a while to make greatness very familiar, if not ridiculous. Now, King Henry making a masque at the Cardinal Wolsey's house, and certain chambers being shot off at his entry, some of the paper, or other stuff, wherewith one of them was stopped, did light on the thatch, where being thought at first but an idle smoke, and their eyes more attentive to the show, it kindled inwardly, and ran round like a train, consuming within less than an hour the whole house to the very grounds. This was the fatal period of that virtuous fabric, wherein yet nothing did perish but wood and straw, and a few forsaken cloaks; only one man had his breeches set on fire, that would perhaps have broiled him, if he had not by the benefit of a provident wit put it out with bottle ale.

Wotton's account reveals how much care the King's Men took in their efforts to represent "pomp and majesty" on stage: from the matting on the floor to the garters and crosses of St. George on the costumes, everything is contrived "to make greatness very familiar." Intriguingly, though, the effect of transforming royal processions through Whitehall and Westminster into passages of a play on the matted stage of a thatched theater in the margins of Southwark is also to make greatness seem just a little ridiculous. The representation of the intrinsic theatricality of state power hints at its flimsiness, its reliance on the same mechanisms of show as those of the theater.

Wotton's insight serves as an epilogue not just on *Henry VIII* but on Shakespeare's whole sequence of English history plays: on his stage, the people of England became intimately familiar for the first time with the story of their great ones, and at the same time they learned—through laughter and through debate—to respect the structures of greatness just a little less. Having witnessed the fall of lords and even monarchs on the boards of the Globe, they were ready some forty years later to erect a scaffold in Whitehall and witness the fall of an axe on the head of a real king.

ABOUT THE TEXT

Shakespeare endures through history. He illuminates later times as well as his own. He helps us to understand the human condition. But he cannot do this without a good text of the plays. Without editions there would be no Shakespeare. That is why every twenty years or so throughout the last three centuries there has been a major new edition of his complete works. One aspect of editing is the process of keeping the texts up to date—modernizing the spelling, punctuation, and typography (though not, of course, the actual words), providing explanatory notes in the light of changing educational practices (a generation ago, most of Shakespeare's classical and biblical allusions could be assumed to be generally understood, but now they can't).

But because Shakespeare did not personally oversee the publication of his plays, editors also have to make decisions about the relative authority of the early printed editions. Half of the sum of his plays only appeared posthumously, in the elaborately produced First Folio text of 1623, the original "Complete Works" prepared for the press by Shakespeare's fellow actors, the people who knew the plays better than anyone else. The other half had appeared in print in his lifetime, in the more compact and cheaper form of "Quarto" editions, some of which reproduced good quality texts, others of which were to a greater or lesser degree garbled and error-strewn. In the case of a few plays there are hundreds of differences between the Quarto and Folio editions, some of them far from trivial.

If you look at printers' handbooks from the age of Shakespeare, you quickly discover that one of the first rules was that, whenever possible, compositors were recommended to set their type from existing printed books rather than manuscripts. This was the age before mechanical typesetting, where each individual letter had to be picked out by hand from the compositor's case and placed on a stick (upside down and back to front) before being laid on the press. It was an age of murky rushlight and of manuscripts written in a secretary hand that had dozens of different, hard-to-decipher forms. Printers' lives were a lot easier when they were reprinting existing books rather than struggling with handwritten copy. Easily the quickest way to have created the First Folio would have been simply to reprint those eighteen plays that had already appeared in Quarto and only work from manuscript on the other eighteen.

But that is not what happened. Whenever Quartos were used, playhouse "promptbooks" were also consulted and stage directions copied in from them. And in the case of several major plays where a reasonably well-printed Quarto was available, the Folio printers were instructed to work from an alternative, playhouse-derived manuscript. This meant that the whole process of producing the first complete Shakespeare took months, even years, longer than it might have done. But for the men overseeing the project, John Hemings and Henry Condell, friends and fellow actors who had been remembered in Shakespeare's will, the additional labor and cost were worth the effort for the sake of producing an edition that was close to the practice of the theater. They wanted all the plays in print so that people could, as they wrote in their prefatory address to the reader, "read him and again and again," but they also wanted "the great variety of readers" to work from texts that were close to the theater-life for which Shakespeare originally intended them. For this reason, the *RSC Shakespeare*, in both *Complete Works* and individual volumes, uses the Folio as base text wherever possible. Significant Quarto variants are, however, noted in the Textual Notes.

Both *King John* and *Henry VIII* were first printed in the Folio. An anonymous two-part play entitled *The Troublesome Reign of King John*, first printed in 1591, was attributed to Shakespeare in both its 1611 and 1622 reprints, though his authorship is extremely unlikely. The Folio text of *King John* is very clean, which argues against it being set from authorial papers, though its lack of theatrical notation seems to suggest otherwise. There are problems with inconsistency of speech headings, though, and the whole picture seems to add up to the printer's copy being a pre-theatrical text copied by multiple scribes. The text of *Henry VIII* is clean and well printed, and is generally considered to have been set from a carefully prepared scribal copy. It features unusually full and detailed stage directions that make large demands on the available cast, although they seem to have been carefully copied from Holinshed, the play's chief source. It does not follow, therefore, that they necessarily reflect performance or that the copy from which the Folio text was set was theatrical.

The following notes highlight various aspects of the editorial process and indicate conventions used in the text of this edition:

Lists of Parts are supplied in the First Folio for only six plays, not including *King John* or *Henry VIII*, so the lists here are editorially supplied. Capitals indicate that part of the name which is used for speech headings in the script (thus "BLANCHE of Castile, John's niece").

Locations are provided by Folio for only two plays, but not for either *King John* or *Henry VIII*. Eighteenth-century editors, working in an age of elaborately realistic stage sets, were the first to provide detailed locations (*"another part of the palace"* or similar). Given that Shakespeare wrote for a bare stage and often an imprecise sense of place, we have relegated locations to the explanatory notes at the foot of the page, where they are given at the beginning of each scene where the imaginary location is different from the one before.

Act and Scene Divisions were provided in Folio in a much more thoroughgoing way than in the Quartos. Sometimes, however, they were erroneous or omitted; corrections and additions supplied by editorial tradition are indicated by square brackets. Five-act division is based on a classical model, and act breaks provided the opportunity to replace the candles in the indoor Blackfriars playhouse the King's Men used after 1608, but Shakespeare did not necessarily think in terms of a five-part structure of dramatic composition. The Folio convention is that a scene ends when the stage is empty. Nowadays, partly under the influence of film, we tend to consider a scene to be a dramatic unit that ends with either a change of imaginary location or a significant passage of time within the narrative. Shakespeare's fluidity of composition accords well with this convention, so in addition to act and scene numbers we provide a *running scene* count in the right margin at the beginning of each new scene, in the typeface used for editorial directions. Where there is a scene break caused by a momentary bare stage, but the location does not change and extra time does not pass, we use the convention *running scene continues*. There is inevitably a degree of editorial judgment in making such calls, but the system is very valuable in suggesting the pace of the plays.

Speakers' Names are often inconsistent in Folio. We have regularized speech headings, but retained an element of deliberate inconsistency in entry directions, in order to give the flavor of Folio.

Verse is indicated by lines that do not run to the right margin and by capitalization of each line. The Folio printers sometimes set verse as prose, and vice versa (either out of misunderstanding or for reasons of space). We have silently corrected in such cases, although in some instances there is ambiguity, in which case we have leaned toward the preservation of Folio layout. Folio sometimes uses contraction ("turnd" rather than "turned") to indicate whether or not the final "-ed" of a past participle is sounded, an area where there is variation for the sake of the five-beat iambic pentameter rhythm. We use the convention of a grave accent to indicate sounding (thus "turnèd" would be two syllables), but would urge actors not to overstress. In cases where one speaker ends with a verse half line and the next begins with the other half of the pentameter, editors since the late eighteenth century have indented the second line. We have abandoned this convention, since the Folio does not use it, and nor did actors' cues in the Shakespearean theater. An exception is made when the second speaker actively interrupts or completes the first speaker's sentence.

Spelling is modernized, but older forms are occasionally maintained where necessary for rhythm or aural effect.

Punctuation in Shakespeare's time was as much rhetorical as grammatical. "Colon" was originally a term for a unit of thought in an argument. The semicolon was a new unit of punctuation (some of the Quartos lack them altogether). We have modernized punctuation throughout, but have given more weight to Folio punctuation than many editors, since, though not Shakespearean, it reflects the usage of his period. In particular, we have used the colon far more than many editors: it is exceptionally useful as a way of indicating how many Shakespearean speeches unfold clause by clause in a developing argument that gives the illusion of enacting the process of thinking in the moment. We have also kept in mind the origin of punctuation in classical times as a way of assisting the actor and orator: the comma suggests the briefest of pauses for breath, the colon a middling one, and a full stop or period a longer pause. Semi-colons, by contrast, belong to an era of punctuation that was only just coming in during Shakespeare's time and that is coming to an end now: we have accordingly only used them where they occur in our copy texts (and not always then). Dashes are sometimes used for parenthetical interjections where the Folio has brackets. They are also used for interruptions and changes in train of thought. Where a change of addressee occurs within a speech, we have used a dash preceded by a full stop (or occasionally another form of punctuation). Often the identity of the respective addressees is obvious from the context. When it is not, this has been indicated in a marginal stage direction.

Entrances and Exits are fairly thorough in Folio, which has accordingly been followed as faithfully as possible. Where characters are omitted or corrections are necessary, this is indicated by square brackets (e.g. "[*and Attendants*]"). *Exit* is sometimes silently normalized to *Exeunt* and *Manet* anglicized to "remains." We trust Folio positioning of entrances and exits to a greater degree than most editors.

Editorial Stage Directions such as stage business, asides, indications of addressee and of characters' position on the gallery stage are only used sparingly in Folio. Other editions mingle directions of this kind with original Folio and Quarto directions, sometimes marking them by means of square brackets. We have sought to distinguish what could be described as *directorial* interventions of this kind from Folio-style directions (either original or supplied) by placing them in the right margin in a different typeface. There is a degree of subjectivity about which directions are of which kind, but the procedure is intended as a reminder to the reader and the actor that Shakespearean stage directions are often dependent upon editorial inference alone and are not set in stone. We also depart from editorial tradition in sometimes admitting uncertainty and thus printing permissive stage directions, such as an ***Aside?*** (often a line may be equally effective as an aside or a direct address—it is for each production or reading to make its own decision) or a ***may exit*** or a piece of business placed between arrows to indicate that it may occur at various different moments within a scene.

Line Numbers in the left margin are editorial, for reference and to key the explanatory and textual notes.

Explanatory Notes at the foot of each page explain allusions and gloss obsolete and difficult words, confusing phraseology, occasional major textual cruces, and so on. Particular attention is given to nonstandard usage, bawdy innuendo, and technical terms (e.g. legal and military language). Where more than one sense is given, commas indicate shades of related meaning, slashes alternative or double meanings.

Textual Notes at the end of the play indicate major departures from the Folio. They take the following form: the reading of our text is given in bold and its source given after an equals sign. For *King John*, "F2" signifies a correction introduced in the Second Folio of 1632 and "Ed" an emendation from the subsequent editorial tradition. The rejected Folio ("F") reading is then given. Thus, for example "**3.1.75 test** = Ed. F = tast. Ed = task" means that at Act 3 Scene 1 line 75 we have accepted the editorial reading "test" and rejected Folio's "tast" in the lines "What earthy name to interrogatories / Can test the free breath of a sacred king?" We have also included the suggested editorial emendation "task" as an interestingly different alternative editorial reading. For *Henry VIII*, "F2" signifies a correction introduced in the Second Folio of 1632, "F3" a correction from the Third Folio of

1663–64, "F4" one from the Fourth Folio of 1685 and "Ed" a correction from the subsequent editorial tradition. Thus, "**4.2.8 think =**
F2. F = thanke" means that at Act 4 Scene 2 line 8, we have accepted
the Second Folio's correction "think" and rejected the First Folio's
"thanke" in the lines "Yes, madam, but I think your grace, / Out of
the pain you suffered, gave no ear to't."

THE LIFE AND DEATH
OF KING JOHN

KEY FACTS: *KING JOHN*

MAJOR PARTS: (*with percentage of lines/number of speeches/scenes on stage*) Bastard (20%/89/11), King John (17%/95/9), Constance (10%/36/3), King Philip of France (7%/44/3), Hubert (6%/52/6), Salisbury (6%/36/6), Lewis the Dauphin (6%/28/5), Cardinal Pandulph (6%/23/4), Arthur (5%/23/5), Pembroke (3%/20/4), Queen Elinor (2%/22/4), Blanche (2%/9/2), Chatillon (2%/5/2).

LINGUISTIC MEDIUM: 100% verse.

DATE: 1595–97? Mentioned by Meres 1598; close relationship to anonymous two-part play *The Troublesome Reign of King John* (published 1591), but stylistically much closer to later histories.

SOURCES: Scholars dispute the play's relationship to *The Troublesome Reign*: is it the principal source or a badly printed text of an early version of Shakespeare's play? On balance, the evidence supports the view that it was an old play that Shakespeare reworked in his own vein (rather as he reworked other anonymously authored chronicle plays such as *The Famous Victories of Henry V* and *King Leir*). The third volume of the 1587 edition of Holinshed's *Chronicles* is the primary historical source behind both the anonymous play and Shakespeare's.

TEXT: The two parts of *The Troublesome Reign* were reprinted together in 1611 with the title-page claim "Written by W. Sh." (reprinted 1622 as "Written by W. Shakespeare"), but this was a sales ploy and not a reliable attribution. The only authoritative text is that in the First Folio. Scholars dispute the nature of the copy from which it was typeset; there is some evidence that it may have been the work of two scribes. There are a number of textual problems, most notably in the name of Hubert: this first appears halfway through Act 2 Scene 1 as speaker's name for the citizen of Angiers (who is initially an anonymous "*Cit.*"), but it is not used in the dialogue at this point, so the citizen is not identifiable by name to the audience. In the theater, "Hubert" is named for the first time when he swears loyalty to King John and is commissioned to imprison Arthur. Is the same person intended? Editors differ in their attempts to untangle this problem: we leave the question open by means of a marginal direction.

LIST OF PARTS

KING JOHN of England

QUEEN ELINOR, his mother, Henry II's widow

PRINCE HENRY, John's son, a child, later Henry III

BLANCHE of Castile, John's niece

LADY FALCONBRIDGE, Sir Robert's widow

ROBERT Falconbridge, her legitimate son

Philip Falconbridge, the BASTARD, her illegitimate son with King Richard I, subsequently knighted and known as Sir Richard Plantagenet

James GURNEY, her servant

William Marshall, Earl of PEMBROKE ⎫

Geoffrey Fitzpeter, Earl of ESSEX ⎬ English lords

William Longsword, Earl of SALISBURY, Henry II's bastard son

Roger BIGOT, Earl of Norfolk ⎭

HUBERT, trusted servant to King John

PETER of Pomfret, a prophet

KING PHILIP II of France

LEWIS the Dauphin, his eldest son

Duke of AUSTRIA, allied to the French

MELUN, a French nobleman

CHATILLON, French nobleman and ambassador to England

CITIZEN of Angiers

CONSTANCE, wife of Geoffrey, John's deceased older brother

ARTHUR, a child, her son and John's nephew, Duke of Bretagne

CARDINAL PANDULPH, Pope Innocent III's representative

FRENCH HERALD

ENGLISH HERALD

FIRST EXECUTIONER

TWO MESSENGERS

A Sheriff and various Lords, Executioners, Messengers, Soldiers, Citizens and Attendants

List of parts   LEWIS anglicized form of French "Louis"

Act 1 Scene 1

Enter King John, Queen Elinor, Pembroke, Essex and Salisbury,
with the Chatillon of France

KING JOHN   Now, say, Chatillon, what would France with us?

CHATILLON   Thus, after greeting, speaks the King of France,
In my behaviour, to the majesty,
The borrowed majesty, of England here.

5   QUEEN ELINOR   A strange beginning: 'borrowed majesty'!

KING JOHN   Silence, good mother: hear the embassy.

CHATILLON   Philip of France, in right and true behalf
Of thy deceasèd brother Geoffrey's son,
Arthur Plantagenet, lays most lawful claim

10   To this fair island and the territories —
To Ireland, Poitiers, Anjou, Touraine, Maine —
Desiring thee to lay aside the sword
Which sways usurpingly these several titles,
And put the same into young Arthur's hand,

15   Thy nephew, and right royal sovereign.

KING JOHN   What follows if we disallow of this?

CHATILLON   The proud control of fierce and bloody war,
To enforce these rights so forcibly withheld—

KING JOHN   Here have we war for war and blood for blood,

20   Controlment for controlment: so answer France.

CHATILLON   Then take my king's defiance from my mouth,
The furthest limit of my embassy.

KING JOHN   Bear mine to him, and so depart in peace:
Be thou as lightning in the eyes of France;

1.1   *Location: England   King John* youngest son of Henry II and Elinor; born 1166,
reigned 1199–1216   ***Queen Elinor*** daughter of William V, Duke of Aquitaine; she married
and divorced Louis VII of France before marrying Henry II of England   **1 would France** does
the King of France want   **3 behaviour** person, i.e. through me   **majesty** sovereignty,
splendor   **4 borrowed** assumed/feigned   **6 embassy** message (from the ambassador)
7 Philip of France King Philip II, son of Louis VII; lived 1165–1223, reigned from 1180
8 Geoffrey fourth son of Henry II   **9 Arthur Plantagenet** son of Geoffrey and Constance
10 territories dominions/dependencies   **11 Poitiers** i.e. the province of Poitou   **12 sword** i.e.
state control   **13 sways** rules, controls   **several** various/individual   **15 right** by right, i.e.
true   **16 disallow of** refuse   **17 control** constraint/mastery   **22 embassy** message/
ambassadorial role

25   For ere thou canst report, I will be there:
        The thunder of my cannon shall be heard.
        So hence: be thou the trumpet of our wrath
        And sullen presage of your own decay.—
        An honourable conduct let him have: *To Pembroke*
30   Pembroke, look to't.— Farewell, Chatillon.

                                        Exeunt Chatillon and Pembroke

        QUEEN ELINOR   What now, my son? Have I not ever said
        How that ambitious Constance would not cease
        Till she had kindled France and all the world,
        Upon the right and party of her son?
35   This might have been prevented and made whole
        With very easy arguments of love,
        Which now the manage of two kingdoms must
        With fearful bloody issue arbitrate.

        KING JOHN   Our strong possession and our right for us.
40   QUEEN ELINOR   Your strong possession much more   *Aside to John*
            than your right,
        Or else it must go wrong with you and me:
        So much my conscience whispers in your ear,
        Which none but heaven, and you, and I, shall hear.

        Enter a Sheriff   *He whispers to Essex*

        ESSEX   My liege, here is the strangest controversy,
45   Come from the country to be judged by you,
        That e'er I heard: shall I produce the men?

        KING JOHN   Let them approach.—   *[Exit Sheriff]*
        Our abbeys and our priories shall pay
        This expeditious charge.

        Enter Robert Falconbridge and Philip [the Bastard]
50   What men are you?

---

25 **ere** before   **report** deliver your message/make the noise of a **cannon** or of **thunder**
27 **hence** go from here   **trumpet** herald/musical wind instrument used to announce
important arrivals   28 **sullen presage** gloomy portent   **decay** downfall/death
29 **conduct** escort   32 **Constance** heiress of Conan IV, Duke of Brittany; married Geoffrey in
1181 with whom she had Arthur   33 **kindled** stirred up, inflamed   **France** king and nation
34 **Upon** on behalf of   **party** part, side   35 **made whole** i.e. resolved   36 **arguments** proofs
love friendship   37 **manage** management, government   38 **issue** outcome   44 **liege** lord
controversy dispute   46 **produce** bring out   49 **expeditious charge** sudden cost

BASTARD   Your faithful subject I, a gentleman,
Born in Northamptonshire and eldest son,
As I suppose, to Robert Falconbridge,
A soldier, by the honour-giving hand
55   Of Coeur-de-lion, knighted in the field.

KING JOHN   What art thou?

ROBERT   The son and heir to that same Falconbridge.

KING JOHN   Is that the elder, and art thou the heir?
You came not of one mother then, it seems.

60   BASTARD   Most certain of one mother, mighty king,
That is well known, and, as I think, one father:
But for the certain knowledge of that truth
I put you o'er to heaven, and to my mother;
Of that I doubt, as all men's children may.

65   QUEEN ELINOR   Out on thee, rude man! Thou dost shame thy
    mother
And wound her honour with this diffidence.

BASTARD   I, madam? No, I have no reason for it.
That is my brother's plea and none of mine,
The which if he can prove, a pops me out
70   At least from fair five hundred pound a year:
Heaven guard my mother's honour and my land.

KING JOHN   A good blunt fellow.— Why, being younger   *Aside /*
    born,   *To Bastard*
Doth he lay claim to thine inheritance?

BASTARD   I know not why, except to get the land:
75   But once he slandered me with bastardy:
But whe'er I be as true begot or no,
That still I lay upon my mother's head:
But that I am as well begot, my liege —
Fair fall the bones that took the pains for me —

---

55 Coeur-de-lion Richard I, nicknamed "the Lionheart"   **field** battlefield   **63 put you o'er**
direct you   **heaven** here and on several subsequent occasions "heaven" may be an alteration
from "God," following 1606 Parliamentary "Act to restrain the Abuses of Players"   **65 Out on**
thee expression of indignation   **rude** uncivilized   **66 diffidence** mistrust   **69 a** he   **pops**
me out disinherits me   **70 fair** fully   **75 once** in a word/at some time   **76 whe'er** whether
true begot honorably conceived, legitimate   **77 lay . . . head** i.e. leave my mother to answer
79 Fair fall may good fortune befall

80　Compare our faces, and be judge yourself
　　If old Sir Robert did beget us both,
　　And were our father and this son like him:
　　O old Sir Robert, father, on my knee
　　I give heaven thanks I was not like to thee!
85　KING JOHN   Why, what a madcap hath heaven lent us here!
　　QUEEN ELINOR   He hath a trick of Coeur-de-lion's face:
　　The accent of his tongue affecteth him.
　　Do you not read some tokens of my son
　　In the large composition of this man?
90　KING JOHN   Mine eye hath well examined his parts,
　　And finds them perfect Richard.— Sirrah, speak,   *To Robert*
　　What doth move you to claim your brother's land?
　　BASTARD   Because he hath a half-face like my father.
　　With half that face would he have all my land —
95　A half-faced groat — five hundred pound a year!
　　ROBERT   My gracious liege, when that my father lived,
　　Your brother did employ my father much—
　　BASTARD   Well, sir, by this you cannot get my land:
　　Your tale must be how he employed my mother.
100　ROBERT   And once dispatched him in an embassy
　　To Germany, there with the emperor
　　To treat of high affairs touching that time.
　　Th'advantage of his absence took the king,
　　And in the meantime sojourned at my father's;
105　Where how he did prevail, I shame to speak.
　　But truth is truth: large lengths of seas and shores
　　Between my father and my mother lay,
　　As I have heard my father speak himself,

84 like similar   85 madcap lunatic/wild fellow   lent brought   86 trick distinctive look,
habit   87 affecteth imitates, assumes the character of   88 tokens signs, evidence   89 large
composition general/robust constitution   90 parts qualities   91 Sirrah sir (used to an
inferior)   92 move prompt   93 half-face profile/thin face   94 face plays on the sense of
"brazen defiance"   95 half-faced groat coin worth four old pence with the monarch's face in
profile; also, "imperfect/insignificant"   96 when that when   97 Your brother i.e. Richard I,
Coeur-de-lion   99 tale story (perhaps plays on sense of "genitals")   employed made use of/
occupied sexually   102 treat of discuss   high important   touching relating to/affecting
104 sojourned stayed   105 prevail gain the mastery/succeed in attaining/persuade

When this same lusty gentleman was got.
110   Upon his death-bed he by will bequeathed
His lands to me, and took it on his death
That this my mother's son was none of his;
And if he were, he came into the world
Full fourteen weeks before the course of time.
115   Then, good my liege, let me have what is mine,
My father's land, as was my father's will.

KING JOHN   Sirrah, your brother is legitimate:
Your father's wife did after wedlock bear him:
And if she did play false, the fault was hers,
120   Which fault lies on the hazards of all husbands
That marry wives. Tell me, how if my brother,
Who, as you say, took pains to get this son,
Had of your father claimed this son for his?
In sooth, good friend, your father might have kept
125   This calf, bred from his cow, from all the world:
In sooth he might. Then if he were my brother's,
My brother might not claim him, nor your father,
Being none of his, refuse him: this concludes,
My mother's son did get your father's heir,
130   Your father's heir must have your father's land.

ROBERT   Shall then my father's will be of no force
To dispossess that child which is not his?

BASTARD   Of no more force to dispossess me, sir,
Than was his will to get me, as I think.

135   QUEEN ELINOR   Whether hadst thou rather be: a Falconbridge,
And like thy brother to enjoy thy land,
Or the reputed son of Coeur-de-lion,
Lord of thy presence, and no land beside?

---

109 lusty vigorous, lively (plays on the sense of "product of lust")   **got** begot, conceived
111 took . . . death i.e. swore most solemnly   **114 before . . . time** i.e. before the full nine
months were up   **119 did play false** was unfaithful   **fault** sin, moral defect (may play on the
sense of "vagina")   **120 lies . . . hazards** i.e. is one of the risks   **121 how** what   **brother** i.e.
Richard I   **124 sooth** truth   **kept . . . world** the owner of a cow has the right to keep any **calf**
born of that cow   **128 refuse him** spurn Philip (the Bastard)   **concludes** settles it   **131 will**
legal testament/wishes   **134 will** wish/carnal desire/penis   **135 Whether** which of the two
137 reputed recognized/supposed   **138 presence** self/personal dignity

BASTARD   Madam, an if my brother had my shape

140   And I had his, Sir Robert's his like him,

And if my legs were two such riding-rods,

My arms, such eel-skins stuffed, my face so thin,

That in mine ear I durst not stick a rose,

Lest men should say, 'Look, where three-farthings goes',

145   And to his shape were heir to all this land,

Would I might never stir from off this place,

I would give it every foot to have this face:

It would not be Sir Nob in any case.

QUEEN ELINOR   I like thee well: wilt thou forsake thy fortune,

150   Bequeath thy land to him and follow me?

I am a soldier and now bound to France.

BASTARD   Brother, take you my land, I'll take my chance.

Your face hath got five hundred pound a year,

Yet sell your face for five pence and 'tis dear.—

155   Madam, I'll follow you unto the death.

QUEEN ELINOR   Nay, I would have you go before me thither.

BASTARD   Our country manners give our betters way.

KING JOHN   What is thy name?

BASTARD   Philip, my liege, so is my name begun,

160   Philip, good old sir Robert's wife's eldest son.

KING JOHN   From henceforth bear his name whose form thou
    bear'st:

Kneel thou down Philip, but rise more great,   *He knights the*

Arise sir Richard, and Plantagenet.   *Bastard*

BASTARD   Brother by th'mother's side, give me your hand:

165   My father gave me honour, yours gave land:

---

139 **an if** if   **shape** appearance   140 **Sir . . . him** i.e. that resembles Sir Robert's   141 **riding-rods** horse whips, i.e. skinny   143 **in** behind   144 **three-farthings** the thin three-farthing coin bore the queen's image in front of a rose   145 **to his shape** in addition to having his inherited physical appearance   146 **Would I might** may I   147 **it every foot** every foot of it this i.e. my own   148 **Nob** nickname for Robert (puns on senses of "head/head of the family") **case** puns on the sense of "face/appearance"   154 **dear** expensive, because more than a groat (fourpence)   156 **thither** i.e. to **death**   157 **give . . . way** allow our superiors to go first, as is polite   161 **form** likeness, image   162 **rise** some editors emend to "arise" for the sake of meter

Now blessèd be the hour by night or day,
When I was got, Sir Robert was away.
QUEEN ELINOR   The very spirit of Plantagenet:
I am thy grandam, Richard: call me so.
170   BASTARD   Madam, by chance, but not by truth: what though?
Something about a little from the right,
In at the window, or else o'er the hatch:
Who dares not stir by day must walk by night,
And have is have, however men do catch:
175   Near or far off, well won is still well shot,
And I am I, howe'er I was begot.
KING JOHN   Go, Falconbridge, now hast thou thy desire:
A landless knight makes thee a landed squire.—
Come, madam, and come, Richard, we must speed
180   For France, for France, for it is more than need.
BASTARD   Brother, adieu: good fortune come to thee,
For thou wast got i'th'way of honesty.   *Exeunt all but Bastard*
A foot of honour better than I was,
But many a many foot of land the worse.
185   Well, now can I make any Joan a lady.
'Good den, Sir Richard' — 'God-a-mercy, fellow' —
And if his name be George, I'll call him Peter;
For new-made honour doth forget men's names:
'Tis too respective and too sociable
190   For your conversion. Now your traveller,
He and his toothpick at my worship's mess,

---

166 hour possible pun on "whore"   169 grandam grandmother   170 truth chaste loyalty
what though what of that   171 Something about in a somewhat indirect way   from the
right distant from the correct way, i.e. legitimacy   172 window with vaginal connotations
hatch lower part of a door (with vaginal connotations)   173 stir plays on the senses of "get an
erection/engage in sex"   walk plays on the sexual sense of "be erect"   174 have (sexual)
possession   catch seize, get hold of   175 Near . . . off i.e. to the target (in archery/sexually)
shot plays on the sense of "ejaculated"   179 speed travel hastily   180 need necessary
181 adieu good-bye   183 foot degree (may pun on French *foutre*, i.e. "fuck")   184 many a
many i.e. many (emphatic)   185 Joan typical name for a country or lower-class woman
186 den evening (from "God give you good even")   God-a-mercy God have mercy on you
189 'Tis i.e. remembering men's names   respective attentive/respectful   190 conversion i.e.
newly titled man   191 toothpick ornate toothpicks were fashionable and seen as a foreign
sophistication   worship's mess company of people eating together (now honored by his title)

And when my knightly stomach is sufficed,
Why then I suck my teeth and catechize
My pickèd man of countries: 'My dear sir,'
195   Thus leaning on mine elbow I begin,
'I shall beseech you'; that is Question now,
And then comes Answer like an Absey book:
'O sir,' says Answer, 'at your best command,
At your employment, at your service, sir.'
200   'No, sir,' says Question, 'I, sweet sir, at yours.'
And so, ere Answer knows what Question would,
Saving in dialogue of compliment,
And talking of the Alps and Apennines,
The Pyrenean and the river Po,
205   It draws toward supper in conclusion so.
But this is worshipful society,
And fits the mounting spirit like myself;
For he is but a bastard to the time
That doth not smack of observation,
210   And so am I whether I smack or no:
And not alone in habit and device,
Exterior form, outward accoutrement,
But from the inward motion to deliver
Sweet, sweet, sweet poison for the age's tooth,
215   Which though I will not practise to deceive,
Yet to avoid deceit I mean to learn;
For it shall strew the footsteps of my rising.
Enter Lady Falconbridge and James Gurney

---

192 **stomach** appetite   **sufficed** satisfied   193 **catechize** question   194 **picked** foppish/
having used the toothpick/specially chosen   **of countries** i.e. well-traveled   197 **Absey book**
book of ABC   201 **would** wants, asks   202 **Saving** except   **dialogue of compliment** polite/
affected conversation   205 **supper** i.e. supper-time   **so** thus   207 **mounting** (socially)
ascending/aspiring   208 **bastard . . . time** not a true son of the current age   209 **smack**
show the characteristics (literally, taste); Folio spelling "smoake" was alternative form of same
word, which could also mean "observe, suspect"   **observation** observance of polite,
fashionable practices   210 **so am I** i.e. a literal bastard   211 **habit** dress   **device** outward
show/ingenuity/heraldic design   212 **accoutrement** formal trappings   213 **motion** desire,
impulse   214 **sweet poison** i.e. flattery   **tooth** appetite, sweet tooth   215 **practise** plot
216 **to . . . learn** i.e. learn how to spot other people's deception by studying it myself
217 **strew** be scattered   **rising** i.e. ascent to greatness

But who comes in such haste in riding-robes?
What woman-post is this? Hath she no husband
220   That will take pains to blow a horn before her?
O me, 'tis my mother.— How now, good lady?
What brings you here to court so hastily?

LADY FALCONBRIDGE   Where is that slave thy brother? Where is he
That holds in chase mine honour up and down?

225   BASTARD   My brother Robert, old Sir Robert's son,
Colbrand the Giant, that same mighty man,
Is it Sir Robert's son that you seek so?

LADY FALCONBRIDGE   Sir Robert's son, ay, thou unreverend boy,
Sir Robert's son. Why scorn'st thou at Sir Robert?

230   He is Sir Robert's son, and so art thou.

BASTARD   James Gurney, wilt thou give us leave a while?

GURNEY   Good leave, good Philip.

BASTARD   Philip Sparrow, James,
There's toys abroad: anon I'll tell thee more.

Exit James [Gurney]

235   Madam, I was not old Sir Robert's son:
Sir Robert might have eat his part in me
Upon Good Friday, and ne'er broke his fast:
Sir Robert could do well, marry, to confess:
Could get me, Sir Robert could not do it;

240   We know his handiwork: therefore, good mother,
To whom am I beholding for these limbs?
Sir Robert never holp to make this leg.

---

218 riding-robes horse-riding clothes   **219 woman-post** female messenger   **220 blow a horn** i.e. to announce her arrival (plays on the fact that her husband has recently been shown to be a cuckold; men with unfaithful wives were popularly imagined to wear horns on their forehead)   **223 slave** wretch, villain   **224 holds in chase** hunts   **up and down** in every respect/everywhere   **226 Colbrand the Giant** part of an invading Danish army defeated by Guy of Warwick, the eponymous hero of a medieval romance story   **228 unreverend** irreverent, disrespectful   **231 give us leave** leave us   **233 Philip Sparrow** the Bastard rejects his former name (since he has been renamed "Sir Richard Plantagenet") as a common name for sparrows (as it resembles their call)   **234 toys** trifling matters   **abroad** about, going on   **anon** soon   **236 eat . . . fast** "He may his part on Good Friday eat and fast never the worse for ought he shall get" was proverbial   **eat** i.e. eaten (pronounced "et")   **in** of   **238 do** perform, achieve/make, produce/copulate   **marry** by the Virgin Mary   **confess** admit/agree   **239 Could get** i.e. were it possible he could conceive   **240 handiwork** i.e. his half-brother, Robert Falconbridge   **241 beholding** beholden, indebted   **242 holp** helped

LADY FALCONBRIDGE   Hast thou conspirèd with thy brother too,
That for thine own gain shouldst defend mine honour?
245   What means this scorn, thou most untoward knave?

BASTARD   Knight, knight, good mother, Basilisco-like!
What! I am dubbed, I have it on my shoulder:
But, mother, I am not Sir Robert's son:
I have disclaimed Sir Robert and my land,
250   Legitimation, name, and all is gone;
Then, good my mother, let me know my father:
Some proper man, I hope: who was it, mother?

LADY FALCONBRIDGE   Hast thou denied thyself a Falconbridge?

BASTARD   As faithfully as I deny the devil.

255   LADY FALCONBRIDGE   King Richard Coeur-de-lion was thy father:
By long and vehement suit I was seduced
To make room for him in my husband's bed:
Heaven lay not my transgression to my charge,
That art the issue of my dear offence
260   Which was so strongly urged past my defence.

BASTARD   Now by this light, were I to get again,
Madam, I would not wish a better father:
Some sins do bear their privilege on earth,
And so doth yours: your fault was not your folly:
265   Needs must you lay your heart at his dispose,
Subjected tribute to commanding love,
Against whose fury and unmatchèd force
The aweless lion could not wage the fight,
Nor keep his princely heart from Richard's hand:
270   He that perforce robs lions of their hearts

---

244 That you who   **245 untoward** unmannerly, improper   **knave** scoundrel; the Bastard
puns on the meaning "servant"   **246 Basilisco** a character in a contemporary play who
insisted on his knighthood being acknowledged   **247 dubbed** knighted, by having a sword
placed on the **shoulder**   **250 Legitimation** legitimacy   **252 proper** fine/respectable
254 deny renounce   **256 suit** urging, courtship   **258 Heaven** may heaven   **charge**
account/responsibility   **259 issue** offspring   **dear** cherished/grievous/costly   **260 defence**
resistance   **261 get** be conceived   **263 privilege** immunity   **264 folly** foolishness/lust
265 dispose disposal, command   **266 Subjected** obedient/as his royal subject   **268 aweless**
fearless   **lion . . . hand** as punishment for killing the Duke of Austria's son, Richard I was
imprisoned with a lion, whose heart he tore out by putting his hand down its throat
270 perforce forcibly

May easily win a woman's: ay, my mother,
With all my heart I thank thee for my father:
Who lives and dares but say thou didst not well
When I was got, I'll send his soul to hell.
275 Come, lady, I will show thee to my kin,
And they shall say, when Richard me begot,
If thou hadst said him nay, it had been sin;
Who says it was, he lies: I say 'twas not.   *Exeunt*

Act 2 Scene 1   *running scene 2*

*Enter before Angiers, [on one side] Philip King of France, Lewis
[the] Dauphin, Constance, [and] Arthur, [on the other side]
Austria*   With their forces

KING PHILIP   Before Angiers well met, brave Austria.—
Arthur, that great forerunner of thy blood,
Richard that robbed the lion of his heart
And fought the holy wars in Palestine,
5 By this brave duke came early to his grave:
And for amends to his posterity,
At our importance hither is he come,
To spread his colours, boy, in thy behalf,
And to rebuke the usurpation
10 Of thy unnatural uncle, English John:
Embrace him, love him, give him welcome hither.
ARTHUR   God shall forgive you Coeur-de-lion's death   To Austria
The rather that you give his offspring life,
Shadowing their right under your wings of war:
15 I give you welcome with a powerless hand,

---

273 **Who** whoever   275 **kin** (new) relations   277 **said him nay** refused him   278 **was** i.e. a
sin   **2.1** **Location: France**   **before Angiers** in front of the gates of Angiers, on the Loire
river   **Dauphin** title for heir to the French throne   **Austria** historically Leopold V; apparently
wearing a lion's skin, supposedly taken from Richard I   **2 that . . . blood** i.e. your predecessor
4 holy . . . Palestine the Crusades   **5 By** i.e. at the hand of   **6 posterity** descendants
7 importance request   **8 spread** display   **colours** battle flags   **9 rebuke** repress
10 unnatural i.e. behaving in a manner that contradicts natural kinship   **13 offspring**
descendants   **14 Shadowing** sheltering   **15 powerless** i.e. without a military force behind it

But with a heart full of unstainèd love:
Welcome before the gates of Angiers, Duke.

LEWIS   A noble boy: who would not do thee right?

AUSTRIA   Upon thy cheek lay I this zealous kiss,

20 As seal to this indenture of my love:
That to my home I will no more return
Till Angiers and the right thou hast in France,
Together with that pale, that white-faced shore,
Whose foot spurns back the ocean's roaring tides

25 And coops from other lands her islanders,
Even till that England, hedged in with the main,
That water-wallèd bulwark, still secure
And confident from foreign purposes,
Even till that utmost corner of the west

30 Salute thee for her king: till then, fair boy,
Will I not think of home, but follow arms.

CONSTANCE   O, take his mother's thanks, a widow's thanks,
Till your strong hand shall help to give him strength
To make a more requital to your love.

35 AUSTRIA   The peace of heaven is theirs that lift their swords
In such a just and charitable war.

KING PHILIP   Well then, to work: our cannon shall be bent
Against the brows of this resisting town.
Call for our chiefest men of discipline,

40 To cull the plots of best advantages:
We'll lay before this town our royal bones,
Wade to the market-place in Frenchmen's blood,
But we will make it subject to this boy.

---

16 **unstainèd** pure, unblemished   19 **zealous** earnest   20 **seal . . . indenture** wax seal on a legal contract   23 **pale . . . shore** i.e. the chalk cliffs of England's southeastern coast (hence England)   **pale** either adjectival (colorless) or a noun (boundary, enclosure)   24 **spurns** kicks, rejects   25 **coops** encloses, protects   26 **main** sea   27 **bulwark** fortification   **still** always   28 **confident from** self-assured against   **purposes** plans, i.e. threats of invasion   31 **follow arms** i.e. take part in military action   34 **more requital to** greater recompense for   37 **bent** directed   38 **brows** i.e. walls/battlements   39 **discipline** military strategy   40 **cull** select   **plots** positions, sites   **advantages** i.e. military advantage in attack   43 **But we will** if necessary to   **subject to** ruled by/answerable to

CONSTANCE   Stay for an answer to your embassy,
45   Lest unadvised you stain your swords with blood:
My lord Chatillon may from England bring
That right in peace which here we urge in war,
And then we shall repent each drop of blood
That hot rash haste so indirectly shed.

Enter Chatillon

50   KING PHILIP   A wonder, lady: lo, upon thy wish,
Our messenger Chatillon is arrived.—
What England says, say briefly, gentle lord:
We coldly pause for thee: Chatillon, speak.

CHATILLON   Then turn your forces from this paltry siege,
55   And stir them up against a mightier task:
England, impatient of your just demands,
Hath put himself in arms: the adverse winds,
Whose leisure I have stayed, have given him time
To land his legions all as soon as I:
60   His marches are expedient to this town,
His forces strong, his soldiers confident:
With him along is come the Mother-Queen,
An Ate stirring him to blood and strife:
With her her niece, the lady Blanche of Spain:
65   With them a bastard of the king's deceased,
And all th'unsettled humours of the land,
Rash, inconsiderate, fiery voluntaries,
With ladies' faces and fierce dragons' spleens,
Have sold their fortunes at their native homes,
70   Bearing their birthrights proudly on their backs,

44 **Stay** wait   **embassy** message   45 **unadvised** rashly, without full thought or information
49 **indirectly** wrongfully   50 **lo** look   52 **England** the King of England   **gentle** noble
53 **coldly** calmly   55 **against** in preparation for   56 **impatient of** angered by   58 **leisure**
convenience   **stayed** waited for   59 **legions** forces   60 **expedient** rapid   62 **Mother-**
Queen Queen-Mother, i.e. Elinor   63 **Ate** Greek goddess of discord and revenge   64 **niece**
female relative; actually Elinor's granddaughter and John's niece   **Blanche of Spain** daughter
of John's sister Eleanor and Alfonso VIII, King of Castile   65 **king's deceased** dead king
(Richard I)   66 **unsettled humours** i.e. unruly persons, malcontents; **humours** four chief
bodily fluids (blood, phlegm, choler, black choler) governing mental qualities and disposition
67 **inconsiderate** reckless   **voluntaries** volunteers   68 **ladies' faces** i.e. beardless and young
spleens tempers, impulses   69 **sold . . . backs** i.e. they have spent everything on armor and
military equipment

To make a hazard of new fortunes here:
In brief, a braver choice of dauntless spirits
Than now the English bottoms have waft o'er
Did never float upon the swelling tide,
75 To do offence and scathe in Christendom.   *Drum beats*
The interruption of their churlish drums
Cuts off more circumstance: they are at hand:
To parley or to fight therefore prepare.

KING PHILIP   How much unlooked-for is this expedition!

80 AUSTRIA   By how much unexpected, by so much
We must awake endeavour for defence,
For courage mounteth with occasion:
Let them be welcome then: we are prepared.

Enter King [John] of England, [the] Bastard, Queen [Elinor], Blanche,
Pembroke and others

KING JOHN   Peace be to France, if France in peace permit
85 Our just and lineal entrance to our own;
If not, bleed France, and peace ascend to heaven,
Whiles we, God's wrathful agent, do correct
Their proud contempt that beats his peace to heaven.

KING PHILIP   Peace be to England, if that war return
90 From France to England, there to live in peace:
England we love, and for that England's sake
With burden of our armour here we sweat:
This toil of ours should be a work of thine;
But thou from loving England art so far,
95 That thou hast underwrought his lawful king,
Cut off the sequence of posterity,
Outfacèd infant state, and done a rape
Upon the maiden virtue of the crown:

71 make ... of risk, venture   72 braver more splendid, finer   choice selection
73 bottoms keels, i.e. ships   waft wafted, i.e. conveyed (suggesting a quick easy journey)
75 scathe damage   76 churlish rough, harsh   77 circumstance details   78 parley
negotiate   79 expedition warlike enterprise/haste   82 occasion (needful) circumstances
83 *others* i.e. troops   85 lineal hereditary   own i.e. territories/role of ruler   88 beats
drives, forces   89 if that if   91 England's i.e. Arthur's   93 toil i.e. supporting Arthur's cause
work duty, undertaking   95 underwrought undermined, sought to overthrow   his its
96 sequence of posterity lawful succession   97 Outfacèd defied/intimidated   infant state
young majesty, i.e. Arthur

Look here upon thy brother Geoffrey's face: *Indicates Arthur*
100   These eyes, these brows, were moulded out of his;
This little abstract doth contain that large
Which died in Geoffrey, and the hand of time
Shall draw this brief into as huge a volume:
That Geoffrey was thy elder brother born,
105   And this his son: England was Geoffrey's right,
And this is Geoffrey's in the name of God:
How comes it then that thou art called a king,
When living blood doth in these temples beat
Which owe the crown that thou o'ermasterest?
110   KING JOHN   From whom hast thou this great commission, France,
To draw my answer from thy articles?
KING PHILIP   From that supernal judge that stirs good thoughts
In any breast of strong authority,
To look into the blots and stains of right:
115   That judge hath made me guardian to this boy,
Under whose warrant I impeach thy wrong,
And by whose help I mean to chastise it.
KING JOHN   Alack, thou dost usurp authority.
KING PHILIP   Excuse it is to beat usurping down.
120   QUEEN ELINOR   Who is it thou dost call usurper, France?
CONSTANCE   Let me make answer: thy usurping son.
QUEEN ELINOR   Out, insolent! Thy bastard shall be king,
That thou mayst be a queen, and check the world.
CONSTANCE   My bed was ever to thy son as true
125   As thine was to thy husband, and this boy
Liker in feature to his father Geoffrey
Than thou and John, in manners being as like
As rain to water, or devil to his dam.

---

99 Geoffrey's i.e. Arthur's father's   **101 abstract** essence, summary   **103 brief** summary
109 owe own   **110 commission** warrant   **111 articles** points/charges   **112 supernal**
judge i.e. God **supernal** celestial   **116 impeach** challenge, accuse   **118 Alack** exclamation of
dissatisfaction, regret   **119 Excuse . . . down** preventing (your) usurpation of authority is a
good enough excuse   **122 Out** expression of irritation and scorn   **123 check** control,
discipline   **126 Liker in feature** more similar in physical appearance   **127 in manners** (who
are) in behavior/character   **128 dam** mother (devil and parent were proverbially similar)

My boy a bastard? By my soul I think
130 His father never was so true begot:
It cannot be, an if thou wert his mother.

QUEEN ELINOR   There's a good mother, boy, that blots thy father.

CONSTANCE   There's a good grandam, boy, that would blot thee.

AUSTRIA   Peace!

135 BASTARD   Hear the crier.

AUSTRIA   What the devil art thou?

BASTARD   One that will play the devil, sir, with you,
An a may catch your hide and you alone:
You are the hare of whom the proverb goes,
140 Whose valour plucks dead lions by the beard.
I'll smoke your skin-coat an I catch you right:
Sirrah, look to't: i'faith I will, i'faith.

BLANCHE   O, well did he become that lion's robe
That did disrobe the lion of that robe.

145 BASTARD   It lies as sightly on the back of him
As great Alcides' shoes upon an ass:
But, ass, I'll take that burden from your back,
Or lay on that shall make your shoulders crack.

AUSTRIA   What cracker is this same that deafs our ears
150 With this abundance of superfluous breath?

KING PHILIP   Lewis, determine what we shall do straight.

LEWIS   Women and fools, break off your conference.
King John, this is the very sum of all:
England and Ireland, Anjou, Touraine, Maine,
155 In right of Arthur do I claim of thee:
Wilt thou resign them and lay down thy arms?

130 His . . . mother Constance insults Elinor by suggesting that it is likelier that Geoffrey was a bastard than that Arthur might be one   131 an if if   132 blots slanders   133 grandam grandmother   blot defile/erase   135 crier announcing officer in a law court/town crier (a mocking reference to Austria)   137 play the devil i.e. make trouble   138 An a if he   catch seize, get hold of   hide i.e. lion's skin   139 hare . . . beard "even hares may pull dead lions by the beard" (proverbial)   141 smoke subject to smoke/disinfect/beat   an if   142 look to't beware   143 become earn/befit   145 sightly appropriately   146 Alcides Hercules (Greek hero, one of whose twelve labors involved killing a lion, whose skin he then wore); some editors emend "shoes" to "shows," i.e. distinctive clothing   148 lay on that i.e. inflict blows   149 cracker boaster (playing on the sense of "supposed breaker of shoulders")   deafs deafens   151 straight straight away   153 very sum final summary, absolute essence

KING JOHN   My life as soon: I do defy thee, France.
Arthur of Bretagne, yield thee to my hand,
And out of my dear love I'll give thee more
160   Than e'er the coward hand of France can win.
Submit thee, boy.

QUEEN ELINOR   Come to thy grandam, child.

CONSTANCE   Do, child, go to it grandam, child:
Give grandam kingdom, and it grandam will
165   Give it a plum, a cherry, and a fig:
There's a good grandam.

ARTHUR   Good my mother, peace.
I would that I were low laid in my grave:
I am not worth this coil that's made for me.

170   QUEEN ELINOR   His mother shames him so, poor boy, he weeps.

CONSTANCE   Now shame upon you, whe'er she does or no:
His grandam's wrongs, and not his mother's shames,
Draws those heaven-moving pearls from his poor eyes,
Which heaven shall take in nature of a fee:
175   Ay, with these crystal beads heaven shall be bribed
To do him justice and revenge on you.

QUEEN ELINOR   Thou monstrous slanderer of heaven and earth!

CONSTANCE   Thou monstrous injurer of heaven and earth,
Call not me slanderer: thou and thine usurp
180   The dominations, royalties, and rights
Of this oppressed boy: this is thy eldest son's son,
Infortunate in nothing but in thee:
Thy sins are visited in this poor child:
The canon of the law is laid on him,
185   Being but the second generation
Removèd from thy sin-conceiving womb.

KING JOHN   Bedlam, have done.

---

158 Bretagne Brittany   **163 it** its   **165 fig** fruit/something valueless/rude gesture   **169 coil** turmoil, fuss   **170 shames** dishonors, embarrasses   **173 pearls** i.e. tears   **174 in . . . fee** as a bribe for divine support   **175 beads** teardrops (plays on the sense of "prayer beads on a rosary")   **177 monstrous** unnatural   **180 dominations** dominions   **royalties** royal rights   **181 eldest son's son** eldest grandson   **182 Infortunate** unfortunate   **183 visited** punished   **184 canon . . . law** scriptural rule (that the sins of the parents will be visited upon their children)   **185 but** only   **186 Removèd** distant   **187 Bedlam** i.e. madwoman

CONSTANCE   I have but this to say:
  That he is not only plaguèd for her sin,
190 But God hath made her sin and her the plague
  On this removèd issue, plagued for her,
  And with her plague her sin: his injury
  Her injury the beadle to her sin,
  All punished in the person of this child,
195 And all for her: a plague upon her!
QUEEN ELINOR   Thou unadvisèd scold, I can produce
  A will that bars the title of thy son.
CONSTANCE   Ay, who doubts that? A will: a wicked will,
  A woman's will, a cankered grandam's will!
200 KING PHILIP   Peace, lady: pause, or be more temperate:
  It ill beseems this presence to cry aim
  To these ill-tunèd repetitions.
  Some trumpet summon hither to the walls
  These men of Angiers: let us hear them speak
205 Whose title they admit, Arthur's or John's.
  Trumpet sounds. Enter a Citizen upon the walls [with others]
CITIZEN   Who is it that hath warned us to the walls?
KING PHILIP   'Tis France, for England.
KING JOHN   England for itself:
  You men of Angiers, and my loving subjects—
210 KING PHILIP   You loving men of Angiers, Arthur's subjects,
  Our trumpet called you to this gentle parle—
KING JOHN   For our advantage; therefore hear us first:
  These flags of France that are advancèd here
  Before the eye and prospect of your town,

190 **her sin** implies John, whom Constance suggests was conceived adulterously (in sin)
191 **removèd issue** relative at one remove, i.e. Arthur   **for** because of   192 **his injury** harm
done to Arthur   193 **beadle** parish officer entitled to punish minor offences, i.e. punisher
195 **for** because of/instead of   196 **unadvisèd** rash, thoughtless   197 **title** legal claim
199 **will** willfulness, wish   **cankered** corrupt   200 **temperate** calm   201 **beseems** befits
presence royal company   **cry aim** shout encouragement (archery term)   202 **ill-tunèd**
harsh-sounding   **repetitions** repeated accusations   203 **trumpet** trumpeter   205 **admit**
grant, recognize   206 **warned** summoned   207 **France, for England** i.e. the French king on
behalf of Arthur (who should be King of England)   211 **gentle** peaceful/noble   **parle**
negotiation   213 **advancèd** raised, displayed   214 **prospect** view

215   Have hither marched to your endamagement.
        The cannons have their bowels full of wrath,
        And ready mounted are they to spit forth
        Their iron indignation gainst your walls:
        All preparation for a bloody siege
220   And merciless proceeding by these French
        Confronts your city's eyes, your winking gates:
        And but for our approach, those sleeping stones,
        That as a waist doth girdle you about,
        By the compulsion of their ordinance
225   By this time from their fixèd beds of lime
        Had been dishabited, and wide havoc made
        For bloody power to rush upon your peace.
        But on the sight of us your lawful king,
        Who painfully with much expedient march
230   Have brought a countercheck before your gates,
        To save unscratched your city's threatened cheeks,
        Behold, the French, amazed, vouchsafe a parle:
        And now instead of bullets wrapped in fire
        To make a shaking fever in your walls,
235   They shoot but calm words, folded up in smoke,
        To make a faithless error in your ears,
        Which trust accordingly, kind citizens,
        And let us in. Your king, whose laboured spirits,
        Forwearied in this action of swift speed,
240   Craves harbourage within your city walls.
        KING PHILIP   When I have said, make answer to us both.
        Lo, in this right hand, whose protection   *He takes Arthur's hand*
        Is most divinely vowed upon the right

---

215 **endamagement** damage, detriment   216 **bowels** entrails   222 **stones** i.e. city
walls   223 **waist** belt   224 **ordinance** artillery   225 **lime** mortar   226 **dishabited**
dislodged   227 **bloody power** violent, fierce troops   229 **much expedient** very hasty
230 **countercheck** rebuke/check to oppose (the course of something)   232 **amazed** stunned/
overwhelmed   **vouchsafe** permit   233 **bullets** cannonballs   235 **folded . . . smoke** i.e.
concealed in deceitful rhetoric   236 **faithless error** untrustworthy lie   237 **accordingly** in
the same manner/as it deserves   238 **laboured** exhausted with hard work   239 **Forwearied**
worn out   240 **harbourage** shelter   241 **said** finished speaking   242 **Lo** see   243 **right** i.e.
just claim

Of him it holds, stands young Plantagenet,
245 Son to the elder brother of this man,
And king o'er him and all that he enjoys:
For this downtrodden equity, we tread
In warlike march these greens before your town,
Being no further enemy to you
250 Than the constraint of hospitable zeal
In the relief of this oppressèd child
Religiously provokes. Be pleasèd then
To pay that duty which you truly owe
To him that owes it, namely this young prince:
255 And then our arms, like to a muzzled bear,
Save in aspect, hath all offence sealed up:
Our cannons' malice vainly shall be spent
Against th'invulnerable clouds of heaven,
And with a blessèd and unvexed retire,
260 With unhacked swords and helmets all unbruised,
We will bear home that lusty blood again
Which here we came to spout against your town,
And leave your children, wives, and you in peace.
But if you fondly pass our proffered offer,
265 'Tis not the roundure of your old-faced walls
Can hide you from our messengers of war,
Though all these English and their discipline
Were harboured in their rude circumference:
Then tell us, shall your city call us lord,
270 In that behalf which we have challenged it?
Or shall we give the signal to our rage,
And stalk in blood to our possession?

---

246 **enjoys** possesses   247 **For** on behalf of   **downtrodden equity** oppressed right   **tread**
picks up on **downtrodden**   248 **greens** grassy areas   250 **constraint** compulsion   254 **owes**
owns   256 **Save** except   **aspect** appearance   **offence** hostility, harm   **sealed up** i.e.
prevented   257 **spent** expended, fired   259 **unvexed** untroubled/unimpeded   **retire** retreat
260 **unhacked** unused/undamaged (from battle)   261 **lusty** vigorous   264 **fondly** foolishly
pass pass up, disregard   265 **roundure** roundness, circumference   266 **messengers of war**
i.e. cannonballs   267 **Though** even if   **discipline** skill in warfare   268 **rude** rough
270 **In . . . which** on behalf of him (Arthur) for whom

CITIZEN   In brief, we are the King of England's subjects:
For him, and in his right, we hold this town.

275   KING JOHN   Acknowledge then the king, and let me in.

CITIZEN   That can we not: but he that proves the king,
To him will we prove loyal: till that time
Have we rammed up our gates against the world.

KING JOHN   Doth not the crown of England prove the king?

280   And if not that, I bring you witnesses:
Twice fifteen thousand hearts of England's breed—

BASTARD   Bastards, and else.   *Aside*

KING JOHN   To verify our title with their lives.

KING PHILIP   As many and as well-born bloods as those—

285   BASTARD   Some bastards too.   *Aside*

KING PHILIP   Stand in his face to contradict his claim.

CITIZEN   Till you compound whose right is worthiest,
We for the worthiest hold the right from both.

KING JOHN   Then God forgive the sin of all those souls

290   That to their everlasting residence,
Before the dew of evening fall, shall fleet
In dreadful trial of our kingdom's king.

KING PHILIP   Amen, amen. Mount, chevaliers: to arms!

BASTARD   Saint George, that swinged the dragon, and e'er since

295   Sits on's horseback at mine hostess' door,
Teach us some fence!— Sirrah, were I at home   *To Austria*
At your den, sirrah, with your lioness,
I would set an ox-head to your lion's hide,
And make a monster of you.

300   AUSTRIA   Peace, no more.

BASTARD   O tremble, for you hear the lion roar.

---

276 proves proves to be   **282 else** others, suchlike   **284 bloods** hot-blooded fellows/
noble men   **286 in his face** against him   **287 compound** agree   **288 for** on behalf of
hold withhold   **290 everlasting residence** i.e. the grave, death   **291 fleet** pass, fly off
292 dreadful terrifying, daunting   **trial** contest, putting to the proof   **293 chevaliers** knights
294 Saint George patron saint of England who famously slew a dragon   **swinged** beat,
thrashed   **295 Sits . . . door** i.e. as a tavern sign   **hostess** tavern landlady   **296 fence**
fencing skill   **297 lioness** i.e. Austria's wife; also means "whore"   **298 set . . . hide** i.e. give
Austria the cuckold's horns by sleeping with his wife   **299 monster** because a combination of
lion and ox

KING JOHN   Up higher to the plain, where we'll set forth
    In best appointment all our regiments.
BASTARD   Speed then, to take advantage of the field.
305 KING PHILIP   It shall be so, and at the other hill
    Command the rest to stand. God and our right!

                    Exeunt [French and English forces] Citizens remain
Here after excursions, enter [at one door] the Herald of   on the walls
France with Trumpets to the gates

FRENCH HERALD   You men of Angiers, open wide your gates,
    And let young Arthur Duke of Bretagne in,
    Who by the hand of France this day hath made
310   Much work for tears in many an English mother,
    Whose sons lie scattered on the bleeding ground:
    Many a widow's husband grovelling lies,
    Coldly embracing the discoloured earth:
    And victory with little loss doth play
315   Upon the dancing banners of the French,
    Who are at hand, triumphantly displayed,
    To enter conquerors, and to proclaim
    Arthur of Bretagne England's king and yours.

Enter [at another door the] English Herald, with Trumpets

ENGLISH HERALD   Rejoice, you men of Angiers, ring your bells:
320   King John, your king and England's, doth approach,
    Commander of this hot malicious day:
    Their armours that marched hence so silver-bright
    Hither return all gilt with Frenchmen's blood:
    There stuck no plume in any English crest
325   That is removèd by a staff of France:
    Our colours do return in those same hands
    That did display them when we first marched forth:
    And like a jolly troop of huntsmen come

---

303 **appointment** order, arrangement   304 **advantage** superior military position/opportunity
306 **God . . . right!** a battle cry   ***excursions*** fighting (across the stage)   ***Trumpets*** trumpeters
309 **by . . . France** with the help of the French king   312 **grovelling** prostrate, face down
316 **displayed** drawn up (if referring to the troops)/unfurled (if referring to the banners)
321 **Commander** victor   **malicious** violent, hostile   322 **hence** from here   323 **gilt** coated/
glittering   324 **crest** i.e. helmet   325 **staff** spear/lance   326 **colours** battle flags
328 **like . . . huntsmen** traditionally huntsmen smeared their hands with blood of the kill

Our lusty English, all with purpled hands,
330   Dyed in the dying slaughter of their foes:
Open your gates and give the victors way.

CITIZEN   Heralds, from off our towers we might   *This Citizen*
  behold   *may be Hubert*
From first to last, the onset and retire
Of both your armies, whose equality
335   By our best eyes cannot be censurèd:
Blood hath bought blood, and blows have answered blows:
Strength matched with strength, and power confronted
  power:
Both are alike, and both alike we like.
One must prove greatest. While they weigh so even,
340   We hold our town for neither, yet for both.

*Enter the two Kings with their powers, at several doors [King John
accompanied by the Bastard, Queen Elinor, Blanche; King Philip by
Lewis the Dauphin and Austria]*

KING JOHN   France, hast thou yet more blood to cast away?
Say, shall the current of our right run on,
Whose passage, vexed with thy impediment,
Shall leave his native channel and o'erswell
345   With course disturbed even thy confining shores,
Unless thou let his silver water keep
A peaceful progress to the ocean.

KING PHILIP   England, thou hast not saved one drop of blood
In this hot trial more than we of France;
350   Rather, lost more. And by this hand I swear,
That sways the earth this climate overlooks,
Before we will lay down our just-borne arms,
We'll put thee down, gainst whom these arms we bear,
Or add a royal number to the dead,

---

333 **onset and retire** attack and retreat   335 **censured** judged   338 **alike** equally   **like**
approve   343 **passage** progress, course   344 **native** natural, habitual   **o'erswell** flood
(John threatens French territory)   347 **progress** journey (may play on the sense of "official
royal tour")   351 **sways** rules   **climate** part of the sky   352 **just-borne** justly carried
353 **put thee down** defeat you   354 **royal number** i.e. a king's name

355 Gracing the scroll that tells of this war's loss
With slaughter coupled to the name of kings.

BASTARD   Ha, majesty! How high thy glory towers,
When the rich blood of kings is set on fire:
O, now doth Death line his dead chaps with steel:
360 The swords of soldiers are his teeth, his fangs:
And now he feasts, mousing the flesh of men
In undetermined differences of kings.
Why stand these royal fronts amazèd thus?
Cry havoc, kings: back to the stainèd field
365 You equal potents, fiery kindled spirits!
Then let confusion of one part confirm
The other's peace: till then, blows, blood and death.

KING JOHN   Whose party do the townsmen yet admit?

KING PHILIP   Speak, citizens, for England. Who's your king?

370 CITIZEN   The King of England, when we know the king.

KING PHILIP   Know him in us, that here hold up his right.

KING JOHN   In us, that are our own great deputy
And bear possession of our person here,
Lord of our presence, Angiers, and of you.

375 CITIZEN   A greater power than we denies all this,
And till it be undoubted, we do lock
Our former scruple in our strong-barred gates:
Kings of our fear, until our fears resolved
Be by some certain king, purged and deposed.

380 BASTARD   By heaven, these scroyles of Angiers flout you, kings,
And stand securely on their battlements,
As in a theatre, whence they gape and point
At your industrious scenes and acts of death.

---

355 **tells of** records/counts   357 **towers** soars, mounts (falconry term)   359 **chaps** jaws
361 **mousing** tearing at (like a cat or an owl with its prey)   362 **undetermined differences**
unresolved disagreements   363 **fronts** faces   364 **havoc** a call for general slaughter
365 **potents** potentates, rulers   366 **confusion** overthrow, destruction   **part** side
367 **peace** i.e. victory   368 **yet admit** now recognize   371 **hold up** support   372 **that . . .**
here i.e. John has no need for a spokesperson, representing himself as rightful king
374 **presence** own existence/majesty   378 **Kings of** i.e. ruled by   379 **some certain** i.e. one
or the other/the particular rightful   **purged and deposed** refers to the fears   380 **scroyles**
scoundrels   **flout** mock, insult   383 **industrious** ingenious/painstaking/hard-working
acts deeds/theatrical actions/parts of a play

Your royal presences be ruled by me:
385 Do like the mutines of Jerusalem,
Be friends awhile, and both conjointly bend
Your sharpest deeds of malice on this town.
By east and west let France and England mount
Their battering cannon chargèd to the mouths,
390 Till their soul-fearing clamours have brawled down
The flinty ribs of this contemptuous city:
I'd play incessantly upon these jades,
Even till unfencèd desolation
Leave them as naked as the vulgar air:
395 That done, dissever your united strengths,
And part your mingled colours once again:
Turn face to face, and bloody point to point:
Then in a moment Fortune shall cull forth
Out of one side her happy minion,
400 To whom in favour she shall give the day,
And kiss him with a glorious victory:
How like you this wild counsel, mighty states?
Smacks it not something of the policy?

KING JOHN   Now, by the sky that hangs above our heads,
405 I like it well.— France, shall we knit our powers,
And lay this Angiers even with the ground,
Then after fight who shall be king of it?

BASTARD   An if thou hast the mettle of a king,
Being wronged as we are by this peevish town,
410 Turn thou the mouth of thy artillery,
As we will ours, against these saucy walls,

---

385 **mutines of Jerusalem** rival Jewish factions who united to fight the Romans besieging Jerusalem in AD 70   **mutines** mutineers, rebels   386 **conjointly bend** jointly aim
388 **mount** raise/prepare for firing   389 **chargèd** loaded   390 **soul-fearing** terrifying **brawled down** destroyed noisily   392 **play** torment by firing at   **jades** wretches (literally, worthless horses)   393 **unfencèd** without walls, i.e. unprotected   **desolation** barren ruin/ despondency   394 **vulgar** common   397 **point** i.e. sword point   398 **cull forth** select
399 **happy minion** fortunate favorite   400 **day** i.e. victory   402 **wild** irregular/audacious **states** sovereigns   403 **Smacks . . . something** has it not a flavor   **the policy** stratagem
405 **knit** unite   406 **lay** level, flatten   407 **who** i.e. to determine who   408 **An if** if   **mettle** spirit, disposition   409 **peevish** obstinate/foolish   411 **saucy** insolent

And when that we have dashed them to the ground,
Why then defy each other, and pell-mell,
Make work upon ourselves, for heaven or hell.

415   KING PHILIP   Let it be so: say, where will you assault?

KING JOHN   We from the west will send destruction
Into this city's bosom.

AUSTRIA   I from the north.

KING PHILIP   Our thunder from the south

420   Shall rain their drift of bullets on this town.

BASTARD   O prudent discipline! From north to south:
Austria and France shoot in each other's mouth:
I'll stir them to it.— Come, away, away!

CITIZEN   Hear us, great kings: vouchsafe awhile to stay,

425   And I shall show you peace and fair-faced league:
Win you this city without stroke or wound:
Rescue those breathing lives to die in beds,
That here come sacrifices for the field.
Persever not, but hear me, mighty kings.

430   KING JOHN   Speak on with favour: we are bent to hear.

CITIZEN   That daughter there of Spain, the lady Blanche,
Is niece to England: look upon the years
Of Lewis the dauphin and that lovely maid.
If lusty love should go in quest of beauty,

435   Where should he find it fairer than in Blanche?
If zealous love should go in search of virtue,
Where should he find it purer than in Blanche?
If love ambitious sought a match of birth,
Whose veins bound richer blood than Lady Blanche?

440   Such as she is, in beauty, virtue, birth,
Is the young dauphin every way complete:

---

412 when that when   413 pell-mell headlong/in hand-to-hand combat   414 ourselves i.e.
each other   heaven or hell i.e. eternal life or damnation   419 thunder i.e. cannon
420 drift shower, deluge   421 discipline military strategy   424 vouchsafe agree, grant
425 league alliance, friendship   427 breathing lives i.e. living people   429 Persever
persevere, proceed   430 favour permission, approval   bent resolved/inclined   432 years
age   434 lusty lively, merry/fertile/lustful   438 birth noble ancestry   439 bound contain
441 complete fully equipped, perfect in

If not complete of, say he is not she:
And she again wants nothing, to name want,
If want it be not that she is not he:
He is the half part of a blessèd man,
Left to be finishèd by such as she:
And she a fair divided excellence,
Whose fullness of perfection lies in him.
O, two such silver currents when they join
Do glorify the banks that bound them in:
And two such shores to two such streams made one,
Two such controlling bounds shall you be, kings,
To these two princes, if you marry them:
This union shall do more than battery can
To our fast-closèd gates: for at this match,
With swifter spleen than powder can enforce,
The mouth of passage shall we fling wide ope,
And give you entrance: but without this match,
The sea enragèd is not half so deaf,
Lions more confident, mountains and rocks
More free from motion, no, not Death himself
In mortal fury half so peremptory,
As we to keep this city.

BASTARD   Here's a stay
That shakes the rotten carcass of old Death
Out of his rags. Here's a large mouth, indeed,
That spits forth death and mountains, rocks and seas,
Talks as familiarly of roaring lions
As maids of thirteen do of puppy-dogs.
What cannoneer begot this lusty blood?
He speaks plain cannon: fire, and smoke, and bounce:

---

442 If . . . she i.e. the only fault in his perfection is that he is not her   **complete of** full of
(those virtues)   **443 wants** lacks   **444 If . . . he** unless it could be a fault that she is not him
446 finishèd completed   **447 divided** incomplete   **452 bounds** boundaries   **453 princes**
royal persons (of either sex)   **454 battery** assault   **455 fast-closèd** firmly, tightly shut
match marriage (puns on the sense of "match that lights gunpowder")   **456 spleen**
eagerness, angry energy   **powder** gunpowder   **457 mouth of passage** i.e. entrance   **ope**
open   **462 mortal** fatal   **peremptory** determined   **464 stay** obstacle   **470 lusty blood**
spirited fellow   **471 plain cannon** i.e. just like a cannon   **bounce** explosion

He gives the bastinado with his tongue:
Our ears are cudgelled: not a word of his
But buffets better than a fist of France:
475 Zounds! I was never so bethumped with words
Since I first called my brother's father dad.

QUEEN ELINOR   Son, list to this conjunction, make this match,
Give with our niece a dowry large enough:
For, by this knot, thou shalt so surely tie
480 Thy now unsured assurance to the crown
That yon green boy shall have no sun to ripe
The bloom that promiseth a mighty fruit.
I see a yielding in the looks of France:
Mark how they whisper: urge them while their souls
485 Are capable of this ambition,
Lest zeal, now melted by the windy breath
Of soft petitions, pity and remorse,
Cool and congeal again to what it was.

CITIZEN   Why answer not the double majesties
490 This friendly treaty of our threatened town?

KING PHILIP   Speak England first, that hath been forward first
To speak unto this city: what say you?

KING JOHN   If that the dauphin there, thy princely son,
Can in this book of beauty read 'I love',
495 Her dowry shall weigh equal with a queen:
For Anjou and fair Touraine, Maine, Poitiers,
And all that we upon this side the sea —
Except this city now by us besieged —
Find liable to our crown and dignity,
500 Shall gild her bridal bed and make her rich

---

472 **bastinado** beating with a stick   474 **buffets** beats, strikes   475 **Zounds** by God's wounds
bethumped pounded, thumped soundly   476 **Since . . . dad** i.e. since I learned to speak
(conceivably suggesting punishment for the illegitimate boy calling Sir Robert "Dad")
477 **list** listen   **conjunction** union   480 **unsured** insecure   481 **yon** yonder, that (one over
there)   **green** youthful/inexperienced   **boy** i.e. Arthur   **sun** i.e. royal patronage
484 **Mark** note, observe   485 **capable of** receptive to   486 **zeal** enthusiasm   487 **soft
petitions** gentle pleas   **remorse** sorrow/compassion   490 **treaty** proposition   491 **forward**
ready   494 **in . . . love** i.e. love Blanche   496 **Anjou** Folio prints "*Angiers*," presumably
mistaking the province of Anjou for the city of Angiers where the scene takes place   497 **the**
of the   499 **liable** subject

In titles, honours, and promotions,
As she in beauty, education, blood,
Holds hand with any princess of the world.

KING PHILIP   What say'st thou, boy? Look in the lady's face.

505 LEWIS   I do, my lord, and in her eye I find
A wonder, or a wondrous miracle,
The shadow of myself formed in her eye:
Which, being but the shadow of your son,
Becomes a sun and makes your son a shadow:

510 I do protest I never loved myself
Till now infixèd I beheld myself
Drawn in the flattering table of her eye.

Whispers with Blanche

BASTARD   Drawn in the flattering table of her eye,
Hanged in the frowning wrinkle of her brow,

515 And quartered in her heart, he doth espy
Himself love's traitor: this is pity now,
That hanged and drawn and quartered there should be
In such a love so vile a lout as he.

BLANCHE   My uncle's will in this respect is mine:

520 If he see aught in you that makes him like,
That anything he sees which moves his liking,
I can with ease translate it to my will:
Or if you will, to speak more properly,
I will enforce it eas'ly to my love.

525 Further I will not flatter you, my lord,
That all I see in you is worthy love,
Than this: that nothing do I see in you,

---

501 **promotions** social advancement   503 **Holds hand with** i.e. is equal to   507 **shadow** reflection, image (sense then shifts to "mere imitation/shadow cast by the sun")   508 **son** plays on "sun" (popular image of royal glory)   509 **makes . . . shadow** i.e. outshines my actual or former self (plays on sense of "dims even your royal glory")   511 **infixèd** fastened firmly   512 **table** tablet, painting surface   513 **Drawn** plays on the sense of "disemboweled" (being **hanged, drawn,** and **quartered** was a traitor's punishment)   515 **quartered** cut into pieces/lodged   **espy** discern   518 **love** expression of love/lover   519 **will** desire, determination   520 **aught** anything   521 **That anything** whatever it is   522 **translate** convert, transform   523 **properly** correctly, decorously   524 **enforce** urge/compel, impose   526 **That** i.e. by saying that   **worthy** worthy of

Though churlish thoughts themselves should be your judge,
That I can find should merit any hate.

530 KING JOHN   What say these young ones? What say you, my
     niece?

BLANCHE   That she is bound in honour still to do
What you in wisdom still vouchsafe to say.

KING JOHN   Speak then, Prince Dauphin, can you love this lady?

LEWIS   Nay, ask me if I can refrain from love,
535 For I do love her most unfeignedly.

KING JOHN   Then do I give Volquessen, Touraine, Maine,
Poitiers and Anjou, these five provinces,
With her to thee, and this addition more:
Full thirty thousand marks of English coin.
540 Philip of France, if thou be pleased withal,
Command thy son and daughter to join hands.

KING PHILIP   It likes us well, young princes: close your hands.

AUSTRIA   And your lips too, for I am well assured
That I did so when I was first assured.   *Lewis and Blanche join*

545 KING PHILIP   Now, citizens of Angiers, ope your   *hands and kiss*
     gates,
Let in that amity which you have made,
For at Saint Mary's chapel presently
The rites of marriage shall be solemnized.
Is not the lady Constance in this troop?
550 I know she is not, for this match made up
Her presence would have interrupted much.
Where is she and her son? Tell me, who knows.

LEWIS   She is sad and passionate at your highness' tent.

KING PHILIP   And by my faith this league that we have made
555 Will give her sadness very little cure.—
Brother of England, how may we content

---

528 churlish harsh/grudging   **529 merit** deserve   **531 still** always   **532 vouchsafe** deign,
graciously condescend   **535 unfeignedly** genuinely   **539 Full** i.e. all of   **mark** monetary
unit (not a coin) worth two thirds of an English pound   **540 withal** with this   **542 likes**
pleases   **close** join   **543 well assured** very certain   **544 assured** betrothed
547 presently immediately   **550 made up** accomplished   **552 who** whoever
553 passionate impassioned/emotional/sorrowful

This widow lady? In her right we came,
Which we, God knows, have turned another way,
To our own vantage.

560   KING JOHN   We will heal up all,
For we'll create young Arthur Duke of Bretagne
And Earl of Richmond, and this rich fair town
We make him lord of. Call the lady Constance:
Some speedy messenger bid her repair

565   To our solemnity: I trust we shall,   [*Exit Salisbury?*]
If not fill up the measure of her will,
Yet in some measure satisfy her so
That we shall stop her exclamation.
Go we as well as haste will suffer us

570   To this unlooked-for, unpreparèd pomp.

                                        Exeunt [all but the Bastard]

      BASTARD   Mad world, mad kings, mad composition!
John, to stop Arthur's title in the whole,
Hath willingly departed with a part,
And France, whose armour conscience buckled on,

575   Whom zeal and charity brought to the field
As God's own soldier, rounded in the ear
With that same purpose-changer, that sly devil,
That broker that still breaks the pate of faith,
That daily break-vow, he that wins of all,

580   Of kings, of beggars, old men, young men, maids,
Who having no external thing to lose
But the word 'maid', cheats the poor maid of that:
That smooth-faced gentleman, tickling commodity,

---

564 **repair** come   565 **solemnity** i.e. the wedding ceremony   566 **measure** magnitude,
capacity   567 **measure** limited extent, proportion   568 **exclamation** outcry, objection
569 **suffer** permit   570 **pomp** celebration   571 **composition** settlement/compromise
572 **title . . . whole** claim to the whole kingdom   573 **departed** parted   576 **rounded**
whispered   577 **With** by   578 **broker** go-between, agent (plays on the notion of breakage)
breaks beats, cracks   **pate** head, skull   **faith** loyalty/truth   579 **wins** gets the better
581 **Who** i.e. the maid's   **thing** plays on the sense of "penis"   582 **'maid'** virgin
583 **smooth-faced** plausible/deceitful   **tickling** amusing, playing with (plays on the sense of
"fondling sexually")   **commodity** convenience, expediency/advantage, profit, self-interest/
woman in her sexual capacity (plays on the sense of "virginity/female sexual goods")

Commodity, the bias of the world,
585 The world who of itself is peisèd well,
Made to run even upon even ground,
Till this advantage, this vile-drawing bias,
This sway of motion, this commodity,
Makes it take head from all indifferency,
590 From all direction, purpose, course, intent:
And this same bias, this commodity,
This bawd, this broker, this all-changing word,
Clapped on the outward eye of fickle France,
Hath drawn him from his own determined aid,
595 From a resolved and honourable war,
To a most base and vile-concluded peace.
And why rail I on this commodity?
But for because he hath not wooed me yet:
Not that I have the power to clutch my hand,
600 When his fair angels would salute my palm;
But for my hand, as unattempted yet,
Like a poor beggar, raileth on the rich.
Well, whiles I am a beggar, I will rail,
And say there is no sin but to be rich:
605 And being rich, my virtue then shall be
To say there is no vice but beggary:
Since kings break faith upon commodity,
Gain be my lord, for I will worship thee.   *Exit*

---

584 **bias** natural inclination (literally the weight in the bowling ball that enables it to be rolled in a curve)   585 **peisèd** poised, weighted   586 **even** level, evenly   587 **vile-drawing** i.e. that attracts evil   588 **sway** guiding power/swerve/change   589 **take head from** rebel against/ roll away from   **indifferency** moderation/equal impartiality   592 **bawd** pimp, go-between   **all-changing** i.e. causing everything to change   593 **Clapped on** fixed on, presented to   **outward eye** eyeball, external eye/hole in the bowling ball through which the bias was inserted   594 **determined** resolved/planned   **aid** i.e. support for Arthur's cause   595 **resolved** determined/settled   596 **base** dishonorable/worthless   597 **rail I on** do I rant about   598 **But for** only   599 **clutch** clench (in refusal of an offer)   600 **angels** gold coins   **salute** greet/touch (plays on the sense of "gold coin" and on the notion of "angelic salutation"—i.e. the angels' greeting to the Virgin Mary)   601 **for** because   **unattempted** untempted/ unapproached   607 **upon** because of

Act 2 [Scene 2]   *running scene 3*

Enter Constance, Arthur and Salisbury

CONSTANCE   Gone to be married? Gone to swear a   *To Salisbury*
       peace?
       False blood to false blood joined! Gone to be friends?
       Shall Lewis have Blanche, and Blanche those provinces?
       It is not so, thou hast misspoke, misheard:
5   Be well advised, tell o'er thy tale again.
       It cannot be, thou dost but say 'tis so.
       I trust I may not trust thee, for thy word
       Is but the vain breath of a common man:
       Believe me, I do not believe thee, man:
10   I have a king's oath to the contrary.
       Thou shalt be punished for thus frighting me,
       For I am sick and capable of fears:
       Oppressed with wrongs, and therefore full of fears:
       A widow, husbandless, subject to fears,
15   A woman naturally born to fears;
       And though thou now confess thou didst but jest
       With my vexed spirits, I cannot take a truce,
       But they will quake and tremble all this day.
       What dost thou mean by shaking of thy head?
20   Why dost thou look so sadly on my son?
       What means that hand upon that breast of thine?
       Why holds thine eye that lamentable rheum,
       Like a proud river peering o'er his bounds?
       Be these sad signs confirmers of thy words?
25   Then speak again, not all thy former tale,
       But this one word: whether thy tale be true.

2.2   4 misspoke spoken inaccurately/expressed badly   **5 Be well advised** consider
carefully/be well informed   **6 but** only   **7 trust** believe   **8 common man** i.e. not a king
11 frighting frightening   **12 capable of** susceptible to   **16 though** even if   **17 take a truce**
make peace   **20 sadly** gravely   **22 lamentable** sorrowful   **rheum** watery discharge, i.e.
tears   **23 proud** swollen/arrogant   **peering o'er his** overflowing its   **24 sad** solemn/
sorrowful

SALISBURY   As true as I believe you think them false
That give you cause to prove my saying true.

CONSTANCE   O, if thou teach me to believe this sorrow,
30 Teach thou this sorrow how to make me die,
And let belief and life encounter so
As doth the fury of two desperate men,
Which in the very meeting fall and die.
Lewis marry Blanche!— O boy, then where art thou?   *To Arthur*
35 France friend with England, what becomes of me?—
Fellow, be gone: I cannot brook thy sight: *To Salisbury*
This news hath made thee a most ugly man.

SALISBURY   What other harm have I, good lady, done,
But spoke the harm that is by others done?

40 CONSTANCE   Which harm within itself so heinous is
As it makes harmful all that speak of it.

ARTHUR   I do beseech you, madam, be content.

CONSTANCE   If thou that bidd'st me be content wert grim,
Ugly and sland'rous to thy mother's womb,
45 Full of unpleasing blots and sightless stains,
Lame, foolish, crooked, swart, prodigious,
Patched with foul moles and eye-offending marks,
I would not care, I then would be content,
For then I should not love thee, no, nor thou
50 Become thy great birth, nor deserve a crown.
But thou art fair, and at thy birth, dear boy,
Nature and Fortune joined to make thee great.
Of Nature's gifts thou mayst with lilies boast,
And with the half-blown rose. But Fortune, O,
55 She is corrupted, changed, and won from thee:

---

27 them either King John and King Philip or simply the French   **28 prove** discover by experience   **31 encounter** meet in combat   **36 brook** tolerate   **42 content** patient, calm
43 wert were   **grim** ugly/destructive   **44 sland'rous** shameful   **45 sightless** unsightly, offensive (possibly "unseen, internal")   **46 crooked** deformed   **swart** swarthy, of dark complexion (considered unattractive)   **prodigious** monstrous, unnatural/ill-omened
47 Patched blotched, marked   **50 Become** befit   **51 fair** handsome/pale-complexioned
54 half-blown half-blossomed, i.e. still young and beautiful

Sh'adulterates hourly with thine uncle John,
And with her golden hand hath plucked on France
To tread down fair respect of sovereignty,
And made his majesty the bawd to theirs.

60   France is a bawd to Fortune and King John,
That strumpet Fortune, that usurping John:—
Tell me, thou fellow, is not France forsworn?   *To Salisbury*
Envenom him with words, or get thee gone
And leave those woes alone, which I alone

65   Am bound to underbear.

SALISBURY   Pardon me, madam,
I may not go without you to the kings.

CONSTANCE   Thou mayst, thou shalt: I will not go with thee:
I will instruct my sorrows to be proud,

70   For grief is proud and makes his owner stoop.
To me and to the state of my great grief
Let kings assemble: for my grief's so great
That no supporter but the huge firm earth
Can hold it up: here I and sorrows sit: *She sits upon the ground*

75   Here is my throne: bid kings come bow to it.

[*Exit Salisbury with Arthur*]   *Constance*

remains seated

Act 3 Scene 1   *running scene 3 continues*

Enter King John, King Philip, Lewis, Blanche, Queen Elinor, the
Bastard [and] Austria

KING PHILIP   'Tis true, fair daughter, and this blessèd day
Ever in France shall be kept festival:

56 **Sh'adulterates** she commits adultery (rather than being faithful to Arthur)   **hourly**
constantly (puns on "whore-ly," i.e. like a whore)   57 **golden** implies offers of money
plucked on drawn on, enticed/dragged in   58 **sovereignty** i.e. Arthur's claim to the throne
59 **his majesty** i.e. King Philip and his power   **theirs** i.e. King John and Fortune's
61 **strumpet** harlot, prostitute   62 **fellow** with connotations of "servant/worthless man"
France i.e. the French king   **forsworn** guilty of perjury, breaking his promise   63 **Envenom**
poison   **words** i.e. curses   65 **underbear** endure   69 **proud** swollen/arrogant   71 **state**
condition/throne   **3.1   1 'Tis true** Philip and Blanche enter mid-conversation   **daughter**
i.e. daughter-in-law

To solemnize this day the glorious sun
Stays in his course and plays the alchemist,
5   Turning with splendour of his precious eye
The meagre cloddy earth to glittering gold:
The yearly course that brings this day about
Shall never see it but a holy day.

CONSTANCE   A wicked day, and not a holy day!   *Rising*
10   What hath this day deserved? What hath it done,
That it in golden letters should be set
Among the high tides in the calendar?
Nay, rather turn this day out of the week,
This day of shame, oppression, perjury.
15   Or if it must stand still, let wives with child
Pray that their burdens may not fall this day,
Lest that their hopes prodigiously be crossed:
But on this day let seamen fear no wreck:
No bargains break that are not this day made;
20   This day all things begun come to ill end,
Yea, faith itself to hollow falsehood change.

KING PHILIP   By heaven, lady, you shall have no cause
To curse the fair proceedings of this day:
Have I not pawned to you my majesty?
25   CONSTANCE   You have beguiled me with a counterfeit
Resembling majesty, which, being touched and tried,
Proves valueless: you are forsworn, forsworn:
You came in arms to spill mine enemies' blood,
But now in arms you strengthen it with yours.
30   The grappling vigour and rough frown of war
Is cold in amity and painted peace,

---

4 Stays . . . course stands still   **plays the alchemist** i.e. turns base metals into gold   **8 holy day** holiday/blessed occasion   **11 golden letters** used to mark feast days in the Church calendar   **12 high tides** important festival dates   **15 stand still** remain   **with child** pregnant   **16 fall** i.e. be born   **17 prodigiously** with ill omen, i.e. with the birth of a deformed child   **crossed** thwarted   **18 But** except   **wreck** shipwreck   **19 No . . . made** break only agreements made on this day   **24 pawned** pledged   **majesty** royal dignity, i.e. his word   **25 beguiled** deceived   **26 touched and tried** put to the test   **27 forsworn** perjured, guilty of breaking your word   **28 in arms** with weapons/in friendship   **29 arms** coat of arms (Blanche and Lewis's heraldic emblems will now be united)   **yours** i.e. your arms/blood   **31 painted** superficial/feigned

And our oppression hath made up this league:
Arm, arm, you heavens, against these perjured kings!
A widow cries: be husband to me, heavens!
35   Let not the hours of this ungodly day
Wear out the days in peace; but, ere sun set,
Set armèd discord 'twixt these perjured kings:
Hear me, O, hear me!

AUSTRIA   Lady Constance, peace!

40   CONSTANCE   War, war, no peace! Peace is to me a war:
O Limoges, O Austria, thou dost shame
That bloody spoil: thou slave, thou wretch, thou coward:
Thou little valiant, great in villainy,
Thou ever strong upon the stronger side;
45   Thou Fortune's champion, that dost never fight
But when her humorous ladyship is by
To teach thee safety: thou art perjured too,
And sooth'st up greatness. What a fool art thou,
A ramping fool, to brag, and stamp, and swear
50   Upon my party: thou cold-blooded slave,
Hast thou not spoke like thunder on my side?
Been sworn my soldier, bidding me depend
Upon thy stars, thy fortune, and thy strength,
And dost thou now fall over to my foes?
55   Thou wear a lion's hide! Doff it for shame,
And hang a calf's-skin on those recreant limbs.

AUSTRIA   O, that a man should speak those words to me!

BASTARD   And hang a calf's-skin on those recreant limbs.

AUSTRIA   Thou dar'st not say so, villain, for thy life.

60   BASTARD   And hang a calf's-skin on those recreant limbs.

---

32 our i.e. Constance and Arthur's   made up composed, accomplished   league alliance
36 Wear out survive/waste   days some editors emend to "day"   41 Limoges i.e. Austria
(Shakespeare combined two historical figures in one character, Duke Leopold of Austria and
Viscount Vidomar of Limoges)   42 bloody spoil i.e. the lion's skin   spoil plunder, booty
45 champion one who fights on behalf of another   46 humorous temperamental   by
nearby   47 safety i.e. the best course of action, how to avoid getting injured   48 sooth'st up
greatness flatter powerful people   49 ramping rampant/roaring/excessive   swear . . . party
declare your support for my cause   54 fall over defect   55 Doff remove   56 calf's-skin
associated with fools and cowards   recreant cowardly

KING JOHN   We like not this: thou dost forget thyself.

Enter Pandulph

KING PHILIP   Here comes the holy legate of the Pope.

CARDINAL PANDULPH   Hail, you anointed deputies of heaven.—
To thee, King John, my holy errand is:
65   I Pandulph, of fair Milan cardinal,
And from Pope Innocent the legate here,
Do in his name religiously demand
Why thou against the Church, our holy mother,
So wilfully dost spurn; and force perforce
70   Keep Stephen Langton, chosen archbishop
Of Canterbury, from that holy see:
This, in our foresaid holy father's name,
Pope Innocent, I do demand of thee.

KING JOHN   What earthy name to interrogatories
75   Can test the free breath of a sacred king?
Thou canst not, cardinal, devise a name
So slight, unworthy, and ridiculous
To charge me to an answer, as the Pope.
Tell him this tale, and from the mouth of England
80   Add thus much more, that no Italian priest
Shall tithe or toll in our dominions:
But as we, under heaven, are supreme head,
So, under him, that great supremacy,
Where we do reign, we will alone uphold
85   Without th'assistance of a mortal hand:
So tell the Pope, all reverence set apart
To him and his usurped authority.

KING PHILIP   Brother of England, you blaspheme in this.

---

61 *Pandulph* a fusion of two historical figures, one a cardinal, the other a **legate**   **62 legate** papal representative   **66 Pope Innocent** Innocent III   **67 religiously** solemnly/in the name of religion   **69 spurn** rebel, kick   **force perforce** with violent compulsion   **70 Stephen Langton** elected Archbishop of Canterbury by Pope Innocent, but rejected by John   **71 see** bishopric/the seat of a bishop in his church   **72 foresaid** aforementioned   **74 earthy** earthly **interrogatories** questions put to an accused person   **75 test** put to the proof   **78 charge** order   **81 tithe** levy a tax (specifically the tenth of one's goods owed to the Church)   **toll** exact a payment   **83 great supremacy** highest authority or power   **84 Where** in which **uphold** maintain/rule   **86 set apart** discarded, ignored   **88 blaspheme** speak irreverently

KING JOHN   Though you and all the kings of Christendom
90   Are led so grossly by this meddling priest,
          Dreading the curse that money may buy out,
          And by the merit of vile gold, dross, dust,
          Purchase corrupted pardon of a man,
          Who in that sale sells pardon from himself:
95   Though you and all the rest so grossly led
          This juggling witchcraft with revenue cherish,
          Yet I alone, alone do me oppose
          Against the Pope, and count his friends my foes.

CARDINAL PANDULPH   Then by the lawful power that I have,
100   Thou shalt stand cursed and excommunicate:
          And blessèd shall he be that doth revolt
          From his allegiance to an heretic:
          And meritorious shall that hand be called,
          Canonizèd and worshipped as a saint,
105   That takes away by any secret course
          Thy hateful life.

CONSTANCE   O, lawful let it be
          That I have room with Rome to curse awhile:
          Good Father Cardinal, cry thou 'Amen'
110   To my keen curses; for without my wrong
          There is no tongue hath power to curse him right.

CARDINAL PANDULPH   There's law and warrant, lady, for my curse.

CONSTANCE   And for mine too: when law can do no right,
          Let it be lawful that law bar no wrong:
115   Law cannot give my child his kingdom here;
          For he that holds his kingdom holds the law:
          Therefore, since law itself is perfect wrong,
          How can the law forbid my tongue to curse?

---

90 grossly foolishly   meddling priest i.e. the Pope   91 the curse i.e. excommunication
buy out cancel   92 vile base   dross impure substance   93 of from   94 sells . . . himself
incurs his own damnation/sells pardons that do not come from God   96 juggling cheating,
deceiving   cherish nourish, maintain   97 me oppose place myself in opposition
100 excommunicate excommunicated   102 heretic one who maintains unorthodox religious
views   108 room space (puns on Rome)   110 keen eager/sharp   my wrong the wrong
done to me (my motivation)   111 right properly, correctly, rightfully (plays on the sense of
"good")   112 warrant authority   114 bar no wrong does not prevent retaliation, i.e. cursing
116 holds maintains, controls   117 perfect completely

CARDINAL PANDULPH   Philip of France, on peril of a curse,
120   Let go the hand of that arch-heretic,
         And raise the power of France upon his head,
         Unless he do submit himself to Rome.
QUEEN ELINOR   Look'st thou pale, France? Do not let go thy hand.
CONSTANCE   Look to that, devil, lest that France repent,
125   And by disjoining hands, hell lose a soul.
AUSTRIA   King Philip, listen to the cardinal.
BASTARD   And hang a calf's-skin on his recreant limbs.
AUSTRIA   Well, ruffian, I must pocket up these wrongs,
         Because—
130 BASTARD   Your breeches best may carry them.
KING JOHN   Philip, what say'st thou to the cardinal?
CONSTANCE   What should he say, but as the cardinal?
LEWIS   Bethink you, father, for the difference
         Is purchase of a heavy curse from Rome,
135   Or the light loss of England for a friend:
         Forgo the easier.
BLANCHE   That's the curse of Rome.
CONSTANCE   O Lewis, stand fast: the devil tempts thee here
         In likeness of a new untrimmèd bride.
140 BLANCHE   The lady Constance speaks not from her faith,
         But from her need.
CONSTANCE   O, if thou grant my need,
         Which only lives but by the death of faith,
         That need must needs infer this principle,
145   That faith would live again by death of need:
         O then tread down my need, and faith mounts up:
         Keep my need up, and faith is trodden down.
KING JOHN   The king is moved, and answers not to this.

---

120 **arch-heretic** chief rebel to the Christian Church   121 **power of France** i.e. army   **his head** him/his army   124 **Look to that** beware of/consider that possibility   128 **pocket up** endure/swallow (the Bastard plays on the literal sense of pockets in **breeches**)   132 **as the cardinal** i.e. as the cardinal says   133 **Bethink you** consider carefully   **difference** disagreement/choice   134 **purchase** acquisition   135 **light** minor   139 **untrimmèd** unadorned/unbedded, i.e. virgin   142 **need** appeal for help   143 **but by** because of   **faith** i.e. King Philip's promise   144 **needs** necessarily   148 **moved** affected with sympathy/angered

CONSTANCE   O, be removed from him, and answer   *To King Philip*
well!

150   AUSTRIA   Do so, King Philip, hang no more in doubt.

BASTARD   Hang nothing but a calf's-skin, most sweet lout.

KING PHILIP   I am perplexed, and know not what to say.

CARDINAL PANDULPH   What canst thou say but will perplex thee
more,
If thou stand excommunicate and cursed?

155   KING PHILIP   Good reverend father, make my person yours,
And tell me how you would bestow yourself.
This royal hand and mine are newly knit,
And the conjunction of our inward souls
Married in league, coupled and linked together
160   With all religious strength of sacred vows:
The latest breath that gave the sound of words
Was deep-sworn faith, peace, amity, true love
Between our kingdoms and our royal selves,
And even before this truce, but new before,
165   No longer than we well could wash our hands
To clap this royal bargain up of peace,
Heaven knows, they were besmeared and overstained
With slaughter's pencil, where revenge did paint
The fearful difference of incensèd kings:
170   And shall these hands, so lately purged of blood,
So newly joined in love, so strong in both,
Unyoke this seizure and this kind regreet?
Play fast and loose with faith, so jest with heaven,
Make such unconstant children of ourselves,
175   As now again to snatch our palm from palm?

---

149 be removed stand apart/separate yourself from his plans/be estranged (plays on **moved**)
151 Hang i.e. wear   **155 make . . . yours** i.e. put yourself in my position   **156 bestow
yourself** behave   **161 latest** last   **164 even** right   **but new** just immediately   **166 clap**
strike hands reciprocally in token of a bargain   **bargain** transaction   **167 overstained**
covered with stains/dyed   **168 pencil** paintbrush   **169 fearful** awesome, fear-inducing
difference dispute, discord   **172 Unyoke this seizure** unclasp this grasp (of hands)   **regreet**
return of salutation   **173 fast and loose** i.e. gamble (literally, game of betting whether the
end of a rope was fastened or not)   **so** in the same manner   **174 unconstant** changeable,
fickle

Unswear faith sworn, and on the marriage-bed
Of smiling peace to march a bloody host,
And make a riot on the gentle brow
Of true sincerity? O holy sir,
180   My reverend father, let it not be so:
Out of your grace, devise, ordain, impose
Some gentle order, and then we shall be blest
To do your pleasure and continue friends.

CARDINAL PANDULPH   All form is formless, order orderless,
185   Save what is opposite to England's love.
Therefore to arms, be champion of our Church,
Or let the Church, our mother, breathe her curse,
A mother's curse, on her revolting son:
France, thou mayst hold a serpent by the tongue,
190   A casèd lion by the mortal paw,
A fasting tiger safer by the tooth,
Than keep in peace that hand which thou dost hold.

KING PHILIP   I may disjoin my hand, but not my faith.

CARDINAL PANDULPH   So mak'st thou faith an enemy to faith,
195   And like a civil war set'st oath to oath,
Thy tongue against thy tongue. O, let thy vow
First made to heaven, first be to heaven performed,
That is, to be the champion of our Church:
What since thou swor'st is sworn against thyself,
200   And may not be performèd by thyself,
For that which thou hast sworn to do amiss
Is not amiss when it is truly done:
And being not done, where doing tends to ill,
The truth is then most done not doing it:
205   The better act of purposes mistook

---

177 **bloody** bloodstained/violent   **host** army   178 **brow** forehead   181 **ordain** establish
188 **revolting** rebelling   189 **hold . . . tongue** "take a serpent by the tongue" (proverbial; a
snake's venom was thought to be located in the tongue)   190 **casèd** wearing a skin, i.e. living
mortal fatal, lethal   193 **faith** promise (to King John)   194 **faith** religious faith, i.e. the
Church   195 **to** against   199 **since** subsequently, i.e. since swearing allegiance to the
Church   **swor'st** i.e. allegiance with John   202 **truly done** i.e. not done at all   203 **to**
toward   205 **act** action   **purposes mistook** misguided aims, erroneous outcomes

Is to mistake again: though indirect,
Yet indirection thereby grows direct,
And falsehood falsehood cures, as fire cools fire
Within the scorchèd veins of one new burned:
210 It is religion that doth make vows kept,
But thou hast sworn against religion:
By what thou swear'st against the thing thou swear'st,
And mak'st an oath the surety for thy truth
Against an oath the truth: thou art unsure
215 To swear, swears only not to be forsworn,
Else what a mockery should it be to swear?
But thou dost swear only to be forsworn,
And most forsworn, to keep what thou dost swear:
Therefore thy later vows against thy first
220 Is in thyself rebellion to thyself:
And better conquest never canst thou make
Than arm thy constant and thy nobler parts
Against these giddy loose suggestions:
Upon which better part our prayers come in,
225 If thou vouchsafe them. But if not, then know
The peril of our curses light on thee
So heavy as thou shalt not shake them off,
But in despair die under their black weight.

AUSTRIA   Rebellion, flat rebellion!
230 BASTARD   Will't not be?
Will not a calf's-skin stop that mouth of thine?

LEWIS   Father, to arms!

BLANCHE   Upon thy wedding day?
Against the blood that thou hast marrièd?

---

206 **mistake again** i.e. break your oath to John   **indirect** roundabout, devious   **208 fire . . .
burned** "one heat drives out another" (proverbial; heat was used to treat burns)   **210 religion**
religious belief, obligation or fear   **212 By . . . swear'st** i.e. you swear against the very faith by
which you swear (in the making of your second oath to John)   **213 And . . . truth** i.e. in
making an oath that apparently guarantees your loyalty and integrity, you in fact violate your
faith   **214 unsure** uncertain, hesitant   **215 swears . . . forsworn** you swear never to break
your word   **224 part** side   **226 light** descend (heavy creates a play on the sense of "of little
weight")   **227 as** that   **228 black** deadly   **229 Rebellion** i.e. Philip's rebellion against the
Church or against himself   **flat** outright   **230 be** i.e. be still and silent   **231 stop** fill/silence
234 blood . . . marrièd i.e. as Blanche is John's niece

235   What, shall our feast be kept with slaughtered men?
       Shall braying trumpets and loud churlish drums,
       Clamours of hell, be measures to our pomp?
       O husband, hear me: ay, alack, how new
       Is 'husband' in my mouth! Even for that name,
240   Which till this time my tongue did ne'er pronounce,
       Upon my knee I beg, go not to arms
       Against mine uncle.   *She may kneel here*

CONSTANCE   O, upon my knee made hard with   *She may kneel*
       kneeling,
       I do pray to thee, thou virtuous dauphin,
245   Alter not the doom forethought by heaven.

BLANCHE   Now shall I see thy love: what motive may
       Be stronger with thee than the name of wife?

CONSTANCE   That which upholdeth him that thee upholds:
       His honour:— O, thine honour, Lewis, thine honour! *To Lewis*

250 LEWIS   I muse your majesty doth seem so cold, *To King Philip*
       When such profound respects do pull you on.

CARDINAL PANDULPH   I will denounce a curse upon his head.

KING PHILIP   Thou shalt not need. England, I will fall from thee.

CONSTANCE   O, fair return of banished majesty!   *She may rise*

255 QUEEN ELINOR   O, foul revolt of French inconstancy!

KING JOHN   France, thou shalt rue this hour within this hour.

BASTARD   Old Time the clock-setter, that bald sexton Time,
       Is it as he will? Well then, France shall rue.

BLANCHE   The sun's o'ercast with blood: fair day, adieu!
260   Which is the side that I must go withal?
       I am with both, each army hath a hand,
       And in their rage, I having hold of both,
       They whirl asunder and dismember me.
       Husband, I cannot pray that thou mayst win:—
265   Uncle, I needs must pray that thou mayst lose:—

---

235 **kept** celebrated   237 **measures** melodious accompaniment   245 **doom** judgment/
destiny   **forethought** anticipated, planned   248 **that thee upholds** who supports you
250 **muse** wonder   251 **profound respects** important considerations   252 **denounce**
proclaim   253 **fall from** desert/renounce   256 **rue** grieve for/regret   257 **bald** proverbially,
Time was hairless   259 **adieu** good-bye   263 **dismember** mutilate, tear limb from limb

Father, I may not wish the fortune thine:—
Grandam, I will not wish thy wishes thrive:
Whoever wins, on that side shall I lose:
Assurèd loss before the match be played.

270   LEWIS   Lady, with me, with me thy fortune   *He may help her rise*
lies.

BLANCHE   There where my fortune lives, there my life dies.

KING JOHN   Cousin, go draw our puissance together.

                                       [Exit the Bastard]

France, I am burned up with inflaming wrath,
A rage whose heat hath this condition:

275   That nothing can allay, nothing but blood,
The blood, and dearest-valued blood, of France.

KING PHILIP   Thy rage shall burn thee up, and thou shalt turn
To ashes, ere our blood shall quench that fire:
Look to thyself, thou art in jeopardy.

280   KING JOHN   No more than he that threats. To arms let's hie!

                                              Exeunt

Act 3 Scene 2   *running scene 4*

Alarums, excursions. Enter [the] Bastard, with Austria's head

BASTARD   Now, by my life, this day grows wondrous hot:
Some airy devil hovers in the sky
And pours down mischief. Austria's head lie there,   *He puts down*
While Philip breathes.   *Austria's head*

Enter [King] John, Arthur [and] Hubert

5   KING JOHN   Hubert, keep this boy.— Philip, make up:
My mother is assailèd in our tent,
And ta'en, I fear.

---

266 **Father** i.e. father-in-law   272 **Cousin** i.e. kinsman   **puissance** power/army
274 **condition** nature/stipulation   276 **dearest-valued** i.e. royal/life-sustaining   280 **threats**
threatens   **hie** hasten   **3.2** *Alarums* calls to battle   *excursions* fighting (across the stage)
2 **airy devil** aerial demons were associated with storms and, here, battle   4 **Philip** i.e. the
Bastard   **breathes** catches his breath   *Hubert* probably based on Hubert de Burgh, chief
judicial officer under King John   5 **keep** look after/guard   **make up** move forward, press on
6 **assailèd** attacked   7 **ta'en** taken, captured

BASTARD   My lord, I rescued her:
Her highness is in safety, fear you not:
10   But on, my liege, for very little pains
Will bring this labour to an happy end.   *Exeunt*

Alarums, excursions, retreat. Enter King John, Queen Elinor, Arthur,
[the] Bastard, Hubert, [and] Lords

KING JOHN   So shall it be: your grace shall stay   *To Queen Elinor*
    behind
So strongly guarded:— Cousin, look not sad: *To Arthur*
Thy grandam loves thee; and thy uncle will
15   As dear be to thee as thy father was.

ARTHUR   O, this will make my mother die with grief.

KING JOHN   Cousin, away for England! Haste before,   *To Bastard*
And ere our coming see thou shake the bags
Of hoarding abbots: imprisoned angels
20   Set at liberty: the fat ribs of peace
Must by the hungry now be fed upon:
Use our commission in his utmost force.

BASTARD   Bell, book and candle shall not drive me back,
When gold and silver becks me to come on.
25   I leave your highness:— grandam, I will pray,
If ever I remember to be holy,
For your fair safety: so I kiss your hand.

ELINOR   Farewell, gentle cousin.

KING JOHN   Coz, farewell.   *[Exit the Bastard]*

30   QUEEN ELINOR   Come hither, little kinsman: hark, a word.   *To Arthur*

KING JOHN   Come hither, Hubert.   *He takes Hubert aside*
                    O my gentle Hubert,
We owe thee much: within this wall of flesh
There is a soul counts thee her creditor

---

10 **liege** lord, superior entitled to feudal allegiance and service   **pains . . . labour** a birth
metaphor   **11 happy end** fortunate outcome/pleasing conclusion   *retreat* call for
withdrawal of army   **12 stay behind** i.e. remain behind in charge of John's territories
17 Haste before hurry ahead (of us)   **19 angels** gold coins (playing on the sense of "heavenly
angels")   **22 commission** warrant/authority   **his** its   **23 Bell . . . candle** items involved in
the ceremony of excommunication   **24 becks** beckons   **28 gentle** kind/noble   **29 Coz**
cousin

And with advantage means to pay thy love:
35 And, my good friend, thy voluntary oath
Lives in this bosom, dearly cherishèd.
Give me thy hand: I had a thing to say,
But I will fit it with some better tune.
By heaven, Hubert, I am almost ashamed
40 To say what good respect I have of thee.

HUBERT I am much bounden to your majesty.

KING JOHN Good friend, thou hast no cause to say so yet,
But thou shalt have: and creep time ne'er so slow,
Yet it shall come for me to do thee good.
45 I had a thing to say, but let it go:
The sun is in the heaven, and the proud day,
Attended with the pleasures of the world,
Is all too wanton and too full of gauds
To give me audience: if the midnight bell
50 Did with his iron tongue and brazen mouth
Sound on into the drowsy race of night:
If this same were a churchyard where we stand,
And thou possessèd with a thousand wrongs:
Or if that surly spirit, melancholy,
55 Had baked thy blood and made it heavy, thick,
Which else runs tickling up and down the veins,
Making that idiot, laughter, keep men's eyes
And strain their cheeks to idle merriment,
A passion hateful to my purposes:
60 Or if that thou couldst see me without eyes,
Hear me without thine ears, and make reply
Without a tongue, using conceit alone,

---

34 **advantage** profit/interest **pay** repay 35 **voluntary** freely offered, willing 36 **bosom** i.e.
heart 38 **tune** i.e. words, speech 40 **respect** regard 41 **bounden** indebted, obliged
48 **wanton** lively, playful **gauds** showy playthings, attractive trifles 49 **give me audience**
listen to me **midnight bell** i.e. bell tolling midnight 50 **brazen** made of brass/shameless
51 **Sound on** continue striking **race** course 56 **else** otherwise 57 **idiot** clown/fool
keep occupy, hold captive 59 **passion** emotion 62 **conceit** thought

Without eyes, ears and harmful sound of words:
Then, in despite of broad-eyed watchful day,
65   I would into thy bosom pour my thoughts.
But, ah, I will not: yet I love thee well,
And by my troth, I think thou lov'st me well.

HUBERT   So well, that what you bid me undertake,
Though that my death were adjunct to my act,
70   By heaven, I would do it.

KING JOHN   Do not I know thou wouldst?
Good Hubert, Hubert, Hubert, throw thine eye
On yon young boy: I'll tell thee what, my friend,
He is a very serpent in my way,
75   And whereso'er this foot of mine doth tread,
He lies before me: dost thou understand me?
Thou art his keeper.

HUBERT   And I'll keep him so,
That he shall not offend your majesty.

80   KING JOHN   Death.

HUBERT   My lord?

KING JOHN   A grave.

HUBERT   He shall not live.

KING JOHN   Enough.

85   I could be merry now: Hubert, I love thee.
Well, I'll not say what I intend for thee:
Remember.— Madam, fare you well:
I'll send those powers o'er to your majesty.

ELINOR   My blessing go with thee.

90   KING JOHN   For England, cousin, go.
Hubert shall be your man, attend on you
With all true duty.— On toward Calais, ho!

Exeunt [Queen Elinor at one door, the rest at another]

---

64 despite spite   watchful wakeful/vigilant   67 troth faith   68 what whatever
69 adjunct to attendant upon, linked to   73 yon yonder, that   78 so in such a way
88 powers forces   90 cousin i.e. Arthur   91 man servant

Act 3 Scene 3   *running scene 5*

Enter King Philip, Lewis, Cardinal Pandulph [and] Attendants

KING PHILIP   So by a roaring tempest on the flood,
     A whole armado of convicted sail
     Is scattered and disjoined from fellowship.

CARDINAL PANDULPH   Courage and comfort: all shall yet go well.

5   KING PHILIP   What can go well when we have run so ill?
     Are we not beaten? Is not Angiers lost?
     Arthur ta'en prisoner? Divers dear friends slain?
     And bloody England into England gone,
     O'erbearing interruption, spite of France?

10   LEWIS   What he hath won, that hath he fortified:
     So hot a speed with such advice disposed,
     Such temperate order in so fierce a cause,
     Doth want example: who hath read or heard
     Of any kindred action like to this?

15   KING PHILIP   Well could I bear that England had this praise,
     So we could find some pattern of our shame.

     Enter Constance   *Distracted, with her hair down*

     Look, who comes here! A grave unto a soul:
     Holding th'eternal spirit against her will,
     In the vile prison of afflicted breath:

20   I prithee, lady, go away with me.

     CONSTANCE   Lo, now: now see the issue of your peace.

     KING PHILIP   Patience, good lady: comfort, gentle Constance.

     CONSTANCE   No, I defy all counsel, all redress,
     But that which ends all counsel, true redress:

25   Death, death, O amiable, lovely death:

3.3   1 **flood** sea   2 **armado** armada, fleet   **convicted** defeated   3 **fellowship** puns on
"fellow ships"   5 **run** fared/followed a course   7 **Divers** various/several   8 **bloody**
bloodstained/violent   **England** the King of England   9 **O'erbearing** overcoming
interruption resistance, obstacles   **spite** in defiance   11 **hot** active, vigorous, quick   **advice**
prudence   **disposed** handled   12 **temperate** calm, composed   13 **want example** lack
precedent   14 **kindred** related, allied in qualities   **like** similar   16 **So** provided that
pattern previous example   17 **grave** i.e. shell of the body, mere container   21 **issue** outcome
peace i.e. agreement, treaty   23 **defy** reject   **counsel** advice   **redress** assistance, comfort
24 **But** except   25 **amiable** lovable

Thou odoriferous stench: sound rottenness:
Arise forth from the couch of lasting night,
Thou hate and terror to prosperity,
And I will kiss thy detestable bones,
30   And put my eyeballs in thy vaulty brows,
And ring these fingers with thy household worms,
And stop this gap of breath with fulsome dust,
And be a carrion monster like thyself:
Come, grin on me, and I will think thou smil'st
35   And buss thee as thy wife: misery's love,
O, come to me!

KING PHILIP   O fair affliction, peace!

CONSTANCE   No, no, I will not, having breath to cry:
O, that my tongue were in the thunder's mouth!
40   Then with a passion would I shake the world,
And rouse from sleep that fell anatomy
Which cannot hear a lady's feeble voice,
Which scorns a modern invocation.

CARDINAL PANDULPH   Lady, you utter madness, and not sorrow.

45   CONSTANCE   Thou art not holy to belie me so:
I am not mad: this hair I tear is mine:
My name is Constance: I was Geoffrey's wife:
Young Arthur is my son, and he is lost:
I am not mad: I would to heaven I were,
50   For then, 'tis like I should forget myself:
O, if I could, what grief should I forget!
Preach some philosophy to make me mad,
And thou shalt be canonized, cardinal:
For, being not mad, but sensible of grief,
55   My reasonable part produces reason
How I may be delivered of these woes,

---

26 **odoriferous** sweet-smelling   **sound** wholesome, healthy   27 **lasting** everlasting
30 **vaulty** empty/sepulchral   32 **gap of breath** i.e. mouth   **fulsome** repulsive   33 **carrion**
skeletal/rotting   35 **buss** kiss   37 **affliction** i.e. afflicted one   41 **fell** terrible/cruel
anatomy skeleton   43 **modern** commonplace, everyday   **invocation** entreaty   45 **belie**
slander   50 **like** likely   54 **sensible of** sensitive to, capable of feeling   55 **reasonable part**
rational faculty   56 **delivered of** released from (perhaps with connotations of childbirth)

And teaches me to kill or hang myself:
If I were mad, I should forget my son,
Or madly think a babe of clouts were he:
60   I am not mad: too well, too well I feel
The different plague of each calamity.

KING PHILIP   Bind up those tresses: O, what love I note
In the fair multitude of those her hairs!
Where but by chance a silver drop hath fallen,
65   Even to that drop ten thousand wiry friends
Do glue themselves in sociable grief,
Like true, inseparable, faithful loves,
Sticking together in calamity.

CONSTANCE   To England, if you will.

70   KING PHILIP   Bind up your hairs.

CONSTANCE   Yes, that I will: and wherefore will I do it?
I tore them from their bonds and cried aloud
'O, that these hands could so redeem my son,
As they have given these hairs their liberty!'
75   But now I envy at their liberty,
And will again commit them to their bonds,
Because my poor child is a prisoner.   *She binds up her hair*
And, Father Cardinal, I have heard you say
That we shall see and know our friends in heaven:
80   If that be true, I shall see my boy again;
For since the birth of Cain, the first male child,
To him that did but yesterday suspire,
There was not such a gracious creature born:
But now will canker-sorrow eat my bud
85   And chase the native beauty from his cheek,

---

59 babe of clouts ragdoll   **clouts** cloths/rags   **61 different** distinct, individual   **plague**
affliction   **62 Bind . . . tresses** in her distress, Constance's hair is loose and disheveled
64 silver drop i.e. tear   **65 wiry friends** i.e. hairs (wiry does not necessarily suggest "coarse,
tough")   **66 sociable** sympathetic   **69 To . . . will** Constance's response to Philip's invitation
earlier in the scene   **71 wherefore** why   **73 redeem** liberate   **75 envy at** resent   **79 know**
recognize/be acquainted with   **81 Cain** in the Bible, Adam and Eve's eldest son (who killed his
brother Abel)   **82 suspire** (first) breathe   **83 gracious** filled with divine grace/virtuous/
delightful   **84 canker-sorrow** the gnawing worm of grief   **bud** i.e. young son   **85 native**
natural

And he will look as hollow as a ghost,
As dim and meagre as an ague's fit,
And so he'll die: and rising so again,
When I shall meet him in the court of heaven
90 I shall not know him: therefore never, never
Must I behold my pretty Arthur more.

CARDINAL PANDULPH   You hold too heinous a respect of grief.

CONSTANCE   He talks to me that never had a son.

KING PHILIP   You are as fond of grief as of your child.

95 CONSTANCE   Grief fills the room up of my absent child:
Lies in his bed, walks up and down with me,
Puts on his pretty looks, repeats his words,
Remembers me of all his gracious parts,
Stuffs out his vacant garments with his form;
100 Then have I reason to be fond of grief?
Fare you well: had you such a loss as I,
I could give better comfort than you do.   *She unbinds her hair*
I will not keep this form upon my head,
When there is such disorder in my wit:
105 O lord, my boy, my Arthur, my fair son,
My life, my joy, my food, my all the world:
My widow-comfort, and my sorrows' cure!   *Exit*

KING PHILIP   I fear some outrage, and I'll follow her.   *Exit*

LEWIS   There's nothing in this world can make me joy:
110 Life is as tedious as a twice-told tale,
Vexing the dull ear of a drowsy man;
And bitter shame hath spoiled the sweet word's taste
That it yields nought but shame and bitterness.

CARDINAL PANDULPH   Before the curing of a strong disease,
115 Even in the instant of repair and health,
The fit is strongest: evils that take leave,

---

87 dim dull/pale   meagre gaunt   an ague's fit (the victim of) a bout of shaking caused by
fever   88 so in that way/in that condition   rising i.e. from death/into heaven   90 know
recognize   92 heinous grave, severe   respect view   94 fond of doting on   95 room place
98 Remembers reminds   103 form orderly arrangement   108 outrage passionate act of
violence (i.e. suicide)   109 joy feel happy, take pleasure   111 dull bored/inattentive/sleepy
112 word's i.e. Life   113 That so that   115 in the instant at the precise moment   repair
recovery   116 fit bout of illness

On their departure most of all show evil:
What have you lost by losing of this day?

LEWIS   All days of glory, joy and happiness.

120 CARDINAL PANDULPH   If you had won it, certainly you had.
No, no: when Fortune means to men most good,
She looks upon them with a threat'ning eye:
'Tis strange to think how much King John hath lost
In this which he accounts so clearly won:

125 Are not you grieved that Arthur is his prisoner?

LEWIS   As heartily as he is glad he hath him.

CARDINAL PANDULPH   Your mind is all as youthful as your blood.
Now hear me speak with a prophetic spirit:
For even the breath of what I mean to speak

130 Shall blow each dust, each straw, each little rub,
Out of the path which shall directly lead
Thy foot to England's throne. And therefore mark:
John hath seized Arthur, and it cannot be
That whiles warm life plays in that infant's veins,

135 The misplaced John should entertain an hour,
One minute, nay, one quiet breath of rest.
A sceptre snatched with an unruly hand
Must be as boisterously maintained as gained:
And he that stands upon a slipp'ry place

140 Makes nice of no vile hold to stay him up:
That John may stand, then Arthur needs must fall:
So be it, for it cannot be but so.

LEWIS   But what shall I gain by young Arthur's fall?

CARDINAL PANDULPH   You, in the right of Lady Blanche your wife,

145 May then make all the claim that Arthur did.

LEWIS   And lose it, life and all, as Arthur did.

CARDINAL PANDULPH   How green you are, and fresh in this old
world!

---

118 day i.e. battle (Lewis employs the more literal sense)   120 had would have (lost all those
things)   121 means intends   124 accounts reckons   130 rub obstacle (a term from the
game of bowls)   132 mark pay attention   134 infant young child/minor, too young to claim
sovereignty (legal term)   135 misplaced i.e. usurping   entertain receive, experience
138 boisterously violently   140 Makes . . . no is not fussy about using any   stay prop, keep
141 That in order that   147 green young, inexperienced

John lays you plots: the times conspire with you:
For he that steeps his safety in true blood
150   Shall find but bloody safety and untrue.
This act, so evilly born, shall cool the hearts
Of all his people and freeze up their zeal,
That none so small advantage shall step forth
To check his reign, but they will cherish it:
155   No natural exhalation in the sky,
No scope of nature, no distempered day,
No common wind, no customèd event,
But they will pluck away his natural cause
And call them meteors, prodigies, and signs,
160   Abortives, presages, and tongues of heaven,
Plainly denouncing vengeance upon John.
LEWIS   Maybe he will not touch young Arthur's life,
But hold himself safe in his prisonment.
CARDINAL PANDULPH   O sir, when he shall hear of your approach,
165   If that young Arthur be not gone already,
Even at that news he dies: and then the hearts
Of all his people shall revolt from him,
And kiss the lips of unacquainted change,
And pick strong matter of revolt and wrath
170   Out of the bloody fingers' ends of John.
Methinks I see this hurly all on foot:
And O, what better matter breeds for you
Than I have named! The Bastard Falconbridge
Is now in England, ransacking the Church,
175   Offending charity: if but a dozen French

---

148 **lays you plots** makes schemes for you   149 **steeps** soaks   **true** legitimate/royal
150 **untrue** deceptive/uncertain   152 **zeal** fervent loyalty   153 **none . . . advantage** not
even the smallest opportunity   154 **check** inhibit, curb, control   **reign** rule (puns on
"rein")   155 **exhalation** vapor/meteor (considered a bad omen)   156 **scope** circumstance
distempered disordered/stormy   157 **customèd** customary, ordinary   158 **pluck away**
disregard   **his** its   **cause** explanation   159 **prodigies** omens   160 **Abortives** abnormalities
presages signs, portents   161 **denouncing** declaring   163 **hold** consider   **himself** i.e. John
in his prisonment i.e. while Arthur is John's prisoner   164 **approach** arrival   168 **kiss . . .**
of i.e. welcome   **unacquainted** unfamiliar   169 **pick** extract/find   **strong matter of**
compelling reason for   170 **Out . . . John** i.e. in John's crimes, symbolized by his bloodstained
hands   171 **hurly** uproar, turmoil   **on foot** underway   172 **breeds** develops

Were there in arms, they would be as a call
To train ten thousand English to their side,
Or, as a little snow, tumbled about,
Anon becomes a mountain. O noble dauphin,
180 Go with me to the king: 'tis wonderful
What may be wrought out of their discontent,
Now that their souls are top-full of offence.
For England go: I will whet on the king.
LEWIS   Strong reasons make strange actions: let us go:
185 If you say ay, the king will not say no.   *Exeunt*

Act 4 Scene 1   *running scene 6*

Enter Hubert and Executioners   *With a rope and irons*

HUBERT   Heat me these irons hot, and look thou stand
Within the arras: when I strike my foot
Upon the bosom of the ground, rush forth
And bind the boy which you shall find with me
5 Fast to the chair: be heedful: hence, and watch.
FIRST EXECUTIONER   I hope your warrant will bear out the deed.
HUBERT   Uncleanly scruples: Fear not you: *The Executioners*
    look to't.   *withdraw*
Young lad, come forth; I have to say with you.   *behind the arras*
Enter Arthur
ARTHUR   Good morrow, Hubert.
10 HUBERT   Good morrow, little prince.
ARTHUR   As little prince, having so great a title
To be more prince, as may be. You are sad.

---

176 **call** decoy, bait/call to arms   177 **train** lure   179 **Anon** instantly   181 **wrought**
fashioned   182 **top-full** brim-full   **offence** hostility, sense of wrong (in reaction to John's
deeds)   183 **whet on** encourage (as if sharpening a sword)   184 **strange actions** unusual/
unexpected military deeds   185 **ay** yes   **4.1   *Location: England, a prison*   1 me** for me
irons branding tools   **look** be sure   2 **Within** behind   **arras** large tapestry wall-hanging
5 **heedful** watchful/careful   6 **bear out** support, authorize   7 **Uncleanly scruples** improper
concerns/concerns about being morally tainted   8 **to say with** something to say to   10 **little**
young, small (Arthur then shifts the sense)   11 **As . . . be** I am as little a prince as possible,
despite having claims to being much greater   12 **sad** serious, solemn

HUBERT   Indeed, I have been merrier.

ARTHUR   'Mercy on me!

15   Methinks nobody should be sad but I:
Yet, I remember, when I was in France,
Young gentlemen would be as sad as night
Only for wantonness: by my christendom,
So I were out of prison and kept sheep,

20   I should be as merry as the day is long:
And so I would be here, but that I doubt
My uncle practises more harm to me:
He is afraid of me, and I of him:
Is it my fault that I was Geoffrey's son?

25   No, indeed, is't not: and I would to heaven
I were your son, so you would love me, Hubert.

HUBERT   If I talk to him, with his innocent prate   *Aside*
He will awake my mercy which lies dead:
Therefore I will be sudden and dispatch.

30   ARTHUR   Are you sick, Hubert? You look pale today:
In sooth, I would you were a little sick,
That I might sit all night and watch with you.
I warrant I love you more than you do me.

HUBERT   His words do take possession of my bosom.—   *Aside*

35   Read here, young Arthur.— How now,   *Showing a paper/Aside*
foolish rheum!
Turning dispiteous torture out of door?
I must be brief, lest resolution drop
Out at mine eyes in tender womanish tears.
Can you not read it? Is it not fair writ?

40   ARTHUR   Too fairly, Hubert, for so foul effect:
Must you with hot irons burn out both mine eyes?

HUBERT   Young boy, I must.

---

14 'Mercy i.e. God's mercy   17 sad serious/mournful/dark-colored   18 Only merely
wantonness foolish behavior/whim   by my christendom i.e. as I am a Christian   19 So
provided that   21 doubt suspect, fear   22 practises plots   25 would wish   26 so if
27 prate chatter   29 dispatch put (him) to death/hurry up   31 sooth truth   32 watch stay
awake   33 warrant assure (you)   35 rheum i.e. tears   36 Turning . . . door banishing
pitiless torture   37 brief quick   resolution determination   39 fair writ written clearly, well
40 effect purpose

ARTHUR   And will you?

HUBERT   And I will.

45   ARTHUR   Have you the heart? When your head did but ache,
        I knit my handkercher about your brows,
        The best I had, a princess wrought it me,
        And I did never ask it you again:
        And with my hand at midnight held your head,
50   And like the watchful minutes to the hour,
        Still and anon cheered up the heavy time,
        Saying 'What lack you?' and 'Where lies your grief?'
        Or 'What good love may I perform for you?'
        Many a poor man's son would have lien still
55   And ne'er have spoke a loving word to you:
        But you at your sick service had a prince:
        Nay, you may think my love was crafty love,
        And call it cunning. Do, an if you will.
        If heaven be pleased that you must use me ill,
60   Why then you must. Will you put out mine eyes?
        These eyes that never did, nor never shall,
        So much as frown on you.

HUBERT   I have sworn to do it:
        And with hot irons must I burn them out.

65   ARTHUR   Ah, none but in this iron age would do it:
        The iron of itself, though heat red-hot,
        Approaching near these eyes, would drink my tears
        And quench this fiery indignation,
        Even in the matter of mine innocence:
70   Nay, after that, consume away in rust
        But for containing fire to harm mine eye:
        Are you more stubborn-hard than hammered iron?

46 knit tied   handkercher handkerchief   47 wrought it embroidered it for   48 it you for it
back from you   50 watchful time-keeping/wakeful/vigilant   51 Still and anon continually
heavy slow-moving/sad   52 lack you i.e. do you need   grief physical pain/sorrow   53 love
act of kindness   54 lien lain   56 at . . . service i.e. to look after you through your illness
57 crafty devious   58 an if if   59 ill badly, wrongfully   65 iron age the present/the last and
worst of the four classical ages: Gold, Silver, Bronze, Iron/a period of wickedness and cruelty
(puns on irons)   66 heat heated   68 this its   69 Even . . . matter in the very substance, i.e.
tears   71 But for containing merely because it contained

And if an angel should have come to me
And told me Hubert should put out mine eyes,
75   I would not have believed him: no tongue but Hubert's.
HUBERT   Come forth.   *Stamps; Executioners come forward*
Do as I bid you do.
ARTHUR   O, save me, Hubert, save me! My eyes are out
Even with the fierce looks of these bloody men.
80   HUBERT   Give me the iron, I say, and bind him here.
ARTHUR   Alas, what need you be so boist'rous-rough?
I will not struggle: I will stand stone-still:
For heaven sake, Hubert, let me not be bound:
Nay, hear me, Hubert, drive these men away,
85   And I will sit as quiet as a lamb:
I will not stir, nor winch, nor speak a word,
Nor look upon the iron angerly:
Thrust but these men away, and I'll forgive you,
Whatever torment you do put me to.
90   HUBERT   Go, stand within: let me alone with him.
FIRST EXECUTIONER   I am best pleased to be from such a deed.
                          [*Exeunt Executioners*]
ARTHUR   Alas, I then have chid away my friend!
He hath a stern look, but a gentle heart:
Let him come back, that his compassion may
95   Give life to yours.
HUBERT   Come, boy, prepare yourself.
ARTHUR   Is there no remedy?
HUBERT   None, but to lose your eyes.
ARTHUR   O heaven, that there were but a mote in yours,
100 A grain, a dust, a gnat, a wandering hair,
Any annoyance in that precious sense:
Then feeling what small things are boisterous there,
Your vile intent must needs seem horrible.

---

73 should have had   **78 out** put out/blinded   **86 winch** wince   **87 angerly** angrily
91 from away from   **92 chid** scolded/driven   **97 remedy** alternative/relief   **99 mote** particle
of dust; making literal the biblical reference to "a mote in the eye," i.e. a minor fault observed
in another person by someone who ignores a greater fault of his or her own (Matthew 7:3)
101 annoyance irritation   **sense** organ of sense, i.e. eye   **102 boisterous** painful

HUBERT   Is this your promise? Go to, hold your tongue.

105 ARTHUR   Hubert, the utterance of a brace of tongues
       Must needs want pleading for a pair of eyes:
       Let me not hold my tongue: let me not, Hubert:
       Or, Hubert, if you will, cut out my tongue,
       So I may keep mine eyes. O, spare mine eyes,
110   Though to no use but still to look on you.
       Lo, by my troth, the instrument is cold
       And would not harm me.

HUBERT   I can heat it, boy.

ARTHUR   No, in good sooth: the fire is dead with grief,
115   Being create for comfort, to be used
       In undeserved extremes: see else yourself:
       There is no malice in this burning coal:
       The breath of heaven hath blown his spirit out,
       And strewed repentant ashes on his head.

120 HUBERT   But with my breath I can revive it, boy.

ARTHUR   An if you do, you will but make it blush
       And glow with shame of your proceedings, Hubert:
       Nay, it perchance will sparkle in your eyes,
       And, like a dog that is compelled to fight,
125   Snatch at his master that doth tarre him on.
       All things that you should use to do me wrong
       Deny their office: only you do lack
       That mercy, which fierce fire and iron extends,
       Creatures of note for mercy, lacking uses.

130 HUBERT   Well, see to live: I will not touch thine eye
       For all the treasure that thine uncle owes:
       Yet am I sworn and I did purpose, boy,
       With this same very iron to burn them out.

---

104 Go to expression of irritated impatience   105 a brace (even) a pair   106 Must . . .
pleading would not be sufficient to plead   107 Let me not do not make me   110 still always
111 troth faith   114 in good sooth truly   115 create created   116 undeserved extremes
unjust cruelties   else otherwise, i.e. if it isn't true   121 but only   123 perchance perhaps
sparkle in send sparks into   125 Snatch snap, bite   tarre provoke, urge   127 office proper
function   128 extends offers   129 Creatures . . . uses instruments noted for compassion
when they are not put to evil uses   131 owes owns   132 purpose intend

ARTHUR	O, now you look like Hubert. All this while
135	You were disguisèd.
HUBERT	Peace; no more. Adieu.
	Your uncle must not know but you are dead.
	I'll fill these doggèd spies with false reports:
	And, pretty child, sleep doubtless, and secure,
140	That Hubert for the wealth of all the world,
	Will not offend thee.
ARTHUR	O heaven! I thank you, Hubert.
HUBERT	Silence, no more: go closely in with me.
	Much danger do I undergo for thee. *Exeunt*

Act 4 Scene 2

running scene 7

Enter King John, Pembroke, Salisbury and other   *King John ascends*
Lords   *the throne*

KING JOHN	Here once again we sit: once again crowned,
	And looked upon, I hope, with cheerful eyes.
PEMBROKE	This 'once again', but that your highness pleased,
	Was once superfluous: you were crowned before,
5	And that high royalty was ne'er plucked off:
	The faiths of men ne'er stainèd with revolt:
	Fresh expectation troubled not the land
	With any longed-for change or better state.
SALISBURY	Therefore, to be possessed with double pomp,
10	To guard a title that was rich before,
	To gild refinèd gold, to paint the lily,
	To throw a perfume on the violet,
	To smooth the ice, or add another hue
	Unto the rainbow, or with taper-light

---

137 but anything other than that   **138 doggèd** doglike/cruel   **139 doubtless** without fear   **141 offend** harm   **143 closely** secretly   **4.2   *Location: England, the court of King John***   **4 once** in a word/one occasion (that was)   **7 Fresh** new   **8 state** state of affairs/monarch   **9 possessed** invested, given possession (of the royal title)   **double pomp** second ceremony   **10 guard** adorn/protect   **11 gild** cover with a thin layer of gold   **14 taper-light** candlelight

15   To seek the beauteous eye of heaven to garnish,
        Is wasteful and ridiculous excess.
    PEMBROKE   But that your royal pleasure must be done,
        This act is as an ancient tale new told,
        And, in the last repeating, troublesome,
20   Being urgèd at a time unseasonable.
    SALISBURY   In this the antique and well-noted face
        Of plain old form is much disfigurèd,
        And, like a shifted wind unto a sail,
        It makes the course of thoughts to fetch about,
25   Startles and frights consideration,
        Makes sound opinion sick and truth suspected,
        For putting on so new a fashioned robe.
    PEMBROKE   When workmen strive to do better than well,
        They do confound their skill in covetousness,
30   And oftentimes excusing of a fault
        Doth make the fault the worse by th'excuse:
        As patches set upon a little breach
        Discredit more in hiding of the fault
        Than did the fault before it was so patched.
35 SALISBURY   To this effect, before you were new crowned,
        We breathed our counsel: but it pleased your highness
        To overbear it, and we are all well pleased,
        Since all and every part of what we would
        Doth make a stand at what your highness will.
40   KING JOHN   Some reasons of this double coronation
        I have possessed you with, and think them strong.
        And more, more strong, than lesser is my fear,

---

15 **eye of heaven** i.e. the sun   17 **But** i.e. were it not   **pleasure** will/desire
20 **unseasonable** unsuitable (probably four syllable; **Being** at beginning of line may be
monosyllabic for sake of meter)   21 **antique** old   **well-noted** well-known   22 **form** custom
disfigurèd altered   23 **shifted** changed (in direction)   24 **It** i.e. having a second coronation
fetch about change tack   25 **consideration** deep reflection   26 **sound** healthy   27 **new a**
fashioned newly made/of new design   29 **confound** ruin   30 **excusing . . . th'excuse** i.e.
excuses draw attention to faults rather than explaining them away   32 **breach** tear, hole
33 **Discredit** bring into disrepute   35 **new crowned** i.e. crowned again   36 **breathed** spoke
37 **overbear** overrule   39 **make . . . at** stop and give way for/resist   41 **possessed you with**
informed you of   42 **more . . . fear** I shall give you further reasons that are as great as my fear
is small

I shall indue you with: meantime but ask
What you would have reformed that is not well,
45   And well shall you perceive how willingly
I will both hear and grant you your requests.

PEMBROKE   Then I, as one that am the tongue of these,
To sound the purposes of all their hearts,
Both for myself and them, but chief of all
50   Your safety, for the which myself and them
Bend their best studies, heartily request
Th'enfranchisement of Arthur, whose restraint
Doth move the murmuring lips of discontent
To break into this dangerous argument:
55   If what in rest you have, in right you hold,
Why then your fears, which, as they say, attend
The steps of wrong, should move you to mew up
Your tender kinsman, and to choke his days
With barbarous ignorance and deny his youth
60   The rich advantage of good exercise.
That the time's enemies may not have this
To grace occasions, let it be our suit
That you have bid us ask his liberty,
Which for our goods we do no further ask
65   Than, whereupon our weal on you depending
Counts it your weal, he have his liberty.

Enter Hubert

KING JOHN   Let it be so: I do commit his youth
To your direction.—
Hubert, what news with you?   *Taking him to one side*

70   PEMBROKE   This is the man should do the bloody deed:
He showed his warrant to a friend of mine:

---

43 **indue** supply   47 **tongue** spokesperson   48 **sound** proclaim/discover the depth of
50 **them** they   51 **Bend** direct, focus   **studies** efforts   52 **enfranchisement** release
55 **rest** peace/freedom from exertion   **in right** rightfully   56 **attend . . . wrong** i.e. are bent
toward wrongdoing   **attend** accompany   57 **mew up** confine   58 **tender** young
60 **exercise** occupations/gentlemanly physical training in the martial arts   61 **That** so that
this i.e. such an argument   62 **grace occasions** suit their purposes   **suit** request (that John
earlier invited them to make)   64 **goods** personal benefits   65 **weal** welfare   66 **Counts**
considers   67 **commit** entrust   68 **direction** responsibility (for Arthur's upbringing)
70 **should do** who was to have done

The image of a wicked heinous fault
Lives in his eye: that close aspect of his
Do show the mood of a much troubled breast,
75   And I do fearfully believe 'tis done,
What we so feared he had a charge to do.

SALISBURY   The colour of the king doth come and go
Between his purpose and his conscience,
Like heralds 'twixt two dreadful battles set:
80   His passion is so ripe, it needs must break.

PEMBROKE   And when it breaks, I fear will issue thence
The foul corruption of a sweet child's death.

KING JOHN   We cannot hold mortality's strong hand.—
Good lords, although my will to give is living,   *To Lords*
85   The suit which you demand is gone and dead.
He tells us Arthur is deceased tonight.

SALISBURY   Indeed we feared his sickness was past cure.

PEMBROKE   Indeed we heard how near his death he was
Before the child himself felt he was sick:
90   This must be answered either here or hence.

KING JOHN   Why do you bend such solemn brows on me?
Think you I bear the shears of destiny?
Have I commandment on the pulse of life?

SALISBURY   It is apparent foul play, and 'tis shame
95   That greatness should so grossly offer it:
So thrive it in your game, and so farewell.

PEMBROKE   Stay yet, Lord Salisbury: I'll go with thee,
And find th'inheritance of this poor child,
His little kingdom of a forcèd grave.

---

72 heinous hateful, odious   **73 Lives** i.e. is apparent   **close** secretive   **aspect** appearance
74 Do most editions since the Fourth Folio emend to "Does," but "Does show" sounds
infelicitous: an elision *Do' show* is possible ("Doth show" is also possible)   **76 charge** order
77 colour i.e. of his complexion (which alternates between pale and red)   **79 'twixt** between
dreadful battles terrifying fighting forces   **80 ripe** swollen (like an abscess)   **break** burst
83 hold hold back   **84 give** i.e. grant your request   **86 tonight** last night   **90 answered**
accounted for/recompensed   **hence** elsewhere/in the future/in the next world   **91 brows**
faces, expressions   **92 shears of destiny** i.e. like Atropos, one of the three Fates, responsible
for cutting the thread of life   **93 commandment on** control over   **94 apparent** evidently
95 greatness i.e. a king   **grossly** blatantly   **offer** undertake, venture to do   **96 So** thus, i.e.
grossly   **game** intrigue, undertaking   **99 forcèd** compelled, brought about by violence

100   That blood which owed the breadth of all this isle,
         Three foot of it doth hold: bad world the while:
         This must not be thus borne: this will break out
         To all our sorrows, and ere long I doubt.   *Exeunt [Lords]*
KING JOHN   They burn in indignation: I repent:
105   There is no sure foundation set on blood:
         No certain life achieved by others' death.

Enter [a] Messenger

         A fearful eye thou hast. Where is that blood
         That I have seen inhabit in those cheeks?
         So foul a sky clears not without a storm:
110   Pour down thy weather: how goes all in France?
MESSENGER   From France to England: never such a power
         For any foreign preparation
         Was levied in the body of a land.
         The copy of your speed is learned by them:
115   For when you should be told they do prepare,
         The tidings comes that they are all arrived.
KING JOHN   O, where hath our intelligence been drunk?
         Where hath it slept? Where is my mother's care,
         That such an army could be drawn in France,
120   And she not hear of it?
MESSENGER   My liege, her ear
         Is stopped with dust: the first of April died
         Your noble mother; and as I hear, my lord,
         The lady Constance in a frenzy died
125   Three days before: but this from Rumour's tongue
         I idly heard: if true or false I know not.
KING JOHN   Withhold thy speed, dreadful Occasion:
         O, make a league with me, till I have pleased

---

100 owed owned   **101 the while** in the meantime/while such things happen   **103 doubt**
fear   **105 sure** secure   **set** i.e. built   **107 fearful** frightened   **110 weather** i.e. stormy news
111 From . . . England the messenger interprets John's **how goes** ("how is it going") in terms of
literal movement (France invading England)   **power** army   **112 preparation** military
expedition   **113 levied** mustered, raised   **body** length and breadth   **114 copy** example
117 intelligence military information, spies   **118 care** diligence   **119 drawn** gathered
124 frenzy madness/fit of agitation   **126 idly** casually   **127 Occasion** course of events
128 league alliance/truce

My discontented peers. What? Mother dead?
130   How wildly then walks my estate in France!—
Under whose conduct came those powers of France
That thou for truth giv'st out are landed here?

MESSENGER   Under the dauphin.

KING JOHN   Thou hast made me giddy
135   With these ill tidings.

Enter [the] Bastard and Peter of Pomfret

                      Now, what says the world
To your proceedings? Do not seek to stuff
My head with more ill news, for it is full.

BASTARD   But if you be afeard to hear the worst,
Then let the worst unheard fall on your head.

140   KING JOHN   Bear with me cousin, for I was amazed
Under the tide: but now I breathe again
Aloft the flood, and can give audience
To any tongue, speak it of what it will.

BASTARD   How I have sped among the clergymen,
145   The sums I have collected shall express:
But as I travelled hither through the land,
I find the people strangely fantasied:
Possessed with rumours, full of idle dreams,
Not knowing what they fear, but full of fear.
150   And here's a prophet that I brought with me
From forth the streets of Pomfret, whom I found
With many hundreds treading on his heels:
To whom he sung in rude harsh-sounding rhymes,
That ere the next Ascension Day at noon,
155   Your highness should deliver up your crown.

---

130 **wildly** disorderedly, without rule   **walks** goes, progresses   **estate** affairs/holdings
131 **conduct** leadership   132 **for . . . out** claim in the name of truth   135 *Pomfret*
Pontefract in Yorkshire   136 **proceedings** course of action, i.e. to collect money from the
monasteries   138 **afeard** afraid   139 **unheard . . . head** befall you without warning, i.e. it is
better to be prepared for the **worst**   140 **amazed** stunned/bewildered   141 **tide** i.e. torrent of
bad news   142 **Aloft** above, afloat in   144 **sped** succeeded/fared   145 **express**
communicate/reveal   147 **strangely fantasied** full of strange imaginings   148 **idle** foolish/
crazy   152 **treading . . . heels** i.e. following him closely   153 **rude** unlearned/lacking in
polish   154 **Ascension Day** celebration of the feast of ascension of Christ into heaven, the
Thursday forty days after Easter   155 **deliver up** surrender

KING JOHN   Thou idle dreamer, wherefore didst thou so?

PETER   Foreknowing that the truth will fall out so.

KING JOHN   Hubert, away with him: imprison him,
And on that day at noon, whereon he says
160   I shall yield up my crown, let him be hanged.
Deliver him to safety, and return,
For I must use thee.—   [*Exeunt Hubert and Peter*]
O my gentle cousin,
Hear'st thou the news abroad, who are arrived?

BASTARD   The French, my lord: men's mouths are full of it.
165   Besides, I met Lord Bigot and Lord Salisbury,
With eyes as red as new-enkindled fire,
And others more, going to seek the grave
Of Arthur, who they say is killed tonight
On your suggestion.

170   KING JOHN   Gentle kinsman, go,
And thrust thyself into their companies.
I have a way to win their loves again:
Bring them before me.

BASTARD   I will seek them out.

175   KING JOHN   Nay, but make haste: the better foot before.
O, let me have no subject enemies,
When adverse foreigners affright my towns
With dreadful pomp of stout invasion.
Be Mercury, set feathers to thy heels,
180   And fly like thought from them to me again.

BASTARD   The spirit of the time shall teach me speed.   *Exit*

KING JOHN   Spoke like a sprightful noble gentleman.
Go after him: for he perhaps shall need
Some messenger betwixt me and the peers,
185   And be thou he.

MESSENGER   With all my heart, my liege.   [*Exit*]

---

161 **safety** safekeeping, i.e. custody   162 **gentle** noble   163 **abroad** out there, in public
168 **is** was   **tonight** last night   169 **suggestion** instigation   175 **the ... before** i.e. quickly
176 **subject enemies** i.e. subjects who are enemies   177 **adverse** hostile   178 **stout** bold/
determined   179 **Mercury** messenger of the Roman gods, often depicted with feathered
sandals or feet   181 **spirit ... time** i.e. circumstances (conceivably **spirit** plays on the
alchemical sense of "mercury")   182 **sprightful** spirited   184 **betwixt** between

KING JOHN   My mother dead!

Enter Hubert

HUBERT   My lord, they say five moons were seen tonight:
Four fixèd, and the fifth did whirl about
190   The other four in wondrous motion.

KING JOHN   Five moons?

HUBERT   Old men and beldams in the streets
Do prophesy upon it dangerously:
Young Arthur's death is common in their mouths,
195   And when they talk of him, they shake their heads
And whisper one another in the ear.
And he that speaks doth grip the hearer's wrist,
Whilst he that hears makes fearful action,
With wrinkled brows, with nods, with rolling eyes.
200   I saw a smith stand with his hammer, thus,
The whilst his iron did on the anvil cool,
With open mouth swallowing a tailor's news,
Who, with his shears and measure in his hand,
Standing on slippers, which his nimble haste
205   Had falsely thrust upon contrary feet,
Told of a many thousand warlike French
That were embattailèd and ranked in Kent.
Another lean, unwashed artificer
Cuts off his tale, and talks of Arthur's death.

210   KING JOHN   Why seek'st thou to possess me with these fears?
Why urgest thou so oft young Arthur's death?
Thy hand hath murdered him: I had a mighty cause
To wish him dead, but thou hadst none to kill him.

HUBERT   No had, my lord! Why, did you not provoke me?

215   KING JOHN   It is the curse of kings to be attended
By slaves that take their humours for a warrant

---

188 tonight last night   **190 wondrous** bizarre, unbelievable   **192 beldams** old women
193 prophesy upon it make predictions based on it   **196 one** to one   **198 fearful action**
frightened gestures   **205 Had . . . feet** he had mistakenly put on the wrong feet   **206 a many
thousand** i.e. many thousands of   **207 embattailèd** drawn up in battle array   **ranked**
arranged in ranks   **208 artificer** artisan   **210 possess** acquaint/occupy   **211 urgest thou**
do you present, bring forward   **oft** often   **212 cause** reason   **214 No had** had none
provoke incite   **216 humours** whims, moods

To break within the bloody house of life,
And on the winking of authority
To understand a law, to know the meaning
220 Of dangerous majesty, when perchance it frowns
More upon humour than advised respect.

HUBERT   Here is your hand and seal for what   *He shows a paper*
I did.

KING JOHN   O, when the last account 'twixt heaven and earth
Is to be made, then shall this hand and seal
225 Witness against us to damnation.
How oft the sight of means to do ill deeds
Make deeds ill done! Hadst not thou been by,
A fellow by the hand of nature marked,
Quoted and signed to do a deed of shame,
230 This murder had not come into my mind.
But taking note of thy abhorred aspect,
Finding thee fit for bloody villainy,
Apt, liable to be employed in danger,
I faintly broke with thee of Arthur's death:
235 And thou, to be endearèd to a king,
Made it no conscience to destroy a prince.

HUBERT   My lord—

KING JOHN   Hadst thou but shook thy head or made a pause
When I spake darkly what I purposèd,
240 Or turned an eye of doubt upon my face,
As bid me tell my tale in express words,
Deep shame had struck me dumb, made me break off,
And those thy fears might have wrought fears in me.
But thou didst understand me by my signs
245 And didst in signs again parley with sin:

---

217 **bloody . . . life** i.e. the body   218 **winking** i.e. subtle signal   219 **understand a law**
interpret it as a mandate   220 **dangerous** threatening   **perchance** perhaps   221 **upon**
humour because of a whim   **advised respect** careful deliberation   222 **hand** signature
223 **account** judgment   226 **means to do** ways of doing, instruments for   227 **by** at hand
228 **marked** physically blemished/taken note of   229 **Quoted** noted, specified   **signed**
marked distinctively   231 **aspect** face/appearance   233 **liable** suitable   234 **faintly** half-
heartedly/tentatively   **broke** spoke   236 **conscience** i.e. matter of moral dilemma
239 **darkly** obscurely   241 **As** as though to   **express** specific   242 **had** would have
243 **wrought** created   245 **parley** negotiate

Yea, without stop, didst let thy heart consent,
And consequently thy rude hand to act
The deed, which both our tongues held vile to name.
Out of my sight, and never see me more!
250   My nobles leave me, and my state is braved,
Even at my gates, with ranks of foreign powers;
Nay, in the body of this fleshly land,
This kingdom, this confine of blood and breath,
Hostility and civil tumult reigns
255   Between my conscience and my cousin's death.
HUBERT   Arm you against your other enemies:
I'll make a peace between your soul and you.
Young Arthur is alive: this hand of mine
Is yet a maiden and an innocent hand,
260   Not painted with the crimson spots of blood.
Within this bosom never entered yet
The dreadful motion of a murderous thought;
And you have slandered nature in my form,
Which, howsoever rude exteriorly,
265   Is yet the cover of a fairer mind
Than to be butcher of an innocent child.
KING JOHN   Doth Arthur live? O, haste thee to the peers:
Throw this report on their incensèd rage,
And make them tame to their obedience.
270   Forgive the comment that my passion made
Upon thy feature, for my rage was blind,
And foul imaginary eyes of blood
Presented thee more hideous than thou art.
O, answer not, but to my closet bring

---

247 **rude** violent/unkind   250 **state** authority, sovereignty   **braved** challenged, defied
252 **body . . . land** refers to England as a body, as well as to the king's own body (the popular
metaphor of monarch as microcosm of state)   253 **confine** territory/limit/prison
254 **tumult** disturbance, insurrection/confused and violent emotion   259 **maiden**
unblemished/virginal (a similarity continued in the idea of hymenal/murderous **blood**)
262 **motion** suggestion/impulse   263 **form** appearance   264 **rude exteriorly** outwardly
harsh-looking   268 **Throw** cast (as if water on the fire of their rage)   269 **tame** submissive
272 **imaginary** imaginative/nonexistent   **eyes of blood** passionate, angry eyes/bloodshot
eyes   274 **closet** private room

275   The angry lords with all expedient haste.
       I conjure thee but slowly: run more fast.   *Exeunt*

Act 4 Scene 3   *running scene 8*

Enter Arthur, on the walls   *Disguised as a ship-boy*

ARTHUR   The wall is high, and yet will I leap down.
          Good ground, be pitiful and hurt me not:
          There's few or none do know me: if they did,
          This ship-boy's semblance hath disguised me quite.
5   I am afraid, and yet I'll venture it.
          If I get down, and do not break my limbs,
          I'll find a thousand shifts to get away:
          As good to die and go, as die and stay.   *He leaps down*
          O me! My uncle's spirit is in these stones:
10   Heaven take my soul, and England keep my bones!   *Dies*
Enter Pembroke, Salisbury and Bigot

SALISBURY   Lords, I will meet him at Saint Edmundsbury:
          It is our safety, and we must embrace
          This gentle offer of the perilous time.
PEMBROKE   Who brought that letter from the cardinal?
15   SALISBURY   The count Melun, a noble lord of France,
          Whose private with me of the dauphin's love
          Is much more general than these lines import.
BIGOT   Tomorrow morning let us meet him then.
SALISBURY   Or rather then set forward; for 'twill be
20   Two long days' journey, lords, or ere we meet.
Enter [the] Bastard

BASTARD   Once more today well met, distempered lords:
          The king by me requests your presence straight.

---

276 **conjure** entreat, ask earnestly   **4.3 *Location: England, a prison*   4 semblance**
appearance   **quite** totally   **5 venture** risk   **7 shifts** stratagems (possibly puns on the sense
of "changes of clothing")   **8 die . . . stay** i.e. risk death by escaping than stay and face certain
death   **11 him** i.e. Lewis the dauphin   **Saint Edmundsbury** Bury St. Edmunds, Suffolk
12 safety best safeguard   **13 gentle** courteous/noble   **16 private** confidential talk
17 general universal, all-embracing   **20 or ere** before   **we** i.e. the English lords and Lewis
21 distempered vexed, discontented   **22 straight** straight away

SALISBURY   The king hath dispossessed himself of us:
We will not line his thin bestainèd cloak
25   With our pure honours, nor attend the foot
That leaves the print of blood where'er it walks.
Return and tell him so: we know the worst.

BASTARD   Whate'er you think, good words, I think, were best.

SALISBURY   Our griefs, and not our manners, reason now.

30   BASTARD   But there is little reason in your grief.
Therefore 'twere reason you had manners now.

PEMBROKE   Sir, sir, impatience hath his privilege.

BASTARD   'Tis true, to hurt his master, no man's else.

SALISBURY   This is the prison. What is he lies   *Sees Arthur's body*
here?

35   PEMBROKE   O, death, made proud with pure and princely
beauty:
The earth had not a hole to hide this deed.

SALISBURY   Murder, as hating what himself hath done,
Doth lay it open to urge on revenge.

BIGOT   Or when he doomed this beauty to a grave,
40   Found it too precious-princely for a grave.

SALISBURY   Sir Richard, what think you? You have beheld,
Or have you read, or heard: or could you think,
Or do you almost think, although you see,
That you do see? Could thought, without this object,
45   Form such another? This is the very top,
The height, the crest, or crest unto the crest,
Of murder's arms: this is the bloodiest shame,
The wildest savagery, the vilest stroke,

---

23 dispossessed himself caused himself to lose possession, i.e. lost our support   **24 line** supply a lining for, i.e. fortify   **bestainèd** marked with stains   **cloak** cover for his deeds   **25 attend the foot** i.e. serve one   **29 griefs** grievances, complaints   **reason** speak, debate (the Bastard shifts the sense to "good sense, rationality")   **32 impatience** anger   **privilege** freedom/advantage   **33 'Tis . . . else** refers to the proverbial saying "anger punishes itself"   **37 as** as if   **38 lay it open** reveal the deed openly   **39 he** i.e. murder   **41 Sir Richard** i.e. the Bastard   **beheld . . . think** i.e. ever encountered or imagined (anything like this)   **43 think** wonder   **44 That . . . see** what you see in front of you/that your eyes are functioning correctly   **object** sight (of Arthur's body)   **46 crest** heraldic device in the upper portion of a coat of arms (sense has shifted from "pinnacle")   **47 arms** coat of arms

That ever wall-eyed wrath or staring rage
50   Presented to the tears of soft remorse.
PEMBROKE   All murders past do stand excused in this:
And this, so sole and so unmatchable,
Shall give a holiness, a purity,
To the yet unbegotten sin of times,
55   And prove a deadly bloodshed but a jest,
Exampled by this heinous spectacle.
BASTARD   It is a damnèd and a bloody work:
The graceless action of a heavy hand,
If that it be the work of any hand.
60   SALISBURY   If that it be the work of any hand?
We had a kind of light what would ensue:
It is the shameful work of Hubert's hand,
The practice and the purpose of the king:
From whose obedience I forbid my soul,
65   Kneeling before this ruin of sweet life,
And breathing to his breathless excellence
The incense of a vow, a holy vow:
Never to taste the pleasures of the world,
Never to be infected with delight,
70   Nor conversant with ease and idleness,
Till I have set a glory to this hand,
By giving it the worship of revenge.
PEMBROKE AND BIGOT   Our souls religiously confirm thy words.
Enter Hubert
HUBERT   Lords, I am hot with haste in seeking you:
75   Arthur doth live: the king hath sent for you.
SALISBURY   O, he is bold, and blushes not at death.—
Avaunt, thou hateful villain, get thee gone!

---

49 wall-eyed pale-eyed/squinting   **50 remorse** pity   **51 excused** pardoned   **in** i.e. in
comparison to   **52 sole** unique, unrivaled   **54 times** the future   **56 Exampled** compared
with the precedent of   **heinous** infamous, wicked   **58 graceless** ungodly/coarse   **heavy**
oppressive/clumsy   **61 light** foresight, indication   **63 practice** plot   **66 breathless** dead/
inexpressible   **67 incense** perfumed smoke/breath   **69 infected** affected, stirred   **71 set**
added   **72 worship** honor   **73 religiously** solemnly/devoutly   **confirm** strengthen, support
77 Avaunt be gone

HUBERT	I am no villain.	
SALISBURY	Must I rob the law?	*Draws his sword*
80 BASTARD	Your sword is bright, sir: put it up again.	
SALISBURY	Not till I sheathe it in a murderer's skin.	
HUBERT	Stand back, Lord Salisbury, stand back, I say:	

HUBERT Stand back, Lord Salisbury, stand back, I say:
By heaven, I think my sword's as sharp as yours.   *Draws his*
I would not have you, lord, forget yourself,   *sword*
85   Nor tempt the danger of my true defence;
Lest I, by marking of your rage, forget
Your worth, your greatness and nobility.

BIGOT   Out, dunghill! Dar'st thou brave a nobleman?

HUBERT   Not for my life: but yet I dare defend
90   My innocent life against an emperor.

SALISBURY   Thou art a murderer.

HUBERT   Do not prove me so:
Yet I am none. Whose tongue soe'er speaks false,
Not truly speaks: who speaks not truly, lies.

95 PEMBROKE   Cut him to pieces.

BASTARD   Keep the peace, I say.

SALISBURY   Stand by, or I shall gall you, Falconbridge.

BASTARD   Thou wert better gall the devil, Salisbury:
If thou but frown on me, or stir thy foot,
100   Or teach thy hasty spleen to do me shame,
I'll strike thee dead. Put up thy sword betime,
Or I'll so maul you and your toasting-iron,
That you shall think the devil is come from hell.

BIGOT   What wilt thou do, renownèd Falconbridge?
105   Second a villain and a murderer?

HUBERT   Lord Bigot, I am none.

BIGOT   Who killed this prince?

---

79 rob the law i.e. by taking the law into my own hands and killing you myself   **81 bright** i.e.
unused   **up** away   **81 murderer's skin** animal leather was the usual material used for sword
scabbards   **85 tempt** test   **danger** damage/peril   **defence** legal defense/self-defense in a
fight   **86 marking** paying sole attention to   **88 brave** challenge, defy   **92 prove me so** i.e.
by making me kill you   **93 Yet** so far   **Whose tongue soe'er** whoever's tongue   **97 by** aside
gall injure   **100 spleen** temper/spirit   **101 betime** at once   **102 toasting-iron** i.e. sword
(contemptuous)   **105 Second** support/act as deputy to

HUBERT   'Tis not an hour since I left him well:
I honoured him, I loved him, and will weep
110   My date of life out for his sweet life's loss.
SALISBURY   Trust not those cunning waters of his eyes,
For villainy is not without such rheum,
And he, long traded in it, makes it seem
Like rivers of remorse and innocency.
115   Away with me, all you whose souls abhor
Th'uncleanly savours of a slaughter-house,
For I am stifled with this smell of sin.
BIGOT   Away toward Bury, to the dauphin there.
PEMBROKE   There tell the king he may inquire us out.

Exeunt Lords

120   BASTARD   Here's a good world! Knew you of this fair work?
Beyond the infinite and boundless reach
Of mercy, if thou didst this deed of death,
Art thou damned, Hubert.
HUBERT   Do but hear me, sir.
125   BASTARD   Ha! I'll tell thee what:
Thou'rt damned as black — nay, nothing is so black —
Thou art more deep damned than Prince Lucifer:
There is not yet so ugly a fiend of hell
As thou shalt be, if thou didst kill this child.
130   HUBERT   Upon my soul—
BASTARD   If thou didst but consent
To this most cruel act, do but despair:
And if thou want'st a cord, the smallest thread
That ever spider twisted from her womb
Will serve to strangle thee: a rush will be a beam
135   To hang thee on: or wouldst thou drown thyself,
Put but a little water in a spoon,
And it shall be as all the ocean,

---

110 **date** duration   112 **rheum** watery matter/tears   113 **traded** practiced   116 **savours**
smells   119 **inquire us out** seek us   126 **black** traditionally the color of the devil
127 **Prince Lucifer** the rebel archangel who fell from heaven to hell, i.e. Satan, the devil
131 **but** nothing but   132 **want'st** lack   **cord** rope (to hang yourself)   134 **rush** reed
135 **wouldst** should you/if you wish to

Enough to stifle such a villain up.
I do suspect thee very grievously.

140 HUBERT   If I in act, consent, or sin of thought,
Be guilty of the stealing that sweet breath
Which was embounded in this beauteous clay,
Let hell want pains enough to torture me:
I left him well.

145 BASTARD   Go, bear him in thine arms:
I am amazed, methinks, and lose my way
Among the thorns and dangers of this world.
How easy dost thou take all England up!
From forth this morsel of dead royalty,
150 The life, the right, and truth of all this realm
Is fled to heaven: and England now is left
To tug and scamble and to part by th'teeth
The unowed interest of proud-swelling state:
Now for the bare-picked bone of majesty
155 Doth doggèd war bristle his angry crest
And snarleth in the gentle eyes of peace:
Now powers from home and discontents at home
Meet in one line: and vast confusion waits,
As doth a raven on a sick-fall'n beast,
160 The imminent decay of wrested pomp.
Now happy he whose cloak and cincture can
Hold out this tempest. Bear away that child
And follow me with speed: I'll to the king:

---

138 stifle suffocate, drown   139 grievously strongly   142 embounded enclosed   clay i.e.
Arthur's flesh   143 want lack   146 amazed confused   148 take . . . up i.e. lift up Arthur's
body (playing on the sense of "cause the English nation to take up arms")   152 scamble
scramble, struggle, make shift   part tear apart   153 unowed interest portion not owned by a
universally recognized king (plays on the financial senses of the words: the nobles do not owe
the king allegiance, imagined as monetary interest to be fought over)   154 for on behalf of
bare-picked . . . majesty sovereign authority that has been almost stripped bare of dignity and
grandeur by being fought over like dogs with a bone   155 doggèd fierce/cruel/doglike
crest hackles/heraldic device on a coat of arms   157 powers armies   from away from
discontents discontented persons   158 line i.e. united purpose   confusion disaster/chaos/
destruction   160 wrested pomp majesty seized by force   161 he is he   cincture belt
162 Hold out weather, endure

A thousand businesses are brief in hand,

165 And heaven itself doth frown upon the land.   *Hubert carrying the*
   Exeunt   body of Arthur

Act 5 Scene 1   *running scene 9*

Enter King John and Pandulph, [with] Attendants

KING JOHN   Thus have I yielded up into your hand   *Giving Cardinal*
The circle of my glory.   *Pandulph the crown*

CARDINAL PANDULPH   Take again   *Returning the crown to King John*
From this my hand, as holding of the Pope

5   Your sovereign greatness and authority.

KING JOHN   Now keep your holy word: go meet the French,
And from his holiness use all your power
To stop their marches 'fore we are inflamed:
Our discontented counties do revolt:

10   Our people quarrel with obedience,
Swearing allegiance and the love of soul
To stranger blood, to foreign royalty;
This inundation of mistempered humour
Rests by you only to be qualified.

15   Then pause not: for the present time's so sick,
That present med'cine must be ministered,
Or overthrow incurable ensues.

CARDINAL PANDULPH   It was my breath that blew this tempest up,
Upon your stubborn usage of the Pope:

20   But since you are a gentle convertite,
My tongue shall hush again this storm of war
And make fair weather in your blust'ring land:

---

164 **brief in hand** will soon be underway/must be dealt with urgently   **5.1** *Location: England, the court of King John*   2 **circle ... glory** i.e. my stately crown   4 **as holding of** in tenure, leasehold from (i.e. John must recognize papal authority once more)   8 **inflamed** consumed by fire   9 **counties** shires/counts, i.e. noblemen   11 **love of soul** deepest love   12 **stranger** foreign   13 **inundation** flood   **mistempered humour** anger, ill-temper/bodily imbalance   14 **Rests** remains   **only** alone   **qualified** calmed   16 **present** instant, taking immediate effect   **ministered** administered, given   17 **overthrow** bodily collapse (with political connotations)   19 **usage** treatment   20 **convertite** convert/penitent   22 **blust'ring** turbulent, stormy

On this Ascension Day, remember well,
Upon your oath of service to the Pope,
25   Go I to make the French lay down their arms.

Exeunt [all but King John]

KING JOHN   Is this Ascension Day? Did not the prophet
Say that before Ascension Day at noon
My crown I should give off? Even so I have:
I did suppose it should be on constraint,
30   But, heav'n be thanked, it is but voluntary.

Enter [the] Bastard

BASTARD   All Kent hath yielded: nothing there holds out
But Dover Castle: London hath received,
Like a kind host, the dauphin and his powers.
Your nobles will not hear you, but are gone
35   To offer service to your enemy:
And wild amazement hurries up and down
The little number of your doubtful friends.

KING JOHN   Would not my lords return to me again
After they heard young Arthur was alive?

40   BASTARD   They found him dead and cast into the streets,
An empty casket, where the jewel of life
By some damned hand was robbed and ta'en away.

KING JOHN   That villain Hubert told me he did live.

BASTARD   So on my soul he did, for aught he knew:
45   But wherefore do you droop? Why look you sad?
Be great in act as you have been in thought:
Let not the world see fear and sad distrust
Govern the motion of a kingly eye:
Be stirring as the time, be fire with fire,
50   Threaten the threat'ner and outface the brow
Of bragging horror: so shall inferior eyes,
That borrow their behaviours from the great,

---

28 give off give up, hand over   **29 constraint** compulsion   **34 hear** listen to, take notice of
37 doubtful fearful/untrustworthy   **45 droop** look downcast   **48 motion** movement
49 stirring as active   **the time** i.e. current events   **50 outface** defy   **brow** countenance
51 bragging boastful/bullying   **inferior eyes** i.e. the king's subjects   **52 borrow . . . from**
model their actions on

Grow great by your example, and put on
The dauntless spirit of resolution.
55　Away, and glisten like the god of war
When he intendeth to become the field:
Show boldness and aspiring confidence:
What, shall they seek the lion in his den,
And fright him there? And make him tremble there?
60　O, let it not be said: forage, and run
To meet displeasure farther from the doors,
And grapple with him ere he come so nigh.

KING JOHN　The legate of the Pope hath been with me,
And I have made a happy peace with him,
65　And he hath promised to dismiss the powers
Led by the dauphin.

BASTARD　O inglorious league!
Shall we, upon the footing of our land,
Send fair-play orders, and make compromise,
70　Insinuation, parley and base truce
To arms invasive? Shall a beardless boy,
A cockered silken wanton, brave our fields,
And flesh his spirit in a warlike soil,
Mocking the air with colours idly spread,
75　And find no check? Let us, my liege, to arms:
Perchance the cardinal cannot make your peace;
Or if he do, let it at least be said
They saw we had a purpose of defence.

KING JOHN　Have thou the ordering of this present time.

80　BASTARD　Away, then, with good courage!— Yet, I know,　*Aside*
Our party may well meet a prouder foe.　*Exeunt*

---

55 **god of war** i.e. the Roman god Mars   56 **become** grace/come to   **field** battlefield
60 **forage** overrun (an area)/pillage   62 **nigh** near   64 **happy** fortunate, opportune
67 **inglorious** shameful   68 **upon . . . land** standing on our own soil/because land is being
paced by foreign soldiers   69 **fair-play** honorable, lacking cunning   70 **Insinuation**
suggestions, attempts to gain favor   **base** dishonorable, cowardly   72 **cockered** pampered
silken effeminate/luxurious/clothed in silk   **wanton** spoiled child   **brave** challenge
73 **flesh** initiate (in warfare)/plunge in (as one would a weapon into flesh)   74 **colours** battle
flags   **idly** foolishly/frivolously   75 **check** resistance   78 **purpose** intention, plan
79 **ordering** management   81 **prouder** superior/more arrogant

Act 5 Scene 2

Enter, in arms, Lewis, Salisbury, Melun, Pembroke, Bigot [and]
Soldiers

LEWIS   My lord Melun, let this be copied out,
And keep it safe for our remembrance:
Return the precedent to these lords again,
That having our fair order written down,
5   Both they and we, perusing o'er these notes,
May know wherefore we took the sacrament
And keep our faiths firm and inviolable.

SALISBURY   Upon our sides it never shall be broken.
And, noble dauphin, albeit we swear
10   A voluntary zeal and an unurged faith
To your proceedings: yet believe me, prince,
I am not glad that such a sore of time
Should seek a plaster by contemned revolt,
And heal the inveterate canker of one wound
15   By making many: O, it grieves my soul
That I must draw this metal from my side
To be a widow-maker: O, and there
Where honourable rescue and defence
Cries out upon the name of Salisbury!
20   But such is the infection of the time,
That for the health and physic of our right,
We cannot deal but with the very hand
Of stern injustice and confusèd wrong:
And is't not pity, O my grievèd friends,
25   That we, the sons and children of this isle,
Was born to see so sad an hour as this,

5.2   *Location: England, the French camp*   3 precedent original (copy)   **4 fair** just/
neatly written   **order** agreement   **6 took the sacrament** received communion (a way of
confirming the sacredness of vows)   **7 faiths** pledges   **9 albeit** although   **12 sore of time**
wound of the present   **13 contemned** despised, contemptible   **14 canker** ulcer/corruption
16 metal i.e. sword   **18 rescue and defence** rescue of England from John/defense of England
against the French   **19 Cries out upon** appeals to/rejects   **21 physic** cure   **22 deal but**
proceed in any way other than   **23 confusèd** disastrous, disorderly

Wherein we step after a stranger, march
Upon her gentle bosom, and fill up
Her enemies' ranks? I must withdraw and weep
30   Upon the spot of this enforcèd cause —
To grace the gentry of a land remote,
And follow unacquainted colours here.
What, here? O nation, that thou couldst remove,
That Neptune's arms who clippeth thee about,
35   Would bear thee from the knowledge of thyself,
And grapple thee unto a pagan shore,
Where these two Christian armies might combine
The blood of malice in a vein of league,
And not to spend it so unneighbourly.
40   LEWIS   A noble temper dost thou show in this,
And great affections wrestling in thy bosom
Doth make an earthquake of nobility.
O, what a noble combat hast thou fought
Between compulsion and a brave respect:
45   Let me wipe off this honourable dew,
That silverly doth progress on thy cheeks:
My heart hath melted at a lady's tears,
Being an ordinary inundation:
But this effusion of such manly drops,
50   This shower, blown up by tempest of the soul,
Startles mine eyes, and makes me more amazed
Than had I seen the vaulty top of heaven
Figured quite o'er with burning meteors.
Lift up thy brow, renownèd Salisbury,
55   And with a great heart heave away this storm:

27 **step after** march behind, support   **stranger** foreigner   **30 spot** place/blemish, moral
stain   **31 grace** honor, support   **32 unacquainted** unfamiliar   **33 remove** move, depart
34 Neptune Roman god of the sea   **clippeth** embrace   **35 bear** carry   **36 grapple** bind,
attach   **pagan . . . league** i.e. the English and French might unite against a common non-
Christian enemy   **39 spend . . . unneighborly** waste it in such an unneighborly manner
40 temper disposition   **41 affections** emotions, loyalties   **42 earthquake** i.e. tumult
44 compulsion necessity (of opposing John)   **brave respect** noble regard (for your country)
45 dew i.e. tears   **48 ordinary** commonplace, everyday   **52 vaulty** arched roof   **53 Figured**
adorned   **55 heave** bear

Commend these waters to those baby eyes
That never saw the giant world enraged,
Nor met with fortune other than at feasts,
Full warm of blood, of mirth, of gossiping:
60   Come, come; for thou shalt thrust thy hand as deep
Into the purse of rich prosperity
As Lewis himself: so, nobles, shall you all,
That knit your sinews to the strength of mine.
And even there methinks an angel spake.

Enter Cardinal Pandulph

65   Look where the holy legate comes apace,
To give us warrant from the hand of heaven
And on our actions set the name of right
With holy breath.

CARDINAL PANDULPH   Hail, noble Prince of France!
70   The next is this: King John hath reconciled
Himself to Rome: his spirit is come in
That so stood out against the Holy Church,
The great metropolis and see of Rome.
Therefore thy threat'ning colours now wind up,
75   And tame the savage spirit of wild war,
That like a lion fostered up at hand,
It may lie gently at the foot of peace,
And be no further harmful than in show.

LEWIS   Your grace shall pardon me, I will not back:
80   I am too high-born to be propertied,
To be a secondary at control,
Or useful serving-man and instrument
To any sovereign state throughout the world.

---

56 **Commend** commit, entrust   **those baby eyes** i.e. babies   59 **blood** liveliness
62 **nobles** may play on the sense of "gold coins"   63 **knit** join   **sinews** muscles, i.e. strength
64 **Even . . . spake** i.e. in this heaven supports us/I see already that the promise of financial
reward will secure your support (alternatively, some editors speculate that the reference is to a
trumpet signaling Pandulph's arrival)   **angel** gold coin/heavenly being   65 **apace** quickly
71 **come in** become reconciled, returned   73 **see** bishopric/seat of a bishop in his church
74 **wind up** furl   76 **fostered . . . hand** brought up by hand   78 **show** appearance   79 **back**
go back   80 **propertied** treated as an object   81 **secondary at control** second in command,
deputy

Your breath first kindled the dead coal of wars
85 Between this chastised kingdom and myself,
And brought in matter that should feed this fire;
And now 'tis far too huge to be blown out
With that same weak wind which enkindled it:
You taught me how to know the face of right,
90 Acquainted me with interest to this land,
Yea, thrust this enterprise into my heart;
And come ye now to tell me John hath made
His peace with Rome? What is that peace to me?
I, by the honour of my marriage-bed,
95 After young Arthur, claim this land for mine:
And, now it is half-conquered, must I back
Because that John hath made his peace with Rome?
Am I Rome's slave? What penny hath Rome borne,
What men provided, what munition sent,
100 To underprop this action? Is't not I
That undergo this charge? Who else but I,
And such as to my claim are liable,
Sweat in this business and maintain this war?
Have I not heard these islanders shout out
105 '*Vive le roi*' as I have banked their towns?
Have I not here the best cards for the game
To win this easy match played for a crown?
And shall I now give o'er the yielded set?
No, no, on my soul, it never shall be said.
110 CARDINAL PANDULPH   You look but on the outside of this work.
LEWIS   Outside or inside, I will not return
Till my attempt so much be glorified

---

89 **right** justice/a rightful claim   90 **Acquainted me with** introduced me to, made me aware of **interest** valid claim   98 **penny . . . borne** expense has Rome sustained   100 **underprop** support   101 **charge** expense   102 **liable** subject   105 '*Vive le roi*' "Long live the king" (French; also a phrase in playing **cards**)   **banked** besieged (within banks of fortifications)/ captured, confined/skirted around ("bank" may also be a card-playing term, perhaps meaning "to secure as a winning" or "a card player's stake")   107 **match** game, contest (may play on the sense of "marriage," given Lewis's union with Blanche)   **crown** royal crown/coin, i.e. bet at cards   108 **set** series of games (won at cards)

As to my ample hope was promisèd
Before I drew this gallant head of war,
115 And culled these fiery spirits from the world
To outlook conquest and to win renown
Even in the jaws of danger and of death.   *Trumpet sounds*
What lusty trumpet thus doth summon us?

Enter [the] Bastard

BASTARD   According to the fair play of the world,
120 Let me have audience: I am sent to speak.
My holy lord of Milan, from the king
I come to learn how you have dealt for him:
And, as you answer, I do know the scope
And warrant limited unto my tongue.

125 CARDINAL PANDULPH   The dauphin is too wilful-opposite,
And will not temporize with my entreaties:
He flatly says he'll not lay down his arms.

BASTARD   By all the blood that ever fury breathed,
The youth says well. Now hear our English king,
130 For thus his royalty doth speak in me:
He is prepared, and reason too he should:
This apish and unmannerly approach,
This harnessed masque and unadvisèd revel,
This unheard sauciness and boyish troops,
135 The king doth smile at, and is well prepared
To whip this dwarfish war, these pigmy arms,
From out the circle of his territories.
That hand which had the strength, even at your door,
To cudgel you and make you take the hatch,

---

113 **ample** complete, great   114 **drew** gathered   **head** army   115 **culled** selected
116 **outlook** overcome/outstare   118 **lusty** vigorous   119 **According to** in accordance with
120 **have audience** be heard   122 **dealt for him** proceeded on his behalf   123 **scope** extent
124 **warrant** authority   **limited** designated, permitted   125 **wilful-opposite** stubbornly
hostile   126 **temporize** negotiate   131 **reason** with good reason   132 **apish** apelike, foolish
unmannerly inappropriate, impolite (puns on "unmanly"—i.e. cowardly/not like a human)
133 **harnessed** armored   **masque** courtly entertainment involving dancing and elaborate
costumes   **unadvisèd** ill-considered   134 **unheard** unheard of, extraordinary (plays on the
literal sense as King John is not present, though he responds through the Bastard; some editors
emend to "unhaired"—i.e. boyishly beardless)   136 **whip** i.e. drive   **pigmy** very small
139 **take the hatch** leap over the lower half of the door, i.e. retreat hastily

140   To dive like buckets in concealèd wells,
           To crouch in litter of your stable planks,
           To lie like pawns locked up in chests and trunks,
           To hug with swine, to seek sweet safety out
           In vaults and prisons, and to thrill and shake
145   Even at the crying of your nation's crow,
           Thinking this voice an armèd Englishman:
           Shall that victorious hand be feebled here,
           That in your chambers gave you chastisement?
           No: know the gallant monarch is in arms
150   And like an eagle o'er his eyrie towers,
           To souse annoyance that comes near his nest:
           And you degenerate, you ingrate revolts,
           You bloody Neroes, ripping up the womb
           Of your dear mother England, blush for shame:
155   For your own ladies and pale-visaged maids
           Like Amazons come tripping after drums:
           Their thimbles into armèd gauntlets change,
           Their needles to lances, and their gentle hearts
           To fierce and bloody inclination.
160   LEWIS   There end thy brave, and turn thy face in peace:
           We grant thou canst outscold us: fare thee well:
           We hold our time too precious to be spent
           With such a brabbler.
      CARDINAL PANDULPH   Give me leave to speak.
165   BASTARD   No, I will speak.
      LEWIS   We will attend to neither.
           Strike up the drums, and let the tongue of war
           Plead for our interest and our being here.

---

141 **litter** animal straw   **planks** floors   142 **pawns** goods pledged in exchange for a loan of
money   143 **hug** i.e. curl up   144 **vaults** cellars/tombs   **thrill** tremble   145 **crow** cockerel,
the French national symbol   150 **eyrie** nest/brood   151 **souse** swoop down on
152 **revolts** rebels   153 **Neroes** the Roman Emperor Nero was supposed to have torn open his
mother's womb after killing her   156 **Amazons** race of warrior women   **tripping** moving
quickly and lightly   157 **gauntlets** armored gloves   160 **brave** challenge   **turn thy face** i.e.
retreat   161 **outscold** outdo us in scolding/have more quarrelsome women than us
163 **brabbler** brawler/quarrelsome fault-finder   166 **attend** listen

BASTARD   Indeed your drums, being beaten, will cry out;
170   And so shall you, being beaten: do but start
An echo with the clamour of thy drum,
And even at hand a drum is ready braced
That shall reverberate all as loud as thine.
Sound but another, and another shall
175   As loud as thine rattle the welkin's ear
And mock the deep-mouthed thunder: for at hand —
Not trusting to this halting legate here,
Whom he hath used rather for sport than need —
Is warlike John: and in his forehead sits
180   A bare-ribbed Death, whose office is this day
To feast upon whole thousands of the French.
LEWIS   Strike up our drums, to find this danger out.
BASTARD   And thou shalt find it, dauphin, do not doubt.

Exeunt [at different doors]

Act 5 Scene 3   *running scene 11*

Alarums. Enter King John and Hubert [at different doors]

KING JOHN   How goes the day with us? O, tell me, Hubert.
HUBERT   Badly, I fear. How fares your majesty?
KING JOHN   This fever that hath troubled me so long
Lies heavy on me: O, my heart is sick!

Enter a Messenger

5   MESSENGER   My lord, your valiant kinsman Falconbridge
Desires your majesty to leave the field
And send him word by me which way you go.
KING JOHN   Tell him toward Swinstead, to the abbey there.
MESSENGER   Be of good comfort, for the great supply
10   That was expected by the dauphin here

---

172 **ready braced** prepared, with the skin tightened   175 **welkin** sky   177 **halting** hesitating
178 **sport** amusement   179 **forehead** countenance   180 **bare-ribbed** skeletal   **office** duty,
task   183 **find** discover/suffer, experience   **5.3** *Location: England, the battlefield*
Alarums battle calls   8 **Swinstead** actually Swineshead, Lincolnshire   9 **supply**
reinforcements

Are wrecked three nights ago on Goodwin Sands.
This news was brought to Richard but even now:
The French fight coldly and retire themselves.

KING JOHN   Ay me, this tyrant fever burns me up,
15   And will not let me welcome this good news.
Set on toward Swinstead: to my litter straight;
Weakness possesseth me, and I am faint.   *Exeunt*

Act 5 Scene 4   *running scene 11 continues*

Enter Salisbury, Pembroke and Bigot

SALISBURY   I did not think the king so stored with friends.

PEMBROKE   Up once again: put spirit in the French:
If they miscarry, we miscarry too.

SALISBURY   That misbegotten devil Falconbridge
5   In spite of spite, alone upholds the day.

PEMBROKE   They say King John, sore sick, hath left the field.

Enter Melun, wounded

MELUN   Lead me to the revolts of England here.

SALISBURY   When we were happy we had other names.

PEMBROKE   It is the count Melun.

10   SALISBURY   Wounded to death.

MELUN   Fly, noble English, you are bought and sold:
Unthread the rude eye of rebellion
And welcome home again discarded faith:
Seek out King John and fall before his feet:
15   For if the French be lords of this loud day,
He means to recompense the pains you take
By cutting off your heads: thus hath he sworn
And I with him, and many more with me,

---

11 Goodwin Sands dangerous sandbanks off the coast of Kent   12 Richard i.e. the Bastard
13 coldly unenthusiastically   retire themselves retreat   16 litter bed for the transport of the
sick or wounded   5.4   1 stored well supplied   2 Up once again i.e. onward, back to battle
3 miscarry fail   4 misbegotten wrongfully conceived   5 In . . . spite despite everything
6 sore grievously   7 revolts rebels   11 Fly flee   bought and sold betrayed   12 Unthread
withdraw (like thread from a needle)   eye needle's eye   16 He i.e. Lewis, the French dauphin

Upon the altar at Saint Edmundsbury;
20   Even on that altar where we swore to you
Dear amity and everlasting love.
SALISBURY   May this be possible? May this be true?
MELUN   Have I not hideous death within my view,
Retaining but a quantity of life,
25   Which bleeds away, even as a form of wax
Resolveth from his figure gainst the fire?
What in the world should make me now deceive,
Since I must lose the use of all deceit?
Why should I then be false, since it is true
30   That I must die here and live hence by truth?
I say again, if Lewis do win the day,
He is forsworn if e'er those eyes of yours
Behold another daybreak in the east:
But even this night, whose black contagious breath
35   Already smokes about the burning crest
Of the old, feeble and day-wearied sun,
Even this ill night, your breathing shall expire,
Paying the fine of rated treachery
Even with a treacherous fine of all your lives,
40   If Lewis by your assistance win the day.
Commend me to one Hubert with your king:
The love of him, and this respect besides,
For that my grandsire was an Englishman,
Awakes my conscience to confess all this.
45   In lieu whereof, I pray you, bear me hence
From forth the noise and rumour of the field,
Where I may think the remnant of my thoughts
In peace, and part this body and my soul
With contemplation and devout desires.

---

24 **quantity** small amount   26 **Resolveth** dissolves, melts   **his figure** its shape   28 **use**
practice/benefit   30 **hence** from now on/in the next world   32 **forsworn** perjured
35 **smokes** grows misty/moves like smoke   38 **fine** penalty   **rated** assessed/rebuked
39 **fine** ending/penalty   42 **respect** factor   45 **lieu** exchange, payment   **whereof** of which
46 **rumour** tumult, noise   47 **remnant** remainder

50   SALISBURY   We do believe thee, and beshrew my soul,
          But I do love the favour and the form
          Of this most fair occasion, by the which
          We will untread the steps of damnèd flight,
          And like a bated and retirèd flood,
55   Leaving our rankness and irregular course,
          Stoop low within those bounds we have o'erlooked
          And calmly run on in obedience
          Even to our ocean, to our great King John.
          My arm shall give thee help to bear thee hence,
60   For I do see the cruel pangs of death
          Right in thine eye. Away, my friends! New flight,
          And happy newness, that intends old right.   *Exeunt*

Act 5 Scene 5

running scene 12

Enter Lewis and his train

    LEWIS   The sun of heaven, methought, was loath to set,
          But stayed and made the western welkin blush,
          When English measure backward their own ground
          In faint retire: O, bravely came we off,
5   When with a volley of our needless shot,
          After such bloody toil, we bid goodnight,
          And wound our tott'ring colours clearly up,
          Last in the field, and almost lords of it.
    Enter a Messenger
    MESSENGER   Where is my prince, the dauphin?
10 LEWIS   Here: what news?

---

50 beshrew curse   51 favour appearance/face/benevolence   form appearance/outcome
53 untread retrace   54 bated diminished   55 rankness swelling, excess (plays on the sense
of "vileness")   56 bounds limits, boundaries   61 Right clearly   New flight i.e. toward
King John   62 happy fortunate   old right i.e. loyalty to King John   **5.5** *Location:
England, the French camp   train* retinue   1 loath reluctant   2 welkin sky   3 measure
travel (over)   4 faint retire weak retreat   bravely splendidly   came we off we left the field
of combat   5 needless superfluous, unnecessary   7 tott'ring waving/tattered (from the
battle)

MESSENGER   The count Melun is slain: the English lords
By his persuasion are again fall'n off,
And your supply, which you have wished so long,
Are cast away and sunk on Goodwin Sands.

15   LEWIS   Ah, foul shrewd news! Beshrew thy very heart!
I did not think to be so sad tonight
As this hath made me. Who was he that said
King John did fly an hour or two before
The stumbling night did part our weary powers?

20   MESSENGER   Whoever spoke it, it is true, my lord.

LEWIS   Well: keep good quarter and good care tonight:
The day shall not be up so soon as I,
To try the fair adventure of tomorrow.   *Exeunt*

Act 5 Scene 6   *running scene 13*

Enter [the] Bastard and Hubert, severally

HUBERT   Who's there? Speak, ho! Speak quickly, or I shoot.

BASTARD   A friend. What art thou?

HUBERT   Of the part of England.

BASTARD   Whither dost thou go?

5   HUBERT   What's that to thee? Why may not I demand
Of thine affairs, as well as thou of mine?

BASTARD   Hubert, I think?

HUBERT   Thou hast a perfect thought:
I will upon all hazards well believe

10   Thou art my friend, that know'st my tongue so well.
Who art thou?

BASTARD   Who thou wilt: and if thou please,
Thou mayst befriend me so much as to think
I come one way of the Plantagenets.

---

12 **are . . . off** have once again withdrawn their allegiance   15 **shrewd** harsh   19 **stumbling**
i.e. causing the men to stumble   21 **quarter** watch   23 **adventure** fortune/hazard
5.6   Location: England, not far from Swinstead Abbey   severally separately   3 **Of the**
part on the side   8 **perfect** accurate   9 **upon all hazards** whatever the risks   14 **come . . .**
of am descended from (via one of my parents)

15   HUBERT   Unkind remembrance! Thou and endless night
             Have done me shame: brave soldier, pardon me,
             That any accent breaking from thy tongue
             Should scape the true acquaintance of mine ear.
      BASTARD   Come, come: *sans* compliment: what news abroad?
20   HUBERT   Why, here walk I in the black brow of night,
             To find you out.
      BASTARD   Brief, then: and what's the news?
      HUBERT   O my sweet sir, news fitting to the night,
             Black, fearful, comfortless and horrible.
25   BASTARD   Show me the very wound of this ill news:
             I am no woman, I'll not swoon at it.
      HUBERT   The king, I fear, is poisoned by a monk:
             I left him almost speechless, and broke out
             To acquaint you with this evil, that you might
30   The better arm you to the sudden time,
             Than if you had at leisure known of this.
      BASTARD   How did he take it? Who did taste to him?
      HUBERT   A monk, I tell you, a resolvèd villain,
             Whose bowels suddenly burst out: the king
35   Yet speaks and peradventure may recover.
      BASTARD   Who didst thou leave to tend his majesty?
      HUBERT   Why, know you not? The lords are all come back,
             And brought Prince Henry in their company,
             At whose request the king hath pardoned them,
40   And they are all about his majesty.
      BASTARD   Withhold thine indignation, mighty heaven,
             And tempt us not to bear above our power.
             I'll tell thee, Hubert, half my power this night,

---

15 Unkind remembrance! Unnatural memory! (Hubert addresses his own memory; **unkind** may play on the sense of "lacking proper kinship")   **17 accent** utterance/way of speaking **breaking** coming   **18 scape** escape, elude   **19 *sans* compliment** without ceremony **abroad** at large, out there   **21 find you out** find you   **22 Brief** be brief   **25 very wound** most painful part, worst   **28 broke out** rushed out, left   **30 to** for   **sudden time** unexpected events, emergency   **31 at leisure** later, without urgency   **32 taste** act as taster (i.e. person who ate some of the king's food to see whether it was poisoned)   **34 bowels** intestines **35 Yet** still   **peradventure** perhaps, by chance   **38 Prince Henry** John's son, the future Henry III, who ruled 1216–72   **42 bear . . . power** endure more than we are able to **43 power** army

Passing these flats, are taken by the tide:
45   These Lincoln Washes have devourèd them:
Myself, well mounted, hardly have escaped.
Away before: conduct me to the king:
I doubt he will be dead or ere I come.   *Exeunt*

Act 5 Scene 7   *running scene 14*

Enter Prince Henry, Salisbury and Bigot

PRINCE HENRY   It is too late: the life of all his blood
Is touched corruptibly, and his pure brain,
Which some suppose the soul's frail dwelling-house,
Doth by the idle comments that it makes
5   Foretell the ending of mortality.
Enter Pembroke
PEMBROKE   His highness yet doth speak, and holds belief
That, being brought into the open air,
It would allay the burning quality
Of that fell poison which assaileth him.
10   PRINCE HENRY   Let him be brought into the orchard here.
                                                [*Exit Bigot*]
Doth he still rage?
PEMBROKE   He is more patient
Than when you left him; even now he sung.
PRINCE HENRY   O vanity of sickness! Fierce extremes
15   In their continuance will not feel themselves.
Death, having preyed upon the outward parts,
Leaves them invisible, and his siege is now
Against the mind, the which he pricks and wounds
With many legions of strange fantasies,

---

44 Passing passing over   flats sandbanks   45 Lincoln Washes sandbanks in Lincolnshire
46 hardly barely/with difficulty   47 Away before lead on, go ahead   48 doubt fear   or ere
before   5.7   *Location: England, the garden of Swinstead Abbey*   2 touched tainted/
endangered   corruptibly in a manner causing decay   pure clear, lucid   4 idle nonsensical
9 fell cruel/fierce   10 orchard garden   11 rage rave   14 vanity absurdity   15 not feel
themselves be unaware/become unaware of physical pain   17 invisible invisibly
19 legions multitudes/armies

20   Which, in their throng and press to that last hold,
        Confound themselves. 'Tis strange that death should sing.
        I am the cygnet to this pale faint swan,
        Who chants a doleful hymn to his own death,
        And from the organ-pipe of frailty sings
25   His soul and body to their lasting rest.
        SALISBURY   Be of good comfort, Prince, for you are born
        To set a form upon that indigest
        Which he hath left so shapeless and so rude.
        King John [is] brought in
        KING JOHN   Ay, marry, now my soul hath elbow-room:
30   It would not out at windows nor at doors:
        There is so hot a summer in my bosom
        That all my bowels crumble up to dust:
        I am a scribbled form, drawn with a pen
        Upon a parchment, and against this fire
35   Do I shrink up.
        PRINCE HENRY   How fares your majesty?
        KING JOHN   Poisoned, ill fare: dead, forsook, cast off:
        And none of you will bid the winter come
        To thrust his icy fingers in my maw,
40   Nor let my kingdom's rivers take their course
        Through my burned bosom, nor entreat the north
        To make his bleak winds kiss my parchèd lips
        And comfort me with cold. I do not ask you much,
        I beg cold comfort: and you are so strait
45   And so ingrateful, you deny me that.
        PRINCE HENRY   O that there were some virtue in my tears,
        That might relieve you!

---

20 hold stronghold (i.e. the mind)   21 Confound destroy, defeat/confuse   22 cygnet young
swan, i.e. Prince Henry, the dying John's youthful son   swan the swan was thought to sing
only once, just before it died   27 indigest shapeless mass/confused situation   28 rude
undefined, rough, disordered   29 elbow-room i.e. enough space   33 scribbled form
indistinctly drawn shape/hasty sketch   37 fare food (plays on the sense of the verb—i.e. "to
do")   forsook rejected, abandoned   39 maw throat/stomach   41 north north wind
44 cold comfort comforting coolness/no comfort   strait severe/stingy ("straight" in Folio)
45 ingrateful ungrateful   46 virtue power/remedy

KING JOHN   The salt in them is hot.
　　　Within me is a hell, and there the poison
50　　Is, as a fiend, confined to tyrannize
　　　On unreprievable condemnèd blood.

Enter [the] Bastard

BASTARD   O, I am scalded with my violent motion
　　　And spleen of speed to see your majesty!

KING JOHN   O cousin, thou art come to set mine eye:
55　　The tackle of my heart is cracked and burnt,
　　　And all the shrouds wherewith my life should sail
　　　Are turnèd to one thread, one little hair:
　　　My heart hath one poor string to stay it by,
　　　Which holds but till thy news be utterèd:
60　　And then all this thou see'st is but a clod
　　　And module of confounded royalty.

BASTARD   The dauphin is preparing hitherward,
　　　Where heaven he knows how we shall answer him:
　　　For in a night the best part of my power,
65　　As I upon advantage did remove,
　　　Were in the Washes all unwarily
　　　Devourèd by the unexpected flood.　　　　*King John dies*

SALISBURY   You breathe these dead news in as dead an ear.—
　　　My liege, my lord!— But now a king, now thus.　　*To King John*
70　PRINCE HENRY   Even so must I run on, and even so stop.
　　　What surety of the world, what hope, what stay,
　　　When this was now a king, and now is clay?

BASTARD   Art thou gone so? I do but stay behind　　*To King John*
　　　To do the office for thee of revenge,
75　　And then my soul shall wait on thee to heaven,

---

52 **motion** urge　53 **spleen** eagerness　54 **set** close (after death)　55 **tackle** rigging and
sails　56 **shrouds** ship's ropes (plays on the sense of "burial sheet")　58 **string** heartstring/
rope　**stay** support/anchor　60 **clod** lump of earth　61 **module** model, image
confounded destroyed　62 **preparing hitherward** on his way here/preparing to come here
63 **heaven he** probably originally "God he," altered because of 1606 Parliamentary "Act to
restrain the Abuses of Players," which sought to put an end to blasphemous language on the
stage　65 **upon** i.e. to gain (tactical)　**remove** move, change the position of　67 **flood**
rushing water/tide　68 **dead** deadly/grave　69 **But** just　**thus** i.e. dead　70 **Even so** in the
same way　71 **stay** support　75 **wait on** escort

As it on earth hath been thy servant still.—
Now, now, you stars that move in your right   *To the Lords*
   spheres,
Where be your powers? Show now your mended faiths,
And instantly return with me again,
80   To push destruction and perpetual shame
Out of the weak door of our fainting land:
Straight let us seek, or straight we shall be sought:
The dauphin rages at our very heels.

SALISBURY   It seems you know not, then, so much as we:
85   The Cardinal Pandulph is within at rest,
Who half an hour since came from the dauphin,
And brings from him such offers of our peace
As we with honour and respect may take,
With purpose presently to leave this war.

90   BASTARD   He will the rather do it when he sees
Ourselves well sinewèd to our defence.

SALISBURY   Nay, 'tis in a manner done already,
For many carriages he hath dispatched
To the seaside, and put his cause and quarrel
95   To the disposing of the cardinal,
With whom yourself, myself and other lords,
If you think meet, this afternoon will post
To consummate this business happily.

BASTARD   Let it be so.— And you, my noble prince,
100   With other princes that may best be spared,
Shall wait upon your father's funeral.

PRINCE HENRY   At Worcester must his body be interred;
For so he willed it.

BASTARD   Thither shall it then,
105   And happily may your sweet self put on

---

76 still always   **77 right spheres** proper orbits   **82 Straight** at once   **88 respect** self-respect
89 presently immediately   **90 rather** sooner   **91 sinewèd** strengthened   **93 carriages** gun-
carriages (i.e. supports for artillery)   **95 disposing** management   **97 meet** fitting   **post**
hasten   **98 consummate** conclude   **100 princes** nobles   **101 wait upon** attend, serve in
105 happily with good fortune

The lineal state and glory of the land,
To whom with all submission, on my knee
I do bequeath my faithful services
And true subjection everlastingly.   *He kneels*

110 SALISBURY   And the like tender of our love we make,
To rest without a spot for ever more.   *The Lords kneel*

PRINCE HENRY   I have a kind soul that would give thanks
And knows not how to do it but with tears.   *He weeps*

BASTARD   O, let us pay the time but needful woe,   *Rising*
115 Since it hath been beforehand with our griefs.
This England never did, nor never shall,
Lie at the proud foot of a conqueror,
But when it first did help to wound itself.
Now these her princes are come home again,
120 Come the three corners of the world in arms,
And we shall shock them. Nought shall make us rue,
If England to itself do rest but true.   *Exeunt*

---

106 **lineal state** i.e. rightfully inherited kingship   108 **bequeath** give   110 **like tender** same
offer   111 **rest** remain   **spot** blot   114 **but** ambiguous here since it can mean both "only"
and "not merely"   **needful woe** necessary mourning   115 **beforehand** in credit, had more
than enough (financial term)   118 **But** except   120 **three corners** i.e. all other parts
121 **shock** repel with force   **rue** grieve   122 **rest** remain

TEXTUAL NOTES

F = First Folio text of 1623, the only authority for the play
F2 = a correction introduced in the Second Folio text of 1632
Ed = a correction introduced by a later editor
SD = stage direction
SH = speech heading (i.e. speaker's name)

List of parts = Ed

1.1.0 SD *the* = F. Ed = them, *but F can be supported if "Chatillon" is regarded as a title rather than a name* **49 expeditious** = F. F2 = expeditions **148 It** = F. F2 = I. F *is taken to refer to the Bastard's **face*** from the previous line **189 too** = F2. F = two **209 smack** = Ed. F = smoake **217 SD** *Enter . . . Gurney* = Ed. *SD five lines down in F* **239 Could** = F. Ed = Could he/a. *Although inserting "he" clarifies the sense, the suggestion is not supported metrically* **259 That** = F. Ed = Thou
Act 2 Scene 1 = Ed. F = *Scæna Secunda* **1 SH KING PHILIP** = Ed. F = *Lewis* **18 SH LEWIS** = F. *Some eds reassign to King Philip* **63 Ate** = Ed. F = Ace **113 breast** = F2. F = beast **146 shoes** = F. Ed = shows **151 SH KING PHILIP** = Ed. F *continues Austria's speech, with line beginning "King Lewis"* **221 Confronts your** = Ed. F = Comfort yours **265 roundure** = Ed. F = rounder **332 SH CITIZEN** = Ed. F = *Hubert. This SH recurs for rest of the scene; editors dispute whether or not the Hubert who is a character from Act 3 scene 2 onward is intended* **342 run** = F2 (runne). F = rome **359 dead** = F. Ed = dread **375 SH CITIZEN** = Ed. F = *Fra* **378 Kings** = F. Ed = Kinged **432 niece** = Ed. F = neere **442 of** = F. Ed = O **496 Anjou** = Ed. F = *Angiers*
Act 2 [Scene 2] = Ed. F = *Actus Secundus*
3.1.75 test = Ed. F = tast. Ed = task **124 that** = F. Ed = it **190 casèd** = F. Ed = crazèd, chafed **213 truth** = F. Ed = troth
3.2.4 SD *Enter . . . Hubert* = Ed. *Placed one line earlier in* F **64 broad-eyed** = Ed. F = brooded
3.3.45 not holy = Ed. F = holy **65 friends** = Ed. F = fiends **112 word's** = F. Ed = world's **151 evilly** = F. Ed = vilely
4.1.68 this = F. Ed = his
4.2.1 again = F3. F = against **42 than** = Ed. F = then. Ed = when **223 account** *spelled* accompt *in* F
4.3.161 cincture = Ed. F = center
Act 5 = Ed. F = *Actus Quartus*

5.1.55 glisten = Ed. F = glister
5.2.36 grapple = Ed. F = cripple. Ed = gripple   **134 unheard** = F. Ed =
    unhaired   **136 these** = Ed. F = this
5.4.18 more = Ed. F = moe
5.5.7 tott'ring = F. Ed = tatt'ring, *secondary sense, i.e. torn*
5.6.15 endless = F. Ed = eyeless
5.7.18 mind = Ed. F = winde   **22 cygnet** = Ed. F = Symet   **44 strait** *spelled*
    straight *in* F

SCENE-BY-SCENE ANALYSIS

ACT 1 SCENE 1

Lines 1–49: The Chatillon of France claims the English throne and lands on behalf of Arthur, King John's nephew, threatening war with France if John refuses. King John, however, is defiant and says that he will be in France with his army before him if Chatillon doesn't hurry. Once Chatillon has left, Queen Elinor reflects that she foresaw that "ambitious Constance" wouldn't stop until she'd provoked French support for Arthur and that the situation could have been prevented if they'd handled her with more tact; it will now involve two kingdoms and a war to sort things out. John protests his "strong possession" and "right" to the crown but his mother points out that his "strong possession" is greater than his "right" in this matter, but she will only admit this privately to him. A Sheriff arrives with news of "the strangest controversy" from the country. John gives permission for the plaintiffs to approach. Returning briefly to the subject of the forthcoming war with France he says he'll make "Our abbeys and our priories" pay for it.

Lines 50–163: Two brothers arrive, Robert Falconbridge, son and heir to the late Robert Falconbridge, and his older brother, Philip. Robert claims that his father made him his heir on his deathbed, although he's the younger brother, because he believed that his older brother was illegitimate, conceived while he was in Germany on business for King Richard. Elinor and John both think that Philip must be Richard's son ("He hath a trick of Coeur-de-lion's face") but John points out that in law, since his mother was married, he is the legal heir to the Falconbridge lands. Elinor asks him if he would rather be son and heir of Falconbridge or acknowledged as King Richard's bastard son with no land. He answers that if he and his brother's places were changed, he'd give away all his land rather than have his brother's face and figure. Elinor likes his bluntness and offers him the chance to leave the Falconbridge estate to his brother, be acknowledged as Richard's bastard son, and follow her to war. He decides at once to follow her "unto the death." John then knights him—he is to be known henceforth as Sir Richard Plantagenet.

Lines 164–278: The brothers say farewell and John and Elinor leave to prepare for war with France. Alone on stage, Richard reflects on his new fortune and status, satirizing the pretensions of the newly risen in the way they treat social inferiors and give themselves airs. He argues that it's the way society works and "fits the mounting spirit like myself" but concludes that he must learn to recognize, although he will not practice, flattery: the "Sweet, sweet, sweet poison for the age's tooth." His mother arrives with a servant, seeking his brother. He dismisses the servant and then confronts his mother, demanding to know his real father's identity. She is shocked at first at the slur on her reputation but finally confesses that "King Richard Coeur-de-lion was thy father," claiming that she was seduced and unable to resist, and asking his pardon. The Bastard is delighted, however, and says he couldn't "wish a better father" and that she should have no regrets since he has none, and takes her to meet his "kin," who will agree it would have been a sin to refuse King Richard's sexual advances and not have borne him.

ACT 2 SCENE 1

Lines 1–83: The French are outside the town of Angiers. King Philip introduces Arthur to the Duke of Austria, who killed his uncle, King Richard, but to make amends has allied himself to the French in support of Arthur's claim to the English crown against John. Arthur welcomes him and Constance offers "his mother's thanks, a widow's thanks" until with his help she is able to offer him a worthy reward. King Philip says they should mount an attack on the town, which refuses to recognize Arthur's claim. Constance advises waiting until Chatillon returns from England to hear John's response. Chatillon appears almost immediately and tells them not to concern themselves with fighting a small town but to expect a greater enemy since John has come with his mother, his niece, bastard nephew and the English army. Philip is surprised but Austria says they must rise to the occasion and prepare to "welcome" them.

Lines 84–150: The English arrive and John greets the French king, saying they can have peace if Philip recognizes his claim to the English throne. Philip says they can have peace if John acknowledges Arthur's claim to it. He asks him to look at Arthur's face, which is like his father Geoffrey's and, since he was John's older brother, this means that he, not John, is the rightful king of England. John asks by whose authority he undertakes this and Philip replies, by God's (the "supernal judge") who has made him Arthur's guardian. John responds that he usurps his authority but Philip replies that preventing usurping is a good enough excuse. Elinor demands to know who he is accusing of usurping and Constance replies Elinor's usurping son, John. Elinor accuses Constance of wanting to make her bastard king so that she can rule. Constance replies that she was never unfaithful to Geoffrey and that her son's less likely to be a bastard than Elinor's. The two women continue to insult each other. Austria calls for peace. The Bastard (Richard) demands to know who speaks and threatens to take the lion-skin, which belonged to King Richard Coeur-de-lion, from his back.

Lines 151–205: Lewis demands that the "women and fools" keep quiet. He claims "England and Ireland, Anjou, Touraine, Maine" for Arthur and asks John to resign his claim and lay down his arms. John refuses but adds that if Arthur yields to him, he'll give him more than France can win by fighting. Elinor tells Arthur to come to her. Constance mocks her offer saying, in exchange for the kingdom, his "grandam" will give Arthur "a plum, a cherry and a fig." Arthur tells his mother to be quiet: he wishes he were dead, he's not worth all this "coil" (fuss). Elinor blames Constance for making Arthur weep and Constance blames Elinor and they resume their slanging match. King John and then King Philip call for peace. Philip suggests that they should ask the men of Angiers which of the two claimants they support—"Whose title they admit, Arthur's or John's." A trumpet is sounded.

Lines 206–306: A Citizen enters upon the walls and demands to know who has summoned them. The two kings each state their case and demand that the men of Angiers should judge between the rival claimants. John says that the French were about to lay siege to the town to destroy it until the English arrived but are now prepared to talk. Philip advances the legitimacy of Arthur's claim to the English crown and says that if the men of Angiers will recognize this, they will leave them in peace. The Citizen claims that the people of Angiers are loyal to the English king. They ask him to say who that is but he is unable to. They must decide between themselves who the rightful king is and Angiers will then be loyal to him. The kings decide they'll have to fight and set their armies in the field. The two armies start fighting.

Lines 307–423: They cease and the French Herald demands that Angiers open the gates to receive Arthur. On the other side the English Herald claims victory for John. The Citizen claims that they have been watching all this while and judge the armies equally matched, that neither has achieved victory; they are not prepared to recognize either—"We hold our town for neither, yet for both." The two kings meet, both still determined to fight on. The Bastard is keen to return to battle till one side has vanquished the other. The kings again appeal to the citizens of Angiers to recognize their right and are again refused. The Bastard then suggests that the two armies join together and turn their power against Angiers for defying them both.

Lines 424–544: The kings agree and are deciding on their positions when the Citizen's spokesperson suggests they can be reconciled peacefully by the marriage of John's niece, "the lady Blanche," and the King of France's son, "Lewis the dauphin." The Bastard is disgusted by the Citizen's long speech in favor of the match. Elinor, however, advises John to accept and to offer a large dowry with Blanche, which will make the French king his ally rather than his enemy. John says that if the dauphin can love Blanche and agree to the match, he will give France all the English lands in France, apart from Angiers, including Anjou, Touraine, Maine and Poitiers. The dauphin looks at Blanche and seeing his own reflection "Drawn in the flattering table of her eye," declares his love. The Bastard is again disgusted by the turn of events but Blanche says that she is willing to do as her uncle asks: all she sees of the dauphin is "worthy love" and she can see nothing that would "merit any hate." The young couple agree to marry and John will give her five provinces plus thirty thousand marks as her dowry.

Lines 545–570: The French king asks Angiers to open their gates so that they can all enter and Blanche and Lewis can be married. He asks where Constance is, knowing she'll be angry. Lewis says she is "sad and passionate" in the king's tent. Philip asks John if there is some way in which she may be compensated. John says he'll make Arthur Duke of Brittany and Earl of Richmond and give him Angiers. He hopes that Constance will be at least partially satisfied and stop complaining. All except the Bastard leave to prepare for the wedding.

Lines 571–608: Alone on stage the Bastard reflects on events: "Mad world, mad kings, mad composition!" In order to stop Arthur's claim to the English crown, John has willingly parted with a large part of his kingdom while the French king, who claimed to be supporting Arthur's legitimate right and posed as "God's own soldier," has listened to the devil in his ear and withdrawn from "a resolved and honourable war / To a most base and vile-concluded peace." He blames all this on "That smooth-faced gentleman, tickling commodity" (profit or self-interest) and rails against its influence in a world in which everyone seems to be out for themselves. He goes on ironically to recognize that the reason he can rail against "commodity" is that he hasn't yet been touched by it personally, being poor he will say there's "no sin but to be rich" but once he's rich he will then say that "there is no vice but beggary." Since kings "break faith" for their own advantage, he will worship "Gain" from now on.

ACT 2 SCENE 2

Constance refuses to believe the Earl of Salisbury's report that Blanche and Lewis are to be married. He assures her that is the case. She's angry and blames him, recognizing that because of this match France will no longer support Arthur's claim. Arthur begs her to "be content" but Constance claims that she might be content if he were ugly or deformed in some way, since then she would not love him, but that he is "fair" and that at his birth "Nature and Fortune joined to make thee great." She blames the "strumpet [whore] Fortune" and claims that France (i.e. the French king) is a "bawd [prostitute] to Fortune and King John." She asks Salisbury whether Philip is not "forsworn" (guilty of breaking his oath) and tells him to curse the king or go. He says he cannot go without her to attend the wedding but she refuses and Salisbury departs with Arthur, leaving Constance alone with her grief.

ACT 3 SCENE 1

Lines 1–61: Blanche and Lewis are married and King Philip declares there will be a holiday in France every year to celebrate "this blessèd day." Constance, however, condemns it as a "wicked day, and not a holy day!" and refusing to be reconciled, calls on the heavens to set "these perjured kings" at odds once more. When Austria calls for peace, Constance immediately retorts, demanding "War, war, no peace!" and declares Austria likewise perjured and, rather than wear a lion's skin, he should take it off for shame and "hang a calf's-skin on those recreant limbs." Austria is furious and says if a man said that to him he'd fight him. The Bastard immediately repeats the words as a challenge and the situation threatens to get out of hand when Cardinal Pandulph, the papal legate, enters.

Lines 62–118: The Cardinal demands to know from John why he refuses to accept Stephen Langton, chosen by Pope Innocent III, as Archbishop of Canterbury. John responds that "no Italian priest" has authority to tell "a sacred king" what to do and argues that he is "supreme head." Philip tells him he "blaspheme[s] in this." John is defiant, arguing that he alone is not led by this "meddling priest," fearful of the Catholic church's power of excommunication and wealth obtained by the corrupt practice of selling pardons. The Cardinal announces that in that case John will be cursed and excommunicated and whoever kills him will be canonized and worshipped as a saint. Constance begs for the right to add her curses to Rome's.

The papal legate argues that he has "law and warrant" for his curse but Constance argues that she does too, "since law itself is perfect wrong." John has stolen Arthur's rightful kingdom and "he that holds his kingdom holds the law."

Lines 119–183: Pandulph then orders Philip, on peril of being excommunicated himself to make war on John, "that arch-heretic," unless he "do submit himself to Rome." Both sides try to sway Philip to support them. Elinor and Constance argue again, as do the Bastard and Austria. Lewis thinks the Pope's curse is heavier than the loss of England's friendship, and his father should "forgo the easier." Blanche suggests that's the Pope's curse but Constance tells Lewis he's being tempted by "the devil." Philip is "perplexed," unsure what to do and asks the Cardinal to put himself in his place—his son and Blanche are just married and peace agreed between their two lands, which have previously been at war. He cannot go back on his word and change his mind. He begs Pandulph to find some peaceful solution.

Lines 184–280: The Cardinal is resolute—Philip cannot remain friends with John. Philip responds that he may let go of John's hand but not his "faith"—his oath of friendship. Pandulph replies that he would then make "faith an enemy to faith" since his duty is to heaven to whom he swore his first vow. He must make war on John. Austria calls it "flat rebellion" and the Bastard taunts him once more. Lewis calls his father "to arms." Blanche is shocked that her husband wants to fight on his wedding day against her own family and begs him not to. Constance urges him on to battle, however. Philip is still undecided until the Cardinal again threatens excommunication at which he reluctantly agrees to fight John. Constance is delighted, Elinor furious, and John threatening; only the Bastard is happy. Blanche is distressed, with her loyalties divided. John tells the Bastard to bring up the army: they are at war with France again.

ACT 3 SCENE 2

Lines 1–30: After more fighting, the Bastard enters with Austria's head. John then enters with Arthur, telling Hubert to look after him.

He fears that Elinor is captured but the Bastard reassures him that he rescued her himself. There is more fighting. John tells Elinor to stay and she'll be strongly guarded and tells Arthur to cheer up since his grandmother loves him and he'll love him like a father. Arthur replies that his mother will "die with grief." John sends the Bastard back to England to extract money from the Church to pay for the wars. Elinor calls Arthur over to her.

Lines 31–92: John takes Hubert to one side and tells him how grateful he is to him and how much he respects him. Hubert says he is much obliged. John then starts a series of evasive, round about hints to Hubert, who, guessing his purpose, says he'll do it: Arthur "shall not live." John is happy. Arthur is to go to England with Hubert while John goes to Calais.

ACT 3 SCENE 3

Lines 1–108: King Philip and Lewis are bemoaning the French defeat while the cardinal attempts to cheer them. Constance enters, blaming Philip and his peace treaty for their defeat. She is distraught, desiring only death: "Death, death, O amiable, lovely death . . . come to me!" Pandulph tells her that what she speaks is "madness" not "sorrow" but she denies it. Philip asks her to tie up her hair. She begs him to make for England. He again asks her to tie up her hair. She agrees, saying that she untied it in her grief, wishing she could have released Arthur as easily, but she will tie it up again since her son is a bound prisoner. She imagines Arthur pale and ill and says she will not recognize him when they meet again in heaven. The Cardinal is impatient and Philip accuses her of being "as fond of grief as of your child." Constance, however, replies that "Grief fills the room up of my absent child": she sees him everywhere. She lets down her hair again since "there is such disorder in my wit" and leaves, still lamenting bitterly. Philip goes after her, fearing she may kill herself.

Lines 109–185: Lewis expresses his discontent to the Cardinal, who replies that in the long run, this will be to his advantage. Lewis does not understand how this can be the case and the Cardinal explains that while Arthur lives, John can have no peace. He will, therefore, have him murdered, at which point Lewis may claim the English throne for himself through his wife, Blanche (her mother was John's older sister, Eleanor). Lewis is unconvinced, believing that he will lose everything, but the Cardinal explains how public opinion will turn against John for Arthur's death: he will be blamed for everything, including the weather. Lewis suggests that perhaps John will let Arthur live but Pandulph assures him that as soon as he learns of the dauphin's approach he will have him killed and then his people will be revolted and desire change. Furthermore "the Bastard Falconbridge" is busy "ransacking the Church / Offending charity" so that even a dozen Frenchmen would gather the support of the English; that support would then snowball. He tells Lewis to go with him to Philip and he will urge him on. The dauphin agrees, "If you say ay, the king will not say no."

ACT 4 SCENE 1

Lines 1–44: Hubert gives instructions to the Executioners to heat irons for branding, hide behind the arras, and when he stamps his foot, to rush out and bind Arthur to the chair. The First Executioner says he hopes Hubert has a warrant for "the deed." Hubert rejects such scruples and calls Arthur to come to him. Arthur greets him and notices that he seems sad. Hubert confesses, "Indeed, I have been merrier." Arthur goes on to say that no one should be as sad as he: he'd be delighted to be free—it's not his fault he's Geoffrey's son; he wishes he were Hubert's son. Hubert is determined to harden his heart. Arthur, however shows his concern, wishing Hubert were ill since he could then sit and watch with him. He believes he cares more for Hubert than Hubert does for him. Hubert is moved and shows Arthur the warrant. Arthur reads it and asks him if he has to burn out his eyes. Hubert replies that he must. Arthur asks him if he will do it and he replies that he will.

Lines 49–51: Arthur goes on to remind Hubert of how when he had a headache, he looked after him, and always asked how he was and what he needed. But he says if Hubert must do it then he must, although his eyes have done him no harm, not so much as to frown on him. Hubert says he's sworn to do it. Arthur believes that such a thing could only happen in "this iron age." Even the iron itself would pity him, drink his tears, and rust away. Arthur asks if Hubert is harder than iron. He would not have believed it, even if an angel told him that Hubert would put out his eyes. Hubert stamps his foot and the Executioners come out. Arthur begs Hubert to save him: the men's looks terrify him. He implores him not to bind him and promises he'll sit quietly, and will forgive him whatever he does. Hubert sends the men away; they're glad to be away from "such a deed."

Lines 92–144: Arthur then regrets sending away one who, he now realizes, despite his harsh looks, was his "friend." Hubert tells him to prepare. Arthur asks if there is no remedy but Hubert assures him there is "None, but to lose your eyes." Arthur wishes there were something in Hubert's eyes and Hubert complains that he promised to sit quietly. Arthur again pleads with him to spare his eyes; he'd rather he cut out his tongue. He thinks the iron has gone cold. Hubert replies that it can be heated again but Arthur says "it's dead for grief"—the breath of heaven has blown it out. Hubert says he can revive it with his breath but Arthur replies that if he does, he'll make it blush for shame. Even iron and fire have more pity than him. Hubert is won over. He will let Arthur live but John mustn't know. He'll report Arthur's death but will not harm him "for the wealth of all the world."

ACT 4 SCENE 2

Lines 1–82: John has had himself crowned a second time, although the Earls of Salisbury and Pembroke think it a pointless waste of time and money—"wasteful and ridiculous excess." John says he's explained it to them and is willing to listen and grant their demands. Pembroke says the lords wish Arthur to be set free—the people think it wrong that he's imprisoned and not at liberty. John agrees and says he will entrust Arthur to them. Hubert enters and John takes him to one side; Pembroke believes he's the one charged with Arthur's murder—he showed the warrant to a friend. He thinks Hubert has a wicked look and believes he's already done "What we so feared he had a charge to do." They note John's changing color as Hubert speaks to him.

Lines 83–135: John announces that unfortunately Arthur is dead. The lords said they feared as much. John wonders why they look so hard at him, arguing that he doesn't hold the power of life or death but Salisbury claims it is "apparent foul play" and that John will have to answer for it, either on earth or in heaven. Pembroke says he'll go and seek Arthur's grave. Once they've gone, John repents the deed since they're so angry and his position is even less secure— "There is no sure foundation set on blood." A messenger arrives to tell him that the French army have arrived led by the dauphin. John is surprised not to have heard of it before—why did his mother not warn him—but the messenger adds that both she and Constance are dead.

Lines 136–187: The Bastard enters with Peter of Pomfret. John says he doesn't want any more bad news—he's had enough. Richard tells him it's better to know and John pulls himself together. He relates how he has traveled up and down the country collecting money for John's wars and on his journeys heard strange rumors. He has brought one with him who prophesies that before the "next Ascension Day at noon" John will deliver up his crown. John orders Hubert to take the man to prison, to be hanged on that day. He asks Richard if he's heard the news. Richard knows about the French and also the lords' anger over Arthur's death, holding John responsible. John orders Richard to go after them and bring them back to him. He sends the messenger off with him. John is alone just long enough on stage to reflect on the news: "My mother dead!"

Lines 188–276: Hubert reenters and says that five moons have been seen. People take it as a dangerous portent: everyone is afraid and rumors are spreading of the arrival of the French, and of Arthur's death. John asks him why he urged him to kill his nephew— Hubert had no reason to wish Arthur dead. Hubert protests that John ordered him. John complains that it's "the curse of kings" to be served by those who take their whims for orders. Hubert shows him the warrant, signed and sealed by John for Arthur's death. John replies that it was Hubert's fault: his presence and villainous appearance put the idea into his head. He blames Hubert for the deed and orders him out of his sight. Finally Hubert tells him that "Young Arthur is alive." John is delighted and tells him to hurry and give the lords the news and bring them to him.

ACT 4 SCENE 3

Lines 1–73: Arthur is high up on the prison wall, planning to escape, disguised as a ship boy. Despite his fear he decides to jump—he might as well "die and go, as die and stay." He falls and is killed. Salisbury, Pembroke, and Bigot are making plans to join with the dauphin. Richard arrives, saying that the king would like to see them straightaway. They reply that they are no longer loyal to him since they do not wish to be stained with his dishonor, claiming they "know the worst." The Bastard tries to persuade them, when they find Arthur's body. They are shocked and horrified by the sight, believing he has been murdered. Salisbury and the others vow to avenge him.

Lines 74–165: Hubert enters to tell them that Arthur is alive but they believe that Hubert has killed him. They threaten him with their swords while Richard strives to keep the peace. Hubert tries to convince them that he's not responsible. They refuse to believe him and leave to meet the dauphin at Bury. Richard asks Hubert if he knew of Arthur's death. If he knew of "this most cruel act," he should despair and kill himself. Hubert tries to convince him of his innocence, assuring Richard that he "left him [Arthur] well." Richard orders him to lift the body up: Richard thinks he's losing his way "Among the thorns and dangers of this world." He foresees all the troubles that will now descend on England through foreign and civil war and John's authority diminished at home. He reflects that he who can survive "this tempest" is fortunate and orders Hubert to follow him, carrying Arthur. There are a "thousand businesses" to attend to and "heaven itself" looks angrily on England.

ACT 5 SCENE 1

Lines 1–30: King John gives up his crown to Cardinal Pandulph who returns it to him with the authority of the Pope. He then asks the Cardinal to go to meet the French and persuade them to return before there's civil war and strife. The Cardinal agrees that since it was he that "blew this tempest up" because John refused to do the Pope's will, now that he's compliant he'll calm the situation down, bidding him remember his oath of service to the Pope "On this Ascension Day." He departs and while briefly alone, John recalls the prophecy that he would give the crown up before noon this day. He believed it meant he would be forced to but is thankful that it was "voluntary" on his part.

Lines 31–81: The Bastard reports that the war with France is going badly: Kent has yielded apart from Dover Castle, and London has welcomed the dauphin. The nobles refuse to listen to John and have gone to offer their services to the enemy; his few friends are all amazed. John asks if the lords wouldn't return after hearing that Arthur was alive but Richard replies that they found his dead body. John says that "villain Hubert" told him he was alive and Richard replies that Hubert believed he was. He encourages John to behave proudly like a king and set a good example to his followers: "Show boldness and aspiring confidence." John tells him the Pope's legate has been with him and they've made peace—he's going to dismiss the dauphin's army. Richard is dismayed: "O inglorious league!" and thinks they should still make their arrangements to fight, in case the Cardinal fails: it should not be said that they didn't try to defend their country. John tells him to organize everything, but privately fears that the French may be superior in strength.

ACT 5 SCENE 2

Lines 1–118: Lewis accepts the services of Salisbury and the other rebel English lords. Salisbury swears to keep faith with him, regretting the need for war, grieving that they should follow a foreign lord and fighting their fellow countrymen, wishing their two Christian armies might join arms against a pagan enemy. Lewis praises those noble sentiments, which do him honour, but is amazed at his tears—

"such manly drops." He tells him to overcome them since he will "thrust [his] hand as deep / Into the purse of rich prosperity" as Lewis will himself. The Cardinal enters and Lewis thinks he has come to authorize their actions. Pandulph greets him and immediately says that John is now reconciled with Rome so the French should pack up their gear and go home. Lewis refuses, claiming that it's too late and he's "too high-born" to be told what to do. The Cardinal started this war and taught him what was right and he now intends to go on. Now that Arthur's dead, by virtue of his marriage to Blanche, he claims the throne of England for himself. It's he not Rome who has done and paid for everything and he believes he can win easily. The Cardinal complains this is a superficial view of things. They hear a trumpet sound.

Lines 119–183: The Bastard enters wanting to know if the Cardinal has succeeded in persuading the dauphin. Pandulph says the dauphin refuses to lay down his arms. Richard is delighted and makes a stirring speech on John's behalf saying that they are prepared. Recalling how they defeated the French in France he asks whether it's not more likely they'll be successful here on their own land. He has special words of anger and scorn for the rebel lords, "you degenerate, you ingrate revolts, / You bloody Neroes . . . , " who would destroy their own land and telling them to blush for shame. Lewis is dismissive, saying he knows the Bastard can "outscold us" but he hasn't got time to listen to "such a brabbler." Richard taunts him that he will be beaten like his drums and claims that John used the Cardinal for "sport" rather than "need." He threatens them that "warlike John" is at hand with "bare-ribbed Death" at his "forehead" who will feast upon "thousands of the French." Each defies the other and they prepare to fight.

ACT 5 SCENE 3

To the sounds of battle, John asks Hubert for news. Hubert thinks it's going badly for the English and John reports feeling ill. A messenger enters from Richard telling John to leave the battlefield and to tell him which way he's going. John replies to Swinstead Abbey. The messenger tells him to cheer up; the French supplies have been shipwrecked on the Goodwin Sands and they're retreating. John repeats how ill he feels and tells them to take him straight to Swinstead.

ACT 5 SCENE 4

Salisbury, Bigot, and Pembroke on the battlefield are surprised by how much support John has but have learned that he's ill. The English success, though, is down to Richard: "That misbegotten devil Falconbridge." Melun enters and warns them that they have been betrayed, that if the French win the dauphin has sworn to cut off their heads and he advises them to make peace with John. They cannot believe it but Melun asks why, since he is facing death himself, he should lie to them. He begs them to remove his body to some quiet place to die. They believe him and are glad that they need be traitors no longer but can return to King John.

ACT 5 SCENE 5

Lewis is reflecting on French successes of a long day of battle when a messenger arrives to say that count Melun is dead, the English rebel lords have returned to John, and French supplies have been lost on Goodwin Sands. Lewis is dismayed by the turn of events but promises to be up before dawn to continue the fight in the morning.

ACT 5 SCENE 6

Hubert seeks Richard with bad news: John has been poisoned by a monk. Richard asks who's left to tend the king and Hubert tells him Prince Henry with the rebel lords who have returned to John. Prince Henry has asked for them to be pardoned. Richard says that he has lost half his army in the Wash and barely escaped himself and asks Hubert to take him to the king.

ACT 5 SCENE 7

Lines 1–51: Prince Henry is discussing his father's serious condition with Salisbury and Bigot. Pembroke enters, saying that John wishes to be brought out into the cool air. He asks if his father is still raging and Pembroke replies that he is calmer now and has just been singing. Prince Henry grieves for his dying father, wondering at the illness' strange effect on his mind. Salisbury comforts him, telling him it's his fate to resolve the confused situation of the times. John is brought into the orchard, relieved to be outside. He is burning inside and desires coolness but complains that none of them will help him. Prince Henry wishes his tears would help his father but John complains they're too hot.

Lines 52–122: Richard rushes in eager to see John, who says he has just enough strength to hear his news. Richard says the dauphin is coming and he has lost half his army, but Salisbury tells him that John is dead. Richard says he will wait just long enough to avenge John and then follow him to the grave. He asks the stars for aid. Salisbury says he obviously doesn't know that Cardinal Pandulph is resting inside, who came half an hour ago to say that he had concluded an honorable peace with the dauphin. Richard thinks he'll be more inclined when he sees them ready to fight but Salisbury says it's already concluded; the dauphin has already sent his troops home and left the Cardinal to arrange the rest with Richard, himself, and the other lords. Richard agrees; Prince Henry should accompany his father's body to Worcester for burial. Richard offers his "faithful services / And true subjection" to the prince, and the other lords follow suit. Prince Henry wishes he could thank them but can only do so with his tears. Richard says they should grieve as befits the time, but England shall never be conquered, now that all are loyal again. Nothing will make them sorry "If England to itself do rest but true."

KING JOHN
IN PERFORMANCE:
THE RSC AND BEYOND

The best way to understand a Shakespeare play is to see it or ideally to participate in it. By examining a range of productions, we may gain a sense of the extraordinary variety of approaches and interpretations that are possible—a variety that gives Shakespeare his unique capacity to be reinvented and made "our contemporary" four centuries after his death.

We begin with a brief overview of the play's theatrical and cinematic life, offering historical perspectives on how it has been performed. We then analyze in more detail a series of productions staged over the last half century by the Royal Shakespeare Company. The sense of dialogue between productions that can only occur when a company is dedicated to the revival and investigation of the Shakespeare canon over a long period, together with the uniquely comprehensive archival resource of promptbooks, programme notes, reviews, and interviews held on behalf of the RSC at the Shakespeare Birthplace Trust in Stratford-upon-Avon, allows an "RSC stage history" to become a crucible in which the chemistry of the play can be explored.

We then go to the horse's mouth. Modern theater is dominated by the figure of the director. He or she must hold together the whole play, whereas the actor must concentrate on his or her part. The director's viewpoint is therefore especially valuable. Shakespeare's plasticity is wonderfully revealed when we hear the directors of two highly successful productions of each play answering the same questions in very different ways.

FOUR CENTURIES OF KING JOHN: AN OVERVIEW

Shakespeare's King John, with its pageantry and anti-Catholicism, appears to have been a popular play during the Elizabethan and early

Jacobean periods. This is evidenced by its mention in Francis Meres' commonplace book *Palladis Tamia* (1598), in which he claims that "As Plautus and Seneca are accounted the best for Comedy and Tragedy among the Latines: so Shakespeare among the English is the most excellent in both kinds for the stage."[1] The inaccurate attribution to Shakespeare in the 1611 and 1622 reprints of the anonymous, strongly anti-Catholic *Troublesome Raigne of King John* (almost certainly one of Shakespeare's key sources), was either a genuine mistake or a deliberate attempt to deceive, but whichever is the case it suggests a degree of popular familiarity with Shakespeare's play in the first two decades of the seventeenth century.

The contemporary reference in Anthony Munday's *Death of Robert, Earl of Huntingdon* (printed in 1601, but commissioned by Philip Henslowe in February 1598), to "Hubert, thou fatall keeper of poore babes"[2] must relate to Shakespeare's play rather than the *Troublesome Raigne* or the historical sources in which Arthur is a youth rather than the much younger child of Shakespeare's play. Since this did not appear in print until the 1623 Folio, the implication is that it had sufficiently impressed itself in the playgoing consciousness by the close of the sixteenth century as to make the reference easily recognizable. Further evidence that the play was regularly staged during this period can be adduced from the fact that it's included in a document dated 12 January 1669 that lists plays "formerly acted at Blackfriars and now allowed of to his Majesties Servants at the New Theatre," which, given that the King's Men did not acquire Blackfriars until 1608, suggests the play's continued stage popularity into the early seventeenth century.

There is, however, no subsequent record of any public performance, until it was revived at Covent Garden in 1737, and evidence suggests that this was after a long period of neglect. This revival was due to the rumored imminent production of a more stridently anti-Catholic adaptation by Colley Cibber, which prompted David Garrick to stage his version at Covent Garden. Defending his adaptation, Cibber wrote in the *Daily Advertiser* in February 1737 that "many of that Fam'd Authors Pieces, for these Hundred Years past, have lain dormant, from, perhaps, a just Suspicion, that they were too weak, for a compleat Entertainment."[3] Similarly, the playbill for the 1745 Drury Lane production proclaimed that it was "Not acted 50 years."

However, from this point onward, and until the third quarter of the nineteenth century, King John becomes a popular, or at least regular, element of the patent houses' repertoires. In the 120 years following the Covent Garden revival, it appeared in at least fifty-eight seasons in either London or the provinces or both, and in three seasons there were rival London productions. During the eighteenth and early to mid-nineteenth centuries the play attracted some of the foremost actors of the day, including Garrick (as both John and the Bastard), Sheridan (who originally played John to Garrick's Bastard), Mrs. Cibber, Mrs. Barry, Mrs. Yates, Mrs. Siddons, John Philip Kemble, and Charles Kemble.

Charles Kemble subsequently staged his own version at Covent Garden in 1823, and by 1830 the play was sufficiently well known for it to receive a burlesque treatment.[4] William Charles Macready, who had made his first appearance in the play in Charles Kemble's company, produced the play himself at Drury Lane in 1842. Shortly afterward, the Theatres Regulation Bill of 1843 ended the duopoly of the London patent theaters and Samuel Phelps (who had earlier played Hubert with Charles Kemble) mounted his own production at Sadler's Wells in 1844 and 1851, and at Drury Lane in 1865 and 1866. Charles Kean also mounted some of the early nonpatent productions of King John at the Princess' Theatre in 1852 and 1858, as well as in American tours in 1846 and 1865. Following Phelps's 1866 production, however, it appears to lapse in popularity once more and does not appear again on the London stage until Herbert Beerbohm Tree's West End revival at Her Majesty's Theatre in 1899, although it was produced at Stratford by Osmond Tearle in 1890.

In the twentieth century, the play was presented at the Old Vic three times in the eight years following the First World War—in 1918, 1921 and 1926—and then appears with less and less frequency in the Old Vic's repertoire: 1931 (with Ralph Richardson as the Bastard); 1953 (directed by George Devine, with Richard Burton, and as part of a project to stage all of the plays in the First Folio), and in 1961. At Stratford there is a similar pattern, with seven productions directed by Michael Benthall between 1901 and 1948, and another in 1957 directed by Douglas Seale, before the five RSC versions discussed in detail below. In the provinces, the play was presented at the Old Vic, Leeds in 1941 (with Sybil Thorndike as Constance), and at the Birmingham Repertory Theatre (with Paul Scofield as the Bastard) in 1945. There was also a BBC radio version in 1944 (again with Ralph Richardson as the Bastard), and a BBC television production in 1984, directed by David Giles. In 2001, however, the play experienced a double revival with both a Northern Broadsides production and Gregory Doran's RSC production at The Swan in Stratford. Josie Rourke directed it again for the RSC's Swan Theatre in 2006; Doran and Rourke discuss their productions in "The Director's Cut."

In summary, therefore, *King John* has enjoyed a chequered stage history, arguably the most variable in stage popularity in the whole Shakespearean canon: popular at the turn of the sixteenth century, it then exits the stage for a century and a half before returning as a staple of the London patent houses' repertoires for some hundred years from the mid-eighteenth century, before seeing its popularity wane in the late nineteenth century and then virtually collapse in the twentieth. What accounts for these shifting fortunes?

One answer lies in the various shifts in styles of acting and theatrical production over the past four hundred years, as well as certain features of the play itself, notably its declamatory style, its emotional range and its episodic nature, which lend themselves well or ill to those fashions. Given these features, especially the play's predominantly declamatory style and its wide emotional range, it's little wonder that in periods which combined, in varying degrees, both "sensibility" and a declamatory style of acting, namely from the mid-eighteenth to the mid-nineteenth centuries, it was relatively popular. Contemporary accounts of productions during this hundred years offer the striking impression of the approbation of the depiction of intense emotion in particular scenes, rather than a particular actor's conception or rendition of a character as a whole, suggesting that the third characteristic discussed above—the play's episodic nature—may also be contributory to its success in this period.

In the 1745 Drury Lane production, Garrick played John to

Susannah Cibber's Constance in a rendition both emphatic and passionate.[5] Similarly, according to contemporary accounts of her performance, Susannah Cibber also seized the opportunity to impress her audience with a number of set pieces in which she displayed an impressive range of emotion, passion, and emphasis,[6] although again it's a particular episode that stands out: in her last, grief-crazed speech she pronounced the words "O Lord! My boy! . . . with such an emphatical scream of agony as will never be forgotten by those who heard her."[7] When, in 1783, at the request of George III, Sarah Siddons succeeded Mrs. Cibber in the part,

> she was ere long regarded as so consummate in the part of *Constance*, that it was not unusual for spectators to leave the house when her part in the tragedy of "King John" was over, as if they could no longer enjoy Shakespeare himself when she ceased to be his interpreter.[8]

As the nineteenth century progressed, however, tastes shifted toward a more natural, realistic style of acting. In Macready's rendition of John in his own 1842 production at Drury Lane, he used a range of contrasting tones and tempos.[9] Such shifts in tempo are in some ways reminiscent of accounts of Edmund Kean's "anarchy of the passions,"[10] although in retaining an overall dignity of delivery, Macready was combining the Romantic and radical techniques of Kean with the more dignified legacy of John Philip Kemble.[11] In particular, Macready appears to have achieved a certain degree of "naturalness" or of "the colloquial" in his acting, without descending to what Coleridge saw in Kean's acting as the vulgarity of "rapid descents from the hyper-tragic to the infra-colloquial."[12] Indeed, according to theatrical historian Alan S. Downer, Macready's style, "refined by science and psychology . . . underlies the whole tradition of naturalism, of Stanislavsky and his heirs."[13] Hence, Macready arguably helped establish the modern system of acting, with its emphasis upon unity of design rather than upon episodic set pieces: "If this was due in part to the spirit of the age, it was due in larger part to Macready's example and practice."[14]

By these standards, and some fifty years after Macready's pioneering work, Herbert Beerbohm Tree's 1899 revival must have seemed remarkably dated, and distaste for the old-fashioned declamatory style, together with a telling iconoclasm for its famous practitioners, is revealed in at least one contemporary review:

> The hysterical grief of Miss Julia Neilson's Constance seems overdone. . . . Mrs. Siddons used to shed real tears as Constance— at least so she said; but that was in the sentimental age. . . . I sometimes think Mrs. Siddons must have been what the Americans call "a holy terror."[15]

Indeed, the part of Constance, which Sarah Siddons so relished because of the emotional range she saw in it,[16] has proved highly problematic for actresses ever since, since to play this role has meant risking the double bind either of being accused of "hysterical grief," as in Julia Neilson's case, or of lifeless understatement of the poetic force of the language. In Douglas Seale's 1957 Stratford production, Joan Miller attempted to play the role with less emphasis on Constance's ranting tirades and greater depth given to her "latent psychosis." The result was generally not well received, with the *Daily Telegraph* reviewer remarking, for example, that she "conveyed little more than that she was rather cross."[17] On the other hand, Susan Engel in Deborah Warner's 1988 RSC production and Claire Bloom in David Giles's 1984 BBC production were both apparently successful in rendering Constance acceptable to a late-twentieth-century audience by playing the part relatively calmly, and effectively questioning whether Constance is actually crazed at all.[18] This impression appears to be confirmed by contemporary reviews, so that, for example, Irving Wardle in *The Times* praised Susan Engel for rendering "the almost unplayably formalized rhetoric into living speech."[19]

However, the Giles and the Warner productions shared an important feature: intimacy with the audience. The Giles production, being for television, allows full-face close-up photography and audible amplification of quiet delivery. Similarly, The Other Place, where Warner mounted her live production, was the smallest and most intimate of all of the RSC's Stratford theaters of the time, and allowed only a tiny audience, which was forced to sit in close proxim-

1. 1957, Douglas Seale production. Joan Miller attempted to play the role with less emphasis on Constance's ranting tirades and greater depth given to her "latent psychosis."

ity to the actors. This suggests that playing Constance successfully in a more restrained fashion accessible to a modern audience requires such intimacy.

Of the two 2001 productions, the critical reception of the Northern Broadsides' Constance suggested that the figure was still not quite at home in the early-twenty-first-century theater, with Charles Spencer in the *Daily Telegraph* opining that Northern Broadsides' "Marie Louise O'Donnell is so stridently histrionic as the grieving Constance . . . that she entirely fails to touch the heart with some of the most poignant and potent poetry in the play,"[20] while Kate Bassett in the *Independent* was even more trenchant: "Marie Louise O'Donnell is ludicrous as the pretender's mother, swishing around like a furious, punctured balloon."[21] Playing Constance in a cooler, more psychoanalytic fashion acceptable to modern audiences requires a realistic, perhaps cinematic acting style that may appear excessively understated unless it is presented in an intimate theater setting, or indeed on film. More generally, complaints about the declamatory nature of the play are rife in the criticism of live performances in the twentieth century, suggesting a reason for its lack of popularity. Thus, a contemporary reviewer of the 1957 Old Vic production commented: "No-one in *King John* ever speaks. They all declaim."[22]

The play's popularity during the early to mid-nineteenth century was also due in some measure to the development in English culture of a taste for extreme historical—indeed "archaeological"—accuracy in the treatment of the subject matter of drama, combined with the spectacular use of costume, stage effects, and supernumeraries. The Shakespeare productions of, in particular, Charles Kemble, William Charles Macready, and Charles Kean, presented costumes and settings that were heavily researched on the basis of scholarship, historical documents, funerary sculpture, and so on. They typically used literally hundreds of supernumeraries in battle scenes and culminated in spectacular final scenes. In part, this trend was commercially based: faced with increasing competition from the nonpatent theaters with their pantomimes and burlesques, the patent theaters had begun in the early nineteenth century to look for new ways to draw the crowds, and so "for all their pieties about only playing the classical repertoire—no burlettas or performing dogs—they relied more and more on 'low' spectacle."[23]

More generally, however, there developed in the mid to late nineteenth century a love of the spectacular, alongside the widespread availability of inventions such as the magic lantern and the stereoscope, paralleled on a grander scale by huge, walk-in, three-dimensional panoramas and dioramas that were popular in London until at least the end of the third quarter of the nineteenth century. Thus, toward the end of William IV's reign, and certainly by the beginning of the second decade of Victoria's (as witnessed by the Great Exhibition in 1851), the English were accustomed first to grandeur and ostentation in their architecture and domestic furniture, and second to looking at the world through pictures rather than through the use of imagination. Thus, the love of the spectacular in the theater, which combined both of these elements, was simply one manifestation of a more general phenomenon in English society.[24] *King John* lent itself well to the pictorial treatment that could be meted out in lavish, spectacular productions, since the very "serial discontinuity"[25] of its episodic structure, together with its medieval subject matter made it ideal for a theatrical magic lantern show that would bring in the crowds. James Robinson Planché, historical advisor to Charles Kemble's 1823 Covent Garden production, recalls with satisfaction the opening night performance:

When the curtain rose, and discovered King John dressed as his effigy appears in Worcester Cathedral, surrounded by his barons sheathed in mail, with cylindrical helmets and correct armorial shields, and his courtiers in the long tunics and mantles of the thirteenth century, there was a roar of approbation, accompanied by four distinct rounds of applause.[26]

In Macready's 1842 Drury Lane production, in addition to recovering the painstaking historical researches of Planché to inform the costume design, fourteen intricate, massive, highly researched painted sets were designed by William Telbin, and huge numbers of supernumeraries were employed.[27] There were fifty-nine persons on stage in the opening scene of the play, as opposed to the six mentioned in the stage directions of the 1623 Folio.[28] Charles Kean's productions at the Princess' Theatre in 1852 and 1858 followed suit and upped the bidding in terms of historical accuracy, so that the throne room in Act 1 Scene 1, for example, was an exact replica of the hall in

Rochester Castle; Kean also made use of large numbers of supernumeraries and used Macready's promptbook to inform his stage directions.[29]

By the time of Tree's 1899 production, however, tastes were beginning to shift again, and may have been given a helping hand by Tree's excessive archaeological-spectacular extravaganza. In an effort to outdo the previous spectacular productions of Kemble, Macready, Phelps, and Kean, Tree included highly researched costumes designed by Percy Anderson, sumptuous sets, vast numbers of supernumeraries, and not only a Magna Carta tableau introduced by Kean but also a further *fifteen* tableaux (with a resulting significant cut in the text). The walls of Angiers were complete with massive Norman archways, a moat, battlements, crenellated parapet walls, corbels, and, in the distance, a faithful painted representation of the medieval chateau of Angiers.[30] Tree's production was distrustful of the text, reliant on props rather than acting conviction, and sentimental. As such, it contradicted virtually all of the precepts of modern theater as they were emerging at the turn of the nineteenth century: overemphasis of archaeological realism was increasingly coming to be seen as artifice and the spectacular as form without content.

Other theatrical trends were also afoot in the early twentieth century which prejudiced against the continuation of the spectacular, most noticeably the rise of the repertory system.[31] Since the basis of the repertory system was a move away from "commercial drama" toward a smaller, more experimental mode of theatrical production, there was no place at all for the high Victorian mode of the spectacular. *King John*'s episodic nature was now a theatrical handicap as the focus of attention shifted from exterior picture show to a more restrained and austere style. Freed from the shackles of historical realism and the distractions of the spectacular, the English theater of the early twentieth century moved toward a greater concentration on the inner coherence of the play and of its characterization.

Absence of any reference to the two things a modern spectator can be guaranteed to know about King John: his legendary relationship with Robin Hood and his signing of Magna Carta at Runnymede in 1215 seem like glaring dramatic omissions today. Shakespeare died twelve years before the 1628 Petition of Right and over sixty

2. 1899, Herbert Beerbohm Tree's production, with Tree himself as John. Tree included highly researched costumes designed by Percy Anderson, sumptuous sets, and vast numbers of supernumeraries.

years before the 1679 Habeas Corpus Act, each of which looks directly back to clause 39 of the charter of 1215.[32] Most importantly, however, Shakespeare could not have known that, within thirty years of his death, England would be plunged into a bloody civil war that was effectively a dispute over the significance of the document, or that the sentiments and even the language of Magna Carta would be used in framing the state and national constitutions of the United States a century and a half later. Palmer sums it up pithily: "As for Magna Carta, the Elizabethans had never heard of it."[33] It is noteworthy that both Kean and Tree should have felt the need to insert the signing of Magna Carta into their nineteenth-century productions in the form of tableaux, although the decline in taste for the dramatic spectacular and the general upward trend in respect for the original text during the twentieth century have not allowed this expedient solution. It seems likely that the lack of reference to Magna Carta has contributed to the play's decline in popularity.

While the absence of any reference to Magna Carta is relatively easy to understand, the lack of any reference to Robin Hood is more puzzling, since there was already a strong popular tradition of Robin Hood plays in the Tudor period.[34] A story about noble outlaws with a reputed link to good King Richard would seem to be prime material for the play's themes of integrity, legitimacy, and kingship, and, moreover, the material would have been well known to Shakespeare's audience: Robin Hood featured in a large number of popular ballads during the medieval and English Renaissance periods.[35] In the last years of the sixteenth century, moreover, there appeared a spate of London plays involving the outlaw, thus demonstrating his popularity with Elizabethan London playgoers but, much to the modern theatergoer's disappointment, there is no reference to Robin Hood in *King John*.

This brief history has outlined the remarkably varying stage popularity of *King John* but not discussed in any detail the play's political elements, which become important during the twentieth century, in particular in a number of the Royal Shakespeare Company productions of the play, to which we now turn.

AT THE RSC

In 2011, the Royal Shakespeare Company celebrated its fiftieth anniversary and marked the event by opening a major extension and refurbishment of the Royal Shakespeare Theatre. While the new RST is boldly forward-looking in its design, it intellectually links with the past both through its apron stage, which harks back to the theaters of Shakespeare's day, and through its brave new tower, homage to the 1879 Shakespeare Memorial Theatre, which stood on an adjoining site before much of it burned down in 1926. It also physically links with the past by conspicuously combining with, rather than replacing, Elizabeth's Scott's elegant 1932 art deco building and by sharing the front-of-theater space in the new RST with the vestiges of the 1879 theater, which, refurbished in 1926, now form the RSC's Swan Theatre. Within this new theater complex, forward-looking but rooted in the past as it is, lies a clue to understanding the shifting stage fortunes of Shakespeare's play, *King John.*

   If a present-day visitor to the RST turns right at the main entrance and skirts the outside of the theater on the west side to come to the Waterside entrance to the Swan, opposite Chapel Lane, and looks up and to the left of the entrance, they will see three stone gothic arches, within each of which is a terra-cotta relief panel. These panels were commissioned and installed in 1885 and survived the disastrous fire of 1926; each depicts a scene from a Shakespeare play, chosen to represent one of the three main genres of the Shakespeare canon, namely comedy, history, and tragedy. The left panel depicts what is clearly a woman in man's clothing standing in a leafy forest, while the right panel depicts a man standing by a graveside staring at a human skull in his hand: our present-day RST visitor, equipped with only a passing knowledge of the most popular plays, is quite likely to identify the first figure as Rosalind disguised as Ganymede and the second as the Danish Prince: *As You Like It* and *Hamlet* would still today be sensible choices to represent Shakespeare's comedies and tragedies. But how many present-day theatergoers—or English literature scholars for that matter—would immediately recognize the central panel as depicting the boy Arthur's moving plea to Hubert not to put out his eyes in Act 4 Scene 1 of *King John?* Certainly, our Shakespeare-loving visitor is likely to shake his head in puzzlement; how the mighty are fallen.

   The fact that in 1885 the Shakespeare Memorial Association chose *King John* as one of three plays to commemorate on the façade of its new theater, and as the single play to represent Shakespeare's histories, says something important about how the play was regarded at that time. However, equally telling about how it was regarded during the second half of the twentieth century is the fact that the Royal Shakespeare Company did not produce *King John* from the date of the ensemble's foundation in 1961 until nearly a decade later in 1970, while both *As You Like It* and *Hamlet* were produced in the RSC's inaugural season and had been produced at Stratford a total of three and four times, respectively, by 1970.

The 1970 production, directed by Buzz Goodbody, and the 1974 production, directed by John Barton, each departed significantly from the text,[36] although Deborah Warner's experimental 1988 production returned to an uncut and unadapted text. The RSC next staged it in 2001, directed by Greg Doran, and then again, as part of the Complete Works Festival in 2006, directed by Josie Rourke. A common feature that unites the RSC productions is the modern political relevance of the play. Much of the play's language appears to be borrowed or adapted from contemporary Elizabethan political anti-Catholic pamphlets. A further political aspect of the play is its general warlike tone, especially toward that perennial enemy of the English, the French. This, together with what audiences and reviewers have perceived as the play's patriotic message, has generally increased its popularity in time of war.[37]

Buzz Goodbody's 1970 "Theatre-go-round" production, which toured schools and community centers around the country, as well as being performed at the RST, was a much simplified, pared-down version of the play. Goodbody took an extreme satirical line by presenting the main characters as shallow and childlike as they charge around the stage, frequently shifting their positions and allegiances, cheerfully indifferent to the carnage they are wreaking. Patrick Stewart's John was, in particular, presented as a childish character taking an irresponsible, whooping glee in the political process. The Goodbody production received some support from contemporary reviewers, with Hilary Spurling in the *Spectator*, for example, arguing that the childlike presentation of the play and deliberate artificiality of the production revealed the futile nature of war and grand politics by likening them to the cruelty and recklessness of children's games, a world in which entire battalions are cheerfully and "boisterously slaughtered between one line and the next."[38] However, a number of contemporary reviewers suggested that the play owed as much to A. A. Milne (quoting Milne's *Now We Are Six* poem about King John) as to W. Shakespeare. Benedict Nightingale, in the *New Statesman*, for example, suggested that Patrick Stewart's John was "a sort of perverted Tigger" in a world in which "War is a hilarious trip to the seaside, and [the nobles] giggle and nudge one another as they prepare to knock down the sandcastles of Angiers. Push, kick, stamp, and then back home for tea."[39] Even more trenchantly, another influential reviewer argued that it was "a pity that this production of

3. 1970, Buzz Goodbody's "Theatre-go-round" production. Patrick Stewart's John was, in particular, presented as a childish character taking an irresponsible, whooping glee in the political process.

King John took place at all. Its flippancy was ill judged and often puerile. Buzz Goodbody . . . imposed on [the play] a single simplified view of politics as a dangerous game incompetently played by caricature kings and councillors who can give and take a giggle but defy respect."[40]

While Goodbody's production was simplified and pared down, John Barton's 1974 RSC production was largely rewritten and incorporated two other plays about King John. In the 1974 programme, Barton explained why:

> Whenever I have seen *King John* on the stage I have been fascinated yet perplexed. When I read it again . . . I was struck by how much the play . . . is about England and us *now*. . . . Even the specific political issues have modern parallels, although I have never seen this emerge fully in performance. So I turned to *The Troublesome Reign of King John* . . . and to the Tudor *King Johan* for clues as to why. . . .

Barton in fact also added lines of his own and cut and transposed Shakespeare's text, as well as interpolating additions from the two other plays. In addition, in production he added a number of visual cues that were meant to illustrate and clarify the narrative. Barton also inserted a number of contemporary political references, including one to the high 1970s inflation rate (". . . the price of goods / Soars meteor-like into the louring heavens / Whiles that our purses dwindle and decline"), although many of these were removed when the production transferred to London the following season, presumably in response to adverse reviewers' comments. Indeed, Barton's adaptation was generally not well received by the critics. Partly this was indignation at Barton's perceived temerity in assuming he could improve on Shakespeare, with the *Observer*, for example, noting that "This year's season at Stratford on Avon began on Wednesday with William Shakespeare's *King John*. So, at least, declared the programme, thereby exposing the Royal Shakespeare Company not merely to criticism, but to possible prosecution under the Trades Descriptions Act."[41] But even reviewers who were willing to entertain the adaptation did not generally applaud Barton's work. Robert

Smallwood, for example, notes that while Barton was attempting to make the play more accessible to a modern audience, "the man who joins together what Shakespeare left asunder and attempts simultaneously to produce three plays is in serious danger of losing the individual focus of them all together in a general blur."[42] A similar criticism was made by Peter Thomson, who has varied praise for the individual performances but, in words reminiscent of Nightingale's comments on Patrick Stewart's interpretation of the same character in the Goodbody production, argues that Emrys James's John was presented as a particularly annoying "nursery king, a mother's boy without an inkling of adult responsibility."[43] The central political message of the Barton production, however, was that of a fatalistic decadence.

Following the generally adverse critical responses to the Goodbody and Barton productions, it is perhaps not surprising that the play was not attempted again at Stratford for nearly a decade and a half, when it was revived by Deborah Warner's experimental but uncut production in 1988. Produced in the small and intimate, corrugated iron, boxlike space of the original Other Place, Warner's production was—as she stated in interview with Geraldine Cousin— "wild, searching," and "deliberately raw, big-brush stroke."[44] The first two weeks of rehearsals were spent in an ensemble exploration of the play in which the cast, as well as reading their own parts, were regularly asked to read other parts and to translate Shakespeare's language into their own words. The eventual production used a sparse set, composed largely of a table, a few chairs, and several ladders, and the costumes were apparently improvised and of no particular period, leading at least one reviewer to note wryly that "some of the characters . . . look as if they have been dressed in a hurry by Oxfam,"[45] while another commented more favorably that "The appearance is timeless-modern, the clothes spattered and well used, greatcoats thrown hastily over civilian trousers and City shirts as though the wearers had been surprised by sudden civil war."[46] The action was delivered at a fast rate, with characters moving on and off stage at high speed, and the production included live, circus-style music during the battle scenes, in order to suggest the farcical nature of politics and war.

Susan Engel, who played Constance, also suggested the modern political relevance of the play when she said in interview that she found natural the scene where Constance sits defiantly (Act 3 Scene 1) "because sitting is what you do when you protest, in Vietnam or in Westminster."[47]

Nicholas Woodeson's John appeared to be in the same satiric vein as Emrys James's interpretation in the Barton adaptation, as well as Patrick Stewart's John in the Goodbody version, with *The Times*, for example, describing him as "a jaunty tinpot monarch"[48] whose insecurity is symbolized by the constant wearing of his crown chained to his waist. Perhaps the most controversial interpretation of the Warner production, however, was David Morrissey's Bastard, which, far from the witty, "pickèd man of parts," was presented as a loud and unpolished young man who appeared to react to events more with a naive spontaneity than "tickling commodity." Critical reception for Morrissey's Bastard was divided, with, on the one hand, Charles Osborne in the *Telegraph* opining that Morrissey "played noisily and often incomprehensibly,"[49] and Paul Taylor in the *Independent* looking for the detachment of a manipulator and opportunist but finding "only the detachment of a football heckler,"[50] and, on the other hand, Michael Coveney in the *Financial Times* describing him as "a ferociously talented and watchable newcomer."[51]

General critical reception of the production was also divided, with some commentators arguing that Warner's "broad-brush" approach was too simplistic, although the overall balance was probably favorable, with several critics applauding Warner's courage in taking on such a difficult play but producing it uncut and unadapted, and welcoming her honest exploration of the play—a view summed up in one review: "It has the distinctive look [Warner] has created of still having one foot in the rehearsal room."[52]

After the Warner production, it again languished at Stratford for over a decade until 2001. Gregory Doran's production certainly seemed to strike a resonant chord of national weariness with politicians and the political process, and was seen by a number of reviewers as "a corrosively satiric study of sordid power struggles."[53] This was partly achieved through comic undercutting of both situations and language. Doran signaled from the outset that having John's

4. 1988, Deborah Warner production. From left to right, Messenger (Julia Ford), The Bastard/Philip Falconbridge (David Morrissey), Arthur (Lyndon Davies). Perhaps the most controversial interpretation was David Morrissey's Bastard, which, far from the witty, "pickèd man of parts," was presented as a loud and unpolished young man who appeared to react to events more with naive spontaneity than "tickling commodity."

late entrance repeatedly heralded by actual fanfares, reminiscent of—or perhaps even an allusion to—a scene from the Marx Brothers' film *Duck Soup* muted the declamatory fanfare. While introducing a comic element, the conspicuously empty throne did immediately raise the central issue of who is legitimately and morally qualified to occupy it. When John—played by Guy Henry, better known for his seriocomic roles—did enter, his dignity already undercut by the late entrance, he was in a farcical hurry, rapidly pulling on his crown and lacking any royal bearing: a nervous, comic mode he retained throughout the play. It soon became clear, however, that this was a political satire. Indeed, both the production itself and the manner in which it was received and discussed seemed to be symptomatic of an underlying distrust of the political process and politicians that's certainly not new in British society, but appeared to be particularly widespread in contemporary Britain at the turn of the twenty-first century. Thus, Charles Spencer, writing in the *Daily Telegraph*, noted:

> The play seems especially resonant at a time when disease haunts the land and when our leader's chief concern seems to be whether he can get away with a quick election. Tony Blair has much in common with King John, whose fine words conceal a devastating lack of conviction. . . . It presents a world in which politicians seek the quick fix and the favourable spin, masking commodity (self-interest) with hollow, tub-thumping rhetoric. And if King John brings Blair to mind, the papal legate, Cardinal Pandulph, is pure Peter Mandelson.[54]

Similarly, Michael Billington, in the *Guardian*, also related the play to modern political spin-doctoring:

> What startles one is the play's modernity: it accords with our own scepticism about politics. . . . And you could hardly have a more outrageous example of spin than the Bastard's belated attempt to terrify the French with the prospect of "warlike John" when the king lies desperately enfeebled.[55]

While Doran's production did succeed in making much of the high declamatory style palatable to a modern audience, effectively by sending it up, this was not without cost. Critics since Adrien Bonjour[56] have noted the X-shaped or chiastic structure of the play: as John descends in regal and, more particularly, moral stature, so the Bastard rises. Indeed, for Bonjour, this balanced structure revealed the central theme of the play as personal integrity and supplied the unity other critics had suggested was lacking. In Doran's production, however, John had little if any distance to fall since his dignity and, by implication, his moral stature were low from the outset. The kingly imprecation of the text, "Be thou as lightning in the eyes of France; / For ere thou canst report, I will be there: / The thunder of my cannon shall be heard" (1.1.24–26), was shouted offstage after Chatillon as John chased after the ambassador and hurled his crown at him. This tended both to disturb a satisfying and symbolic structural aspect of the play and to undermine both the Bastard's moral rise and his role in the early part of the play as cynical debunker. "Mad world, mad kings, mad composition!"—the audience needed not a love child of Coeur-de-lion come from the country to tell them this: it was already patently obvious.

Even the temptation scene (Act 3 Scene 3) was played in a black comic fashion, with the staccato climax delivered in a rapid-fire exchange that, although it seemed to lack a final "boom-boom," nevertheless elicited hearty laughter from the audience. Yet this scene has historically been treated with gravity. In a contemporary review of Macready's 1842 Drury Lane production, for example, *The Times* recorded Macready's own interpretation of John in this scene in the following terms:

> A gloom, which came in sudden contrast to the previous bustle of the drama, seemed to usher in the conversation between John and Hubert. It was a foreboding look that John cast on Arthur, the tongue faltered as the horrible mission was entrusted to Hubert. For a moment the countenance of the king beamed as he said "Good Hubert," but the gloom returned when he said "Throw thine eye on yonder boy." That he did not look Hubert in the face when he proposed "death" was a fine conception.[57]

The contrast with Doran's version of the temptation scene is striking, prompting us to contemplate whether it is modern embarrassment at the potential sentimentality of the scene that makes a contemporary director prefer a black comic version. Given that, in the Doran production, Guy Henry's John was a comic "nervy twerp"[58] from the outset, however, it is perhaps hard to imagine how it could have been played otherwise. Indeed, while the strongly satirical aspects of the Doran production were generally well recognized and received, nevertheless certain of the comic aspects appeared to generate a degree of irritation in several reviewers. John Peter, in the *Sunday Times*, panned the production as "medieval England as Fawlty Towers,"[59] while Michael Billington, in a generally favorable review for the *Guardian*, was forced to admit that the production had "occasional hints of Woody Allen in medieval England."[60]

To return to the contemporary political relevance of the Doran production, however, it seemed that this was largely highlighted by bringing out features already present in the text. Consider, for example, Act 4 Scene 3, where John yields up to Pandulph "The circle of [his] glory" and then reveals the other side of the deal—"Now keep your holy word: go meet the French." In Doran's production, this was done with sufficient bathetic contrast between John the prostrate penitent, stripped to a loincloth, and John the brusque wheeler-dealer, suddenly dropping the mask, as to emphasize strongly the cynicism involved and evoke laughter from the audience. The production also introduced other gentle political nuances. For example, Pandulph, after his insinuating persuasion of the dauphin to invade England is left alone on stage momentarily and, finding himself alone, he very slowly bursts into deep gales of laughter, revealing the pleasure he is taking in manipulating the political process.

While Doran's success in treating the play as a political satire may have been largely due to the readiness of an early-twenty-first-century, spin-doctoring-weary British audience to accept such an interpretation, the fact that much of the language of the play draws on contemporary political pamphlets, as discussed earlier, is key to understanding its modern political appeal: Shakespeare built the essence of political language—its equivocating, declamatory, chop-logic nature—into the text by drawing on actual political propaganda documents of his day, the essential features of which are still present in political discourse of the present day. More generally, the play's episodic structure allows for a series of set debates, which are also redolent of the political process. In several of these, however, notably the debate before the walls of Angiers (Act 2 Scene 1), the process is constantly interrupted by the Bastard's series of asides and punctuated by his cynical soliloquizing ("Mad world, mad kings, mad composition!"). This serves to undercut the political gravity and reveal it as political posturing. To make matters worse, the Bastard's own entrance into the political arena—his plan to combine the English and French forces against the "peevish town" of Angiers—is accompanied with a certain pride ("Smacks it not something of the policy?"), leading us still to harbor suspicions about his sincerity even at the end of the play. The implication, then, is that Shakespeare's text, in its structure, characterization, and language, presents an ironic, detached, and to a large extent cynical view of the political process. The relative success of Doran's 2001 production of the play as a political satire may therefore be due to the rediscovery of this facet of the play.

Given its Stratford track record, one might have expected to have waited at least another decade for another RSC production, but the RSC Complete Works Festival in 2006 occasioned its revival by Josie Rourke just five years later at the Swan. Rourke's set was sparse, with two pivoting doors being the main prop, and some attempt at historical accuracy in the costumes. The production received mixed reviews, and seemed to suffer from comparison with the relatively recent Doran production. Rhoda Koenig, in the *Independent*, for example, argued that "The part of John, who is mean and craven, is not one of Shakespeare's best, and one might think Richard McCabe's plodding interpretation sufficient had one not seen Guy Henry's mesmerising, creepily whimsical monarch. This actor is indecisive when he should suggest a deeper defect, and when he tries to be fierce, he does it with popped eyes or arms akimbo."[61] Similarly, Tamsin Greig, as Constance, had to live up to Kelly Hunter's impressive interpretation of five years earlier, although her understated performance was by and large favorably received. Joseph Millson's Bastard was generally perceived as powerful and mesmerizing, although Rhoda Koenig, while acknowledging the "impishness and sex appeal" of Millson's interpretation, goes on to lament that "this actor, who seems to have attended the Douglas Fairbanks School for Bastards, becomes tiresome halfway through his first appearance, with his antic mannerisms. In the second half, the Bastard does act more normally, but before that he is exhausting rather than enlivening."[62]

Although Rourke's production did not seem to resonate so strongly with the public concerning the politics of spin-doctoring as the Doran production had—perhaps because Doran's production had taken place at a period of significant change in British politics, toward the end of the first "New Labour" administration—the political relevance was still noted, with Dominic Cavendish in the *Daily Telegraph* observing, "The parallels with our own disordered times are plain for all to see—and it's hard not to think of the carnage in the Middle East on hearing Tamsin Greig's beautifully understated Constance deliver her heartbroken lament for her lost Arthur (Ralph Davis) in the play's most heart-piercing speech: 'Grief fills the room up of my absent child.'"[63]

Overall, the stage history of the RSC productions of *King John* reveals the fundamental problems in producing the play for a modern audience. In particular, while an Elizabethan audience would have had the Tudor image of the historical King John firmly planted in their mind, the modern popular image of King John does not quite accord with the image presented in the play. This, together with the large chunks of rhetorical and declamatory language, which do not particularly suit modern, realistic acting styles, has tempted some directors to produce the play with a comic aspect, which sits uneasily with the play's bleak subject matter. Because of these problems, every production of *King John* is in some sense experimental in that the director has to experiment with ways in which to make the play relevant and enjoyable to a modern audience. A unifying theme of the RSC productions has been to examine the play's modern political relevance, and in particular its political cynicism, which seems to be hardwired into its construction and language. In that sense, the RSC productions from Goodbody to Rourke may indeed have rediscovered in *King John* "a tract for the times."

THE DIRECTOR'S CUT: INTERVIEWS WITH GREGORY DORAN AND JOSIE ROURKE

Gregory Doran, born in 1958, studied at Bristol University and the Bristol Old Vic theater school. He began his career as an actor, before becoming associate director at the Nottingham Playhouse. He played some minor roles in the RSC ensemble before directing for the company, first as a freelance, then as Associate and subsequently chief associate director. His productions, several of which have starred his partner Antony Sher, are characterized by extreme intelligence and lucidity. He has made a particular mark with several of Shakespeare's lesser-known plays, including *King John* (2001), which he is discussing here, as well as the revival of works by other contemporary Elizabethan and Jacobean writers.

Josie Rourke went to school in Eccles and attended sixth-form college in Salford before going on to train on the Donmar Warehouse's resident assistant director scheme in 2000. Her first major breakthrough was as assistant director to Peter Gill at the Lowry Theatre in Salford Quays in 2002 for the premiere of his play *The York Realist*. She worked as a freelance director from 2002 to 2007 and as associate director of the Sheffield Theatres as well as a trainee associate director at the Royal Court. Josie directed Philip Massinger's *Believe What You Will* and Shakespeare's *King John* for the RSC in 2006, which she's discussing here, and was appointed as artistic director of London's Bush Theatre in 2007. She recently directed *Men Should Weep* for the National Theatre, while her *Much Ado About Nothing* with David Tennant and Catherine Tate opened in June 2011 at Wyndham's Theatre. Widely regarded as one of Britain's most exciting young directors, she takes over as director of the Donmar Warehouse in 2012.

King John used to be a popular play which enjoyed spectacular "authentic" Victorian stagings but its popularity has steadily declined in the twentieth and twenty-first centuries; why do you think this is the case and was it an advantage or disadvantage for your production?

Doran: On the front of the Swan Theatre in Stratford there are three terracotta plaques representing Shakespeare's Histories, Comedies, and Tragedies. Tragedy, not unsurprisingly, is represented by *Hamlet*; *As You Like It* represents Comedy; the third plaque, representing History, is not as you might expect *Henry V* or *Richard III* but *King John*; which suggests that when the plaques went up, within a few years of the theater being built in 1879, it was regarded as an extremely popular play.

From a selfish point of view I was glad that the play didn't have a recent weight of precedence; it meant that I could see it afresh. With *Henry VIII* I had gone into rehearsals weighed down with research material and historical references. With *King John* I just went in with the script. I wasn't interested in the historical King John. I wasn't even that interested in the period in which Shakespeare was writing, though I am pretty sure that it is a later play than it has often been claimed to be, because ultimately I decided it was a much more sophisticated play than it is often given credit for. It allowed us to take the play on its own terms and see how it spoke to us now. I have to say that we understood it in a completely different way by the time we came to perform it than we had done at the beginning of rehearsals.

I thought, and indeed I think, it to be a highly satirical play in the first half, but to begin with I thought the whole play was satirical; in particular through the character of Cardinal Pandulph, who can say at any one moment that black is white and then argue that black is black. That is quite clearly a satire on politics. Then some very significant events happened during the final rehearsals and then during the run itself. TV footage of a young Palestinian boy called Muhammed al-Durrah, who was shot while he crouched behind his father during a gunfight in a street in the Gaza Strip, was beamed around the world. The death of the innocent brought about an international outcry, but ultimately it didn't change anything. It helped us realize that the death of Prince Arthur had a really significant impact on the play.

The other event that intensified and deepened my respect for the play took place during a Tuesday matinee. The matinee began at 1:30 p.m. and backstage the company had started to gather around a TV monitor: it was the Tuesday afternoon that two hijacked planes flew into the Twin Towers of the World Trade Center. At about 2:58 p.m. the South Tower collapsed, and nearly two hours into the production the North Tower collapsed in twelve seconds. The company were following this backstage and didn't know what to do, whether to continue with the production. The audience knew nothing. At the moment when Prince Arthur slips from the walls, the Bastard comes on stage to say, I "lose my way / Among the thorns and dangers of this world." He describes how "vast confusion waits, / As doth a raven on a sick-fall'n beast"; those words were intensified by what was happening in New York. Somehow the play grew from being a satirical portrait of politics into a devastating account of how human lives can be affected by the absurdity of politics and people's individual agendas. Shakespeare is like a magnet for the iron filings of contemporary events. Our respect deepened throughout the run, and the play emerged for us anew.

Rourke: I think it's important to remember that almost all of Shakespeare's plays have waxed and waned in their popularity. At any particular time there are sets of critical thinking around a play that tend to influence how much it gets done. For example, the Victorians couldn't get enough of *King John*. I think that is also partly because of the pageant; that would have appealed to their theater. It's also because of the deeply moving and sentimental portrait of grief embodied by Constance in the latter part of her character's journey. It is certainly important to note that *King John* is a heavily rhetorical play and currently rhetorical theater is not particularly fashionable. Of course, since the Complete Works production of *King John* we've had the Obama campaign that reignited our interest in rhetoric, but at the time that I was directing *King John* it was more about the art of spin than that of persuasion. I think that the other thing to bear in mind is that, whilst King John is a great part for an actor, it's not a part that actors that enjoy long soliloquies are particularly drawn to: he has one line of soliloquy. I think that's probably why you don't see many actors saying, "I really want to give my King John."

King John is an immensely demanding play for actors and audiences with its mix of genres, political debates, and ambiguous characterization—it's been called a "failure" on account of these features. How did you approach and manage this complexity and did you find your production in danger of veering too far one way or the other?

Rourke: The critics were very kind and the audiences were tremendously responsive to our production; I don't think that it has to be heavy going. I think that depends on whether or not the production and the performances are intelligent and gripping.

While the historical King John reigned in the thirteenth century, Shakespeare's plays were performed in modern (i.e. Elizabethan) dress, which highlighted contemporary political and religious concerns for Shakespeare's audiences; when was your production set and did it make allusion to early modern or contemporary political debates in any way?

Doran: I viewed the play in the context of a continuum of productions in Stratford. In 1974 John Barton had done a production in which he had included some of his own writing, and Michael Billington described it in the *Guardian* as "one of the best new plays we've seen this year." I wanted to look at the play entirely on its own merits and in the context of our own world. We staged it with a sort of eleventh- or twelfth-century look. I didn't want to put it specifically in modern dress but I did want to allow the metaphor to apply to the modern world.

Rourke: We did a medieval production of the play. For a number of reasons, actually. One is that I was struck by the idea that Shakespeare was writing, in some sense, a "period" drama and was enjoying the different sensibilities of a period of history that was not his own. Also, the pageantry of the medieval world was extremely helpful to the storytelling of the production—all the bright, distinct colors of the different armies both looked amazing and did a great job of clarity when it came to the gates of Angiers, where the powers of England, France, and Austria are all assembled (that's even before Rome turns up). However, there were modern touches to the style of playing. When I directed the play it was around the end of the Blair government. Sometime later, when Gordon Brown was faltering as prime minister, I nearly called Michael Boyd to ask if we could revive the production, I was so struck by the parallels. In *King John*, the play offers us a dazzlingly acute portrayal of a man with a thirst for power, who clears everything out of his path without any moral compunction about what is needed in order to achieve the throne.

Then once he achieves his goal, he finds that he can't rule, he can't cut it, and his reign fails through a series of terrible and quixotic judgment calls.

The thing about the play that was a big revelation to me when we did it in Stratford is the jingoism of it. I was astonished at the response to the vitriolic language about the French. The audience response was completely rapturous. It was fascinating to see how, even in the relatively middle-class milieu of a Stratford audience, a character urging a crowd to "get the French" awakes something really violent and vocal in our national character.

One of the things that must have interested Shakespeare about John was that he was the only king before Henry VIII to be excommunicated. We took great pains to stage the excommunication, with bell, book, and candle. We did it in a big moment of pageantry and then later, when John tells the Bastard to rob the monasteries and he replies, "Bell, book and candle shall not drive me back, / When gold and silver becks me to come on," it would always get a massive laugh because you could see it was excommunication that he meant. The deep-seated nationalistic and antipapist reformation undercurrents of the play still connect with audiences now in the most extraordinary way.

History hasn't been kind to King John on the whole—his reputation is based on the pantomime villain of the Robin Hood myth, defeat in the barons' revolt, and subsequent signing of Magna Carta; did you find him a more complex, shaded character in Shakespeare?

Doran: I had the sublime Guy Henry as King John. I had perceived the character as having a comic element to it. Guy thought that King John had no soliloquies but then discovered one: the moment when he hears that his mother has died and he says the line, "My mother dead!" Guy suddenly produced a sense of deep shock, which was beautiful and gave the character a greater depth. John is a pusillanimous, feeble, weak man and of course delightful in terms of comedy. Although it is the Bastard who guides us through the play, I think

King John achieves a kind of elevation at the end. When he is sick at Swinstead Abbey and declares "now my soul hath elbow-room," I think that deepens your appreciation of the character.

I think King John is balanced by Constance, in the same way that the Bastard is balanced by the dauphin. Kelly Hunter played Constance as having a fanatical belief in her rights, to an almost fundamentalist degree. She provided a rigor that was balanced against everybody else constantly compromising and shifting their positions. The one certain mooring in the first half of the play was Constance's faith in the rights of her son, and that existed in balance with King John's feeble vacillation.

Rourke: I think he is terribly complex. Richard McCabe, who played him, was absolutely fantastic at showing us that complexity; his psychological understanding of John's rise, falter, and fall was astonish-

5. 2006, Josie Rourke production. Richard McCabe (King John), Sam Cox (Hubert). "For Richard, John was someone who was continually teetering on the precipice of an immoral act. King John struggles and struggles for power, attains it, and then finds out he is a terrible king."

ing. For Richard, John was someone who was continually teetering on the precipice of an immoral act. King John struggles and struggles for power, attains it, and then finds out that he is a terrible king. There is something fascinating about a character who pushes and pushes at their ambition, gets there, and then can't deliver. And then he has what is effectively a nervous breakdown. His mother is dead; Arthur is dead; the French are attacking; the country is in revolt. When he learnt of his mother's death he was left alone on stage and said the line "My mother dead!" quietly to himself, then he acted this extraordinary sort of collapse, his whole frame slumped down into the throne and you saw, in that private instant, that he was finished. It was an incredibly powerful and intimate moment for the audience to watch this tiny but infinitely powerful gesture on the Swan stage. I always found it quite terrifying to witness, it was as if he sank down into his clothes; you could see him physically shrink. Then we forced this enormous pause and Hubert came in with his news about Arthur's death, and it was the final nail in the coffin of his sanity. We created a sequence where he came on around his next entrance and haunted the battlefield: he was wandering around in a nightshirt being sick into a bucket in the midst of this chaos.

The unhistorical Bastard undergoes a profound personal journey in the play and is the most compelling, charismatic character on stage; he is sometimes seen as Shakespeare's representative within the play. Is that how you saw him and how did you manage that shift from the exuberant personality of the first three acts to the political realist of the last two?

Doran: I do think that the Bastard provides our window into the Court and how that world operates. He's initially thrilled by seeing how he's going to be encouraged to pursue his agenda. It's very funny to see how he exploits the situation—how this young man realizes how to get on in this environment—but also crucial to see how he matures. The Bastard is introduced into this mad world, is fascinated by how you get on within it and concludes that it's all about commodity, expediency, about looking after number one. Then the death of Arthur changes the whole nature of the play and

6. 2001, Gregory Doran production. Guy Henry (King John), Jo Stone-Fewings (Bastard). "[T]he Bastard provides our window into the Court and how that world operates. . . . It's very funny to see how he exploits the situation—how this young man realizes how to get on in this environment—but also crucial to see how he matures."

changes the Bastard's view of how the world works. He develops from being an opportunist to become to some extent the moral center of the play.

There's an extraordinary scene conducted entirely in the dark, in the "eyeless night," where the Bastard meets Hubert, who of course has been through his own moral journey in deciding whether or not to carry out the blinding of Prince Arthur. The two of them meet trying to find their way to each other. It was a wonderful metaphor, demonstrating perhaps the difficulty and necessity of finding your ethical route through a very complex political quagmire. I thought that one scene gave an insight into a deeper reality of the play, one that transcended the sometimes cartoon versions of it that we had previously seen.

Rourke: I think that the journey that he makes is quite an accessible one in the twenty-first century. It's essentially a filmic one. When we open the play you get what I called a POV Bastard: if it were being told as a film, the narrative would be shot from his point of view. At the top of the play there is a lot of information you need to give to audiences who aren't necessarily familiar with medieval history, but instead you have to listen to something else, which is the Bastard's personal history. That's tricky for audiences, I think. It's a bit like at the beginning of *Henry IV Part I*, where there is a really long speech about the crusade and then a shift into something else. It's a tricky beginning to do.

To continue with the filmic metaphor, if you think of it as his POV and it being shot from his perspective, the idea that he then gets pulled into becoming more and more the protagonist and more and more at the center of the drama is fantastic. Joseph Millson, who played that part, was doubling it with Benedick in *Much Ado* in the same season. Benedick is another character that starts off as the sort of joker on the periphery of events and then gets personally pulled in because of something that happens to him. Having already played Benedick that season Joe had become used to making that leap from someone who is on the periphery commenting, to someone who is driving the plot and who is at the center of the story. I think that's a story that audiences really understand; a regular guy, who wears his ordinariness in a very public way, suddenly winds up over the course of the play having to fight for England and everything it stands for in the midst of a rebellion. If you pitch that as a movie, someone would make that; that's a good journey. Circumstances changing around a character, and then the character changing because of those circumstances, is a very playable thing for an actor.

Women play central roles in both dynastic and personal terms. Unusually there are three mothers in the play but in each case the mother/son relationship is seen as problematic: affection is compromised by self-interest. How did you find these relationships worked theatrically?

Doran: John's mother, Elinor, is the power behind the throne. Lady Falconbridge is clearly rather ashamed of having produced a bastard son. And then of course you have Constance, who is terrifying in her self-belief but devastating in her loss. She provides another moment when the play grows and deepens because in "Grief fills the room up of my absent child" she produces one of the most harrowing and beautiful speeches about the loss of a child that I know of. It's an incredibly beautifully written speech and must have come from a deep place within Shakespeare. I suspect the death of his own son must have affected how he came to write that speech.

Rourke: There are three mothers in the play. You only see two of them, but we also put in Isabella of Angoulême, who is Henry's mother, so you get another mother and son moment. Eleanor of Aquitaine is one of the most arresting and important women in history and Sorcha Cusack really enjoyed getting into the meat of that role and playing someone who very clearly could and should be running the show. She had moments of real impatience with her son's rule. She saw everything and knew everything and was ahead of the game. There is a lot of reversal in the play. Constance reverts from this sort of horrific stage mother pushing her son forward towards the throne to a childless, grief-stricken widow. It seems to me a real theme running through that play and that's why we were interested in having Isabella of Angoulême so you've got another instance of a mother ruling through a son. I think actually if they'd just let these women reign, Europe would probably be in a much better place.

Shakespeare made Prince Arthur younger than the historical character, presumably for his own dramatic purposes; what problems did this pose, working with such a young actor (or more than one) and how did you overcome them? How did you manage the harrowing scenes of his threatened torture and then his death?

Doran: Initially I was very wary about it. I have been very wary about child actors on the stage. He does have to be young: it's absolutely deliberate Shakespeare's making him younger. I was very lucky that Barbara Roberts, who looked after the children's casting, found and nurtured two particularly good young boys—one of whom, Joshua McGuire, is now playing Hamlet at the Globe. It was as important a role for me to cast as John, the Bastard, or Constance.

In this cynical world of shifting allegiances, Prince Arthur's selfless love stands as a really important parameter. We had defined the moment of Arthur's death as needing to jolt the play, to be a real shock. The designer Stephen Brimson Lewis managed to produce one of the most spectacular moments of shock that we've seen in the Swan: Arthur, all of twelve or thirteen years old, seemed to walk along the rail of the top gallery and then to fall from there to his death, a distance of some eighteen feet (5.5 meters). I remember a lot of mothers in the audience clutching their neighbors, terrified by the vulnerability of this young child. Of course it was all a rather brilliantly devised trick of substituting a dummy just at the moment when the child fell with a sickening thud onto the stage. But it did cause a shock and often a scream in the audience, which I think was required in the play: it's almost like you're being slapped by that moment.

It has to bring home the reality of how politics can destroy the innocent. We had images in our heads of Kim Phuc, the little girl running from the napalm attack in South Vietnam—moments where innocence had been caught in the crossfire. It felt as though that was a key moment to deliver: to stop the play running away with itself as a political satire.

Rourke: That's interesting because after *King John* I went and did a Mamet play called *The Cryptogram* at the Donmar Warehouse, which had an enormous part for a ten-year-old boy in it as well. It was my year for working with ten-year-old boys! They were fantastic. It was one of my greatest experiences working with those lads on that role because I think Shakespeare understood something—and I realized through the play—about the incredible power of a child who is just at the point of losing his childhood. When I worked with those two boys on that play they were nine and ten. I saw them a year later and they were getting ready to be teenagers, they weren't children anymore. There's something about those liminal points in our lives, when we are between one thing and the next, that give this incredible dramatic potency. On press night there was an amazing moment when one of the boys went completely method, and when Hubert thrust the warrant at him was so angry he knocked it out of his hand—in the moment. He was feeling it so powerfully. Thank goodness that the actor playing Hubert was so ready to respond!

There was another great moment: I will never forget seeing an audience member, when Hubert was standing over Arthur with the poker, ready to blind him, holding his programme in front of his face because he couldn't bear it. You really believed it.

In the play, Arthur throws himself off a high wall in order to escape imprisonment and dies. It was very important to us that we could actually fly the child—drop them and fly them forward—so we could do the descent. We worked really hard technically on that moment. There was a great moment where you thought that we'd dropped him because it happened so quickly and then he moved and groaned in pain and it was a great theatrical shock to people.

I remember when I was a kid, down at the bottom of my street there was a wall where the ground gradually fell away then inclined, and we'd dare each other to drop higher and higher off it. There's a very basic, very human thing about a child misjudging a height. As we grow up we learn that we shouldn't touch hot things, and that cold things are cold, we learn what distance means, and what we should do with our body. Arthur is not pushed. He doesn't jump out of some kind of strange, tormented suicide bid. He genuinely believes he can have a go and jump it and survive, when he clearly can't. I find that enormously moving.

The play's language is dense and almost impenetrable at times; did your actors encounter problems in understanding what it meant and more importantly conveying that meaning to the audience?

Doran: We spent a lot of time unpicking the text with the entire company, and then seeing how the conflicting rhetoric worked. Once the company had got an understanding of what the language meant, they really began to enjoy how people used argument: how they deployed and marshaled their arguments rhetorically. You could see how people twisted argument and in the Swan, which is a sort of debating chamber, it became particularly exciting; the sheer thrill of an argument well debated. We had great verse-speakers like Guy Henry, Geoffrey Freshwater (Philip of France), Kelly Hunter, Jo Stone-Fewings (the Bastard), and John Hopkins as the dauphin, so the verse was in very good hands. If you didn't attend to the complexities of that verse, and if you didn't have somebody as brilliant as David Collings playing Cardinal Pandulph, then I could see how you could get lost, or as the Bastard says at one point, be "bethumped with words." But there is great wit in how the argument shifts. When it suits him Pandulph can turn an argument completely upside down.

Rourke: We did a lot of work on this in rehearsal. I had a friend of mine who is a barrister and a public speaking champion called Benet Brandreth who did some fantastic work with us. What he said about rhetoric is that it is the art of persuasion. What's really interesting about the play is that people have the ability to persuade other people of their position; it's a real muscular force within the play. The way we use rhetoric to steady, or to change, or to state a claim—all of those persuasive grounds are really fascinating. It would be great if rhetoric was to come back more strongly into the theater and a passion for how ideas work would be reignited—I think that is starting to happen now. In 2006 when we did the play something in British politics was deeply unrhetorical. Politics wasn't about persuading people of your position; it was about continually canvassing opinion, trying to move along as smoothly as possible and taking as many people with you as you could. It was a different kind of persuasion; it was following the latest opinion poll. There wasn't anyone taking a stand, or saying "This is what I think, what do you think? Let's argue the point." That had blown out of our culture a little bit, but I hope it's returning now.

The play is sometimes seen as a debate as to who should be king and who the hero is; did you see it in those terms or as a more complicated exploration of legal and moral rights of inheritance and political legitimacy?

Rourke: I really hate the term "problem play"; I think "problem play" is a term used by literary critics to analyze plays which do not have clear protagonists. The term problem play is as unhelpful to a play like *King John* as it is unhelpful to a play like *Measure for Measure*. Audiences don't always need a clear protagonist. Audiences are interested in moral relativism, in exploring behavior and choice through a clearly defined context. One thing that *King John* has really got going for it is that it's a terribly clear world. It's so clear that you can have a character like the Bastard slide through it with his particular perspective. I was most interested in figuring it as a struggle for power, and what happens when you gain advantage and then can't play it. Constance, John, France, even to an extent the Bastard, take up all the oxygen in the room in order to persuade people that they are right, to get their advantage and gain position.

The Bastard calls the nobles "distempered lords"; is he right? Do they place morality above patriotism or is that a smokescreen for "that smooth-faced gentleman, tickling commodity"?

Rourke: Within all Shakespeare's plays you can see him asserting and reasserting his idea of Englishness. One of the things that is great in the writing of this play is that so many concepts (abstracts) are defined by people doing them badly, by Shakespeare showing us what they are not: motherhood; kingship; piety. Apart from the Bastard's courage (and you could argue that was bloodlust) most things are defined by acts of rebellion, or departures from what is expected. So when the nobles remove themselves from loyalty to England we get a very clear and very beautiful overview in a rhetorical picture of what English loyalty is. Loyalty is more sharply defined by the lords rebelling than it is in their uneasy allegiance.

THE FAMOUS HISTORY
OF THE LIFE OF
KING HENRY
THE EIGHTH

KEY FACTS: *HENRY VIII*

MAJOR PARTS: *(with percentage of lines/number of speeches/scenes on stage)* Henry VIII (14%/81/9), Cardinal Wolsey (14%/79/7), Queen Katherine (12%/50/4), Duke of Norfolk (7%/48/5), Duke of Buckingham (6%/26/2), Lord Chamberlain (5%/38/7), Thomas Cranmer (4%/21/4), Duke of Suffolk (3%/30/4), Gardiner (3%/22/3), Earl of Surrey (3%/24/2), Sir Thomas Lovell (2%/21/4), Old Lady (2%/14/2), Surveyor (2%/9/1), Griffith (2%/13/2), Anne Bullen (2%/18/2), Cardinal Campeius (2%/14/3), Thomas Cromwell (2%/21/2), Lord Sands (2%/17/2).

LINGUISTIC MEDIUM: 98% verse, 2% prose.

DATE: 1613. The first Globe Theatre burned down in a fire that started during a performance of the play on 29 June 1613. A letter by Sir Henry Wotton describes it as "a new play" at this time.

SOURCES: principally based on the third volume of Holinshed's *Chronicles*, probably in the 1587 edition; the Stephen Gardiner sequence in Act 5 draws on John Foxe's virulently anti-Catholic *Actes and Monuments* (perhaps in 1583 edition); John Stow's *Annals* (1592) and John Speed's *Theatre of the Empire of Great Britain* (1611) also seem to have been consulted and there may be some influence from an earlier play in celebration of the birth of one of Henry VIII's children, Samuel Rowley's *When you see me, You know me. Or the famous Chronicle Historie of king Henrie the eighth, with the birth and vertuous life of Edward Prince of Wales* (1605).

TEXT: First Folio is only early text. Good quality of printing, probably set from a scribal transcript of the authorial manuscript.

LIST OF PARTS

PROLOGUE/EPILOGUE

KING HENRY VIII

QUEEN KATHERINE (of Aragon),
Henry's first wife, later
Princess Dowager

CARDINAL WOLSEY, Lord Chancellor
and Archbishop of York

ANNE Bullen, later Queen, Henry's
second wife

CARDINAL CAMPEIUS, legate from the
Pope

Thomas CRANMER, later
Archbishop of Canterbury

Stephen GARDINER, the king's
secretary, later Bishop of
Winchester

Bishop of LINCOLN

Lord CHAMBERLAIN

Lord CHANCELLOR, after Wolsey's
fall

Thomas CROMWELL, Wolsey's
servant and later secretary to
the King's Council

Duke of BUCKINGHAM

Duke of NORFOLK

Duke of SUFFOLK

Earl of SURREY ⎤ sons-in-law to
Lord ABERGAVENNEY ⎦ Buckingham

Lord SANDS

Sir Thomas LOVELL

Sir Henry (Harry) GUILDFORD

Sir Nicholas VAUX

Sir Anthony DENNY

GRIFFITH, Gentleman-usher to
Katherine

WOMAN (who sings), attendant on
Katherine

PATIENCE, attendant on Katherine

OLD LADY, friend to Anne

SECRETARY to Wolsey

BRANDON

SERGEANT-at-Arms

SURVEYOR to the Duke of
Buckingham

Three GENTLEMEN

SCRIBE to the court

CRIER to the court

KEEPER of the door of the Council
Chamber

MESSENGER at Kimbolton

Lord CAPUTIUS, an ambassador
from the Emperor Charles V

PAGE to Gardiner

DR BUTTS, the king's physician

PORTER and his MAN

GARTER King-at-Arms

List of parts   CHANCELLOR . . . fall in Act 3 Scene 2, it is announced that Sir Thomas More
has been made Chancellor in Wolsey's place; historically, More resigned before the coronation
of Queen Anne, so the character who marches in the procession in Act 4 Scene 1 and speaks in
Act 5 Scene 2 would have been Sir Thomas Audley, but he is unnamed in the text

SERVANT to Wolsey

Lord Mayor of London

Marquis of Dorset

Marchioness of Dorset

Old Duchess of Norfolk

Guards, Tipstaves, Halberds,
Secretaries, Scribes, Bishops,
Priests, Gentlemen, Vergers,
Aldermen, Lords, Ladies,
Women, Spirits, Attendants

The Prologue

[Enter Prologue]

I come no more to make you laugh: things now
That bear a weighty and a serious brow,
Sad, high, and working, full of state and woe:
Such noble scenes as draw the eye to flow
5   We now present. Those that can pity here
May, if they think it well, let fall a tear:
The subject will deserve it. Such as give
Their money out of hope they may believe,
May here find truth too. Those that come to see
10   Only a show or two, and so agree
The play may pass, if they be still, and willing,
I'll undertake may see away their shilling
Richly in two short hours. Only they
That come to hear a merry, bawdy play,
15   A noise of targets, or to see a fellow
In a long motley coat guarded with yellow,
Will be deceived. For, gentle hearers, know
To rank our chosen truth with such a show
As fool and fight is, beside forfeiting

The Prologue   3 Sad serious, solemn   high lofty/important   working emotive, moving
state stateliness, dignity   10 show spectacle   11 pass be approved, pass muster   still, and
willing attentive and well-inclined   12 shilling the cost of some of the most expensive seats in
the theater   13 two short hours i.e. the length of the play   15 targets shields   16 long . . .
yellow a fool's customary costume   motley parti- or multicolored   guarded trimmed
17 deceived disappointed   know understand (that)   19 forfeiting . . . brains abandoning
our intelligence

20   Our own brains, and the opinion that we bring
        To make that only true we now intend,
        Will leave us never an understanding friend.
        Therefore, for goodness' sake, and as you are known
        The first and happiest hearers of the town,
25   Be sad, as we would make ye. Think ye see
        The very persons of our noble story
        As they were living: think you see them great,
        And followed with the general throng and sweat
        Of thousand friends: then, in a moment, see
30   How soon this mightiness meets misery:
        And if you can be merry then, I'll say
        A man may weep upon his wedding day.   [*Exit*]

Act 1 Scene 1   *running scene 1*

Enter the Duke of Norfolk at one door. At the other, the Duke of
Buckingham and the Lord Abergavenny

BUCKINGHAM   Good morrow, and well met. How have ye done
        Since last we saw in France?
NORFOLK   I thank your grace:
        Healthful, and ever since a fresh admirer
5   Of what I saw there.
BUCKINGHAM   An untimely ague
        Stayed me a prisoner in my chamber when
        Those suns of glory, those two lights of men,
        Met in the vale of Andres.
10 NORFOLK   'Twixt Guînes and Ardres:
        I was then present, saw them salute on horseback,
        Beheld them when they lighted, how they clung

---

20 opinion . . . intend reputation we have for presenting truthfully what we intend to perform
22 understanding comprehending (plays on the sense of audience members "standing under"
the stage, in the yard)   **24 happiest** most favored   **25 sad** serious   **27 As** as if   **great**
influential, of high rank   **1.1**   *Location: the royal court, London*   **2 saw** saw one
another   **4 fresh** untired, eager   **5 what . . . there** Norfolk refers to the meeting of Henry
VIII and the French King François I at the Field of the Cloth of Gold   **6 untimely ague** badly
timed fever   **7 Stayed** detained   **10 'Twixt** between   **Guînes and Ardres** towns near Calais
in northern France   **12 lighted** alighted, dismounted

In their embracement as they grew together,
Which had they, what four throned ones could have
   weighed
15   Such a compounded one?

BUCKINGHAM   All the whole time
I was my chamber's prisoner.

NORFOLK   Then you lost
The view of earthly glory: men might say
20   Till this time pomp was single, but now married
To one above itself. Each following day
Became the next day's master, till the last
Made former wonders its. Today the French,
All clinquant, all in gold, like heathen gods
25   Shone down the English; and tomorrow they
Made Britain India: every man that stood
Showed like a mine. Their dwarfish pages were
As cherubins, all gilt: the madams too,
Not used to toil, did almost sweat to bear
30   The pride upon them, that their very labour
Was to them as a painting. Now this masque
Was cried incomparable, and th'ensuing night
Made it a fool and beggar. The two kings,
Equal in lustre, were now best, now worst,
35   As presence did present them: him in eye,
Still him in praise, and being present both,
'Twas said they saw but one, and no discerner

---

13 as as if   **14 Which had they** i.e. had they grown together   **throned ones** i.e. kings
weighed balanced, equaled   **20 pomp** splendor, ceremony   **21 Each . . . master** i.e. each
day learned something from the one before it   **following** succeeding   **22 master** teacher
23 its i.e. its own   **24 clinquant** glittering   **25 Shone down** outshone   **tomorrow** i.e. the
next day   **they** i.e. the English   **26 India** i.e. seem as wealthy as the Indies (whose mines were
thought to be sources of immeasurable riches)   **27 Showed** appeared   **28 cherubins** (statues
of) angels   **madams** high-ranking ladies   **30 pride** magnificent finery, rich clothing, and
accessories   **that** so that   **labour . . . painting** efforts caused them to flush, so that they looked
as if they were wearing rouge   **31 masque** courtly entertainment involving elaborate costume
32 cried proclaimed   **night** i.e. night's entertainments   **33 Made . . . beggar** i.e. seemed
trivial and cheap in comparison   **34 were . . . them** were deemed more or less splendid
depending on which one was on view at the time   **35 him . . . praise** the king on view always
being the one praised   **36 being . . . one** when both kings were present they appeared
indistinguishable in their splendor   **37 discerner** observer/one who perceives a difference

Durst wag his tongue in censure. When these suns —
For so they phrase 'em — by their heralds challenged
40   The noble spirits to arms, they did perform
Beyond thought's compass, that former fabulous story,
Being now seen possible enough, got credit,
That Bevis was believed.

BUCKINGHAM   O, you go far.

45   NORFOLK   As I belong to worship, and affect
In honour honesty, the tract of ev'rything
Would by a good discourser lose some life,
Which action's self was tongue to. All was royal:
To the disposing of it nought rebelled:
50   Order gave each thing view. The office did
Distinctly his full function.

BUCKINGHAM   Who did guide —
I mean, who set the body and the limbs
Of this great sport together, as you guess?

55   NORFOLK   One, certes, that promises no element
In such a business.

BUCKINGHAM   I pray you who, my lord?

NORFOLK   All this was ordered by the good discretion
Of the right reverend Cardinal of York.

60   BUCKINGHAM   The devil speed him! No man's pie is freed
From his ambitious finger. What had he
To do in these fierce vanities? I wonder

---

38 Durst dared   censure judgment (in favor of one rather than the other)   39 phrase call, term   40 perform . . . compass enact unimaginable feats   compass bounds, limit   41 that . . . credit so that tales formerly thought to be mythical and far-fetched gained such credibility   43 Bevis the tale of Bevis of Hampton; the hero of an early English romance, he carried out legendary feats of chivalry and skill   44 go far are making very great claims/ exaggerate   45 belong to worship hold high rank, am a nobleman   affect . . . honesty respect integrity in matters of honor   46 tract narrative, course of events   47 discourser narrator   lose . . . to fall short in describing the actual vivid events   49 To . . . rebelled i.e. nothing interfered with the arrangement and handling of events   50 Order . . . view good preparations meant that everything was visible   The . . . function officials carried out their respective duties properly   54 sport entertainment   55 certes certainly   promises no element is not in his usual role   58 ordered organized   discretion judgment   59 Cardinal of York i.e. Wolsey   60 speed prosper, i.e. dispatch, hasten to his death   62 fierce high-spirited/warlike   vanities entertainments/extravagances

That such a keech can with his very bulk
Take up the rays o'th'beneficial sun
65 And keep it from the earth.

NORFOLK   Surely, sir,
There's in him stuff that puts him to these ends:
For being not propped by ancestry, whose grace
Chalks successors their way, nor called upon
70 For high feats done to th'crown, neither allied
To eminent assistants, but spider-like,
Out of his self-drawing web, a gives us note,
The force of his own merit makes his way
A gift that heaven gives for him, which buys
75 A place next to the king.

ABERGAVENNY   I cannot tell
What heaven hath given him — let some graver eye
Pierce into that — but I can see his pride
Peep through each part of him: whence has he that,
80 If not from hell? The devil is a niggard,
Or has given all before, and he begins
A new hell in himself.

BUCKINGHAM   Why the devil,
Upon this French going out, took he upon him,
85 Without the privity o'th'king, t'appoint
Who should attend on him? He makes up the file
Of all the gentry: for the most part such
To whom as great a charge as little honour
He meant to lay upon: and his own letter,

---

63 **keech** lump of animal fat (probably alludes to Wolsey's origins as a butcher's son as well as to his size)   64 **Take up** absorb, occupy   **o'th'beneficial** plays on the sense of "granting benefices" (ecclesiastical positions)   **sun** i.e. King Henry VIII   67 **stuff** substance, personal traits (plays on the sense of "meat for stuffing a pie")   **puts** encourages, provokes   68 **ancestry** i.e. high birth   **grace** honor, renown, virtue   69 **Chalks** shows   70 **high feats** important services   71 **eminent assistants** noble patrons/influential helpers   72 **self-drawing** self-made   **a . . . note** he lets us know   **a** he   75 **next to** intimately close to/next in status to   77 **graver** more reverend, wiser   80 **niggard** miser   81 **he** i.e. Wolsey   84 **going out** expedition   85 **privity** private knowledge and consent   86 **attend on him** i.e. accompany the king to France (a costly enterprise)   **file** register, list   87 **such . . . upon** i.e. those listed will have to pay a disproportionately large amount for the small honor bestowed on them   89 **own letter** personal summons (to **attend**)

90   The honourable board of council out,
       Must fetch him in, he papers.
       ABERGAVENNY   I do know
       Kinsmen of mine, three at the least, that have
       By this so sickened their estates, that never
95   They shall abound as formerly.
       BUCKINGHAM   O, many
       Have broke their backs with laying manors on 'em
       For this great journey. What did this vanity
       But minister communication of
100   A most poor issue?
       NORFOLK   Grievingly I think
       The peace between the French and us not values
       The cost that did conclude it.
       BUCKINGHAM   Every man,
105   After the hideous storm that followed, was
       A thing inspired, and, not consulting, broke
       Into a general prophecy: that this tempest,
       Dashing the garment of this peace, aboded
       The sudden breach on't.
110   NORFOLK   Which is budded out,
       For France hath flawed the league, and hath attached
       Our merchants' goods at Bordeaux.
       ABERGAVENNY   Is it therefore
       Th'ambassador is silenced?
115   NORFOLK   Marry, is't.

---

90 board of council i.e. Privy Council, the king's advisers   out disregarded, not consulted
91 fetch . . . papers summon whoever is listed   papers sets down on paper   94 sickened
weakened, depleted   95 abound prosper, be wealthy   97 laying . . . 'em selling property to
pay for fine clothes   98 vanity foolish extravagance (i.e. the lavish meeting of the two kings)
99 minister . . . issue provide the opportunity for a useless discussion (communication may
possibly play on the sense of "sexual procreation," and poor issue does play on the sense of
"impoverished children"; the sale of assets will affect the noblemen's heirs)   101 Grievingly
sadly   102 not values is not worth   106 inspired i.e. with divine, prophetic power   not
consulting without consulting one another, independently   107 general universal
108 Dashing destroying   aboded predicted, foretold   109 on't of it   110 is budded out has
developed, come to pass   111 flawed broken, contravened   attached seized   113 therefore
for that reason   114 silenced placed under house arrest   115 Marry by the Virgin Mary

ABERGAVENNY   A proper title of a peace, and purchased
At a superfluous rate.
BUCKINGHAM   Why, all this business
Our reverend cardinal carried.
120   NORFOLK   Like it your grace,
The state takes notice of the private difference
Betwixt you and the cardinal. I advise you —
And take it from a heart that wishes towards you
Honour and plenteous safety — that you read
125   The cardinal's malice and his potency
Together: to consider further that
What his high hatred would effect wants not
A minister in his power. You know his nature,
That he's revengeful: and I know his sword
130   Hath a sharp edge: it's long and't may be said,
It reaches far, and where 'twill not extend,
Thither he darts it. Bosom up my counsel,
You'll find it wholesome. Lo, where comes that rock
That I advise your shunning.

Enter Cardinal Wolsey, the purse borne before him, certain of the Guard,
and two Secretaries with papers. The Cardinal in his passage fixeth his
eye on Buckingham, and Buckingham on him, both full of disdain

135   CARDINAL WOLSEY   The Duke of Buckingham's surveyor, ha?
Where's his examination?
SECRETARY   Here, so please you.
CARDINAL WOLSEY   Is he in person ready?
SECRETARY   Ay, please your grace.
140   CARDINAL WOLSEY   Well, we shall then know more, and
Buckingham
Shall lessen this big look.   *Exeunt Cardinal and his train*

---

116 **proper title of** fine name for   117 **superfluous rate** very high cost   119 **carried**
managed   120 **Like it** may it please   121 **state** Privy Council/the king   **difference** dispute,
discord   124 **read** consider/interpret   125 **potency** power   127 **would** wishes to   **wants**
lacks   128 **minister** agent   132 **darts** thrusts   **Bosom up** keep secret/take to heart
133 **wholesome** healthy, beneficial   **Lo** look   134 *purse* containing the great seal of
England, used by the king to authenticate documents; the Lord Chancellor (Wolsey) was its
official keeper   135 **surveyor** estate manager   136 **examination** deposition, statement
141 **big** proud, haughty   *train* retinue, attendants

BUCKINGHAM   This butcher's cur is venom-mouthed, and I
Have not the power to muzzle him: therefore best
Not wake him in his slumber. A beggar's book
145   Outworths a noble's blood.

NORFOLK   What, are you chafed?
Ask God for temp'rance: that's th'appliance only
Which your disease requires.

BUCKINGHAM   I read in's looks
150   Matter against me, and his eye reviled
Me as his abject object: at this instant
He bores me with some trick: he's gone to th'king:
I'll follow, and outstare him.

NORFOLK   Stay, my lord,
155   And let your reason with your choler question
What 'tis you go about: to climb steep hills
Requires slow pace at first. Anger is like
A full hot horse, who being allowed his way,
Self-mettle tires him: not a man in England
160   Can advise me like you: be to yourself
As you would to your friend.

BUCKINGHAM   I'll to the king,
And from a mouth of honour quite cry down
This Ipswich fellow's insolence, or proclaim
165   There's difference in no persons.

NORFOLK   Be advised:
Heat not a furnace for your foe so hot
That it do singe yourself. We may outrun,
By violent swiftness, that which we run at,
170   And lose by overrunning: know you not

---

142 **butcher's cur** another reference to Wolsey's origins as a butcher's son   **cur** dog
144 **beggar's . . . blood** a poor man's (i.e. Wolsey's) learning is more highly valued than a
nobleman's lineage   146 **chafed** irritated, angry   147 **temp'rance** self-control, moderation
th'appliance only the only remedy   150 **Matter** substance, something significant (plays on
the sense of "rheum, infected ocular discharge")   151 **abject object** despicable view
152 **bores** cheats   155 **choler** anger   158 **full hot** very headstrong, overly hasty   159 **Self-
mettle** his own vigorous spirit   163 **mouth of honour** i.e. gentleman's mouth   **quite**
completely   164 **Ipswich** Wolsey's birthplace, a town in Suffolk in eastern England
165 **difference** distinction of rank   166 **advised** warned   170 **overrunning** running past it

The fire that mounts the liquor till't run o'er,
In seeming to augment it wastes it? Be advised:
I say again there is no English soul
More stronger to direct you than yourself,
175   If with the sap of reason you would quench
Or but allay the fire of passion.

BUCKINGHAM   Sir,
I am thankful to you, and I'll go along
By your prescription: but this top-proud fellow —
180   Whom from the flow of gall I name not, but
From sincere motions — by intelligence,
And proofs as clear as founts in July when
We see each grain of gravel, I do know
To be corrupt and treasonous.

185   NORFOLK   Say not 'treasonous'.

BUCKINGHAM   To th'king I'll say't, and make my vouch as strong
As shore of rock: attend. This holy fox,
Or wolf, or both — for he is equal rav'nous
As he is subtle, and as prone to mischief
190   As able to perform't, his mind and place
Infecting one another, yea, reciprocally —
Only to show his pomp as well in France
As here at home, suggests the king our master
To this last costly treaty, th'interview
195   That swallowed so much treasure, and like a glass
Did break i'th'wrenching.

NORFOLK   Faith, and so it did.

BUCKINGHAM   Pray give me favour, sir: this cunning cardinal
The articles o'th'combination drew
200   As himself pleased: and they were ratified

171 **mounts** causes to rise up, i.e. boils   176 **allay** diminish, moderate/mix, alloy
179 **prescription** direction, advice   **top-proud** proud to the highest degree   180 **gall** bile,
bitterness   181 **motions** motives   **intelligence** secret information   182 **founts** springs
186 **vouch** affirmation, allegation   188 **equal** just as   189 **subtle** cunning   190 **place**
official position (as Lord Chancellor)   192 **pomp** greatness, splendor   193 **suggests**
persuades, encourages, tempts   194 **last** recent   **th'interview** the meeting (between the
French and English kings)   195 **treasure** money, wealth   196 **i'th'wrenching** in the rinsing/
distortion of meaning   198 **give me favour** i.e. permit me to continue   199 **articles** clauses,
terms   **o'th'combination** of the treaty   **drew** drafted, drew up

As he cried 'Thus let be', to as much end
As give a crutch to th'dead. But our count-cardinal
Has done this, and 'tis well: for worthy Wolsey,
Who cannot err, he did it. Now this follows —
205 Which, as I take it, is a kind of puppy
To th'old dam treason — Charles the Emperor,
Under pretence to see the queen his aunt —
For 'twas indeed his colour, but he came
To whisper Wolsey — here makes visitation:
210 His fears were that the interview betwixt
England and France might through their amity
Breed him some prejudice, for from this league
Peeped harms that menaced him. He privily
Deals with our cardinal, and as I trow —
215 Which I do well, for I am sure the emperor
Paid ere he promised, whereby his suit was granted
Ere it was asked — but when the way was made
And paved with gold, the emperor thus desired
That he would please to alter the king's course,
220 And break the foresaid peace. Let the king know,
As soon he shall by me, that thus the cardinal
Does buy and sell his honour as he pleases,
And for his own advantage.

NORFOLK   I am sorry
225 To hear this of him, and could wish he were
Something mistaken in't.

BUCKINGHAM   No, not a syllable:
I do pronounce him in that very shape
He shall appear in proof.

Enter Brandon, a Sergeant-at-Arms before him, and two or three of
the Guard

---

201 end effect, use   **202 count-cardinal** i.e. cardinal behaving like an aristocrat
(contemptuous); often emended to "court-cardinal"   **206 dam** mother   **Charles the**
Emperor Holy Roman Emperor, Charles V, Katherine of Aragon's nephew   **208 colour** pretext
209 whisper whisper to   **213 privily** privately, secretly   **214 trow** believe   **216 ere** before
217 but only   **219 he** i.e. Wolsey   **222 his** i.e. the king's   **he** i.e. Wolsey   **226 Something**
somewhat   **mistaken** misunderstood, misrepresented   **229 in proof** when put to the test/in
fact, according to evidence

230 BRANDON   Your office, sergeant: execute it.

SERGEANT   Sir,   *To Buckingham*
My lord the Duke of Buckingham, and Earl
Of Hertford, Stafford and Northampton, I
Arrest thee of high treason, in the name
235 Of our most sovereign king.

BUCKINGHAM   Lo you, my lord,
The net has fall'n upon me: I shall perish
Under device and practice.

BRANDON   I am sorry
240 To see you ta'en from liberty, to look on
The business present. 'Tis his highness' pleasure
You shall to th'Tower.

BUCKINGHAM   It will help me nothing
To plead mine innocence, for that dye is on me
245 Which makes my whit'st part black. The will of heav'n
Be done in this and all things: I obey.
O my Lord Aberga'nny, fare you well.

BRANDON   Nay, he must bear you company.—   *To Abergavenny*
The king
Is pleased you shall to th'Tower, till you know
250 How he determines further.

ABERGAVENNY   As the duke said,
The will of heaven be done, and the king's pleasure
By me obeyed.

BRANDON   Here is a warrant from
255 The king t'attach Lord Montague and the bodies
Of the duke's confessor, John de la Car,
One Gilbert Perk, his chancellor—

BUCKINGHAM   So, so;
These are the limbs o'th'plot: no more, I hope.

260 BRANDON   A monk o'th'Chartreux.

BUCKINGHAM   O, Nicholas Hopkins?

---

230 **office** duty, task   233 **Hertford** historically Hereford, to which some editors emend
238 **device and practice** plots and stratagems   240 **look on** witness   241 **pleasure** will
242 **th'Tower** the Tower of London   243 **nothing** in no way   255 **t'attach** to arrest   **bodies**
persons   260 **o'th'Chartreux** of the Carthusian order—a monastical order noted for its severity

BRANDON   He.

BUCKINGHAM   My surveyor is false: the o'er-great cardinal
Hath showed him gold: my life is spanned already:
265   I am the shadow of poor Buckingham,
Whose figure even this instant cloud puts on,
By dark'ning my clear sun. My lord, farewell.   *Exeunt*

Act 1 Scene 2   *Running scene 2*

*Cornets. Enter King Henry [VIII], leaning on the Cardinal [Wolsey]'s
shoulder, the Nobles, [Wolsey's Secretary] and Sir Thomas Lovell: the
Cardinal places himself under the King's feet on his right side*

KING HENRY VIII   My life itself, and the best heart of it,
Thanks you for this great care: I stood i'th'level
Of a full-charged confederacy, and give thanks
To you that choked it. Let be called before us
5   That gentleman of Buckingham's: in person
I'll hear him his confessions justify,
And point by point the treasons of his master
He shall again relate.

*A noise within crying 'Room for the Queen, ushered by the Duke of
Norfolk'. Enter the Queen [Katherine], Norfolk and Suffolk: she kneels.
[The] King riseth from his state, takes her up, kisses and placeth her by him*

QUEEN KATHERINE   Nay, we must longer kneel: I am a suitor.

10   KING HENRY VIII   Arise, and take place by us: half your   *The Queen*
suit   *moves to his side*
Never name to us: you have half our power:
The other moiety ere you ask is given:
Repeat your will and take it.

263 **false** disloyal   264 **showed him gold** bribed him (to betray Buckingham; whether the
surveyor lies or reveals an actual plot is unclear)   **spanned** measured out   265 **shadow . . .
Buckingham** the shadowy likeness of my former self   266 **Whose . . . sun** my form being now
obscured by cloud and its former innocent brightness (**clear sun**) dimmed/my form being
shrouded by a sudden cloud that darkens my king's favor (**sun**)   **1.2** *Cornets* hornlike
wind instruments (here announcing the king's arrival)   **under . . . feet** standing at the foot of
the king's throne or dais on which it sits   1 **best heart** very essence   2 **level** aim, target
sights   3 **full-charged** fully loaded   **confederacy** conspiracy, plot   6 **justify** prove, confirm
8 *state* throne   9 **we** the royal plural   **suitor** person with a request to make, favor to ask
10 **place** your official place as queen   12 **moiety** half   13 **Repeat your will** utter your desire

QUEEN KATHERINE   Thank your majesty.
15   That you would love yourself, and in that love
        Not unconsidered leave your honour, nor
        The dignity of your office, is the point
        Of my petition.
        KING HENRY VIII   Lady mine, proceed.
20   QUEEN KATHERINE   I am solicited, not by a few,
        And those of true condition, that your subjects
        Are in great grievance: there have been commissions
        Sent down among 'em which hath flawed the heart
        Of all their loyalties: wherein, although,
25   My good lord cardinal, they vent reproaches
        Most bitterly on you, as putter-on
        Of these exactions, yet the king our master —
        Whose honour heaven shield from soil — even he escapes not
        Language unmannerly, yea, such which breaks
30   The sides of loyalty, and almost appears
        In loud rebellion.
        NORFOLK   Not 'almost appears',
        It doth appear: for, upon these taxations,
        The clothiers all, not able to maintain
35   The many to them longing, have put off
        The spinsters, carders, fullers, weavers, who,
        Unfit for other life, compelled by hunger
        And lack of other means, in desperate manner
        Daring th'event to th'teeth, are all in uproar,
40   And danger serves among them.
        KING HENRY VIII   Taxation?
        Wherein, and what taxation? My lord cardinal,

14 **Thank** i.e. I thank   17 **dignity** honor, kingly status   20 **solicited** urged, entreated
21 **true condition** loyal disposition   22 **grievance** distress   **commissions** official
authorization (to collect taxes)   23 **flawed** cracked, damaged   26 **putter-on** instigator
27 **exactions** extortionate charges   28 **soil** dishonorable stain   34 **clothiers** cloth workers,
who dealt with woollen fabric   35 **longing** belonging, i.e. dependent on them for employment
put off dismissed   36 **spinsters** spinners of wool into thread for weaving into cloth   **carders**
those who prepared wool for spinning by combing out impurities and aligning the fibres
fullers those who beat cloth to clean and thicken it   37 **life** i.e. ways of making a living
39 **Daring . . . th'teeth** pushing the situation to the extreme, challenging matters to the limit
40 **danger** i.e. the potential for outright revolt   **serves** has joined ranks

You that are blamed for it alike with us,
Know you of this taxation?

45   CARDINAL WOLSEY   Please you, sir,
I know but of a single part in aught
Pertains to th'state, and front but in that file
Where others tell steps with me.

QUEEN KATHERINE   No, my lord?

50   You know no more than others? But you frame
Things that are known alike, which are not wholesome
To those which would not know them, and yet must
Perforce be their acquaintance. These exactions,
Whereof my sovereign would have note, they are

55   Most pestilent to th'hearing, and to bear 'em
The back is sacrifice to th'load. They say
They are devised by you, or else you suffer
Too hard an exclamation.

KING HENRY VIII   Still 'exaction':

60   The nature of it? In what kind, let's know,
Is this exaction?

QUEEN KATHERINE   I am much too venturous
In tempting of your patience, but am boldened
Under your promised pardon. The subjects' grief

65   Comes through commissions, which compels from each
The sixth part of his substance, to be levied
Without delay, and the pretence for this
Is named your wars in France: this makes bold mouths:
Tongues spit their duties out, and cold hearts freeze

70   Allegiance in them: their curses now
Live where their prayers did: and it's come to pass

---

46 **single part** individual role, i.e. only my share   **aught** anything   47 **front . . . me** merely
march in the front rank along with others who keep the same pace   48 **tell** count
50 **you . . . acquaintance** you devise matters that are known to everyone, which are damaging
to those who would rather not know of them but who are obliged to endure them nevertheless
54 **have note** be informed   55 **bear** carry   56 **is . . . th'load** i.e. is bowed down painfully
by the burden   58 **exclamation** outcry, reproach   60 **In what kind** of what nature
62 **venturous** adventurous, daring   63 **tempting of** testing   **boldened Under** made bold by
64 **grief** grievance, complaint   66 **substance** wealth   67 **pretence** alleged reason/pretext
71 **prayers** i.e. for the king

This tractable obedience is a slave
To each incensèd will. I would your highness
Would give it quick consideration, for
75 There is no primer baseness.
  KING HENRY VIII   By my life,
This is against our pleasure.
  CARDINAL WOLSEY   And for me,
I have no further gone in this than by
80 A single voice, and that not passed me but
By learnèd approbation of the judges: if I am
Traduced by ignorant tongues, which neither know
My faculties nor person, yet will be
The chronicles of my doing, let me say
85 'Tis but the fate of place, and the rough brake
That virtue must go through: we must not stint
Our necessary actions, in the fear
To cope malicious censurers, which ever,
As rav'nous fishes, do a vessel follow
90 That is new trimmed, but benefit no further
Than vainly longing. What we oft do best,
By sick interpreters, once weak ones, is
Not ours, or not allowed: what worst, as oft,
Hitting a grosser quality, is cried up
95 For our best act: if we shall stand still,
In fear our motion will be mocked or carped at,
We should take root here where we sit,
Or sit state-statues only.

---

72 **tractable** compliant   **slave . . . will** i.e. now governed by wrath   73 **would** wish
75 **primer baseness** greater manifestation of low, dishonorable behavior   77 **pleasure**
wishes   80 **single voice** (his) individual vote/unanimous vote (of the Privy Council)
passed ratified, approved by   81 **approbation** consent   82 **Traduced** slandered, dishonored
83 **faculties** capabilities/qualities   85 **place** high office   **brake** thicket   86 **stint** restrain,
withhold   88 **To cope** of encountering   **censurers** critics   90 **new trimmed** newly fitted
out   91 **vainly longing** i.e. hoping in vain for the refurbished and seaworthy boat to sink and
provide food   **What . . . allowed** malicious or essentially foolish interpreters often refuse to
believe in or give us credit for our best actions   93 **what . . . act** our worst actions, which often
appeal to baser people, are declared the best we ever did   96 **In** for   **motion** action/proposal
carped at complained of   98 **state-statues** images of statesmen

KING HENRY VIII   Things done well,
100   And with a care, exempt themselves from fear:
Things done without example, in their issue
Are to be feared. Have you a precedent
Of this commission? I believe not any.
We must not rend our subjects from our laws,
105   And stick them in our will. Sixth part of each?
A trembling contribution; why, we take
From every tree lop, bark, and part o'th'timber:
And though we leave it with a root, thus hacked
The air will drink the sap. To every county
110   Where this is questioned send our letters, with
Free pardon to each man that has denied
The force of this commission: pray, look to't;
I put it to your care.

CARDINAL WOLSEY   A word with you.   *To the Secretary*
115   Let there be letters writ to every shire,
Of the king's grace and pardon.— The grievèd
        commons   *Aside to Secretary*
Hardly conceive of me. Let it be noised
That through our intercession this revokement
And pardon comes: I shall anon advise you
120   Further in the proceeding.   *Exit Secretary*

Enter Surveyor

QUEEN KATHERINE   I am sorry that the Duke of   *To the King*
        Buckingham
Is run in your displeasure.

KING HENRY VIII   It grieves many:
The gentleman is learnèd, and a most rare speaker,
125   To nature none more bound: his training such
That he may furnish and instruct great teachers,

---

101 **example** precedent   **issue** outcome   103 **Of** for   104 **rend . . . will** i.e. force the subjects
to obey the changing will of the monarch rather than the law   106 **trembling** fearful
107 **lop** lopped-off branch   109 **The . . . sap** i.e. the tree will die   110 **questioned**
challenged, resisted   116 **grace** good will/mercy   **commons** common people   117 **Hardly**
conceive think harshly   **noised** rumored, reported   118 **our** Wolsey uses the royal plural
revokement repeal   119 **anon** shortly   122 **Is run in** has incurred, come into   124 **rare**
splendid/exceptional   125 **To . . . bound** no one is more indebted to nature for such qualities

And never seek for aid out of himself: yet see,
When these so noble benefits shall prove
Not well disposed, the mind growing once corrupt,
130 They turn to vicious forms, ten times more ugly
Than ever they were fair. This man so complete,
Who was enrolled 'mongst wonders — and when we,
Almost with ravished listening, could not find
His hour of speech a minute — he, my lady,
135 Hath into monstrous habits put the graces
That once were his, and is become as black
As if besmeared in hell. Sit by us: you shall hear —
This was his gentleman in trust — of him
Things to strike honour sad.— Bid him recount *To Wolsey*
140 The fore-recited practices, whereof
We cannot feel too little, hear too much.

CARDINAL WOLSEY Stand forth, and with bold *To the Surveyor*
 spirit relate what you
Most like a careful subject have collected
Out of the Duke of Buckingham.

145 **KING HENRY VIII** Speak freely.

SURVEYOR First, it was usual with him — every day
It would infect his speech — that if the king
Should without issue die, he'll carry it so
To make the sceptre his. These very words
150 I've heard him utter to his son-in-law,
Lord Aberga'nny, to whom by oath he menaced
Revenge upon the cardinal.

CARDINAL WOLSEY Please your highness note
His dangerous conception in this point,
155 Not friended by his wish to your high person:

---

127 **out of** beyond 129 **disposed** applied, directed 130 **vicious** wicked, immoral
131 **complete** accomplished, perfect 133 **ravished** entranced 135 **monstrous** unnatural
habits clothing/behavior, practices 138 **gentleman in trust** trusted servant 140 **practices**
plots 141 **hear too much** i.e. for our own protection 143 **careful** dutiful, full of care (for
the king) **collected** picked up, gathered (as evidence) 148 **issue** children **carry**
manage 149 **sceptre** staff carried as a symbol of sovereignty 151 **menaced** threatened
154 **conception** intention, plan 155 **Not . . . person** not being gratified in his wish regarding
you (i.e. that the king should die childless)

His will is most malignant, and it stretches
Beyond you to your friends.

QUEEN KATHERINE   My learnèd lord cardinal,
Deliver all with charity.

160   KING HENRY VIII   Speak on: *To the Surveyor*
How grounded he his title to the crown
Upon our fail? To this point hast thou heard him
At any time speak aught?

SURVEYOR   He was brought to this

165   By a vain prophecy of Nicholas Hopkins.

KING HENRY VIII   What was that Hopkins?

SURVEYOR   Sir, a Chartreux friar,
His confessor, who fed him every minute
With words of sovereignty.

170   KING HENRY VIII   How know'st thou this?

SURVEYOR   Not long before your highness sped to France,
The Duke being at the Rose, within the parish
St Lawrence Poultney, did of me demand
What was the speech among the Londoners

175   Concerning the French journey. I replied
Men feared the French would prove perfidious
To the king's danger: presently the duke
Said 'twas the fear indeed and that he doubted
'Twould prove the verity of certain words

180   Spoke by a holy monk that oft, says he,
'Hath sent to me, wishing me to permit
John de la Car, my chaplain, a choice hour
To hear from him a matter of some moment:
Whom after under the confession's seal

185   He solemnly had sworn that what he spoke

---

157 **friends** i.e. Wolsey   159 **Deliver** speak   161 **How . . . fail?** On what did he base his claim
to the throne in the event of my death without an heir?   162 **To this point** on this subject
167 **Chartreux** Carthusian, i.e. one of a strict monastic order from Chartreux near Grenoble in
France   172 **the Rose** the name of a manor house belonging to Buckingham   173 **St
Lawrence Poultney** a church on Candlewick Street in London   174 **speech** talk, gossip,
prevailing opinion   176 **perfidious** treacherous   177 **To . . . danger** resulting in danger for
the king   **presently** instantly   178 **doubted** feared/suspected   182 **choice** chosen,
appointed   183 **moment** importance

My chaplain to no creature living but
To me should utter, with demure confidence
This pausingly ensued: "Neither the king nor's heirs,
Tell you the duke, shall prosper: bid him strive
190 To gain the love o'th'commonalty: the duke
Shall govern England."'

QUEEN KATHERINE   If I know you well,
You were the duke's surveyor, and lost your office
On the complaint o'th'tenants: take good heed
195 You charge not in your spleen a noble person
And spoil your nobler soul: I say, take heed:
Yes, heartily beseech you.

KING HENRY VIII   Let him on:
Go forward.   *To the Surveyor*

200 SURVEYOR   On my soul, I'll speak but truth.
I told my lord the duke, by th'devil's illusions
The monk might be deceived, and that 'twas dangerous
For him to ruminate on this so far, until
It forged him some design, which being believed,
205 It was much like to do: he answered, 'Tush,
It can do me no damage', adding further,
That had the king in his last sickness failed,
The cardinal's and Sir Thomas Lovell's heads
Should have gone off.

210 KING HENRY VIII   Ha? What, so rank? Ah, ha!
There's mischief in this man: canst thou say further?

SURVEYOR   I can, my liege.

KING HENRY VIII   Proceed.

SURVEYOR   Being at Greenwich,
215 After your highness had reproved the duke
About Sir William Bulmer—

---

187 **demure confidence** grave assurance, solemn certainty   190 **o'th'commonalty** of the
common people   195 **spleen** anger, malice   196 **nobler** i.e. as the immortal soul is more
important than worldly rank   198 **on** go on   200 **but** only   204 **forged** formed, created (in)
205 **much . . . do** very likely to be carried out   207 **failed** died   210 **rank** foul, corrupt, gross
214 **Greenwich** a royal palace south of the River Thames

KING HENRY VIII   I remember
Of such a time: being my sworn servant,
The duke retained him his. But on: what hence?
220 SURVEYOR   'If', quoth he, 'I for this had been committed' —
As to the Tower, I thought, — 'I would have played
The part my father meant to act upon
Th'usurper Richard, who, being at Salisbury,
Made suit to come in's presence: which if granted,
225 As he made semblance of his duty, would
Have put his knife to him.'
KING HENRY VIII   A giant traitor.
CARDINAL WOLSEY   Now, madam, may his highness live in
freedom,
And this man out of prison?
230 QUEEN KATHERINE   God mend all.
KING HENRY VIII   There's something more would out of thee:
what say'st?
SURVEYOR   After 'the duke his father', with 'the knife',
He stretched him, and with one hand on his dagger,
Another spread on's breast, mounting his eyes,
235 He did discharge a horrible oath, whose tenor
Was, were he evil used, he would outgo
His father by as much as a performance
Does an irresolute purpose.
KING HENRY VIII   There's his period:
240 To sheathe his knife in us: he is attached:
Call him to present trial: if he may
Find mercy in the law, 'tis his: if none,
Let him not seek't of us: by day and night,
He's traitor to th'height.   *Exeunt*

---

219 his as his own (instead of the king's)   **220 committed** imprisoned   **223 Richard** i.e.
Richard III   **Salisbury** town in Wiltshire, southwest England   **224 suit** a formal request
225 made . . . duty i.e. by kneeling before Richard in feigned respect   **230 God mend all** may
God put everything right   **233 stretched him** stood fully upright   **234 mounting** raising
236 evil used badly treated   **outgo** surpass   **238 irresolute** shaky, undecided/not
accomplished   **239 period** end, purpose   **240 attached** arrested   **241 present** immediate
244 to th'height in the highest degree

Act 1 Scene 3

Enter [the] Lord Chamberlain and Lord Sands

CHAMBERLAIN   Is't possible the spells of France should juggle
Men into such strange mysteries?

SANDS   New customs,
Though they be never so ridiculous,
5 Nay, let 'em be unmanly, yet are followed.

CHAMBERLAIN   As far as I see, all the good our English
Have got by the late voyage is but merely
A fit or two o'th'face: but they are shrewd ones,
For when they hold 'em, you would swear directly
10 Their very noses had been counsellors
To Pepin or Clotharius, they keep state so.

SANDS   They have all new legs, and lame ones: one would
take it,
That never see 'em pace before, the spavin
Or springhalt reigned among 'em.

15 CHAMBERLAIN   Death, my lord,
Their clothes are after such a pagan cut to't
That sure they've worn out Christendom.

Enter Sir Thomas Lovell

How now?
What news, Sir Thomas Lovell?

LOVELL   Faith, my lord,
20 I hear of none, but the new proclamation
That's clapped upon the court gate.

CHAMBERLAIN   What is't for?

1.3   **1 spells** magic charms   **juggle** trick, deceive, conjure   **2 mysteries** enigmatic behavior (i.e. the imitation of French courtly fashions)   **5 let 'em be** even if they are   **7 late** recent   **8 fit . . . o'th'face** one or two grimaces, contrived facial expressions   **shrewd** cunning, artful/sharp, clever   **9 hold 'em** assume such facial expressions   **11 Pepin or Clotharius** eighth- and sixth-century Kings of the Franks   **keep state so** maintain such affected dignity (presumably those referred to are walking around with their noses in the air)   **12 legs** i.e. ways of walking/bowing   **take it** think, assume/affirm, swear   **13 spavin** tumor on a horse's leg caused by inflammation of cartilage   **14 springhalt** stringhalt, a disease of a horse's hind legs, causing spasmodic muscle contractions   **15 Death** contracted form of the oath "by God's death"   **16 after . . . to't** fashioned in such a pagan manner   **17 worn out** exhausted (all the styles available in)   **21 clapped** placed

LOVELL   The reformation of our travelled gallants,
That fill the court with quarrels, talk and tailors.

25 CHAMBERLAIN   I'm glad 'tis there: now I would pray our monsieurs
To think an English courtier may be wise,
And never see the Louvre.

LOVELL   They must either,
For so run the conditions, leave those remnants
30 Of fool and feather that they got in France,
With all their honourable points of ignorance
Pertaining thereunto — as fights and fireworks,
Abusing better men than they can be
Out of a foreign wisdom, renouncing clean
35 The faith they have in tennis and tall stockings,
Short blistered breeches, and those types of travel —
And understand again like honest men,
Or pack to their old playfellows: there, I take it,
They may *cum privilegio* 'oui' away
40 The lag end of their lewdness and be laughed at.

SANDS   'Tis time to give 'em physic, their diseases
Are grown so catching.

CHAMBERLAIN   What a loss our ladies
Will have of these trim vanities!

---

27 Louvre French royal palace in Paris   **30 fool and feather** foolishness and elaborate dress (such as feathers worn on hats)   **31 honourable . . . ignorance** foolish trivia they consider worthy (**points** plays on the sense of "laces used for fastening clothing")   **32 as** such as **fights** i.e. duels   **fireworks** fighting/whoring (perhaps also with associations of "elaborate pyrotechnic displays")   **33 Abusing** dishonoring, mocking   **34 Out . . . wisdom** using the so-called wisdom they have gained abroad   **renouncing clean** they must now renounce totally   **35 tall . . . breeches** i.e. French fashions, playing on notion of venereal disease **blistered** short and puffed/covered in blisters, symptomatic of venereal disease   **36 types** marks, indications   **travel** plays on sense of sexual travail, exertion   **37 understand** comprehend/stand up properly (with sexual connotations)   **honest** honorable/true **38 pack** depart   **playfellows** (sexual) partners   **39 *cum privilegio*** "with immunity" (Latin; an abbreviated form of the phrase announcing the exclusive right of a printer to publish a book)   **oui** "yes" (French)   **40 lag end** latter part, tail end (with phallic connotations) **lewdness** foolishness/wickedness/lechery   **41 physic** medicine, specifically perhaps a cure for venereal disease   **44 trim vanities** smart dandies/worthless fripperies/handsome playthings

45 LOVELL   Ay, marry,
There will be woe indeed, lords: the sly whoresons
Have got a speeding trick to lay down ladies:
A French song and a fiddle has no fellow.

SANDS   The devil fiddle 'em! I am glad they are going,
50 For sure there's no converting of 'em: now
An honest country lord, as I am, beaten
A long time out of play, may bring his plainsong
And have an hour of hearing, and, by'r lady,
Held current music too.

55 CHAMBERLAIN   Well said, Lord Sands:
Your colt's tooth is not cast yet?

SANDS   No, my lord,
Nor shall not, while I have a stump.

CHAMBERLAIN   Sir Thomas,   *To Lovell*
60 Whither were you a-going?

LOVELL   To the cardinal's:
Your lordship is a guest too.

CHAMBERLAIN   O, 'tis true:
This night he makes a supper, and a great one,
65 To many lords and ladies: there will be
The beauty of this kingdom, I'll assure you.

LOVELL   That churchman bears a bounteous mind indeed,
A hand as fruitful as the land that feeds us:
His dews fall everywhere.

70 CHAMBERLAIN   No doubt he's noble:
He had a black mouth that said other of him.

SANDS   He may, my lord, he's wherewithal in him:
Sparing would show a worse sin than ill doctrine:

---

45 **marry** by the Virgin Mary   46 **whoresons** bastards, wretches (a coarse term of abuse)
47 **speeding** successful/speedy   **lay down** seduce/have sex with   48 **fiddle** musical
instrument/penis/mirth-maker, jester   **fellow** equal   49 **fiddle** play with/cheat
50 **converting of 'em** i.e. reforming their behavior   52 **play** performing music/sexual play
plainsong simple melody, i.e. straightforward manner of wooing   53 **hearing** i.e. audience
(with a woman)   **by'r lady** by Our Lady (the Virgin Mary)   54 **Held** be considered   **current**
fashionable   56 **colt's tooth** youthful lust   **cast** discarded   58 **stump** remains of a tooth/
penis   64 **makes** gives   68 **fruitful** generous   69 **dews** i.e. favors, benevolence (puns on
"dues" or taxes)   71 **black** slanderous/sinful   **other** otherwise   72 **he's wherewithal** he has
the necessary means   73 **Sparing** frugality, economy

Men of his way should be most liberal:
75   They are set here for examples.

CHAMBERLAIN   True, they are so:
But few now give so great ones. My barge stays:
Your lordship shall along. Come, good Sir Thomas,   *To Lovell*
We shall be late else, which I would not be,
80   For I was spoke to, with Sir Henry Guildford,
This night to be comptrollers.

SANDS   I am your lordship's.   *Exeunt*

Act 1 Scene 4   *running scene 3*

*Hautboys. A small table under a state for the Cardinal, a longer table
for the guests. Then enter Anne Bullen, and divers other Ladies and
Gentlemen, as guests at one door; at another door enter Sir Henry
Guildford*

GUILDFORD   Ladies, a general welcome from his grace
Salutes ye all: this night he dedicates
To fair content and you: none here, he hopes,
In all this noble bevy, has brought with her
5   One care abroad: he would have all as merry
As, first, good company, good wine, good welcome,
Can make good people.

Enter Lord Chamberlain, Lords Sands and Lovell

O, my lord, you're tardy: *To Chamberlain*
The very thought of this fair company
Clapped wings to me.

10   CHAMBERLAIN   You are young, Sir Harry Guildford.

SANDS   Sir Thomas Lovell, had the cardinal
But half my lay thoughts in him, some of these

---

74 **way** way of life, i.e. as a cardinal   77 **ones** i.e. **examples**   **stays** waits   78 **along** i.e. come
along   80 **spoke to** asked   81 **comptrollers** stewards, masters of ceremonies   82 **your
lordship's** i.e. entirely at your disposal   **1.4** *Location: York Place (now Whitehall)—
Wolsey's residence   Hautboys* oboelike instruments   *state* canopy   *divers* various,
several   4 **bevy** company   5 **abroad** out with her, from home   7 **tardy** slow, late
9 **Clapped** fixed   12 **lay** secular/sexual

Should find a running banquet ere they rested

I think would better please 'em: by my life,

15   They are a sweet society of fair ones.

LOVELL   O, that your lordship were but now confessor

To one or two of these.

SANDS   I would I were:

They should find easy penance.

20 LOVELL   Faith, how easy?

SANDS   As easy as a down bed would afford it.

CHAMBERLAIN   Sweet ladies, will it please you sit?—   *To Guildford*

Sir Harry,

Place you that side, I'll take the charge of this:

His grace is ent'ring. Nay, you must not freeze:

25   Two women placed together makes cold weather:

My lord Sands, you are one will keep 'em waking:

Pray sit between these ladies.

SANDS   By my faith,

And thank your lordship.—   *He sits between Anne and another lady*

By your leave, sweet ladies,

30   If I chance to talk a little wild, forgive me:

I had it from my father.

ANNE   Was he mad, sir?

SANDS   O, very mad, exceeding mad, in love too:

But he would bite none: just as I do now,

35   He would kiss you twenty with a breath.   *He kisses her*

CHAMBERLAIN   Well said, my lord.

So now you're fairly seated: gentlemen,

The penance lies on you, if these fair ladies

Pass away frowning.

---

13 **running banquet** hasty meal/rewarding sexual pursuit or sex itself   15 **society** group
16 **confessor** plays on the sense of "sexual partner"   19 **easy penance** with sexual
connotations   21 **down** feather   23 **Place you** you arrange the seating   25 **cold** plays on
the sense of "sexually unresponsive"   26 **waking** awake, lively (with suggestion of sexual
activity)   29 **thank** I thank   30 **wild** erratically, madly/recklessly, excitably/lustfully
32 **mad** insane/uncontrollable, high-spirited   34 **bite** biting was thought to be a common
trait of madmen   35 **twenty** i.e. twenty ladies   **with a breath** in one breath, in a very short
space of time   36 **said** done   37 **fairly** properly/favorably/fully   39 **Pass away** leave

40 SANDS　For my little cure,
　　　　Let me alone.

Hautboys. Enter Cardinal Wolsey, and takes his state

CARDINAL WOLSEY　You're welcome, my fair guests: that noble
　　　　lady
　　　　Or gentleman that is not freely merry,
　　　　Is not my friend. This, to confirm my welcome,
45　　　And to you all, good health.　　　　　　　*He drinks*

SANDS　Your grace is noble:
　　　　Let me have such a bowl may hold my thanks,
　　　　And save me so much talking.

CARDINAL WOLSEY　My lord Sands,
50　　　I am beholding to you: cheer your neighbours:
　　　　Ladies, you are not merry: gentlemen,
　　　　Whose fault is this?

SANDS　The red wine first must rise
　　　　In their fair cheeks, my lord, then we shall have 'em
55　　　Talk us to silence.

ANNE　You are a merry gamester,
　　　　My lord Sands.

SANDS　Yes, if I make my play:
　　　　Here's to your ladyship: and pledge it, madam,
60　　　For 'tis to such a thing—

ANNE　You cannot show me.

SANDS　I told your grace they would talk anon.

Drum and Trumpet: chambers discharged

CARDINAL WOLSEY　What's that?

CHAMBERLAIN　Look out there, some of ye.　　　*To Servants*

65　CARDINAL WOLSEY　What warlike voice,　　　*Exit Servants*
　　　　And to what end is this? Nay, ladies, fear not:
　　　　By all the laws of war you're privileged.

Enter a Servant

---

40 For as for　**cure** spiritual duty/remedy (for frowning)/sexual remedy　**41 Let me alone**
leave it to me　**47 bowl** i.e. full of wine　**may** as may　**50 beholding** beholden, indebted
cheer entertain/encourage/cheer up　**56 gamester** sporting, fun-loving person/gambler/one
fond of sex　**58 make my play** score (in cards/in love)　**59 pledge it** drink to my toast
60 thing plays on the sense of "penis"　**62 anon** soon　*chambers* small cannon　**65 voice**
i.e. noise　**67 privileged** protected

CHAMBERLAIN How now, what is't?

SERVANT   A noble troop of strangers,
70   For so they seem: they've left their barge and landed,
    And hither make, as great ambassadors
    From foreign princes.

CARDINAL WOLSEY   Good Lord Chamberlain,
    Go, give 'em welcome: you can speak the French tongue:
75   And pray receive 'em nobly, and conduct 'em
    Into our presence, where this heaven of beauty
    Shall shine at full upon them. Some attend him.

                [*Exit Chamberlain, attended*]
All rise, and tables removed
    You have now a broken banquet, but we'll mend it.
    A good digestion to you all: and once more
80   I shower a welcome on ye: welcome all.
Hautboys. Enter King [Henry] and others as Masquers, habited like
shepherds, ushered by the Lord Chamberlain. They pass directly before
the Cardinal, and gracefully salute him
    A noble company: what are their pleasures?

CHAMBERLAIN   Because they speak no English, thus they prayed
    To tell your grace: that having heard by fame
    Of this so noble and so fair assembly
85   This night to meet here, they could do no less,
    Out of the great respect they bear to beauty,
    But leave their flocks, and under your fair conduct,
    Crave leave to view these ladies, and entreat
    An hour of revels with 'em.
90   CARDINAL WOLSEY   Say, Lord Chamberlain,
    They have done my poor house grace; for which I pay 'em
    A thousand thanks, and pray 'em take their pleasures.
[The Masquers] choose Ladies [for the dance]. [The] King [chooses]
Anne Bullen

---

69 strangers foreigners   **71 make** make their way   **76 heaven of beauty** i.e. gathering of
beautiful ladies   **78 broken** disrupted   **80 *Masquers*** costumed nobles taking part in a
courtly entertainment involving dancing   ***habited*** dressed   **81 pleasures** wills, desires
83 fame report, rumor   **87 conduct** guidance, permission   **89 revels** merriment/courtly
entertainment

KING HENRY VIII   The fairest hand I ever touched. O beauty,
Till now I never knew thee!   *Music. [They] dance*

95 CARDINAL WOLSEY   My lord.

CHAMBERLAIN   Your grace?

CARDINAL WOLSEY   Pray, tell 'em thus much from me:
There should be one amongst 'em, by his person,
More worthy this place than myself, to whom,
100 If I but knew him, with my love and duty
I would surrender it.

CHAMBERLAIN   I will, my lord.

[He talks in a] whisper [to the Masquers]

CARDINAL WOLSEY   What say they?

CHAMBERLAIN   Such a one, they all confess,
105 There is indeed, which they would have your grace
Find out, and he will take it.

CARDINAL WOLSEY   Let me see, then.
By all your good leaves, gentlemen, here I'll make
My royal choice.

110 KING HENRY VIII   Ye have found him, cardinal: *He unmasks*
You hold a fair assembly: you do well, lord.
You are a churchman, or I'll tell you, cardinal,
I should judge now unhappily.

CARDINAL WOLSEY   I am glad
115 Your grace is grown so pleasant.

KING HENRY VIII   My Lord Chamberlain,
Prithee come hither: what fair lady's that?

CHAMBERLAIN   An't please your grace, Sir Thomas Bullen's
daughter —
The Viscount Rochford — one of her highness' women.

120 KING HENRY VIII   By heaven, she is a dainty one.—
Sweetheart,   *To Anne*
I were unmannerly to take you out

---

99 this place i.e. the chair of state   **100 but** only   **106 it** i.e. the chair of state   **111 fair** fine/
virtuous/beautiful   **112 You . . . unhappily** i.e. if you were not a rightfully minded clergyman,
I should look unfavorably upon this gathering of beautiful women   **115 pleasant** merry
117 Prithee please (literally "I pray thee")   **118 An't** if it   **119 her highness' women** i.e.
lady-in-waiting to Queen Katherine   **120 dainty** delicately pretty   **121 take you out** i.e. to
dance

And not to kiss you. A health, gentlemen: *He drinks*
Let it go round.

CARDINAL WOLSEY   Sir Thomas Lovell, is the banquet ready
125   I'th'privy chamber?

LOVELL   Yes, my lord.

CARDINAL WOLSEY   Your grace,   *To the King*
I fear, with dancing is a little heated.

KING HENRY VIII   I fear too much.

130   CARDINAL WOLSEY   There's fresher air, my lord,
In the next chamber.

KING HENRY VIII   Lead in your ladies, ev'ry one: sweet
partner,   *To Anne*
I must not yet forsake you:— let's be merry,   *To Cardinal Wolsey*
Good my lord cardinal: I have half a dozen healths
135   To drink to these fair ladies, and a measure
To lead 'em once again, and then let's dream
Who's best in favour. Let the music knock it.

Exeunt with Trumpets

Act 2 Scene 1   *running scene 4*

Enter two Gentlemen at several doors

FIRST GENTLEMAN   Whither away so fast?

SECOND GENTLEMAN   O, God save ye:
Ev'n to the hall, to hear what shall become
Of the great Duke of Buckingham.

5   FIRST GENTLEMAN   I'll save you
That labour, sir. All's now done but the ceremony
Of bringing back the prisoner.

SECOND GENTLEMAN   Were you there?

FIRST GENTLEMAN   Yes, indeed was I.

---

122 **health** toast   124 **banquet** separate course of sweetmeats after the main feast, served in a different room   125 **I'th'privy chamber** i.e. in a private inner room   128 **heated** hot, but in his reply Henry plays on the sense of "lustful, hot-blooded"   133 **forsake** leave, give up   135 **measure** slow stately dance   136 **dream** focus on/conjecture   137 **best in favour** best-looking/most popular with the ladies   **knock it** strike up   **2.1** *Location: a street in Westminster, London*   **several** separate   3 **hall** i.e. Westminster Hall

10   SECOND GENTLEMAN   Pray speak what has happened.

FIRST GENTLEMAN   You may guess quickly what.

SECOND GENTLEMAN   Is he found guilty?

FIRST GENTLEMAN   Yes, truly is he, and condemned upon't.

SECOND GENTLEMAN   I am sorry for't.

15   FIRST GENTLEMAN   So are a number more.

SECOND GENTLEMAN   But pray, how passed it?

FIRST GENTLEMAN   I'll tell you in a little. The great duke
Came to the bar, where to his accusations
He pleaded still not guilty, and alleged
20   Many sharp reasons to defeat the law.
The king's attorney, on the contrary,
Urged on the examinations, proofs, confessions
Of divers witnesses, which the duke desired
To him brought *viva voce* to his face:
25   At which appeared against him his surveyor,
Sir Gilbert Perk his chancellor, and John Car,
Confessor to him, with that devil monk,
Hopkins, that made this mischief.

SECOND GENTLEMAN   That was he
30   That fed him with his prophecies.

FIRST GENTLEMAN   The same:
All these accused him strongly, which he fain
Would have flung from him, but indeed he could not:
And so his peers, upon this evidence,
35   Have found him guilty of high treason. Much
He spoke, and learnedly, for life, but all
Was either pitied in him or forgotten.

SECOND GENTLEMAN   After all this, how did he bear himself?

FIRST GENTLEMAN   When he was brought again to th'bar, to hear
40   His knell rung out, his judgement, he was stirred
With such an agony, he sweat extremely,

---

16 passed it did the trial proceed   **17 a little** brief   **18 to his accusations** in response to the accusations brought against him   **19 still** consistently   **alleged** brought forward   **20 law** i.e. case against him   **22 examinations** testimonies, statements   **proofs** evidence   **23 divers** various, several   **24 him brought** i.e. have brought to him   *viva voce* "in person, in live speech" (Latin)   **32 fain** gladly   **37 pitied in him** i.e. prompted useless pity   **forgotten** i.e. was ineffectual   **40 knell** funeral bell, i.e. death sentence   **41 sweat** sweated

And something spoke in choler, ill and hasty:
But he fell to himself again, and sweetly
In all the rest showed a most noble patience.

45 SECOND GENTLEMAN   I do not think he fears death.

FIRST GENTLEMAN   Sure he does not:
He never was so womanish: the cause
He may a little grieve at.

SECOND GENTLEMAN   Certainly
50   The cardinal is the end of this.

FIRST GENTLEMAN   'Tis likely
By all conjectures: first, Kildare's attainder,
Then deputy of Ireland, who, removed,
Earl Surrey was sent thither, and in haste too,
55   Lest he should help his father.

SECOND GENTLEMAN   That trick of state
Was a deep envious one.

FIRST GENTLEMAN   At his return
No doubt he will requite it: this is noted,
60   And generally, whoever the king favours,
The card'nal instantly will find employment,
And far enough from court too.

SECOND GENTLEMAN   All the commons
Hate him perniciously and, o'my conscience,
65   Wish him ten fathom deep: this duke as much
They love and dote on, call him 'bounteous Buckingham,
The mirror of all courtesy'—

Enter Buckingham from his arraignment, Tipstaves before him, the axe
with the edge towards him, Halberds on each side, accompanied with
Sir Thomas Lovell, Sir Nicholas Vaux, Sir William Sands, and Common
People etc.

---

42 choler anger   **ill** unfavorable/wicked/bitter   **43 fell to** recovered   **50 end** root, bottom
52 Kildare's attainder the accusation and disgrace of the Earl of Kildare; he was imprisoned on
a number of charges and his role as Lord Deputy in Ireland was given to the **Earl of Surrey,**
Buckingham's son-in-law   **53 deputy** governor   **55 father** father-in-law   **56 trick of state**
political contrivance   **57 envious** malicious   **58 his** i.e. Surrey's   **59 requite** avenge, repay
60 generally universally, by all   **64 perniciously** deeply, desiring his death or ruin   **67 mirror**
image, model   **Tipstaves** court officers, named after their badge of office, a metal-tipped staff
axe . . . him signifying that the prisoner had been condemned to death   **Halberds** i.e. halberdiers,
carrying long-handled weapons topped with a combination of spearhead and axe blade

FIRST GENTLEMAN   Stay there, sir,
And see the noble ruined man you speak of.

70   SECOND GENTLEMAN   Let's stand close and behold him.

BUCKINGHAM   All good people,
You that thus far have come to pity me:
Hear what I say, and then go home and lose me.
I have this day received a traitor's judgement,

75   And by that name must die: yet heaven bear witness,
And if I have a conscience, let it sink me,
Even as the axe falls, if I be not faithful.
The law I bear no malice for my death,
'T has done upon the premises, but justice:

80   But those that sought it I could wish more Christians:
Be what they will, I heartily forgive 'em:
Yet let 'em look they glory not in mischief,
Nor build their evils on the graves of great men,
For then my guiltless blood must cry against 'em.

85   For further life in this world I ne'er hope,
Nor will I sue, although the king have mercies
More than I dare make faults. You few that loved me,
And dare be bold to weep for Buckingham,
His noble friends and fellows, whom to leave

90   Is only bitter to him, only dying:
Go with me like good angels to my end,
And as the long divorce of steel falls on me,
Make of your prayers one sweet sacrifice,
And lift my soul to heaven.— Lead on, i'God's name.   *To Lovell*

95   LOVELL   I do beseech your grace, for charity,
If ever any malice in your heart
Were hid against me, now to forgive me frankly.

BUCKINGHAM   Sir Thomas Lovell, I as free forgive you
As I would be forgiven: I forgive all.

---

70 close out of sight/quietly   **73 lose** forget   **74 judgement** sentence   **76 sink** ruin/damn
79 premises evidence (submitted in court)   **80 more** better   **82 look** beware, watch out
83 evils wrongdoings, evil careers/hovels or privies   **86 sue** plead   **87 More . . . faults** i.e.
much greater than the magnitude of offense I would dare to commit   **90 only . . . dying** the
only thing that is bitter to him, the only real death he experiences   **92 divorce of steel** i.e.
separation of body and soul by the axe   **93 sacrifice** offering

100 There cannot be those numberless offences
Gainst me that I cannot take peace with: no black envy
Shall make my grave. Commend me to his grace:
And if he speak of Buckingham, pray tell him
You met him half in heaven: my vows and prayers
105 Yet are the king's, and, till my soul forsake,
Shall cry for blessings on him. May he live
Longer than I have time to tell his years:
Ever beloved and loving may his rule be:
And when old time shall lead him to his end,
110 Goodness and he fill up one monument.

LOVELL   To th'water-side I must conduct your grace,
Then give my charge up to Sir Nicholas Vaux,
Who undertakes you to your end.

VAUX   Prepare there,
115 The duke is coming: see the barge be ready,
And fit it with such furniture as suits
The greatness of his person.

BUCKINGHAM   Nay, Sir Nicholas,
Let it alone: my state now will but mock me.
120 When I came hither, I was Lord High Constable
And Duke of Buckingham: now, poor Edward Bohun:
Yet I am richer than my base accusers,
That never knew what truth meant. I now seal it,
And with that blood will make 'em one day groan for't.
125 My noble father, Henry of Buckingham,
Who first raised head against usurping Richard,
Flying for succour to his servant Banister,
Being distressed, was by that wretch betrayed,
And without trial fell: God's peace be with him.
130 Henry the Seventh succeeding, truly pitying
My father's loss, like a most royal prince,

---

101 take make   envy malice   105 Yet still   forsake leaves (my body)   107 tell count
109 old time perhaps a personification here   110 monument tomb   112 charge duty, role
113 undertakes takes responsibility for   116 furniture furnishings, equipment   119 state
rank   122 base dishonorable, unworthy/low-born   123 truth loyalty/honesty   seal
confirm, ratify   126 head an army   Richard i.e. Richard III

Restored me to my honours, and out of ruins
Made my name once more noble. Now his son,
Henry the Eighth, life, honour, name and all
135   That made me happy, at one stroke has taken
For ever from the world. I had my trial,
And must needs say a noble one, which makes me
A little happier than my wretched father:
Yet thus far we are one in fortunes: both
140   Fell by our servants, by those men we loved most:
A most unnatural and faithless service.
Heaven has an end in all: yet, you that hear me,
This from a dying man receive as certain:
Where you are liberal of your loves and counsels,
145   Be sure you be not loose: for those you make friends
And give your hearts to, when they once perceive
The least rub in your fortunes, fall away
Like water from ye, never found again
But where they mean to sink ye. All good people,
150   Pray for me. I must now forsake ye: the last hour
Of my long weary life is come upon me. Farewell:
And when you would say something that is sad,
Speak how I fell. I have done, and God forgive me.

Exeunt Duke and train

FIRST GENTLEMAN   O, this is full of pity. Sir, it calls,
155   I fear, too many curses on their heads
That were the authors.
SECOND GENTLEMAN   If the duke be guiltless,
'Tis full of woe: yet I can give you inkling
Of an ensuing evil, if it fall,
160   Greater than this.
FIRST GENTLEMAN   Good angels keep it from us.
What may it be? You do not doubt my faith, sir?

---

135 **stroke** action/executioner's blow   138 **happier** more fortunate   142 **end** purpose
143 **from . . . certain** the words of a dying man were considered especially wise or prophetic
144 **liberal of** generous with   145 **loose** careless   147 **rub** obstacle (bowling term)
149 **But** except   156 **authors** originators, causes   159 **fall** happens   162 **faith** reliability, trustworthiness

SECOND GENTLEMAN   This secret is so weighty, 'twill require
A strong faith to conceal it.

165   FIRST GENTLEMAN   Let me have it:
I do not talk much.

SECOND GENTLEMAN   I am confident:
You shall, sir: did you not of late days hear
A buzzing of a separation

170   Between the king and Katherine?

FIRST GENTLEMAN   Yes, but it held not:
For when the king once heard it, out of anger
He sent command to the Lord Mayor straight
To stop the rumour, and allay those tongues

175   That durst disperse it.

SECOND GENTLEMAN   But that slander, sir,
Is found a truth now: for it grows again
Fresher than e'er it was, and held for certain
The king will venture at it. Either the cardinal,

180   Or some about him near, have, out of malice
To the good queen, possessed him with a scruple
That will undo her: to confirm this too,
Cardinal Campeius is arrived, and lately,
As all think, for this business.

185   FIRST GENTLEMAN   'Tis the cardinal:
And merely to revenge him on the emperor
For not bestowing on him at his asking
The archbishopric of Toledo, this is purposed.

SECOND GENTLEMAN   I think you have hit the mark: but is't not
cruel

---

167 am confident i.e. trust you   168 shall i.e. shall **have it**   **late** recent   169 **buzzing** rumor
171 **held not** did not stand firm, did not last   173 **straight** straight away   174 **allay** subdue,
silence   178 **held for** it is thought   179 **venture at it** risk acting on it   180 **about him near**
who are close to him   181 **possessed . . . scruple** put a doubt into his mind (perhaps with
connotations of demonic possession; the doubt is that Henry's marriage is invalid because
Katherine had originally been married to his older brother Arthur; marrying one's brother's
widow is prohibited in Leviticus 20:21)   183 **Cardinal Campeius** the Pope's legate sent from
Rome to determine the legality of the king's marriage   186 **emperor** Holy Roman Emperor,
Charles V, Queen Katherine's nephew   188 **purposed** intended, planned   189 **have . . .
mark** i.e. are accurate   **mark** target (in archery)

190   That she should feel the smart of this? The cardinal
         Will have his will, and she must fall.

FIRST GENTLEMAN   'Tis woeful.
         We are too open here to argue this:
         Let's think in private more.   *Exeunt*

Act 2 Scene 2   *running scene 5*

Enter Lord Chamberlain, reading this letter

CHAMBERLAIN   'My lord, the horses your lordship sent for, with
   all the care I had, I saw well chosen, ridden and furnished.
   They were young and handsome, and of the best breed in the
   north. When they were ready to set out for London, a man of
5 my lord cardinal's, by commission and main power, took 'em
   from me, with this reason: his master would be served before
   a subject, if not before the king, which stopped our mouths,
   sir.' I fear he will indeed: well, let him have them: he will have
   all, I think.

Enter to the Lord Chamberlain the Dukes of Norfolk and Suffolk

10 NORFOLK   Well met, my Lord Chamberlain.

CHAMBERLAIN   Good day to both your graces.

SUFFOLK   How is the king employed?

CHAMBERLAIN   I left him private,
         Full of sad thoughts and troubles.

15 NORFOLK   What's the cause?

CHAMBERLAIN   It seems the marriage with his brother's wife
         Has crept too near his conscience.

SUFFOLK   No, his conscience
         Has crept too near another lady.

20 NORFOLK   'Tis so:
         This is the cardinal's doing: the king-cardinal,

---

190 smart pain   193 open exposed, public   **2.2   *Location: the royal court, London***
2 ridden broken in   furnished equipped   5 commission warrant   main considerable
13 private on his own   14 sad serious   18 conscience Suffolk plays on the sexual sense of
"genital expansiveness"

That blind priest, like the eldest son of fortune,
Turns what he list. The king will know him one day.

SUFFOLK   Pray God he do: he'll never know himself else.

25 NORFOLK   How holily he works in all his business,
And with what zeal! For now he has cracked the league
Between us and the emperor, the queen's great-nephew,
He dives into the king's soul, and there scatters
Dangers, doubts, wringing of the conscience,
30 Fears, and despairs, and all these for his marriage.
And out of all these, to restore the king,
He counsels a divorce, a loss of her
That like a jewel has hung twenty years
About his neck, yet never lost her lustre:
35 Of her that loves him with that excellence
That angels love good men with: even of her
That when the greatest stroke of fortune falls
Will bless the king: and is not this course pious?

CHAMBERLAIN   Heaven keep me from such counsel: 'tis most true
40 These news are everywhere, every tongue speaks 'em,
And every true heart weeps for't. All that dare
Look into these affairs see this main end:
The French king's sister. Heaven will one day open
The king's eyes, that so long have slept upon
45 This bold bad man.

SUFFOLK   And free us from his slavery.

NORFOLK   We had need pray,
And heartily, for our deliverance,
Or this imperious man will work us all
50 From princes into pages: all men's honours
Lie like one lump before him, to be fashioned
Into what pitch he please.

---

22 **blind** without regard for others; **fortune** was commonly depicted as a blind woman who
turns the wheel of people's fortunes   23 **list** pleases   **know** understand, recognize   25 **he**
i.e. Wolsey   42 **end** purpose/outcome   43 **French king's sister** the Duchess of Alençon,
suggested by Wolsey as a second wife for Henry   44 **slept upon** failed to notice, not perceived
truly   45 **bold** daring, overconfident   51 **lump** probably lump of clay   52 **pitch** height, i.e.
stature

SUFFOLK   For me, my lords,
I love him not, nor fear him: there's my creed:
55   As I am made without him, so I'll stand,
If the king please: his curses and his blessings
Touch me alike: they're breath I not believe in.
I knew him, and I know him: so I leave him
To him that made him proud: the Pope.

60   NORFOLK   Let's in,
And with some other business put the king
From these sad thoughts, that work too much upon him:
My lord, you'll bear us company?

CHAMBERLAIN   Excuse me,
65   The king has sent me otherwhere: besides,
You'll find a most unfit time to disturb him:
Health to your lordships.

NORFOLK   Thanks, my good Lord Chamberlain.

*Exit Lord Chamberlain, and the King [Henry] draws the curtain and
sits reading pensively*

SUFFOLK   How sad he looks: sure, he is much afflicted.

70   KING HENRY VIII   Who's there? Ha?

NORFOLK   Pray God he be not angry.

KING HENRY VIII   Who's there, I say? How dare you thrust
yourselves
Into my private meditations?
Who am I? Ha?

75   NORFOLK   A gracious king that pardons all offences
Malice ne'er meant: our breach of duty this way
Is business of estate, in which we come
To know your royal pleasure.

KING HENRY VIII   Ye are too bold:
80   Go to: I'll make ye know your times of business:
Is this an hour for temporal affairs? Ha?

---

53 For as for   55 made i.e. successful, of noble rank   stand remain, stand firm   57 breath
i.e. mere words   65 otherwhere elsewhere   68 *curtain* separating the main stage from the
discovery space or recess at the back of the stage   76 this way in this respect   77 estate state
80 Go to expression of impatient dismissal   81 temporal worldly, secular

Enter [Cardinal] Wolsey and [Cardinal] Campeius with a commission
    Who's there? My good lord cardinal? O my Wolsey,
    The quiet of my wounded conscience:
    Thou art a cure fit for a king.— You're welcome,   *To Cardinal*
85   Most learnèd reverend sir, into our kingdom: *Campeius*
    Use us and it.— My good lord, have great care   *To Cardinal*
    I be not found a talker.   *Wolsey*
CARDINAL WOLSEY   Sir, you cannot:
    I would your grace would give us but an hour
90   Of private conference.
KING HENRY VIII   We are busy: go.   *To Norfolk and Suffolk*
NORFOLK   This priest has no pride in him?   *Norfolk and Suffolk speak*
SUFFOLK   Not to speak of: *aside*
    I would not be so sick though for his place:
95   But this cannot continue.
NORFOLK   If it do,
    I'll venture one have-at-him.
SUFFOLK   I another.   *Exeunt Norfolk and Suffolk*
CARDINAL WOLSEY   Your grace has given a precedent of wisdom
100   Above all princes, in committing freely
    Your scruple to the voice of Christendom:
    Who can be angry now? What envy reach you?
    The Spaniard, tied by blood and favour to her,
    Must now confess, if they have any goodness,
105   The trial just and noble. All the clerks,
    I mean the learnèd ones in Christian kingdoms,
    Have their free voices. Rome, the nurse of judgement,
    Invited by your noble self, hath sent
    One general tongue unto us: this good man,

---

commission warrant (from the Pope)   **83 quiet** calm   **84 cure** physical remedy (but with connotations of spiritual care)   **87 talker** i.e. man of words rather than action   **92 priest** i.e. Wolsey   **94 sick** envious   **97 have-at-him** thrust, attack (fencing term)   **99 precedent** example   **101 scruple** doubt   **voice of Christendom** i.e. the Pope and the various clergymen who were consulted over Henry's problem of conscience   **102 envy** malice   **103 Spaniard** i.e. Charles V (Katherine's nephew), or the Spanish in general   **her** i.e. Queen Katherine   **104 confess** admit, allow   **105 clerks** scholars   **107 Have . . . voices** may vote as they please   **109 general tongue** i.e. representative spokesperson

110   This just and learnèd priest, Card'nal Campeius,
       Whom once more I present unto your highness.
   KING HENRY VIII   And once more in mine arms I bid him welcome,
       And thank the holy conclave for their loves:
       They have sent me such a man I would have wished for.
115 CARDINAL CAMPEIUS   Your grace must needs deserve all
           strangers' loves,
       You are so noble: to your highness' hand
       I tender my commission, by whose virtue,
       The court of Rome commanding, you my lord
       Cardinal of York, are joined with me their servant
120   In the unpartial judging of this business.
   KING HENRY VIII   Two equal men: the queen shall be acquainted
       Forthwith for what you come. Where's Gardiner?
   CARDINAL WOLSEY   I know your majesty has always loved her
       So dear in heart, not to deny her that
125   A woman of less place might ask by law:
       Scholars allowed freely to argue for her.
   KING HENRY VIII   Ay, and the best she shall have, and my favour
       To him that does best, God forbid else. Cardinal,
       Prithee call Gardiner to me, my new secretary.
130   I find him a fit fellow.   *Cardinal Wolsey calls Gardiner*
   Enter Gardiner
   CARDINAL WOLSEY   Give me your hand: much joy and favour to
           you;
       You are the king's now.   *Aside to Gardiner*
   GARDINER   But to be commanded   *Aside to Wolsey*
       For ever by your grace, whose hand has raised me.
135 KING HENRY VIII   Come hither, Gardiner.
       [*The King*] *walks and whispers* [*with Gardiner*]
   CARDINAL CAMPEIUS   My lord of York, was not one Doctor Pace
       In this man's place before him?

---

113 **conclave** body of cardinals (in Rome)   115 **strangers** foreigners   117 **tender** submit
virtue power   120 **unpartial** impartial   124 **that** that which   125 **place** rank   130 **fit**
suitable, able

CARDINAL WOLSEY   Yes, he was.

CARDINAL CAMPEIUS   Was he not held a learnèd man?

140   CARDINAL WOLSEY   Yes, surely.

CARDINAL CAMPEIUS   Believe me, there's an ill opinion spread
then,
Even of yourself, lord cardinal.

CARDINAL WOLSEY   How? Of me?

CARDINAL CAMPEIUS   They will not stick to say you envied him,

145   And fearing he would rise, he was so virtuous,
Kept him a foreign man still, which so grieved him,
That he ran mad and died.

CARDINAL WOLSEY   Heav'n's peace be with him:
That's Christian care enough: for living murmurers

150   There's places of rebuke. He was a fool,
For he would needs be virtuous. That good fellow,
If I command him, follows my appointment:
I will have none so near else. Learn this, brother,
We live not to be griped by meaner persons.

155   KING HENRY VIII   Deliver this with modesty to th'queen.   *To Gardiner*

Exit Gardiner

The most convenient place that I can think of
For such receipt of learning is Blackfriars:
There ye shall meet about this weighty business.
My Wolsey, see it furnished. O, my lord,

160   Would it not grieve an able man to leave
So sweet a bedfellow? But, conscience, conscience:
O, 'tis a tender place, and I must leave her.   *Exeunt*

---

144 stick hesitate   **146 Kept . . . still** i.e. always had him traveling abroad (on diplomatic missions)   **149 murmurers** gossips, rumormongers/troublemakers   **152 appointment** order   **153 none . . . else** i.e. no one else so close to the king   **154 griped** seized, clutched at   **meaner** lower ranking   **155 Deliver** tell, report   **modesty** propriety/consideration   **157 For . . . learning** to receive, play host to such a learned discussion   **Blackfriars** Dominican monastery in London   **159 furnished** equipped   **160 able** (sexually) vigorous   **161 bedfellow** i.e. Katherine   **conscience** perhaps playing on "con-science" meaning "knowledge of the vagina" (i.e. Anne Bullen's)

Act 2 Scene 3   *running scene 6*

Enter Anne Bullen and an Old Lady

ANNE   Not for that neither: here's the pang that pinches:
His highness having lived so long with her, and she
So good a lady that no tongue could ever
Pronounce dishonour of her — by my life,
5   She never knew harm-doing — O, now, after
So many courses of the sun enthroned,
Still growing in a majesty and pomp, the which
To leave a thousandfold more bitter than
'Tis sweet at first to acquire — after this process,
10   To give her the avaunt, it is a pity
Would move a monster.

OLD LADY   Hearts of most hard temper
Melt and lament for her.

ANNE   O, God's will! Much better
15   She ne'er had known pomp: though't be temporal,
Yet, if that quarrel, fortune, do divorce
It from the bearer, 'tis a sufferance panging
As soul and body's severing.

OLD LADY   Alas, poor lady,
20   She's a stranger now again.

ANNE   So much the more
Must pity drop upon her: verily,
I swear, 'tis better to be lowly born,
And range with humble livers in content,
25   Than to be perked up in a glist'ring grief,
And wear a golden sorrow.

OLD LADY   Our content
Is our best having.

2.3   1 Not . . . neither Anne and the Old Lady enter mid-conversation   pinches torments
4 Pronounce declare/utter   6 courses . . . sun i.e. years   9 process course (of events)
10 avaunt order to be gone   pity pity-provoking situation   12 temper substance,
hardness/disposition   15 temporal worldly (rather than heavenly)   16 quarrel quarreler
17 sufferance panging hardship as tormenting   20 stranger outsider/foreigner   24 range
roam/live/be ranked   humble livers those of low rank   25 perked up decked out   glist'ring
glittering, sparkling   28 having possession

ANNE   By my troth and maidenhead,
30   I would not be a queen.

OLD LADY   Beshrew me, I would,
And venture maidenhead for't, and so would you,
For all this spice of your hypocrisy:
You, that have so fair parts of woman on you,
35   Have, too, a woman's heart, which ever yet
Affected eminence, wealth, sovereignty:
Which, to say sooth, are blessings: and which gifts,
Saving your mincing, the capacity
Of your soft cheverel conscience would receive,
40   If you might please to stretch it.

ANNE   Nay, good troth.

OLD LADY   Yes, troth and troth: you would not be a queen?

ANNE   No, not for all the riches under heaven.

OLD LADY   'Tis strange: a three-pence bowed would hire me,
45   Old as I am, to queen it: but, I pray you,
What think you of a duchess? Have you limbs
To bear that load of title?

ANNE   No, in truth.

OLD LADY   Then you are weakly made: pluck off a little:
50   I would not be a young count in your way,
For more than blushing comes to: if your back
Cannot vouchsafe this burden, 'tis too weak
Ever to get a boy.

ANNE   How you do talk!
55   I swear again, I would not be a queen
For all the world.

---

29 troth faith   maidenhead virginity   31 Beshrew curse   33 spice dash, touch   34 so
fair parts such beauty/such good qualities   36 Affected likes, is drawn to   37 sooth truth
38 Saving despite   mincing pretentious manner, affectations   39 cheverel kid leather (noted
for its softness)   41 troth truth, faith   44 bowed bent, i.e. worthless (puns on "bawd")
45 queen it play the queen; puns on "quean" meaning "prostitute"   47 bear endure/support
during sex/give birth to   load of title title of duchess/duke himself/duke's child   49 pluck off
come down (in aspiration; literally "undress")   50 count i.e. rank lower than a duke; puns on
"cunt"   way path/condition (of being a virgin)   51 For . . . to i.e. on account of sexual
modesty   52 vouchsafe permit, accept   burden i.e. of a man's body during sex   53 get
beget, conceive

OLD LADY   In faith, for little England
   You'd venture an emballing: I myself
   Would for Caernarvonshire, although there longed
60   No more to th'crown but that. Lo, who comes here?

Enter Lord Chamberlain

CHAMBERLAIN   Good morrow, ladies: what were't worth to know
   The secret of your conference?

ANNE   My good lord,
   Not your demand: it values not your asking:
65   Our mistress' sorrows we were pitying.

CHAMBERLAIN   It was a gentle business, and becoming
   The action of good women: there is hope
   All will be well.

ANNE   Now I pray God, amen.

70   CHAMBERLAIN   You bear a gentle mind, and heav'nly blessings
   Follow such creatures. That you may, fair lady,
   Perceive I speak sincerely, and high note's
   Ta'en of your many virtues: the king's majesty
   Commends his good opinion of you, and
75   Does purpose honour to you no less flowing
   Than Marchioness of Pembroke: to which title
   A thousand pound a year, annual support,
   Out of his grace he adds.

ANNE   I do not know
80   What kind of my obedience I should tender:
   More than my all is nothing: nor my prayers
   Are not words duly hallowed, nor my wishes
   More worth than empty vanities: yet prayers and wishes
   Are all I can return. Beseech your lordship,

---

57 little England affectionate term for England itself/Pembrokeshire, south Wales, where most people spoke English rather than Welsh/Westminster Hall   **58 emballing** to be invested with the orb of sovereignty (as queen)/sexual intercourse   **59 Caernarvonshire** a poor rural county in north Wales   **longed** belonged   **62 conference** conversation   **64 values not** is not worth   **66 gentle** noble/kind   **74 Commends** declares, offers   **75 purpose** intend   **78 grace** favor   **80 kind** manifestation   **tender** offer (in return)   **81 More . . . nothing** more than all I am able to offer is still insufficient (**nothing** may pick up on the sense of "vagina," which is of course what Anne is required to supply)   **82 hallowed** blessed, sanctified   **83 More** of more

85   Vouchsafe to speak my thanks and my obedience,
    As from a blushing handmaid to his highness,
    Whose health and royalty I pray for.

CHAMBERLAIN   Lady,
    I shall not fail t'approve the fair conceit
90   The king hath of you.— I have perused her well: *Aside*
    Beauty and honour in her are so mingled
    That they have caught the king: and who knows yet
    But from this lady may proceed a gem
    To lighten all this isle.— I'll to the king   *To Anne*
95   And say I spoke with you.

ANNE   My honoured lord.   *Exit Lord Chamberlain*

OLD LADY   Why, this it is: see, see!
    I have been begging sixteen years in court,
    Am yet a courtier beggarly, nor could
100   Come pat betwixt too early and too late
    For any suit of pounds, and you — O fate! —
    A very fresh fish here — fie, fie, fie upon
    This compelled fortune! — have your mouth filled up
    Before you open it.

105 ANNE   This is strange to me.

OLD LADY   How tastes it? Is it bitter? Forty pence, no:
    There was a lady once, 'tis an old story,
    That would not be a queen, that would she not
    For all the mud in Egypt: have you heard it?

110 ANNE   Come, you are pleasant.

OLD LADY   With your theme, I could
    O'ermount the lark. The Marchioness of Pembroke?

---

85 **Vouchsafe** agree   89 **t'approve** to corroborate, confirm   **conceit** opinion, notion
90 **perused** observed, examined   93 **gem** i.e. an heir (anticipating Elizabeth's birth)
94 **lighten** illuminate (some jewels were thought to emit light)   99 **beggarly** still poor
100 **Come . . . late** i.e. ask at the appropriate time   **pat** neatly   101 **suit of pounds** request
for money   **pound** plays on the sense of rags/(fish) ponds   102 **fresh** young/blooming   **fish**
woman/whore   **fie** expression of reproach   103 **compelled** enforced/unsought   **have . . .**
it i.e. to get plenty without even needing to ask (probably also refers to oral sex)   105 **strange**
odd, incomprehensible/new, unfamiliar   106 **tastes** probably continues to play on the idea of
oral sex   **Forty pence** i.e. I'll bet a small amount   108 **queen** continues to pun of "quean"
(i.e. prostitute)   109 **mud** i.e. wealth, since Egypt was known for its rich soil   110 **pleasant**
merry, joking   111 **your theme** your subject (i.e. the same advancement as you)
112 **O'ermount** rise higher than

A thousand pounds a year for pure respect?
No other obligation? By my life,

115   That promises more thousands: honour's train
Is longer than his foreskirt: by this time
I know your back will bear a duchess. Say,
Are you not stronger than you were?

ANNE   Good lady,

120   Make yourself mirth with your particular fancy,
And leave me out on't. Would I had no being
If this salute my blood a jot: it faints me,
To think what follows.
The queen is comfortless, and we forgetful

125   In our long absence: pray, do not deliver
What here you've heard to her.

OLD LADY   What do you think me?   *Exeunt*

Act 2 Scene 4   *running scene 7*

*Trumpets, sennet and cornets. Enter two Vergers, with short silver
wands; next them two Scribes in the habit of doctors [and a Crier]:
after them, the [Arch]bishop of Canterbury alone: after him, the
Bishops of Lincoln, Ely, Rochester and St Asaph: next them, with
some small distance, follows a Gentleman bearing the purse, with the
great seal, and a cardinal's hat: then two Priests, bearing each a silver
cross: then a Gentleman-usher bare-headed, accompanied with a
Sergeant-at-arms, bearing a silver mace: then two Gentlemen bearing
two great silver pillars: after them, side by side, the two Cardinals*

---

115 honour's . . . foreskirt i.e. more rewards will follow, just as the train of a dress is longer
than the front of the skirt (perhaps with some sexual suggestion of lifting one's skirt)
117 your . . . duchess i.e. you will marry a duke and bear his children   **120 particular fancy**
personal imaginings   **121 on't of** it   **122 salute** affects, excites   **blood** passions, spirits
(perhaps with play on "sexual desires")   **faints me** makes me faint   **125 deliver** report
2.4   *Location: Blackfriars (a Dominican monastery in London)*   sennet trumpet fanfare
signaling a procession   ***Vergers*** officials carrying rods of office who process in front of
Church dignitaries   ***habit of doctors*** academic robes worn by Doctors of Law, i.e. black
gowns and flat hats   ***St Asaph*** Llanelwy, an ancient bishopric in north Wales   ***purse*** it
contained the ***great seal*** of England, used by the king to authenticate documents; the Lord
Chancellor (Wolsey) was its official keeper   ***two . . . pillars*** like the **mace**, emblems of Wolsey's
role as cardinal

[Wolsey and Campeius], two Noblemen, with the sword and mace. The
King [Henry] takes place under the cloth of state. The two Cardinals sit
under him as judges. The Queen [Katherine, attended by Griffith] takes
place some distance from the King. The Bishops place themselves on
each side the court in manner of a consistory: below them, the Scribes.
The Lords sit next the Bishops. The rest of the Attendants stand in
convenient order about the stage

CARDINAL WOLSEY   Whilst our commission from Rome is read,
　　Let silence be commanded.

KING HENRY VIII   What's the need?
　　It hath already publicly been read,
5　　And on all sides th'authority allowed:
　　You may then spare that time.

CARDINAL WOLSEY   Be't so. Proceed.

SCRIBE   Say, 'Henry, King of England, come into the court.'

CRIER   Henry, King of England, come into the court.

10　KING HENRY VIII   Here.

SCRIBE   Say, 'Katherine, Queen of England, come into the
　　court.'

CRIER   Katherine, Queen of England, come into the court.
The Queen makes no answer, rises out of her chair, goes about the
court, comes to the King, and kneels at his feet: then speaks

QUEEN KATHERINE   Sir, I desire you do me right and justice,
15　And to bestow your pity on me, for
　　I am a most poor woman, and a stranger,
　　Born out of your dominions, having here
　　No judge indifferent, nor no more assurance
　　Of equal friendship and proceeding. Alas, sir,
20　In what have I offended you? What cause
　　Hath my behaviour given to your displeasure,
　　That thus you should proceed to put me off,
　　And take your good grace from me? Heaven witness,

---

cloth of state canopy over a throne   *consistory* ecclesiastical court   **5 th'authority allowed**
its authority recognized   **16 stranger** foreigner   **18 indifferent** impartial   **19 equal** fair
proceeding course of action/legal proceedings   **22 proceed . . . off** go about to dismiss me/
take legal action to discard me   **23 grace** favor/royal person

I have been to you a true and humble wife,
25   At all times to your will conformable,
Ever in fear to kindle your dislike,
Yea, subject to your countenance, glad or sorry,
As I saw it inclined. When was the hour
I ever contradicted your desire,
30   Or made it not mine too? Or which of your friends
Have I not strove to love, although I knew
He were mine enemy? What friend of mine,
That had to him derived your anger, did I
Continue in my liking? Nay, gave notice
35   He was from thence discharged? Sir, call to mind
That I have been your wife, in this obedience,
Upward of twenty years, and have been blessed
With many children by you. If, in the course
And process of this time, you can report,
40   And prove it too, against mine honour aught,
My bond to wedlock, or my love and duty
Against your sacred person, in God's name,
Turn me away, and let the foul'st contempt
Shut door upon me, and so give me up
45   To the sharp'st kind of justice. Please you, sir,
The king your father was reputed for
A prince most prudent, of an excellent
And unmatched wit and judgement. Ferdinand
My father, King of Spain, was reckoned one
50   The wisest prince that there had reigned by many
A year before. It is not to be questioned
That they had gathered a wise council to them
Of every realm, that did debate this business,
Who deemed our marriage lawful. Wherefore I humbly
55   Beseech you, sir, to spare me, till I may

25 **conformable** compliant, obedient   26 **dislike** displeasure   27 **countenance** facial
expression/favor/disposition   33 **to him derived** drawn upon himself   38 **many children**
Katherine had six children by Henry, of whom only one (Mary) survived infancy   40 **honour**
good name   **aught** anything   42 **Against** toward   48 **wit** wisdom   49 **one The wisest** the
very wisest   54 **Wherefore** for which reason

Be by my friends in Spain advised, whose counsel
I will implore. If not, i'th'name of God,
Your pleasure be fulfilled.

CARDINAL WOLSEY   You have here, lady,
60 And of your choice, these reverend fathers, men
Of singular integrity and learning,
Yea, the elect o'th'land, who are assembled
To plead your cause. It shall be therefore bootless
That longer you desire the court, as well
65 For your own quiet, as to rectify
What is unsettled in the king.

CARDINAL CAMPEIUS   His grace
Hath spoken well and justly: therefore, madam,
It's fit this royal session do proceed,
70 And that, without delay, their arguments
Be now produced and heard.

QUEEN KATHERINE   Lord cardinal,
To you I speak.

CARDINAL WOLSEY   Your pleasure, madam?

75 QUEEN KATHERINE   Sir,
I am about to weep: but, thinking that
We are a queen, or long have dreamed so, certain
The daughter of a king, my drops of tears
I'll turn to sparks of fire.

80 CARDINAL WOLSEY   Be patient yet.

QUEEN KATHERINE   I will, when you are humble: nay, before,
Or God will punish me. I do believe,
Induced by potent circumstances, that
You are mine enemy, and make my challenge
85 You shall not be my judge. For it is you
Have blown this coal betwixt my lord and me,
Which God's dew quench. Therefore, I say again,

---

60 **reverend fathers** clergymen   62 **elect** best, most choice men   63 **bootless** useless
64 **longer** any longer   **desire** request (i.e. the trial's postponement)   65 **quiet** peace of mind
69 **session** court, judicial gathering   77 **certain** certainly   81 **before** i.e. before you are
humble (which you'll never be)   84 **challenge** formal objection (legal term)   86 **blown this
coal** i.e. stirred up trouble (proverbial)

I utterly abhor, yea, from my soul,
Refuse you for my judge, whom yet once more
90   I hold my most malicious foe, and think not
At all a friend to truth.

CARDINAL WOLSEY   I do profess
You speak not like yourself, who ever yet
Have stood to charity, and displayed th'effects
95   Of disposition gentle, and of wisdom
O'ertopping woman's power. Madam, you do me wrong:
I have no spleen against you, nor injustice
For you or any: how far I have proceeded,
Or how far further shall, is warranted
100   By a commission from the consistory,
Yea, the whole consistory of Rome. You charge me
That I have blown this coal: I do deny it:
The king is present: if it be known to him
That I gainsay my deed, how may he wound,
105   And worthily, my falsehood: yea, as much
As you have done my truth. If he know
That I am free of your report, he knows
I am not of your wrong. Therefore in him
It lies to cure me, and the cure is to
110   Remove these thoughts from you: the which before
His highness shall speak in, I do beseech
You, gracious madam, to unthink your speaking
And to say so no more.

QUEEN KATHERINE   My lord, my lord,
115   I am a simple woman, much too weak
T'oppose your cunning. You're meek and humble-mouthed:
You sign your place and calling, in full seeming,
With meekness and humility: but your heart
Is crammed with arrogancy, spleen and pride.
120   You have by fortune and his highness' favours,

---

88 **abhor** reject   94 **stood to** upheld   97 **spleen** malice   104 **gainsay** deny   105 **worthily** justly   107 **free** innocent   **report** condemnation, allegation   108 **your wrong** the wrong you do me in making such statements   111 **in** about, with regard to   117 **sign** display   **in full seeming** to all appearances

Gone slightly o'er low steps, and now are mounted
Where powers are your retainers, and your words,
Domestics to you, serve your will as't please
Yourself pronounce their office. I must tell you,
125   You tender more your person's honour than
Your high profession spiritual, that again
I do refuse you for my judge, and here,
Before you all, appeal unto the Pope,
To bring my whole cause 'fore his holiness,
130   And to be judged by him.

She curtsies to the King, and offers to depart

CARDINAL CAMPEIUS   The queen is obstinate,
Stubborn to justice, apt to accuse it, and
Disdainful to be tried by't: 'tis not well.
She's going away.
135   KING HENRY VIII   Call her again.   *To the Crier*
CRIER   Katherine, Queen of England, come into the court.
GRIFFITH   Madam, you are called back.   *To Queen Katherine*
QUEEN KATHERINE   What need you note it? Pray you keep your
          way:
When you are called, return. Now the Lord help:
140   They vex me past my patience. Pray you, pass on:
I will not tarry: no, nor ever more
Upon this business my appearance make
In any of their courts.   *Exeunt Queen and her Attendants*
KING HENRY VIII   Go thy ways, Kate.
145   That man i'th'world who shall report he has
A better wife, let him in nought be trusted
For speaking false in that: thou art alone —
If thy rare qualities, sweet gentleness,
Thy meekness saint-like, wife-like government,

---

121 **slightly** with ease   122 **powers** officials in power/power of position   **retainers** servants
123 **Domestics** servants   **as't . . . office** in whatever manner you wish, as soon as you utter
their tasks   125 **tender** regard, are concerned with   126 **that** so that   129 **cause** legal case
130 *offers* attempts, makes to   132 **Stubborn** resistant   **apt** quick, ready   138 **keep your
way** keep going   141 **tarry** stay, linger   148 **rare** excellent/exceptional   149 **government**
control (of self and others)

150   Obeying in commanding, and thy parts
       Sovereign and pious else, could speak thee out —
       The queen of earthly queens: she's noble born:
       And like her true nobility, she has
       Carried herself towards me.

155 CARDINAL WOLSEY   Most gracious sir,
       In humblest manner I require your highness,
       That it shall please you to declare in hearing
       Of all these ears — for where I am robbed and bound,
       There must I be unloosed, although not there

160   At once and fully satisfied — whether ever I
       Did broach this business to your highness, or
       Laid any scruple in your way, which might
       Induce you to the question on't, or ever
       Have to you, but with thanks to God for such

165   A royal lady, spake one the least word that might
       Be to the prejudice of her present state,
       Or touch of her good person?

     KING HENRY VIII   My lord cardinal,
       I do excuse you: yea, upon mine honour,

170   I free you from't: you are not to be taught
       That you have many enemies, that know not
       Why they are so, but like to village curs,
       Bark when their fellows do. By some of these
       The queen is put in anger. You're excused:

175   But will you be more justified? You ever
       Have wished the sleeping of this business, never desired
       It to be stirred, but oft have hindered, oft,
       The passages made toward it: on my honour,
       I speak my good lord card'nal to this point,

180   And thus far clear him. Now, what moved me to't,

---

150 **Obeying in commanding** behaving with restraint even when issuing orders/behaving
both like a queen and a dutiful wife   **parts . . . else** other superior and pious qualities
Sovereign excellent/royal   **151 speak thee out** declare themselves as being in you
154 Carried conducted   **156 require** request   **160 satisfied** compensated   **166 prejudice**
detriment   **state** situation/rank   **167 touch** taint, stain   **169 excuse** exonerate
170 you . . . taught i.e. you know full well   **172 curs** dogs   **178 passages** proceedings
179 speak support

I will be bold with time and your attention:
Then mark th'inducement. Thus it came: give heed to't:
My conscience first received a tenderness,
Scruple, and prick, on certain speeches uttered
185 By th'Bishop of Bayonne, then French ambassador,
Who had been hither sent on the debating
A marriage 'twixt the Duke of Orléans and
Our daughter Mary: i'th'progress of this business,
Ere a determinate resolution, he,
190 I mean the bishop, did require a respite,
Wherein he might the king his lord advertise
Whether our daughter were legitimate,
Respecting this our marriage with the dowager,
Sometimes our brother's wife. This respite shook
195 The bosom of my conscience, entered me,
Yea, with a spitting power, and made to tremble
The region of my breast, which forced such way,
That many mazed considerings did throng
And pressed in with this caution. First, methought
200 I stood not in the smile of heaven, who had
Commanded nature that my lady's womb,
If it conceived a male child by me, should
Do no more offices of life to't than
The grave does to th'dead: for her male issue
205 Or died where they were made, or shortly after
This world had aired them. Hence I took a thought,
This was a judgement on me, that my kingdom,
Well worthy the best heir o'th'world, should not
Be gladded in't by me. Then follows that
210 I weighed the danger which my realms stood in
By this my issue's fail, and that gave to me

182 mark th'inducement note what persuaded me   183 tenderness sensitivity   187 'twixt
between   189 determinate resolution conclusive outcome   191 advertise notify, discuss
with   193 dowager i.e. Katherine, the widow of Henry's brother Arthur   194 Sometimes
formerly   196 spitting piercing, stabbing   198 mazed considerings bewildered thoughts,
confused wonderings   200 smile i.e. favor   203 offices duties, services   205 Or either
206 This . . . them i.e. birth   209 gladded made glad   211 issue's offspring's

Many a groaning throe: thus hulling in
The wild sea of my conscience, I did steer
Toward this remedy, whereupon we are
215   Now present here together: that's to say,
I meant to rectify my conscience, which
I then did feel full sick, and yet not well,
By all the reverend fathers of the land
And doctors learned. First I began in private
220   With you, my lord of Lincoln: you remember
How under my oppression I did reek
When I first moved you.

LINCOLN   Very well, my liege.

KING HENRY VIII   I have spoke long: be pleased yourself to say
225   How far you satisfied me.

LINCOLN   So please your highness,
The question did at first so stagger me,
Bearing a state of mighty moment in't
And consequence of dread, that I committed
230   The daring'st counsel which I had to doubt,
And did entreat your highness to this course
Which you are running here.

KING HENRY VIII   I then moved you,   *To Canterbury*
My lord of Canterbury, and got your leave
235   To make this present summons: unsolicited
I left no reverend person in this court,
But by particular consent proceeded
Under your hands and seals: therefore, go on:
For no dislike i'th'world against the person
240   Of the good queen, but the sharp thorny points
Of my alleged reasons, drives this forward:
Prove but our marriage lawful, by my life

---

212 **throe** pain (a word often used of labor pains)   **hulling** drifting (with sails furled)   **217 full**
very   **yet** still (now)   **219 doctors** scholars   **221 oppression** burdensome distress   **reek**
sweat   **222 moved** put the matter to, appealed to   **225 satisfied** reassured   **228 Bearing . . .**
dread given that it concerned a matter of great importance and potentially alarming
consequences   **229 committed . . . doubt** questioned the most extreme, audacious advice I was
inclined to give (i.e. to pursue divorce)   **237 particular** individual   **238 Under . . . seals** i.e. with
your formal written agreement   **hands** signatures   **242 Prove but** if you can only prove

And kingly dignity, we are contented
To wear our mortal state to come with her,
245   Katherine our queen, before the primest creature
That's paragoned o'th'world.

CARDINAL CAMPEIUS   So please your highness,
The queen being absent, 'tis a needful fitness
That we adjourn this court till further day:
250   Meanwhile must be an earnest motion
Made to the queen, to call back her appeal
She intends unto his holiness.

KING HENRY VIII   I may perceive   *Aside*
These cardinals trifle with me: I abhor
255   This dilatory sloth and tricks of Rome.
My learned and well-belovèd servant, Cranmer,
Prithee return: with thy approach, I know,
My comfort comes along.— Break up the court: *Aloud*
I say, set on.   *Exeunt in manner as they entered*

Act 3 Scene 1   *running scene 8*

Enter Queen [Katherine] and her Women, as at work   *One with a lute*

QUEEN KATHERINE   Take thy lute, wench: my soul grows sad with
troubles:
Sing, and disperse 'em, if thou canst: leave working.

WOMAN   Orpheus with his lute made trees,   *Sings*
And the mountain tops that freeze,
5   Bow themselves when he did sing.
To his music plants and flowers

244 **wear . . . come** spend our remaining life (or perhaps "our earthly sovereignty")
245 **primest** most supreme (perhaps plays on the sense of "youngest, freshest")
246 **paragoned** put forth as an ideal model   248 **a needful fitness** necessarily appropriate
behavior   249 **further** another   250 **motion** request   252 **his holiness** i.e. the Pope
255 **dilatory** delaying (with specifically legal sense of entering a dilatory plea to delay
proceedings)   257 **return** the clergyman Thomas **Cranmer** was at this point in Europe,
gathering support for Henry's divorce   259 **set on** advance, proceed   **3.1**   *Location: the
royal court, London*   1 **lute** stringed musical instrument played like a guitar   2 **leave** stop
3 **Orpheus** legendary Greek poet, whose music had the power to charm trees, animals, and
stones   **made** i.e. made them bow

Ever sprung, as sun and showers
There had made a lasting spring.
Every thing that heard him play,
Even the billows of the sea,
Hung their heads, and then lay by.
In sweet music is such art,
Killing care and grief of heart
Fall asleep, or hearing, die.

Enter [Griffith] a Gentleman

QUEEN KATHERINE   How now?

GRIFFITH   An't please your grace, the two great cardinals
Wait in the presence.

QUEEN KATHERINE   Would they speak with me?

GRIFFITH   They willed me say so, madam.

QUEEN KATHERINE   Pray their graces
To come near.   [*Exit Griffith*]
What can be their business
With me, a poor weak woman, fall'n from favour?
I do not like their coming: now I think on't,
They should be good men, their affairs as righteous:
But all hoods make not monks.

Enter the two Cardinals, Wolsey and Campeius

CARDINAL WOLSEY   Peace to your highness.

QUEEN KATHERINE   Your graces find me here part of a housewife:
I would be all, against the worst may happen.
What are your pleasures with me, reverend lords?

CARDINAL WOLSEY   May it please you, noble madam, to withdraw
Into your private chamber: we shall give you
The full cause of our coming.

QUEEN KATHERINE   Speak it here.
There's nothing I have done yet, o' my conscience,
Deserves a corner: would all other women

---

7 **as** as if   10 **billows** swelling waves   11 **lay by** subsided, became calm   13 **Killing** fatal, deadly   17 **presence** royal reception chamber   19 **willed** ordered   20 **Pray** ask (politely) 24 **as righteous** i.e. as their goodness   27 **part of** partly   28 **all** i.e. wholly a housewife **against** in anticipation of   **worst** i.e. divorce from Henry (which would necessitate careful domestic and economic management for a woman living alone)   35 **corner** i.e. secrecy

Could speak this with as free a soul as I do.
My lords, I care not, so much I am happy
Above a number, if my actions
Were tried by ev'ry tongue, ev'ry eye saw 'em,
40   Envy and base opinion set against 'em,
I know my life so even. If your business
Seek me out, and that way I am wife in,
Out with it boldly: truth loves open dealing.

CARDINAL WOLSEY   *Tanta est erga te mentis integritas, Regina*
        serenissima—

45   QUEEN KATHERINE   O, good my lord, no Latin:
I am not such a truant since my coming,
As not to know the language I have lived in:
A strange tongue makes my cause more strange,
        suspicious:
Pray, speak in English: here are some will thank you,
50   If you speak truth, for their poor mistress' sake:
Believe me, she has had much wrong. Lord cardinal,
The willing'st sin I ever yet committed
May be absolved in English.

CARDINAL WOLSEY   Noble lady,
55   I am sorry my integrity should breed,
And service to his majesty and you,
So deep suspicion, where all faith was meant:
We come not by the way of accusation,
To taint that honour every good tongue blesses,
60   Nor to betray you any way to sorrow:
You have too much, good lady: but to know
How you stand minded in the weighty difference
Between the king and you, and to deliver,
Like free and honest men, our just opinions
65   And comforts to your cause.

---

36 **free** innocent   37 **happy** fortunate   38 **a number** many others   40 **Envy** malice
41 **even** straightforward, constant   42 **that . . . in** it concerns my wifely status   44 ***Tanta . . .***
serenissima "So great is my integrity toward you, most serene queen" (Latin)   46 **truant**
negligent student   **coming** i.e. to England from Spain   48 **strange** foreign   52 **willing'st**
most deliberate   57 **all** only   **faith** loyalty, integrity, honesty   58 **by the way** for the purpose
of   62 **minded** inclined   **difference** disagreement   64 **free** honorable, upright

CARDINAL CAMPEIUS   Most honoured madam,
My lord of York, out of his noble nature,
Zeal and obedience he still bore your grace,
Forgetting, like a good man, your late censure
70   Both of his truth and him, which was too far,
Offers, as I do, in a sign of peace,
His service and his counsel.

QUEEN KATHERINE   To betray me.—   *Aside*
My lords, I thank you both for your good wills: *Aloud*
75   Ye speak like honest men:— pray God ye prove so.   *Aside?*
But how to make ye suddenly an answer
In such a point of weight, so near mine honour —
More near my life, I fear — with my weak wit,
And to such men of gravity and learning:
80   In truth I know not. I was set at work
Among my maids, full little, God knows, looking
Either for such men or such business:
For her sake that I have been — for I feel
The last fit of my greatness — good your graces,
85   Let me have time and counsel for my cause:
Alas, I am a woman friendless, hopeless.

CARDINAL WOLSEY   Madam, you wrong the king's love with
        these fears.
Your hopes and friends are infinite.

QUEEN KATHERINE   In England
90   But little for my profit: can you think, lords,
That any Englishman dare give me counsel?
Or be a known friend gainst his highness' pleasure,
Though he be grown so desperate to be honest,
And live a subject? Nay forsooth, my friends,
95   They that must weigh out my afflictions,
They that my trust must grow to, live not here:

---

76 **suddenly** immediately, spontaneously   78 **wit** intelligence   80 **set** seated   81 **looking**
prepared   83 **her . . . been** i.e. my sake as the queen I was till now   84 **fit** brief period
90 **profit** benefit   93 **desperate** reckless   94 **live a subject** i.e. continue to be treated as a
loyal subject to Henry (despite supporting the queen)   **forsooth** in truth   95 **weigh out**
counterbalance, compensate for/outweigh/assess fully

They are, as all my other comforts, far hence
In mine own country, lords.

CARDINAL CAMPEIUS   I would your grace

100 Would leave your griefs, and take my counsel.

QUEEN KATHERINE   How, sir?

CARDINAL CAMPEIUS   Put your main cause into the king's
protection:
He's loving and most gracious. 'Twill be much
Both for your honour better and your cause:

105 For if the trial of the law o'ertake ye,
You'll part away disgraced.

CARDINAL WOLSEY   He tells you rightly.

QUEEN KATHERINE   Ye tell me what ye wish for both — my ruin:
Is this your Christian counsel? Out upon ye.

110 Heaven is above all yet: there sits a judge
That no king can corrupt.

CARDINAL CAMPEIUS   Your rage mistakes us.

QUEEN KATHERINE   The more shame for ye: holy men I
thought ye,
Upon my soul, two reverend cardinal virtues:

115 But cardinal sins and hollow hearts I fear ye:
Mend 'em for shame, my lords. Is this your comfort?
The cordial that ye bring a wretched lady?
A woman lost among ye, laughed at, scorned?
I will not wish ye half my miseries:

120 I have more charity. But say I warned ye:
Take heed, for heaven's sake, take heed, lest at once
The burden of my sorrows fall upon ye.

CARDINAL WOLSEY   Madam, this is a mere distraction:
You turn the good we offer into envy.

---

106 **part away** depart   109 **Out upon ye** dismissive exclamation, "Away with you"
112 **mistakes** causes you to misunderstand   114 **cardinal virtues** there were four of these:
justice, prudence, temperance, and fortitude   115 **cardinal sins** the seven deadly sins: pride,
covetousness, envy, wrath, gluttony, sloth, and lechery (**cardinal**, as well as playing on the
men's ecclesiastical titles, may pun on "carnal")   117 **cordial** heart-restoring remedy
121 **at once** suddenly/all at once   123 **mere distraction** complete frenzy   124 **envy** hatred,
ill will

125   QUEEN KATHERINE   Ye turn me into nothing. Woe upon ye
      And all such false professors. Would you have me —
      If you have any justice, any pity,
      If ye be anything but churchmen's habits —
      Put my sick cause into his hands that hates me?
130   Alas, he's banished me his bed already,
      His love, too long ago. I am old, my lords,
      And all the fellowship I hold now with him
      Is only my obedience. What can happen
      To me above this wretchedness? All your studies
135   Make me a curse like this.
      CARDINAL CAMPEIUS   Your fears are worse.
      QUEEN KATHERINE   Have I lived thus long — let me speak myself,
      Since virtue finds no friends — a wife, a true one?
      A woman, I dare say without vainglory,
140   Never yet branded with suspicion?
      Have I with all my full affections
      Still met the king? Loved him next heaven? Obeyed him?
      Been, out of fondness, superstitious to him?
      Almost forgot my prayers to content him?
145   And am I thus rewarded? 'Tis not well, lords.
      Bring me a constant woman to her husband,
      One that ne'er dreamed a joy beyond his pleasure,
      And to that woman, when she has done most,
      Yet will I add an honour, a great patience.
150   CARDINAL WOLSEY   Madam, you wander from the good we aim at.
      QUEEN KATHERINE   My lord, I dare not make myself so guilty,
      To give up willingly that noble title
      Your master wed me to: nothing but death
      Shall e'er divorce my dignities.
155   CARDINAL WOLSEY   Pray, hear me.

---

126 professors those who profess to be Christians   128 habits garments, i.e. the mere outer
appearance   130 his from his   132 fellowship partnership/sexual intimacy   134 above
more than   studies efforts   137 speak speak for, defend   139 vainglory boasting   141 full
affections complete love   142 Still always, with constancy   next next to   143 fondness
affection/foolishness   superstitious excessively devoted, idolatrous   150 wander from stray
from/mistake   154 dignities nobleness, high rank

QUEEN KATHERINE   Would I had never trod this English earth,
Or felt the flatteries that grow upon it:
Ye have angels' faces, but heaven knows your hearts.
What will become of me now, wretched lady?
160   I am the most unhappy woman living.
Alas, poor wenches, where are now your fortunes?
Shipwrecked upon a kingdom, where no pity,
No friends, no hope, no kindred weep for me?
Almost no grave allowed me? Like the lily
165   That once was mistress of the field and flourished,
I'll hang my head and perish.
CARDINAL WOLSEY   If your grace
Could but be brought to know our ends are honest,
You'd feel more comfort. Why should we, good lady,
170   Upon what cause, wrong you? Alas, our places,
The way of our profession is against it:
We are to cure such sorrows, not to sow 'em.
For goodness' sake, consider what you do,
How you may hurt yourself, ay, utterly
175   Grow from the king's acquaintance, by this carriage.
The hearts of princes kiss obedience,
So much they love it, but to stubborn spirits
They swell and grow as terrible as storms.
I know you have a gentle, noble temper,
180   A soul as even as a calm: pray think us
Those we profess: peacemakers, friends and servants.
CARDINAL CAMPEIUS   Madam, you'll find it so: you wrong your
        virtues
With these weak women's fears. A noble spirit,
As yours was put into you, ever casts
185   Such doubts as false coin from it. The king loves you:
Beware you lose it not: for us, if you please
To trust us in your business, we are ready
To use our utmost studies in your service.

---

156 Would I wish   **168 ends** intentions   **170 places** (Church) positions   **175 carriage**
behavior   **179 temper** temperament   **180 even** level   **calm** calm sea   **184 casts** rejects
(plays on sense of melting metal to form coins)   **188 studies** efforts

QUEEN KATHERINE   Do what ye will, my lords: and pray forgive me

190   If I have used myself unmannerly.
        You know I am a woman, lacking wit
        To make a seemly answer to such persons.
        Pray do my service to his majesty:
        He has my heart yet, and shall have my prayers

195   While I shall have my life. Come, reverend fathers,
        Bestow your counsels on me. She now begs,
        That little thought, when she set footing here,
        She should have bought her dignities so dear.   *Exeunt*

Act 3 Scene 2   *running scene 9*

Enter the Duke of Norfolk, Duke of Suffolk, Lord Surrey and Lord
Chamberlain

NORFOLK   If you will now unite in your complaints,
        And force them with a constancy, the cardinal
        Cannot stand under them. If you omit
        The offer of this time, I cannot promise

5   But that you shall sustain more new disgraces,
        With these you bear already.
    SURREY   I am joyful
        To meet the least occasion that may give me
        Remembrance of my father-in-law the duke,

10   To be revenged on him.
    SUFFOLK   Which of the peers
        Have uncontemned gone by him, or at least
        Strangely neglected? When did he regard
        The stamp of nobleness in any person

15   Out of himself?
    CHAMBERLAIN   My lords, you speak your pleasures:
        What he deserves of you and me I know:

190 **used** conducted   193 **do my service** pay my respects   197 **That** who   **set footing**
here arrived in England   **3.2**   2 **force** urge, press   **a constancy** persistence   3 **omit . . .**
time neglect this current opportunity   9 **duke** i.e. of Buckingham   10 **him** i.e. Wolsey
12 **uncontemned** unscorned, not treated contemptuously   13 **neglected** disregarded/slighted
15 **Out of** beyond

What we can do to him, though now the time
Gives way to us, I much fear. If you cannot
20   Bar his access to th'king, never attempt
Anything on him: for he hath a witchcraft
Over the king in's tongue.

NORFOLK   O, fear him not:
His spell in that is out: the king hath found
25   Matter against him that forever mars
The honey of his language. No, he's settled,
Not to come off, in his displeasure.

SURREY   Sir,
I should be glad to hear such news as this
30   Once every hour.

NORFOLK   Believe it, this is true.
In the divorce his contrary proceedings
Are all unfolded, wherein he appears
As I would wish mine enemy.

35 SURREY   How came
His practices to light?

SUFFOLK   Most strangely.

SURREY   O, how, how?

SUFFOLK   The cardinal's letters to the Pope miscarried,
40   And came to th'eye o'th'king, wherein was read
How that the cardinal did entreat his holiness
To stay the judgment o'th'divorce, for if
It did take place, 'I do', quoth he, 'perceive
My king is tangled in affection to
45   A creature of the queen's, Lady Anne Bullen.'

SURREY   Has the king this?

SUFFOLK   Believe it.

SURREY   Will this work?

---

19 Gives way favors   **fear** doubt   **22 in's** in his   **24 out** ended, lost   **26 he's** may apply to
Wolsey or to Henry   **27 come off** escape (if Wolsey)/desist (if Henry)   **his** i.e. Henry's
32 contrary oppositional/contradictory   **33 unfolded** exposed   **36 practices** schemes
39 miscarried went astray/were intercepted   **42 stay** delay   **45 creature** dependant,
servant

CHAMBERLAIN   The king in this perceives him how he coasts
50   And hedges his own way. But in this point
        All his tricks founder, and he brings his physic
        After his patient's death: the king already
        Hath married the fair lady.

SURREY   Would he had.

55 SUFFOLK   May you be happy in your wish, my lord,
        For I profess you have it.

SURREY   Now, all my joy
        Trace the conjunction.

SUFFOLK   My amen to't.

60 NORFOLK   All men's.

SUFFOLK   There's order given for her coronation:
        Marry, this is yet but young, and may be left
        To some ears unrecounted. But, my lords,
        She is a gallant creature, and complete
65   In mind and feature. I persuade me, from her
        Will fall some blessing to this land, which shall
        In it be memorized.

SURREY   But will the king
        Digest this letter of the cardinal's?

70   The Lord forbid!

NORFOLK   Marry, amen.

SUFFOLK   No, no:
        There be more wasps that buzz about his nose
        Will make this sting the sooner. Cardinal Campeius
75   Is stol'n away to Rome: hath ta'en no leave:
        Has left the cause o'th'king unhandled, and
        Is posted as the agent of our cardinal

---

49 perceives him perceives   coasts And hedges is indirect and devious (as if traveling in a
roundabout manner along a coastline or by hedgerows)   51 physic remedy   58 Trace the
conjunction follow the marriage   60 All men's puns on amen   62 Marry by the Virgin Mary
(picks up on the notion of marriage)   young i.e. recent news   may . . . unrecounted perhaps
not everyone will have heard it/not everyone needs to hear it   64 gallant fine, splendid
complete perfect   65 persuade me am convinced   66 fall befall/be born   67 memorized
made memorable   69 Digest endure, stomach   76 cause i.e. the divorce   unhandled
unresolved, without management   77 Is posted has gone in haste

To second all his plot. I do assure you
The king cried 'Ha!' at this.

80 CHAMBERLAIN   Now, God incense him,
And let him cry 'Ha!' louder.

NORFOLK   But, my lord,
When returns Cranmer?

SUFFOLK   He is returned in his opinions, which
85 Have satisfied the king for his divorce,
Together with all famous colleges
Almost in Christendom: shortly, I believe,
His second marriage shall be published, and
Her coronation. Katherine no more
90 Shall be called 'Queen', but 'Princess Dowager'
And 'widow to Prince Arthur'.

NORFOLK   This same Cranmer's
A worthy fellow, and hath ta'en much pain
In the king's business.

95 SUFFOLK   He has, and we shall see him
For it an archbishop.

NORFOLK   So I hear.

SUFFOLK   'Tis so.

Enter [Cardinal] Wolsey and Cromwell
The cardinal.

100 NORFOLK   Observe, observe, he's moody.

CARDINAL WOLSEY   The packet, Cromwell: gave't you the king?

CROMWELL   To his own hand, in's bedchamber.

CARDINAL WOLSEY   Looked he
O'th'inside of the paper?

105 CROMWELL   Presently
He did unseal them, and the first he viewed,
He did it with a serious mind: a heed

---

84 He . . . opinions i.e. letters from him have been received ahead of his arrival; the **opinions** may be Cranmer's own or, more likely, those that he was sent to gather on the divorce 88 **published** announced publicly   100 **moody** sullen, angry   101 **packet** dispatch, packet of letters   103 **Looked . . . paper?** i.e. Did he open it?   105 **Presently** immediately 107 **heed** care, attention

Was in his countenance. You he bade
Attend him here this morning.

110 CARDINAL WOLSEY   Is he ready
To come abroad?

CROMWELL   I think by this he is.

CARDINAL WOLSEY   Leave me awhile.—   *Exit Cromwell*
It shall be to the Duchess of Alençon,   *Aside*

115 The French king's sister: he shall marry her.
Anne Bullen? No, I'll no Anne Bullens for him:
There's more in't than fair visage. Bullen?
No, we'll no Bullens. Speedily I wish
To hear from Rome. The Marchioness of Pembroke?

120 NORFOLK   He's discontented.

SUFFOLK   Maybe he hears the king
Does whet his anger to him.

SURREY   Sharp enough,
Lord, for thy justice.

125 CARDINAL WOLSEY   The late queen's gentlewoman? A knight's
daughter,   *Aside*
To be her mistress' mistress? The queen's queen?
This candle burns not clear: 'tis I must snuff it,
Then out it goes. What though I know her virtuous
And well deserving? Yet I know her for

130 A spleeny Lutheran, and not wholesome to
Our cause, that she should lie i'th'bosom of
Our hard-ruled king. Again, there is sprung up
An heretic, an arch-one: Cranmer, one
Hath crawled into the favour of the king,

135 And is his oracle.

NORFOLK   He is vexed at something.

Enter King [Henry], reading of a schedule [and Lovell]

---

111 **abroad** out of his **bedchamber**   112 **this** this time   117 **visage** face   125 **late** former
127 **clear** bright   **snuff it** trim its wick   130 **spleeny Lutheran** hot-headed Protestant
wholesome beneficial, healthy   131 **lie i'th'bosom of** i.e. have sex with/share the secrets of
132 **hard-ruled** difficult to manage; possible erectile connotations   133 **arch-one** major,
principal one (plays on "archbishop")   134 **Hath** who has   136 *schedule* document

SURREY   I would 'twere something that would fret the string,
The master-cord on's heart!
SUFFOLK   The king, the king!
140 KING HENRY VIII   What piles of wealth hath he accumulated   *Aside*
To his own portion? And what expense by th'hour
Seems to flow from him? How i'th'name of thrift
Does he rake this together?— Now, my lords,   *Aloud*
Saw you the cardinal?
145 NORFOLK   My lord, we have
Stood here observing him. Some strange commotion
Is in his brain: he bites his lip, and starts,
Stops on a sudden, looks upon the ground,
Then lays his finger on his temple, straight
150 Springs out into fast gait, then stops again,
Strikes his breast hard, and anon he casts
His eye against the moon: in most strange postures
We have seen him set himself.
KING HENRY VIII   It may well be,
155 There is a mutiny in's mind. This morning
Papers of state he sent me to peruse,
As I required: and wot you what I found
There, on my conscience put unwittingly?
Forsooth, an inventory, thus importing
160 The several parcels of his plate, his treasure,
Rich stuffs and ornaments of household, which
I find at such proud rate, that it outspeaks
Possession of a subject.
NORFOLK   It's heaven's will:
165 Some spirit put this paper in the packet,
To bless your eye withal.

---

137 **fret** gnaw, fray/add frets or ridges (to aid tuning on a stringed instrument)   138 **master-cord** main sinew, chief string   **on's** of his   141 **portion** share   146 **commotion** agitation   149 **straight** straight away   152 **against** toward   157 **wot** know   159 **importing** concerning   160 **several parcels** various pieces   **plate** gold or silver tableware   161 **stuffs** material, cloth   **ornaments of household** furnishings   162 **proud rate** great cost/vast quantity   **outspeaks . . . subject** far exceeds what a subject ought to own   166 **withal** with

KING HENRY VIII   If we did think
His contemplation were above the earth,
And fixed on spiritual object, he should still
170   Dwell in his musings: but I am afraid
His thinkings are below the moon, not worth
His serious considering.

King takes his seat; [and] whispers [with] Lovell, who goes to the Cardinal

CARDINAL WOLSEY   Heaven forgive me!—
Ever God bless your highness.   *To the king*

175   KING HENRY VIII   Good, my lord,
You are full of heavenly stuff, and bear the inventory
Of your best graces in your mind, the which
You were now running o'er: you have scarce time
To steal from spiritual leisure a brief span
180   To keep your earthly audit: sure, in that
I deem you an ill husband, and am glad
To have you therein my companion.

CARDINAL WOLSEY   Sir,
For holy offices I have a time: a time
185   To think upon the part of business which
I bear i'th'state: and nature does require
Her times of preservation, which perforce
I, her frail son, amongst my brethren mortal,
Must give my tendance to.

190   KING HENRY VIII   You have said well.

CARDINAL WOLSEY   And ever may your highness yoke together,
As I will lend you cause, my doing well
With my well saying.

---

168 **contemplation** thoughts/religious musing   169 **should** would be allowed (to)
171 **below the moon** i.e. worldly   176 **stuff** matter (plays on the sense of "(rich) fabric"; the king's loaded language continues with **inventory, steal, audit)**   177 **graces** virtues
179 **leisure** time for contemplation   180 **keep . . . audit** see to your worldly accounts (as opposed to the spiritual reckoning at Judgment Day)   181 **ill husband** poor domestic manager   **glad** i.e. because Wolsey is so unconcerned with self-seeking material matters (ironic)   187 **times of preservation** life-sustaining activities (i.e. eating, sleeping)   **perforce** of necessity   189 **tendance** attention

KING HENRY VIII   'Tis well said again,
195   And 'tis a kind of good deed to say well:
And yet words are no deeds. My father loved you:
He said he did, and with his deed did crown
His word upon you. Since I had my office,
I have kept you next my heart, have not alone
200   Employed you where high profits might come home,
But pared my present havings, to bestow
My bounties upon you.

CARDINAL WOLSEY   What should this mean?   *Aside*

SURREY   The Lord increase this business!   *Aside*

205   KING HENRY VIII   Have I not made you,
The prime man of the state? I pray you tell me
If what I now pronounce you have found true:
And if you may confess it, say withal
If you are bound to us or no. What say you?

210   CARDINAL WOLSEY   My sovereign, I confess your royal graces,
Showered on me daily, have been more than could
My studied purposes requite, which went
Beyond all man's endeavours. My endeavours
Have ever come too short of my desires,
215   Yet filed with my abilities: mine own ends
Have been mine so that evermore they pointed
To th'good of your most sacred person and
The profit of the state. For your great graces
Heaped upon me, poor undeserver, I
220   Can nothing render but allegiant thanks,
My prayers to heaven for you, my loyalty,
Which ever has and ever shall be growing,
Till death, that winter, kill it.

KING HENRY VIII   Fairly answered:
225   A loyal and obedient subject is

---

197 **crown . . . you** i.e. by investing Wolsey with Church promotions   199 **alone** only
201 **pared** trimmed, reduced   **havings** fortune   206 **prime** foremost, most powerful (under
the king)   207 **pronounce** declare   208 **withal** moreover, in addition   210 **graces** favors
211 **could . . . requite** my most deliberate efforts could repay   215 **filed** kept pace   216 **so**
only to the extent   220 **allegiant** loyal

Therein illustrated: the honour of it
Does pay the act of it, as i'th'contrary
The foulness is the punishment. I presume
That as my hand has opened bounty to you,
230   My heart dropped love, my power rained honour, more
On you than any: so your hand and heart,
Your brain, and every function of your power,
Should, notwithstanding that your bond of duty,
As 'twere in love's particular, be more
235   To me, your friend, than any.

CARDINAL WOLSEY   I do profess
That for your highness' good I ever laboured
More than mine own: that am, have and will be —
Though all the world should crack their duty to you,
240   And throw it from their soul: though perils did
Abound, as thick as thought could make 'em, and
Appear in forms more horrid — yet my duty,
As doth a rock against the chiding flood,
Should the approach of this wild river break,
245   And stand unshaken yours.

KING HENRY VIII   'Tis nobly spoken:
Take notice, lords, he has a loyal breast,
For you have seen him open't. Read o'er this,   *Gives Wolsey a paper*
And after, this, and then to breakfast with   *Gives him another paper*
250   What appetite you have.   *Exit King, frowning upon the*
                                                Cardinal, the Nobles throng after him,
                                                        smiling and whispering

CARDINAL WOLSEY   What should this mean?
What sudden anger's this? How have I reaped it?
He parted frowning from me, as if ruin
Leaped from his eyes. So looks the chafèd lion

---

226 the . . . it "honor is the reward of virtue" was proverbial   228 foulness dishonor, public
shame   232 power faculties   233 notwithstanding . . . duty despite your duty to the
Church/beyond the debt of allegiance of any subject to his king   that your i.e. that   234 in
love's particular on account of the intimacy of close friendship   238 that . . . be I who am,
have been and will be (after digressing, Wolsey never in fact finishes this sentence)   239 crack
violate, destroy   242 horrid frightening   243 chiding tumultuous, angry   244 break
interrupt/stem   254 chafèd enraged

255   Upon the daring huntsman that has galled him:
         Then makes him nothing. I must read this paper:
         I fear the story of his anger.— 'Tis so: *He reads one of the papers*
         This paper has undone me: 'tis the account
         Of all that world of wealth I have drawn together
260   For mine own ends — indeed, to gain the popedom,
         And fee my friends in Rome. O negligence,
         Fit for a fool to fall by! What cross devil
         Made me put this main secret in the packet
         I sent the king? Is there no way to cure this?
265   No new device to beat this from his brains?
         I know 'twill stir him strongly. Yet I know
         A way, if it take right, in spite of fortune
         Will bring me off again. What's this? 'To th'Pope'?
         The letter, as I live, with all the business
270   I writ to's holiness. Nay then, farewell:
         I have touched the highest point of all my greatness,
         And from that full meridian of my glory,
         I haste now to my setting. I shall fall
         Like a bright exhalation in the evening,
275   And no man see me more.
         Enter to Wolsey, the Dukes of Norfolk and Suffolk, the Earl of Surrey
         and the Lord Chamberlain
         NORFOLK   Hear the king's pleasure, cardinal, who
             commands you
         To render up the great seal presently
         Into our hands, and to confine yourself
         To Asher House, my lord of Winchester's,
280   Till you hear further from his highness.

---

255 **galled** wounded/angered   256 **makes him nothing** destroys him (the **huntsman**)
257 **story** cause/narrative   258 **undone** ruined   **account** may play on the sense of "**story,**
narrative"   259 **world** vast quantity   261 **fee** pay/bribe   262 **cross** perverse, thwarting
263 **main** chief, significant   265 **device** strategy, trick   266 **stir** anger   267 **take right** works
properly, succeeds   268 **bring me off** rescue me   272 **meridian** highest point (of the sun)
273 **setting** decline, sunset   274 **exhalation** shooting star, meteor   277 **presently**
immediately   279 **Asher House** Esher House, Surrey, which belonged to Wolsey as Bishop of
Winchester

CARDINAL WOLSEY   Stay:
Where's your commission, lords? Words cannot carry
Authority so weighty.

SUFFOLK   Who dare cross 'em,

285   Bearing the king's will from his mouth expressly?

CARDINAL WOLSEY   Till I find more than will or words to do it —
I mean your malice — know, officious lords,
I dare and must deny it. Now I feel
Of what coarse metal ye are moulded: envy.

290   How eagerly ye follow my disgraces,
As if it fed ye, and how sleek and wanton
Ye appear in everything may bring my ruin!
Follow your envious courses, men of malice:
You have Christian warrant for 'em, and no doubt

295   In time will find their fit rewards. That seal
You ask with such a violence, the king,
Mine and your master, with his own hand gave me:
Bade me enjoy it, with the place and honours,
During my life: and to confirm his goodness,

300   Tied it by letters patents. Now, who'll take it?

SURREY   The king, that gave it.

CARDINAL WOLSEY   It must be himself, then.

SURREY   Thou art a proud traitor, priest.

CARDINAL WOLSEY   Proud lord, thou liest:

305   Within these forty hours Surrey durst better
Have burnt that tongue than said so.

SURREY   Thy ambition,
Thou scarlet sin, robbed this bewailing land
Of noble Buckingham, my father-in-law:

310   The heads of all thy brother cardinals,
With thee, and all thy best parts bound together,

---

282 commission warrant, authority   **284 cross** challenge   **286 it** i.e. obey their orders
289 metal material/mettle (i.e. disposition, spirit)   **envy** malice   **291 sleek** fawning, oily
wanton unprincipled, lawless, merciless   **295 rewards** i.e. punishments   **298 enjoy** use,
benefit from   **300 Tied** authorized, confirmed   **letters patents** documents signed by the king
conferring land, title or official position   **305 forty hours** used indefinitely to convey a broad
period of time   **308 scarlet sin** refers to the color of a cardinal's robes; also to Isaiah 1:18
which describes sins as "red like scarlet"   **311 parts** qualities

Weighed not a hair of his. Plague of your policy,
You sent me deputy for Ireland,
Far from his succour, from the king, from all
315   That might have mercy on the fault thou gav'st him:
Whilst your great goodness, out of holy pity,
Absolved him with an axe.

CARDINAL WOLSEY   This, and all else
This talking lord can lay upon my credit,
320   I answer is most false. The duke by law
Found his deserts. How innocent I was
From any private malice in his end,
His noble jury and foul cause can witness.
If I loved many words, lord, I should tell you
325   You have as little honesty as honour,
That in the way of loyalty and truth
Toward the king, my ever royal master,
Dare mate a sounder man than Surrey can be,
And all that love his follies.

330   SURREY   By my soul,
Your long coat, priest, protects you: thou shouldst feel
My sword i'th'life-blood of thee else. My lords,
Can ye endure to hear this arrogance?
And from this fellow? If we live thus tamely,
335   To be thus jaded by a piece of scarlet,
Farewell nobility: let his grace go forward,
And dare us with his cap, like larks.

CARDINAL WOLSEY   All goodness
Is poison to thy stomach.

340   SURREY   Yes, that goodness
Of gleaning all the land's wealth into one,

---

312 **Weighed** equaled in weight   **of** on   **policy** political strategy, cunning   314 **his**
succour being able to help him (Buckingham)   315 **fault** offense   **gav'st** assigned to
319 **credit** reputation   322 **From** of   323 **cause** case (tried in court)   326 **That** I who
328 **mate** be a match for, contend with   334 **fellow** common man/servant/good-for-nothing
(a contemptuous term for one of Wolsey's status)   335 **jaded** deceived, made fools of (plays
on the sense of "made green")   337 **dare . . . larks** birds could be caught by being distracted
with a piece of scarlet cloth while nets were dropped on them; there may be an implicit
reference to Joan Larke, Wolsey's mistress   **dare** daze

Into your own hands, Card'nal, by extortion:
The goodness of your intercepted packets
You writ to th'Pope against the king: your goodness,
345   Since you provoke me, shall be most notorious.
My lord of Norfolk, as you are truly noble,
As you respect the common good, the state
Of our despised nobility, our issues,
Whom if he live will scarce be gentlemen,
350   Produce the grand sum of his sins, the articles
Collected from his life. I'll startle you
Worse than the sacring bell, when the brown wench
Lay kissing in your arms, lord cardinal.

CARDINAL WOLSEY   How much, methinks, I could despise   *Aside*
   this man,
355   But that I am bound in charity against it.

NORFOLK   Those articles, my lord, are in the king's hand:
But thus much: they are foul ones.

CARDINAL WOLSEY   So much fairer
And spotless shall mine innocence arise,
360   When the king knows my truth.

SURREY   This cannot save you:
I thank my memory, I yet remember
Some of these articles, and out they shall.
Now, if you can blush and cry 'Guilty', cardinal,
365   You'll show a little honesty.

CARDINAL WOLSEY   Speak on, sir:
I dare your worst objections: if I blush,
It is to see a nobleman want manners.

SURREY   I had rather want those than my head. Have at you!
370   First, that without the king's assent or knowledge,

---

348 **issues** children, i.e. sons   349 **he** i.e. Wolsey   350 **articles** items in a list of formal charges
352 **sacring bell** small bell rung at the consecration of the host, the holiest part of the Mass
(after the Reformation it signified the bell rung to announce morning prayers)   **brown**
brunette/dark-complexioned (or sunburned; another dig at Wolsey, suggesting this particular
lover is a common peasant)   **wench** girl of the rustic or working class/mistress   356 **hand**
possession/handwriting   357 **thus much** I can say this much   **foul** plays on the sense of
"illegible, blotted"   363 **out** be revealed   367 **dare** challenge, defy   **objections** accusations
368 **want** lack   369 **Have at you!** i.e. here I come (standard utterance at the opening of a fight)

You wrought to be a legate, by which power
You maimed the jurisdiction of all bishops.

NORFOLK   Then, that in all you writ to Rome, or else
To foreign princes, '*Ego et Rex meus*'
375   Was still inscribed, in which you brought the king
To be your servant.

SUFFOLK   Then, that without the knowledge
Either of king or council, when you went
Ambassador to the emperor, you made bold
380   To carry into Flanders the great seal.

SURREY   *Item*, you sent a large commission
To Gregory de Cassado, to conclude
Without the king's will or the state's allowance,
A league between his highness and Ferrara.

385   SUFFOLK   That out of mere ambition, you have caused
Your holy hat to be stamped on the king's coin.

SURREY   Then, that you have sent innumerable substance —
By what means got, I leave to your own conscience —
To furnish Rome, and to prepare the ways
390   You have for dignities, to the mere undoing
Of all the kingdom. Many more there are,
Which since they are of you, and odious,
I will not taint my mouth with.

CHAMBERLAIN   O my lord,
395   Press not a falling man too far. 'Tis virtue:
His faults lie open to the laws, let them,

---

371 **wrought** planned, connived, worked   **legate** one of the Pope's representatives
374 '*Ego . . . meus*' "My king and I" (Latin); literally "I and my king," which leads Norfolk
to claim that Wolsey places himself before the king; however, this is the required Latin word
order and Wolsey's real offense is to equate himself with the monarch   375 **still** always
379 **Ambassador** i.e. as Henry's ambassador   **emperor** the Holy Roman Emperor, Charles V
made bold dared   380 **carry . . . seal** taking the great seal of England out of the country
was forbidden   **Flanders** part of the Netherlands   381 *Item* next (on the list; Latin)
commission delegation with specific instructions   382 **Gregory de Cassado** English
ambassador to the Pope   383 **allowance** permission   384 **Ferrara** the Duke of Ferrara
(one of the Italian city-states)   385 **mere** absolute, utter   387 **innumerable substance**
incalculable wealth   389 **furnish . . . dignities** bribe Rome as a means of paving your way to
personal titles and offices   390 **to . . . kingdom** i.e. at England's expense   391 **Many more** i.e.
accusations, offenses   395 **virtue** i.e. virtuous not to list the offenses   396 **lie open** are
exposed, i.e. are at the mercy (of)

Not you, correct him. My heart weeps to see him
So little of his great self.

SURREY   I forgive him.

400   SUFFOLK   Lord cardinal, the king's further pleasure is,
Because all those things you have done of late
By your power legative within this kingdom,
Fall into th'compass of a praemunire,
That therefore such a writ be sued against you,
405   To forfeit all your goods, lands, tenements,
Castles, and whatsoever, and to be
Out of the king's protection. This is my charge.

NORFOLK   And so we'll leave you to your meditations
How to live better. For your stubborn answer
410   About the giving back the great seal to us,
The king shall know it, and, no doubt, shall thank you.
So fare you well, my little good lord cardinal.

Exeunt all but Wolsey

CARDINAL WOLSEY   So farewell to the little good you bear me.
Farewell? A long farewell to all my greatness.
415   This is the state of man: today he puts forth
The tender leaves of hopes: tomorrow blossoms,
And bears his blushing honours thick upon him:
The third day comes a frost, a killing frost,
And when he thinks, good easy man, full surely
420   His greatness is a-ripening, nips his root,
And then he falls, as I do. I have ventured,
Like little wanton boys that swim on bladders,
This many summers in a sea of glory,
But far beyond my depth: my high-blown pride

---

402 **legative** as a papal legate   403 **praemunire** the offense of recognizing papal legal
authority over that of the English monarch   404 **sued** instituted, legally enforced
405 **tenements** houses/leased land or property   406 **Castles** some editors emend to
"chattels" on the basis of the equivalent passage in Holinshed, but the Folio reading is a
suitable climax to the list   407 **charge** order, instruction   409 **For** as for   416 **tender**
young, fresh   417 **blushing** glowing, vibrant (perhaps with reference to the red robes of a
cardinal)   419 **easy** comfortable, complacent   422 **wanton** playful, wild, careless
bladders inflated animal bladders used as floats   423 **This** (for) these   424 **high-blown** over-
inflated (like the **bladders**; also a suggestion of "fully blooming," recalling the vegetation
imagery of a few lines earlier)

425　At length broke under me, and now has left me
　　Weary, and old with service, to the mercy
　　Of a rude stream, that must for ever hide me.
　　Vain pomp and glory of this world, I hate ye:
　　I feel my heart new opened. O, how wretched
430　Is that poor man that hangs on princes' favours?
　　There is betwixt that smile we would aspire to,
　　That sweet aspect of princes, and their ruin,
　　More pangs and fears than wars or women have:
　　And when he falls, he falls like Lucifer,
435　Never to hope again.

Enter Cromwell, standing amazed

　　　　　　　　　　　　　Why, how now, Cromwell?

CROMWELL　I have no power to speak, sir.

CARDINAL WOLSEY　What, amazed
　　At my misfortunes? Can thy spirit wonder
　　A great man should decline? Nay, an you weep
440　I am fall'n indeed.

CROMWELL　How does your grace?

CARDINAL WOLSEY　Why, well:
　　Never so truly happy, my good Cromwell.
　　I know myself now, and I feel within me
445　A peace above all earthly dignities,
　　A still and quiet conscience. The king has cured me,
　　I humbly thank his grace, and from these shoulders,
　　These ruined pillars, out of pity, taken
　　A load would sink a navy: too much honour.
450　O, 'tis a burden, Cromwell, 'tis a burden
　　Too heavy for a man that hopes for heaven.

CROMWELL　I am glad your grace has made that right use of it.

---

427 **rude stream** rough current　428 **Vain** proud/empty, meaningless/foolish, frivolous
432 **aspect** facial appearance/gaze (with astrological connotations of "influential position of a
planet")　**their ruin** the ruin they can cause　433 **pangs** pains (often applied to labor pains)
434 **Lucifer** the brightest angel in heaven, who rebelled, was cast into hell and became the devil
435 *amazed* stunned　439 **decline** fall　**an** if　443 **happy** fortunate　448 **pillars** may recall
the silver pillars that were emblems of Wolsey's role as cardinal　452 **it** i.e. self-knowledge

CARDINAL WOLSEY   I hope I have: I am able now, methinks,
Out of a fortitude of soul I feel,
455   To endure more miseries and greater far
Than my weak-hearted enemies dare offer.
What news abroad?
CROMWELL   The heaviest and the worst
Is your displeasure with the king.
460   CARDINAL WOLSEY   God bless him.
CROMWELL   The next is that Sir Thomas More is chosen
Lord Chancellor in your place.
CARDINAL WOLSEY   That's somewhat sudden,
But he's a learnèd man. May he continue
465   Long in his highness' favour, and do justice
For truth's sake and his conscience, that his bones,
When he has run his course and sleeps in blessings,
May have a tomb of orphans' tears wept on him.
What more?
470   CROMWELL   That Cranmer is returned with welcome,
Installed Lord Archbishop of Canterbury.
CARDINAL WOLSEY   That's news indeed.
CROMWELL   Last, that the Lady Anne,
Whom the king hath in secrecy long married,
475   This day was viewed in open as his queen,
Going to chapel, and the voice is now
Only about her coronation.
CARDINAL WOLSEY   There was the weight that pulled me down.
O Cromwell,
480   The king has gone beyond me: all my glories
In that one woman I have lost for ever.
No sun shall ever usher forth mine honours,
Or gild again the noble troops that waited
Upon my smiles. Go, get thee from me, Cromwell:
485   I am a poor fall'n man, unworthy now

---

458 heaviest saddest/most weighty   459 displeasure disgrace   466 that so that
468 orphans the Lord Chancellor was the legal guardian of all orphans under the age of
twenty-one   475 open public   476 voice talk   480 gone beyond overreached   481 In i.e.
because of   483 troops retinues, groups of followers

To be thy lord and master. Seek the king —
That sun I pray may never set — I have told him
What and how true thou art: he will advance thee:
Some little memory of me will stir him —
490   I know his noble nature — not to let
Thy hopeful service perish too. Good Cromwell,
Neglect him not: make use now, and provide
For thine own future safety.

CROMWELL   O my lord,
495   Must I then leave you? Must I needs forgo
So good, so noble and so true a master?
Bear witness, all that have not hearts of iron,
With what a sorrow Cromwell leaves his lord.
The king shall have my service: but my prayers
500   For ever and for ever shall be yours.

CARDINAL WOLSEY   Cromwell, I did not think to shed a
        tear   *He weeps*
In all my miseries: but thou hast forced me,
Out of thy honest truth, to play the woman.
Let's dry our eyes: and thus far hear me Cromwell,
505   And when I am forgotten, as I shall be,
And sleep in dull cold marble, where no mention
Of me more must be heard of, say I taught thee:
Say Wolsey, that once trod the ways of glory,
And sounded all the depths and shoals of honour,
510   Found thee a way, out of his wreck, to rise in:
A sure and safe one, though thy master missed it.
Mark but my fall, and that that ruined me:
Cromwell, I charge thee, fling away ambition:
By that sin fell the angels: how can man then,
515   The image of his maker, hope to win by it?
Love thyself last: cherish those hearts that hate thee:
Corruption wins not more than honesty.

---

491 **hopeful** promising   492 **make use** take advantage, profit   495 **forgo** forsake   503 **truth**
loyalty   **play the woman** i.e. weep   506 **dull** lifeless   509 **sounded** fathomed, probed the
depth of   **shoals** shallows   510 **wreck** shipwreck/ruin   512 **Mark** note, heed

Still in thy right hand carry gentle peace
To silence envious tongues. Be just, and fear not:
520   Let all the ends thou aim'st at be thy country's,
Thy God's, and truth's. Then if thou fall'st, O Cromwell,
Thou fall'st a blessèd martyr.
Serve the king: and prithee lead me in:
There take an inventory of all I have:
525   To the last penny 'tis the king's. My robe,
And my integrity to heaven, is all
I dare now call mine own. O Cromwell, Cromwell,
Had I but served my God with half the zeal
I served my king, he would not in mine age
530   Have left me naked to mine enemies.

CROMWELL   Good sir, have patience.

CARDINAL WOLSEY   So I have. Farewell
The hopes of court: my hopes in heaven do dwell.   *Exeunt*

Act 4 Scene 1   *running scene 10*

Enter two Gentlemen, meeting one another [the First holding a paper]

FIRST GENTLEMAN   You're well met once again.

SECOND GENTLEMAN   So are you.

FIRST GENTLEMAN   You come to take your stand here, and behold
The Lady Anne pass from her coronation?

5   SECOND GENTLEMAN   'Tis all my business. At our last encounter,
The Duke of Buckingham came from his trial.

FIRST GENTLEMAN   'Tis very true. But that time offered sorrow,
This, general joy.

SECOND GENTLEMAN   'Tis well: the citizens,
10   I am sure, have shown at full their royal minds —
As, let 'em have their rights, they are ever forward —
In celebration of this day with shows,
Pageants and sights of honour.

---

518 Still always   530 naked defenseless   **4.1**   *Location: a street in Westminster,*
London   5 all my business what I'm here for   8 general public, universal   10 royal
generous/supportive of the monarchy   11 let . . . rights to give them their due   forward
eager, ready

FIRST GENTLEMAN Never greater,

15   Nor, I'll assure you, better taken, sir.

SECOND GENTLEMAN May I be bold to ask what that contains,
        That paper in your hand?

FIRST GENTLEMAN Yes, 'tis the list
        Of those that claim their offices this day

20   By custom of the coronation.
        The Duke of Suffolk is the first, and claims
        To be High Steward: next, the Duke of Norfolk,
        He to be Earl Marshal: you may read the rest.

SECOND GENTLEMAN I thank you, sir: had I not known those
        customs,

25   I should have been beholding to your paper:
        But I beseech you, what's become of Katherine,
        The Princess Dowager? How goes her business?

FIRST GENTLEMAN That I can tell you too. The Archbishop
        Of Canterbury, accompanied with other

30   Learnèd and reverend fathers of his order,
        Held a late court at Dunstable, six miles off
        From Ampthill, where the princess lay: to which
        She was often cited by them, but appeared not:
        And, to be short, for not appearance and

35   The king's late scruple, by the main assent
        Of all these learnèd men she was divorced,
        And the late marriage made of none effect,
        Since which she was removed to Kimbolton,
        Where she remains now sick.

40 SECOND GENTLEMAN Alas, good lady.   *Trumpets*
        The trumpets sound: stand close, the queen is coming.

---

15 taken received   **22 High Steward** the officer presiding over the coronation   **23 Earl
Marshal** a high-ranking state office   **25 beholding** beholden, indebted   **30 order** rank, status
(i.e. other bishops)   **31 late** recent   Dunstable Bedfordshire town, about thirty-five miles
north of London   **32 Ampthill** Ampthill Castle, in fact nearer ten miles north of Dunstable
lay lodged   **33 cited** summoned   **34 short** brief   **35 late scruple** recent doubt (over the
validity of his marriage to Katherine)   **main assent** general agreement   **37 of none effect**
null and void   **38 Kimbolton** a castle in Cambridgeshire, not far from Huntingdon   **41 close**
quiet/to one side

Hautboys

The Order of the Coronation

1. *A lively flourish of Trumpets.*
2. *Then, [enter] two Judges.*
3. *Lord Chancellor, with purse and mace before him.*
4. *Choristers, singing. Music [being played by musicians].*
5. *Mayor of London, bearing the mace. Then Garter, in his coat of arms, and on his head he wore a gilt copper crown.*
6. *Marquis Dorset, bearing a sceptre of gold, on his head a demi-coronal of gold. With him, the Earl of Surrey, bearing the rod of silver with the dove, crowned with an earl's coronet. Collars of esses.*
7. *Duke of Suffolk, in his robe of estate, his coronet on his head, bearing a long white wand, as High Steward. With him, the Duke of Norfolk, with the rod of marshalship, a coronet on his head. Collars of esses.*
8. *A canopy, borne by four [Barons] of the Cinque Ports, under it the Queen [Anne] in her robe, in her hair, richly adorned with pearl, crowned. On each side her, the Bishops of London and Winchester.*
9. *The old Duchess of Norfolk, in a coronal of gold, wrought with flowers, bearing the Queen's train.*
10. *Certain Ladies or Countesses, with plain circlets of gold without flowers.*

Exeunt, first passing over the stage in order and state
[while being discussed by the Gentlemen]

SECOND GENTLEMAN   A royal train, believe me: these I know.
Who's that that bears the sceptre?

FIRST GENTLEMAN   Marquis Dorset,

45   And that the Earl of Surrey, with the rod.

---

flourish fanfare   *Garter* Garter King-at-Arms, chief herald of the College of Arms and a key official in the management of royal ceremonies   *demi-coronal* small coronet   *dove* emblematic of peace   *Collars of esses* ornamental gold chains composed of S-shaped links   *estate* state   *Cinque Ports* five ports on the southeast coast of England, originally Dover, Hastings, Sandwich, Hythe and Romney; their barons had the right to hold the canopy over the king during processions   *in her hair* with her hair loose, as was customary for brides   *coronal* coronet   *train* excess material at the back of a dress   **42 train** retinue

SECOND GENTLEMAN   A bold brave gentleman. That should be
      The Duke of Suffolk?

FIRST GENTLEMAN   'Tis the same: High Steward.

SECOND GENTLEMAN   And that my lord of Norfolk?

50   FIRST GENTLEMAN   Yes.

SECOND GENTLEMAN   Heaven bless thee!   *He sees Anne*
      Thou hast the sweetest face I ever looked on.—
      Sir, as I have a soul, she is an angel:
      Our king has all the Indies in his arms,

55   And more, and richer, when he strains that lady:
      I cannot blame his conscience.

FIRST GENTLEMAN   They that bear
      The cloth of honour over her, are four barons
      Of the Cinque Ports.

60   SECOND GENTLEMAN   Those men are happy,
      And so are all are near her.
      I take it she that carries up the train
      Is that old noble lady, Duchess of Norfolk.

FIRST GENTLEMAN   It is, and all the rest are countesses.

65   SECOND GENTLEMAN   Their coronets say so. These are stars indeed,
      And sometimes falling ones.

FIRST GENTLEMAN   No more of that.

                            [*Exit the end of the procession,*] *and then*
                                    a great flourish of Trumpets

Enter a Third Gentleman

FIRST GENTLEMAN   God save you, sir. Where have you been
      broiling?

THIRD GENTLEMAN   Among the crowd i'th'Abbey, where a finger

70   Could not be wedged in more: I am stifled
      With the mere rankness of their joy.

---

46 should must   **54 Indies** i.e. great wealth   **55 strains** embraces, with suggestion of sexual
exertion   **56 conscience** plays on the sense of "genitals"   **58 cloth of honour** royal canopy
59 Cinque Ports five (later seven) ports on the southeast coast of England that provided the
navy and were granted privileges in return   **66 falling** plays on the sense of "sexually
receptive"   **68 broiling** becoming heated, sweating (from struggling for a good view amongst
a **crowd** of onlookers)   **69 i'th'Abbey** in Westminster Abbey, venue for coronations
finger . . . more perhaps with sexual connotations (especially if **rankness** is given its sexual
sense)   **71 mere** absolute, utter   **rankness** exuberance/foul (sweaty) smell/lustfulness

SECOND GENTLEMAN You saw
  The ceremony?

THIRD GENTLEMAN That I did.

75 FIRST GENTLEMAN How was it?

THIRD GENTLEMAN Well worth the seeing.

SECOND GENTLEMAN Good sir, speak it to us.

THIRD GENTLEMAN As well as I am able. The rich stream
  Of lords and ladies, having brought the queen
80 To a prepared place in the choir, fell off
  A distance from her, while her grace sat down
  To rest a while, some half an hour or so,
  In a rich chair of state, opposing freely
  The beauty of her person to the people.
85 Believe me, sir, she is the goodliest woman
  That ever lay by man: which when the people
  Had the full view of, such a noise arose
  As the shrouds make at sea in a stiff tempest,
  As loud, and to as many tunes. Hats, cloaks —
90 Doublets, I think — flew up, and had their faces
  Been loose, this day they had been lost. Such joy
  I never saw before. Great-bellied women,
  That had not half a week to go, like rams
  In the old time of war, would shake the press
95 And make 'em reel before 'em. No man living
  Could say 'This is my wife' there, all were woven
  So strangely in one piece.

SECOND GENTLEMAN But, what followed?

THIRD GENTLEMAN At length her grace rose, and with modest
  paces
100 Came to the altar, where she kneeled, and saint-like
  Cast her fair eyes to heaven and prayed devoutly.

---

77 speak describe   **80 fell off** withdrew   **83 opposing** displaying   **85 goodliest** finest, most
good-looking   **87 arose** perhaps with connotations of penile erection   **88 shrouds** ropes
attached to the mast, standard part of a ship's rigging (perhaps with phallic connotations; a
rope was a slang image for a penis)   **stiff** strong; again with connotations of penile erection
90 Doublets men's close-fitting jackets   **92 Great-bellied** i.e. pregnant   **93 rams** battering
rams   **94 press** crowd, throng

Then rose again and bowed her to the people:
When by the Archbishop of Canterbury
She had all the royal makings of a queen,
105 As holy oil, Edward Confessor's crown,
The rod, and bird of peace, and all such emblems
Laid nobly on her: which performed, the choir,
With all the choicest music of the kingdom,
Together sung *Te Deum*. So she parted,
110 And with the same full state paced back again
To York Place, where the feast is held.

FIRST GENTLEMAN   Sir,
You must no more call it York Place, that's past:
For, since the cardinal fell, that title's lost:
115 'Tis now the king's, and called Whitehall.

THIRD GENTLEMAN   I know it;
But 'tis so lately altered, that the old name
Is fresh about me.

SECOND GENTLEMAN   What two reverend bishops
120 Were those that went on each side of the queen?

THIRD GENTLEMAN   Stokesley and Gardiner, the one of
Winchester,
Newly preferred from the king's secretary:
The other, London.

SECOND GENTLEMAN   He of Winchester
125 Is held no great good lover of the archbishop's,
The virtuous Cranmer.

THIRD GENTLEMAN   All the land knows that:
However, yet there is no great breach: when it comes,
Cranmer will find a friend will not shrink from him.

130 SECOND GENTLEMAN   Who may that be, I pray you?

THIRD GENTLEMAN   Thomas Cromwell;
A man in much esteem with th'king, and truly
A worthy friend. The king has made him

---

104 royal makings trappings of royalty bestowed during a coronation   **105 As** such as
108 music musicians   **109 *Te Deum*** thanksgiving hymn "*Te Deum laudamus*" (Latin; "We
praise thee O God")   **parted** departed   **110 state** procession/pomp/dignity   **117 lately**
recently   **121 the one** i.e. Gardiner   **122 preferred** promoted   **129 will** who will

Master o'th'Jewel House,

135   And one already of the Privy Council.

SECOND GENTLEMAN   He will deserve more.

THIRD GENTLEMAN   Yes, without all doubt.

Come, gentlemen, ye shall go my way,

Which is to th'court, and there ye shall be my guests:

140   Something I can command. As I walk thither,

I'll tell ye more.

FIRST *and* SECOND GENTLEMEN   You may command us, sir.   *Exeunt*

Act 4 Scene 2   *running scene 11*

Enter Katherine Dowager, sick, led between Griffith, her
Gentleman-usher, and Patience, her Woman

GRIFFITH   How does your grace?

KATHERINE   O Griffith, sick to death:

My legs like loaden branches, bow to th'earth,

Willing to leave their burden. Reach a chair: *She sits*

5   So now, methinks, I feel a little ease.

Didst thou not tell me, Griffith, as thou led'st me,

That the great child of honour, Cardinal Wolsey, was dead?

GRIFFITH   Yes, madam, but I think your grace,

Out of the pain you suffered, gave no ear to't.

10   KATHERINE   Prithee, good Griffith, tell me how he died.

If well, he stepped before me happily

For my example.

GRIFFITH   Well, the voice goes, madam:

For after the stout Earl Northumberland

15   Arrested him at York, and brought him forward,

As a man sorely tainted, to his answer,

He fell sick suddenly, and grew so ill

He could not sit his mule.

---

134 **Master o'th'Jewel House** i.e. responsible for the Crown Jewels in the Tower of London
140 **Something . . . command** i.e. I have some degree of influence   **4.2**   *Location:*
Kimbolton Castle, Cambridgeshire   3 **loaden** laden, overburdened   11 **happily** fittingly/
fortunately/perhaps   13 **voice** word, rumor   14 **stout** brave, resolute   15 **brought him**
forward escorted him   16 **tainted** disgraced/corrupted   **answer** trial   18 **sit** sit on

KATHERINE   Alas, poor man.

20   GRIFFITH   At last, with easy roads, he came to Leicester,
Lodged in the abbey, where the reverend abbot,
With all his convent, honourably received him,
To whom he gave these words: 'O father abbot,
An old man, broken with the storms of state,

25   Is come to lay his weary bones among ye:
Give him a little earth for charity.'
So went to bed, where eagerly his sickness
Pursued him still: and three nights after this,
About the hour of eight, which he himself

30   Foretold should be his last, full of repentance,
Continual meditations, tears, and sorrows,
He gave his honours to the world again,
His blessèd part to heaven, and slept in peace.

KATHERINE   So may he rest: his faults lie gently on him.

35   Yet thus far, Griffith, give me leave to speak him,
And yet with charity. He was a man
Of an unbounded stomach, ever ranking
Himself with princes: one that by suggestion
Tied all the kingdom. Simony was fair play:

40   His own opinion was his law. I'th'presence
He would say untruths, and be ever double
Both in his words and meaning. He was never,
But where he meant to ruin, pitiful.
His promises were, as he then was, mighty:

45   But his performance, as he is now, nothing:
Of his own body he was ill, and gave
The clergy ill example.

GRIFFITH   Noble madam,
Men's evil manners live in brass, their virtues

---

20 **roads** stages (of the journey)   **Leicester** chief town of Leicestershire, in central England
22 **convent** members of the monastery   26 **little earth** i.e. grave   27 **eagerly** keenly/fiercely
33 **blessèd part** i.e. soul   35 **speak** speak of/describe   37 **stomach** pride/ambitious appetite
38 **suggestion** incitement, prompting (to wrongdoing)   39 **Tied** subjected, tied up   **Simony**
buying and selling ecclesiastical posts   40 **I'th'presence** in the royal reception chamber/
presence of the king   41 **double** duplicitous/ambiguous   43 **pitiful** merciful, compassionate
46 **body** i.e. sexual appetites, love of worldly pleasures   **ill** immoral

50   We write in water. May it please your highness
        To hear me speak his good now?

    KATHERINE   Yes, good Griffith,
        I were malicious else.

    GRIFFITH   This cardinal,
55   Though from an humble stock, undoubtedly
        Was fashioned to much honour. From his cradle
        He was a scholar, and a ripe and good one:
        Exceeding wise, fair-spoken, and persuading:
        Lofty and sour to them that loved him not:
60   But to those men that sought him, sweet as summer.
        And though he were unsatisfied in getting,
        Which was a sin, yet in bestowing, madam,
        He was most princely: ever witness for him
        Those twins of learning that he raised in you,
65   Ipswich and Oxford: one of which fell with him,
        Unwilling to outlive the good that did it:
        The other, though unfinished, yet so famous,
        So excellent in art, and still so rising,
        That Christendom shall ever speak his virtue.
70   His overthrow heaped happiness upon him:
        For then, and not till then, he felt himself,
        And found the blessedness of being little.
        And, to add greater honours to his age
        Than man could give him, he died fearing God.
75   KATHERINE   After my death I wish no other herald,
        No other speaker of my living actions,
        To keep mine honour from corruption,
        But such an honest chronicler as Griffith.
        Whom I most hated living, thou hast made me,
80   With thy religious truth and modesty,

---

51 good goodness, virtues   **56 to** for   **57 ripe** mature, sophisticated   **59 Lofty** haughty
61 unsatisfied in getting never satisfied with what he had acquired   **64 you** Griffith addresses
Ipswich and Oxford   **65 Ipswich and Oxford** Wolsey founded colleges in both towns, though
only that at Oxford survived him; originally intended to be Cardinal's College, it was renamed
Christ Church   **66 did** made, founded   **68 art** scholarship   **rising** growing (in reputation
and excellence; plays on the idea of physical completion)   **72 little** humble   **79 Whom** he
whom (i.e. Wolsey)   **80 religious** conscientious   **modesty** moderation, restraint

Now in his ashes honour: peace be with him.
Patience, be near me still, and set me lower: *To Patience*
I have not long to trouble thee. Good Griffith,
Cause the musicians play me that sad note

85 I named my knell, whilst I sit meditating
On that celestial harmony I go to.

                                     Sad and solemn music   She sleeps

GRIFFITH   She is asleep: good wench, let's sit down quiet
For fear we wake her. Softly, gentle Patience.

The Vision

Enter, solemnly tripping one after another, six personages, clad in white
robes, wearing on their heads garlands of bays, and golden vizards on
their faces, branches of bays or palm in their hands. They first congee
unto her, then dance: and at certain changes, the first two hold a spare
garland over her head, at which the other four make reverent curtsies.
Then the two that held the garland deliver the same to the other next
two, who observe the same order in their changes, and holding the
garland over her head. Which done, they deliver the same garland to the
last two, who likewise observe the same order. At which, as it were by
inspiration, she makes in her sleep signs of rejoicing, and holdeth up
her hands to heaven. And so, in their dancing vanish, carrying the
garland with them. The music continues

KATHERINE   Spirits of peace, where are ye? Are ye all gone,

90 And leave me here in wretchedness behind ye?

GRIFFITH   Madam, we are here.

KATHERINE   It is not you I call for:
Saw ye none enter since I slept?

GRIFFITH   None, madam.

95 KATHERINE   No? Saw you not even now a blessèd troop
Invite me to a banquet, whose bright faces
Cast thousand beams upon me, like the sun?
They promised me eternal happiness,

---

82 **set me lower** i.e. help me to lie back or sit lower in the chair   84 **note** tune   85 **knell**
funeral bell   86 **celestial harmony** i.e. heaven   *tripping* moving nimbly and lightly   *bays*
bay-tree leaves, a symbol of triumph   *vizards* masks   *congee* make a formal bow
changes turns or stages of the dance   *in their* i.e. still

And brought me garlands, Griffith, which I feel
100   I am not worthy yet to wear: I shall, assuredly.
GRIFFITH   I am most joyful, madam, such good dreams
Possess your fancy.
KATHERINE   Bid the music leave,
They are harsh and heavy to me.   *Music ceases*
105   PATIENCE   Do you note   *Patience and Griffith speak aside*
How much her grace is altered on the sudden?
How long her face is drawn? How pale she looks,
And of an earthy cold? Mark her eyes!
GRIFFITH   She is going, wench: pray, pray.
110   PATIENCE   Heaven comfort her.
Enter a Messenger
MESSENGER   An't like your grace—
KATHERINE   You are a saucy fellow:
Deserve we no more reverence?
GRIFFITH   You are to blame,   *To the Messenger*
115   Knowing she will not lose her wonted greatness,
To use so rude behaviour. Go to, kneel.
MESSENGER   I humbly do entreat your highness' pardon:
My haste made me unmannerly. There is staying
A gentleman sent from the king to see you.
120   KATHERINE   Admit him entrance, Griffith. But this fellow
Let me ne'er see again.   *Exit Messenger*
Enter Lord Caputius [ushered by Griffith]
                              If my sight fail not,
You should be lord ambassador from the emperor,
My royal nephew, and your name Caputius.
CAPUTIUS   Madam, the same. Your servant.
125   KATHERINE   O my lord,
The times and titles now are altered strangely
With me since first you knew me. But I pray you,
What is your pleasure with me?

---

102 fancy imagination   **103 music leave** musicians cease   **104 heavy** oppressive/sorrowful
111 An't like if it please   **112 saucy** insolent   **115 lose** give up   **wonted** accustomed
118 staying waiting   **122 emperor** Holy Roman Emperor Charles V, Katherine's **nephew**

CAPUTIUS   Noble lady,

130   First mine own service to your grace: the next,
        The king's request that I would visit you,
        Who grieves much for your weakness, and by me
        Sends you his princely commendations,
        And heartily entreats you take good comfort.

135   KATHERINE   O my good lord, that comfort comes too late,
        'Tis like a pardon after execution:
        That gentle physic given in time had cured me,
        But now I am past all comforts here but prayers.
        How does his highness?

140   CAPUTIUS   Madam, in good health.

        KATHERINE   So may he ever do, and ever flourish,
        When I shall dwell with worms, and my poor name
        Banished the kingdom. Patience, is that letter
        I caused you write yet sent away?

145   PATIENCE   No, madam.   *Gives it to Katherine*

        KATHERINE   Sir, I most humbly pray you to deliver
        This to my lord the king.   *Gives the letter to Caputius*

        CAPUTIUS   Most willing, madam.

        KATHERINE   In which I have commended to his goodness

150   The model of our chaste loves, his young daughter —
        The dews of heaven fall thick in blessings on her —
        Beseeching him to give her virtuous breeding.
        She is young, and of a noble modest nature:
        I hope she will deserve well — and a little

155   To love her for her mother's sake, that loved him,
        Heaven knows how dearly. My next poor petition
        Is that his noble grace would have some pity
        Upon my wretched women, that so long
        Have followed both my fortunes faithfully:

160   Of which there is not one, I dare avow,
        And now I should not lie, but will deserve

---

137 physic medicine   **had** would have   **148 willing** willingly   **150 model** image   **daughter**
i.e. Mary   **152 breeding** upbringing   **159 both my fortunes** i.e. good and bad, as queen and
subsequently

For virtue and true beauty of the soul,
For honesty and decent carriage,
A right good husband — let him be a noble —
165   And sure those men are happy that shall have 'em.
The last is for my men — they are the poorest,
But poverty could never draw 'em from me —
That they may have their wages duly paid 'em,
And something over to remember me by.
170   If heaven had pleased to have given me longer life
And able means, we had not parted thus.
These are the whole contents, and, good my lord,
By that you love the dearest in this world,
As you wish Christian peace to souls departed,
175   Stand these poor people's friend, and urge the king
To do me this last right.

CAPUTIUS   By heaven, I will,
Or let me lose the fashion of a man.

KATHERINE   I thank you, honest lord. Remember me
180   In all humility unto his highness:
Say his long trouble now is passing
Out of this world. Tell him in death I blessed him,
For so I will. Mine eyes grow dim. Farewell,
My lord. Griffith, farewell. Nay, Patience,
185   You must not leave me yet. I must to bed:
Call in more women. When I am dead, good wench,
Let me be used with honour: strew me over
With maiden flowers, that all the world may know
I was a chaste wife to my grave: embalm me,
190   Then lay me forth: although unqueened, yet like
A queen and daughter to a king inter me.
I can no more.   *Exeunt leading Katherine*

---

163 **honesty** chastity/virtue   **carriage** behavior   165 **happy** fortunate   169 **over** extra
171 **able** sufficient   178 **fashion** form, nature, character   179 **honest** honorable   187 **used**
treated   188 **maiden flowers** i.e. those flowers befitting chastity   190 **forth** i.e. out for burial
192 **can** i.e. say or do

Act 5 Scene 1

Enter Gardiner, Bishop of Winchester, a Page with a torch before him,
met by Sir Thomas Lovell

GARDINER   It's one o'clock, boy, is't not?

PAGE   It hath struck.

GARDINER   These should be hours for necessities,
Not for delights: times to repair our nature
5   With comforting repose, and not for us
To waste these times. Good hour of night, Sir Thomas:
Whither so late?

LOVELL   Came you from the king, my lord?

GARDINER   I did, Sir Thomas, and left him at primero
10   With the Duke of Suffolk.

LOVELL   I must to him too,
Before he go to bed. I'll take my leave.

GARDINER   Not yet, Sir Thomas Lovell. What's the matter?
It seems you are in haste: an if there be
15   No great offence belongs to't, give your friend
Some touch of your late business: affairs that walk,
As they say spirits do, at midnight, have
In them a wilder nature than the business
That seeks dispatch by day.

20   LOVELL   My lord, I love you,
And durst commend a secret to your ear
Much weightier than this work. The queen's in labour —
They say in great extremity — and feared
She'll with the labour end.

25   GARDINER   The fruit she goes with
I pray for heartily, that it may find
Good time, and live: but for the stock, Sir Thomas,
I wish it grubbed up now.

5.1 *Location: the royal court, London*   **3 necessities** essential activities, i.e. sleep
7 Whither where are you going   **9 primero** gambling card game   **11 must** must go   **14 an if**
if   **15 offence** harm   **16 touch** sense, hint   **late** recent/late night   **21 durst commend**
dare entrust   **22 this work** i.e. what he has been engaged in   **23 feared** it is feared   **25 fruit**
i.e. child   **goes with** carries/is in the throes of labor with   **27 time** delivery, outcome   **stock**
tree that bore the fruit, i.e. Anne   **28 grubbed up** uprooted

LOVELL   Methinks I could
30   Cry the amen, and yet my conscience says
        She's a good creature and, sweet lady, does
        Deserve our better wishes.

GARDINER   But, sir, sir,
        Hear me, Sir Thomas: you're a gentleman
35   Of mine own way. I know you wise, religious,
        And let me tell you, it will ne'er be well —
        'Twill not, Sir Thomas Lovell, take't of me —
        Till Cranmer, Cromwell, her two hands, and she
        Sleep in their graves.

40 LOVELL   Now, sir, you speak of two
        The most remarked i'th'kingdom. As for Cromwell,
        Beside that of the Jewel House, is made Master
        O'th'Rolls and the king's secretary. Further, sir,
        Stands in the gap and trade of more preferments,
45   With which the time will load him. Th'archbishop
        Is the king's hand and tongue, and who dare speak
        One syllable against him?

GARDINER   Yes, yes, Sir Thomas,
        There are that dare, and I myself have ventured
50   To speak my mind of him: and indeed this day,
        Sir, I may tell it you, I think I have
        Incensed the lords o'th'council, that he is —
        For so I know he is, they know he is —
        A most arch-heretic, a pestilence
55   That does infect the land: with which they, moved,
        Have broken with the king, who hath so far
        Given ear to our complaint, of his great grace
        And princely care, foreseeing those fell mischiefs

---

30 Cry the amen i.e. agree   **35 way** of thinking, i.e. Catholic religious views   **38 hands** i.e. assistants, supporters   **41 remarked** notable/conspicuous   **42 Master O'th'Rolls** a high-ranking legal position   **44 gap and trade** opening and path   **45 time** age, state of affairs/time to come/opportunity   **49 are** are those   **52 Incensed** angered   **54 arch-heretic** major, principal holder of unorthodox religious views (puns on "archbishop")   **55 moved** angered, stirred   **56 broken** broached (the matter)   **58 fell** fierce, terrible   **mischiefs** evils, misfortunes

Our reasons laid before him, hath commanded
60   Tomorrow morning to the council board
He be convented. He's a rank weed, Sir Thomas,
And we must root him out. From your affairs
I hinder you too long. Goodnight, Sir Thomas.

LOVELL   Many good nights, my lord: I rest your servant.

Exeunt Gardiner and Page
Enter King [Henry] and Suffolk

65   KING HENRY VIII   Charles, I will play no more tonight: *To Suffolk*
My mind's not on't: you are too hard for me.

SUFFOLK   Sir, I did never win of you before.

KING HENRY VIII   But little, Charles,
Nor shall not when my fancy's on my play.

70   Now, Lovell, from the queen what is the news?

LOVELL   I could not personally deliver to her
What you commanded me, but by her woman
I sent your message, who returned her thanks
In the great'st humbleness, and desired your highness
75   Most heartily to pray for her.

KING HENRY VIII   What say'st thou? Ha?
To pray for her? What, is she crying out?

LOVELL   So said her woman, and that her suff'rance made
Almost each pang a death.

80   KING HENRY VIII   Alas, good lady.

SUFFOLK   God safely quit her of her burden, and
With gentle travail, to the gladding of
Your highness with an heir!

KING HENRY VIII   'Tis midnight, Charles.
85   Prithee to bed, and in thy prayers remember
Th'estate of my poor queen. Leave me alone,
For I must think of that which company
Would not be friendly to.

---

61 **convented** summoned to appear   **rank** rapidly growing, abundant   64 **rest** remain
66 **hard** strong (a player)   69 **fancy** mind, inclination   78 **suff'rance** suffering   81 **God**
may God   **quit** release, relieve   82 **travail** labor   **gladding** delighting   86 **estate** state,
situation

SUFFOLK   I wish your highness
90 A quiet night, and my good mistress will
Remember in my prayers.

KING HENRY VIII   Charles, goodnight.   *Exit Suffolk*

Enter Sir Anthony Denny

Well, sir, what follows?

DENNY   Sir, I have brought my lord the archbishop,
95 As you commanded me.

KING HENRY VIII   Ha? Canterbury?

DENNY   Ay, my good lord.

KING HENRY VIII   'Tis true: where is he, Denny?

DENNY   He attends your highness' pleasure.

100 KING HENRY VIII   Bring him to us.   [*Exit Denny*]

LOVELL   This is about that which the bishop spake.   *Aside*
I am happily come hither.

Enter Cranmer and Denny

KING HENRY VIII   Avoid the gallery.   *Lovell seems to stay*
Ha? I have said. Be gone.

        Exeunt Lovell and Denny

What?

105 CRANMER   I am fearful: wherefore frowns he thus?   *Aside*
'Tis his aspect of terror. All's not well.

KING HENRY VIII   How now, my lord? You desire to know
Wherefore I sent for you.

CRANMER   It is my duty   *He kneels*
110 T'attend your highness' pleasure.

KING HENRY VIII   Pray you, arise,
My good and gracious lord of Canterbury.
Come, you and I must walk a turn together:
I have news to tell you. Come, come, give me your
hand.   *Cranmer stands. They walk*
115 Ah, my good lord, I grieve at what I speak,
And am right sorry to repeat what follows.
I have, and most unwillingly, of late

99 **attends** awaits   101 **bishop** i.e. Gardiner   102 **happily** fortunately, opportunely
103 **Avoid** leave   **gallery** long room used for walking in   106 **aspect of terror** angry
expression

Heard many grievous — I do say, my lord,
Grievous — complaints of you, which, being considered,
120   Have moved us and our council, that you shall
This morning come before us, where I know
You cannot with such freedom purge yourself,
But that, till further trial in those charges
Which will require your answer, you must take
125   Your patience to you, and be well contented
To make your house our Tower. You a brother of us,
It fits we thus proceed, or else no witness
Would come against you.

CRANMER   I humbly thank your highness,   *He kneels*
130   And am right glad to catch this good occasion
Most throughly to be winnowed, where my chaff
And corn shall fly asunder. For I know
There's none stands under more calumnious tongues
Than I myself, poor man.

135   KING HENRY VIII   Stand up, good Canterbury:
Thy truth and thy integrity is rooted
In us, thy friend. Give me thy hand, stand up:
Prithee, let's walk. Now, by my halidom,   *Cranmer stands. They walk*
What manner of man are you? My lord, I looked
140   You would have given me your petition that
I should have ta'en some pains to bring together
Yourself and your accusers, and to have heard you
Without endurance further.

CRANMER   Most dread liege,
145   The good I stand on is my truth and honesty:
If they shall fail, I with mine enemies
Will triumph o'er my person, which I weigh not,

118 **grievous** serious   120 **moved** prompted, decided   122 **with such freedom** so freely,
easily   **purge** clear, exonerate   124 **take . . . you** be patient   126 **Tower** Tower of London
brother of us being a fellow member of the council   127 **fits** is fitting   131 **throughly**
thoroughly   **winnowed** i.e. cleared of impurity, as **corn** is exposed to wind in order to separate
it from worthless husks (**chaff**)   133 **stands under** endures/is subject to   **calumnious**
slanderous   138 **my halidom** all I consider holy   139 **looked** anticipated   140 **given . . .**
petition requested   143 **endurance further** further hardship/forthcoming imprisonment
144 **dread** revered   147 **triumph** exult (at the downfall of)   **weigh** value

Being of those virtues vacant. I fear nothing
What can be said against me.

150 **KING HENRY VIII**   Know you not
How your state stands i'th'world, with the whole world?
Your enemies are many, and not small: their practices
Must bear the same proportion, and not ever
The justice and the truth o'th'question carries

155 The dew o'th'verdict with it: at what ease
Might corrupt minds procure knaves as corrupt
To swear against you? Such things have been done.
You are potently opposed, and with a malice
Of as great size. Ween you of better luck —

160 I mean in perjured witness — than your master,
Whose minister you are, whiles here he lived
Upon this naughty earth? Go to, go to:
You take a precipice for no leap of danger,
And woo your own destruction.

165 **CRANMER**   God and your majesty
Protect mine innocence, or I fall into
The trap is laid for me.

KING HENRY VIII   Be of good cheer:
They shall no more prevail than we give way to.

170 Keep comfort to you, and this morning see
You do appear before them. If they shall chance,
In charging you with matters, to commit you,
The best persuasions to the contrary
Fail not to use, and with what vehemency

175 Th'occasion shall instruct you. If entreaties
Will render you no remedy, this ring
Deliver them, and your appeal to us
There make before them. Look, the good man weeps: *Cranmer*
He's honest, on mine honour. God's blest mother,   *weeps*

148 **Being** should it be   **nothing** not at all   152 **small** insignificant   **practices** plots
153 **bear . . . proportion** be correspondingly powerful   **ever** always   155 **The dew o'th'verdict**
i.e. a successful outcome   **at** with   157 **swear** testify   159 **Ween you of** do you expect
160 **perjured witness** false testimony   **your master** i.e. Christ   162 **naughty** wicked
163 **take . . . danger** behave as though jumping off a cliff were not dangerous   164 **woo** invite,
court   167 **is** that is   169 **give way to** i.e. allow   171 **chance** happen   172 **commit** imprison

180   I swear he is true-hearted, and a soul
       None better in my kingdom. Get you gone,
       And do as I have bid you.   *Exit Cranmer*
                            He has strangled
       His language in his tears.
       Enter Old Lady
       LOVELL   Come back: what mean you?   *Within*
185   OLD LADY   I'll not come back: the tidings that I bring
       Will make my boldness manners.— Now good angels   *To the*
       Fly o'er thy royal head, and shade thy person   *King*
       Under their blessèd wings.
       KING HENRY VIII   Now by thy looks
190   I guess thy message. Is the queen delivered?
       Say, 'Ay, and of a boy.'
       OLD LADY   Ay, ay, my liege,
       And of a lovely boy: the God of heaven
       Both now and ever bless her. 'Tis a girl
195   Promises boys hereafter. Sir, your queen
       Desires your visitation, and to be
       Acquainted with this stranger: 'tis as like you
       As cherry is to cherry.
       KING HENRY VIII   Lovell.
200   LOVELL   Sir?
       KING HENRY VIII   Give her an hundred marks. I'll to the queen.
                                                           Exit King
       OLD LADY   An hundred marks? By this light, I'll ha' more.
       An ordinary groom is for such payment.
       I will have more, or scold it out of him.
205   Said I for this, the girl was like to him? I'll
       Have more, or else unsay't: and now, while 'tis hot,
       I'll put it to the issue.   *Exit [Old] Lady [with Lovell]*

---

186 **Now** now may   190 **Is . . . delivered?** Has the queen given birth?   194 **girl** may apply
either to Anne or to the newly born Elizabeth   195 **Promises** i.e. who promises to give birth to
196 **and** and for you   201 **marks** a mark was a monetary unit (rather than a coin) worth two
thirds of a pound   203 **groom** servingman   **for** suitable for   206 **hot** "to strike while the
iron is hot" was proverbial   207 **put . . . issue** undertake it, insist on it (**issue** may play on the
sense of "child")

Act 5 Scene 2   *running scene 13*

Enter Cranmer, Archbishop of Canterbury

CRANMER   I hope I am not too late, and yet the gentleman
      That was sent to me from the council prayed me
      To make great haste. All fast? What means this? Ho!
      Who waits there?

Enter [Door] Keeper

                        Sure you know me?

5   KEEPER   Yes, my lord,
      But yet I cannot help you.

CRANMER   Why?

KEEPER   Your grace must wait till you be called for.

Enter Doctor Butts [passing over the stage]

CRANMER   So.

10   DOCTOR BUTTS   This is a piece of malice. I am glad   *Aside*
      I came this way so happily. The king
      Shall understand it presently.   *Exit [Doctor] Butts*

CRANMER   'Tis Butts,   *Aside*
      The king's physician: as he passed along
15   How earnestly he cast his eyes upon me:
      Pray heaven he sound not my disgrace: for certain
      This is of purpose laid by some that hate me —
      God turn their hearts, I never sought their malice —
      To quench mine honour: they would shame to make me
20   Wait else at door, a fellow councillor,
      'Mong boys, grooms, and lackeys. But their pleasures
      Must be fulfilled, and I attend with patience.

Enter the King [Henry] and [Doctor] Butts at a window above

DOCTOR BUTTS   I'll show your grace the strangest sight—

KING HENRY VIII   What's that, Butts?

25   DOCTOR BUTTS   I think your highness saw this many a day.

KING HENRY VIII   Body o'me, where is it?

5.2   **3 fast** locked up   **4 Sure** surely   **9 So** so be it/I see   **11 happily** fortunately/by chance
12 understand it presently be informed of it at once   **16 sound** perceive/proclaim   **17 laid**
arranged (like a trap)   **18 turn** alter   **22 attend** wait   *above* i.e. on the upper staging level
or gallery   **26 Body o'me** upon my body (i.e. life)

DOCTOR BUTTS   There, my lord:
The high promotion of his grace of Canterbury,
Who holds his state at door, 'mongst pursuivants,
30   Pages, and footboys.

KING HENRY VIII   Ha? 'Tis he, indeed.
Is this the honour they do one another?
'Tis well there's one above 'em yet: I had thought
They had parted so much honesty among 'em —
35   At least good manners — as not thus to suffer
A man of his place, and so near our favour,
To dance attendance on their lordships' pleasures —
And at the door, too, like a post with packets.
By holy Mary, Butts, there's knavery:
40   Let 'em alone, and draw the curtain close:
We shall hear more anon.   [*Exeunt above*]

A council table brought in with chairs and stools, and placed under the
state. Enter Lord Chancellor, places himself at the upper end of the
table, on the left hand: a seat being left void above him, as for
Canterbury's seat. Duke of Suffolk, Duke of Norfolk, Surrey, Lord
Chamberlain, Gardiner, seat themselves in order on each side. Cromwell
at lower end, as secretary

CHANCELLOR   Speak to the business, master secretary: *To Cromwell*
Why are we met in council?

CROMWELL   Please your honours,
45   The chief cause concerns his grace of Canterbury.

GARDINER   Has he had knowledge of it?

CROMWELL   Yes.

NORFOLK   Who waits there?

KEEPER   Without, my noble lords?

50   GARDINER   Yes.

KEEPER   My lord archbishop:
And has done half an hour to know your pleasures.

---

29 Who . . . state who maintains his dignity/is detained according to his status (ironic)
pursuivants state messengers   30 footboys boy servants, often assistants to footmen
33 one above 'em i.e. the king/God   34 parted divided   honesty integrity/decorum
35 suffer permit   36 place status   37 dance attendance be kept waiting   38 post courier
packets i.e. of letters   40 close shut   state throne   above next to, at the upper end of the
table; the seating arrangements reflect the men's positions   49 Without outside

CHANCELLOR   Let him come in.

KEEPER   Your grace may enter now.

Cranmer [enters below and] approaches the council table

55 CHANCELLOR   My good lord archbishop, I'm very sorry
To sit here at this present, and behold
That chair stand empty: but we all are men,
In our own natures frail, and capable
Of our flesh: few are angels: out of which frailty
60 And want of wisdom, you that best should teach us,
Have misdemeaned yourself, and not a little:
Toward the king first, then his laws, in filling
The whole realm, by your teaching and your chaplains —
For so we are informed — with new opinions,
65 Divers and dangerous, which are heresies,
And, not reformed, may prove pernicious.

GARDINER   Which reformation must be sudden too,
My noble lords, for those that tame wild horses
Pace 'em not in their hands to make 'em gentle,
70 But stop their mouths with stubborn bits and spur 'em
Till they obey the manage. If we suffer,
Out of our easiness and childish pity
To one man's honour, this contagious sickness,
Farewell all physic: and what follows then?
75 Commotions, uproars, with a general taint
Of the whole state, as of late days our neighbours,
The upper Germany, can dearly witness,
Yet freshly pitied in our memories.

CRANMER   My good lords, hitherto, in all the progress
80 Both of my life and office, I have laboured,

---

56 **present** present time   57 **chair** i.e. Cranmer's vacant chair next to the Lord Chancellor
58 **capable Of** susceptible to   59 **flesh** bodily urges, mortal weakness   60 **want** lack
61 **misdemeaned yourself** behaved improperly   65 **Divers** various/different/perverse, cruel
heresies views contrary to orthodox religious opinion   66 **pernicious** destructive
69 **Pace . . . hands** do not train them gently, by hand   70 **stubborn** unyielding   71 **obey the**
manage perform the specific movements correctly (from French *manège*, "horsemanship")
suffer permit   72 **easiness** indulgence, leniency   74 **physic** medicine   75 **taint** corruption/
infection   77 **upper . . . witness** a reference either to the Saxony peasants' revolt of 1524 or
to the rising of the Anabaptists in Münster in 1535   **upper** higher/inland

And with no little study, that my teaching
And the strong course of my authority
Might go one way, and safely: and the end
Was ever to do well: nor is there living —
85   I speak it with a single heart, my lords —
A man that more detests, more stirs against,
Both in his private conscience and his place,
Defacers of a public peace than I do:
Pray heaven the king may never find a heart
90   With less allegiance in it. Men that make
Envy and crooked malice nourishment
Dare bite the best. I do beseech your lordships
That in this case of justice, my accusers,
Be what they will, may stand forth face to face,
95   And freely urge against me.

SUFFOLK   Nay, my lord,
That cannot be: you are a councillor,
And by that virtue no man dare accuse you.

GARDINER   My lord, because we have business of more
    moment,
100   We will be short with you. 'Tis his highness' pleasure
And our consent, for better trial of you,
From hence you be committed to the Tower,
Where being but a private man again,
You shall know many dare accuse you boldly,
105   More than, I fear, you are provided for.

CRANMER   Ah, my good lord of Winchester, I thank you:
You are always my good friend: if your will pass,
I shall both find your lordship judge and juror,
You are so merciful. I see your end:
110   'Tis my undoing. Love and meekness, lord,
Become a churchman better than ambition:
Win straying souls with modesty again:

82 course current/series of undertakings   85 single united, honest   87 place official public position   95 urge make allegations   98 by that virtue by virtue of that   99 moment importance   100 short brief   103 private i.e. not exercising public office   105 provided prepared   107 pass be approved, prevail   109 end aim, purpose   111 Become befit, suit

Cast none away. That I shall clear myself,
Lay all the weight ye can upon my patience,
115   I make as little doubt as you do conscience
In doing daily wrongs. I could say more,
But reverence to your calling makes me modest.

GARDINER   My lord, my lord, you are a sectary,
That's the plain truth: your painted gloss discovers
120   To men that understand you, words and weakness.

CROMWELL   My lord of Winchester, you're a little,
By your good favour, too sharp: men so noble,
However faulty, yet should find respect
For what they have been: 'tis a cruelty
125   To load a falling man.

GARDINER   Good Master Secretary,
I cry your honour mercy: you may worst
Of all this table say so.

CROMWELL   Why, my lord?

130   GARDINER   Do not I know you for a favourer
Of this new sect? Ye are not sound.

CROMWELL   Not sound?

GARDINER   Not sound, I say.

CROMWELL   Would you were half so honest:
135   Men's prayers then would seek you, not their fears.

GARDINER   I shall remember this bold language.

CROMWELL   Do.
Remember your bold life, too.

CHANCELLOR   This is too much:
140   Forbear for shame, my lords.

GARDINER   I have done.

CROMWELL   And I.

CHANCELLOR   Then thus for you, my lord: it stands
agreed,   *To Cranmer*

---

115 doubt i.e. of my innocence   conscience i.e. trouble your conscience   118 sectary
follower of a heretical sect   119 painted counterfeit/superficial   discovers reveals
120 words i.e. mere words   122 By . . . favour if you will permit me (to say so)   127 cry . . .
mercy beg your honor's pardon   worst least   131 sound orthodox, honest   136 bold
audacious, impertinent   140 Forbear stop, desist

I take it, by all voices, that forthwith
145 You be conveyed to th'Tower a prisoner,
There to remain till the king's further pleasure
Be known unto us: are you all agreed, lords?

ALL   We are.

CRANMER   Is there no other way of mercy,
150 But I must needs to th'Tower, my lords?

GARDINER   What other
Would you expect? You are strangely troublesome:
Let some o'th'guard be ready there.

Enter the Guard

CRANMER   For me?
155 Must I go like a traitor thither?

GARDINER   Receive him,   *To the Guard*
And see him safe i'th'Tower.

CRANMER   Stay, good my lords,
I have a little yet to say. Look there, my lords,   *He shows the*
160 By virtue of that ring, I take my cause   *King's ring*
Out of the gripes of cruel men, and give it
To a most noble judge, the king my master.

CHAMBERLAIN   This is the king's ring.

SURREY   'Tis no counterfeit.

165 SUFFOLK   'Tis the right ring, by heaven: I told ye all,
When we first put this dangerous stone a-rolling,
'Twould fall upon ourselves.

NORFOLK   Do you think, my lords,
The king will suffer but the little finger
170 Of this man to be vexed?

CHAMBERLAIN   'Tis now too certain:
How much more is his life in value with him?
Would I were fairly out on't.

CROMWELL   My mind gave me,
175 In seeking tales and informations

---

156 **Receive** take into custody   157 **safe** securely confined   161 **gripes** grips, clutches
163 CHAMBERLAIN some editors reassign this line to the Chancellor   172 **in . . . him** of value
to the king   173 **on't** of it (the present business)   174 **gave** misgave, prompted fearful doubts
(in)   175 **informations** pieces of intelligence/accusations/tales

Against this man, whose honesty the devil
And his disciples only envy at,
Ye blew the fire that burns ye: now have at ye!

Enter King [Henry] frowning on them: takes his seat

GARDINER   Dread sovereign, how much are we bound to
    heaven

180   In daily thanks, that gave us such a prince,
Not only good and wise, but most religious:
One that, in all obedience, makes the Church
The chief aim of his honour and, to strengthen
That holy duty out of dear respect,

185   His royal self in judgement comes to hear
The cause betwixt her and this great offender.

KING HENRY VIII   You were ever good at sudden commendations,
Bishop of Winchester. But know I come not
To hear such flattery now, and in my presence

190   They are too thin and base to hide offences:
To me you cannot reach. You play the spaniel,
And think with wagging of your tongue to win me:
But whatsoe'er thou tak'st me for, I'm sure
Thou hast a cruel nature and a bloody.—

195   Good man, sit down.— Now let me see the
    proudest   *To Cranmer,*
He, that dares most, but wag his finger at thee.   *who sits in*
By all that's holy, he had better starve   *vacant seat at head of table*
Than but once think his place becomes thee not.

SURREY   May it please your grace—

200   KING HENRY VIII   No, sir, it does not please me.
I had thought I had had men of some understanding
And wisdom of my council, but I find none.
Was it discretion, lords, to let this man,
This good man — few of you deserve that title —

205   This honest man, wait like a lousy footboy
At chamber door? And one as great as you are?

---

seat throne   **183 aim** i.e. beneficiary   **184 dear respect** earnest regard (for the Church)
187 sudden hasty/spontaneous   **190 They** i.e. the **commendations**   **194 bloody** bloodthirsty,
destructive   **196 He** i.e. man   **197 starve** die   **203 discretion** prudence, wisdom

Why, what a shame was this? Did my commission
Bid ye so far forget yourselves? I gave ye
Power as he was a councillor to try him,
210 Not as a groom. There's some of ye, I see,
More out of malice than integrity,
Would try him to the utmost, had ye mean,
Which ye shall never have while I live.

CHANCELLOR   Thus far,
215 My most dread sovereign, may it like your grace
To let my tongue excuse all. What was purposed
Concerning his imprisonment, was rather —
If there be faith in men — meant for his trial,
And fair purgation to the world than malice,
220 I'm sure, in me.

KING HENRY VIII   Well, well, my lords, respect him:
Take him, and use him well: he's worthy of it.
I will say thus much for him: if a prince
May be beholding to a subject, I
225 Am for his love and service so to him.
Make me no more ado, but all embrace him:
Be friends, for shame, my lords.— My lord of
    Canterbury,   *To Cranmer*
I have a suit which you must not deny me:
That is, a fair young maid that yet wants baptism:
230 You must be godfather, and answer for her.

CRANMER   The greatest monarch now alive may glory
In such an honour: how may I deserve it
That am a poor and humble subject to you?

KING HENRY VIII   Come, come, my lord, you'd spare your spoons:
235 you shall have two noble partners with you: the old Duchess
of Norfolk, and Lady Marquess Dorset: will these please you?
Once more, my lord of Winchester, I charge you   *To Gardiner*
Embrace and love this man.

---

209 **try** put on trial (sense then shifts to "afflict, torment")   212 **mean** the means   215 **like** please   216 **purposed** intended   219 **purgation** clearing of his name   222 **use** treat   226 **ado** fuss   229 **wants** lacks   234 **spoons** a set of spoons was a common christening gift

GARDINER   With a true heart   *He embraces Cranmer*
240   And brother-love I do it.
CRANMER   And let heaven   *He weeps*
Witness how dear I hold this confirmation.
KING HENRY VIII   Good man, those joyful tears show thy true
heart:
The common voice, I see, is verified
245   Of thee, which says thus: 'Do my lord of Canterbury
A shrewd turn, and he's your friend for ever.'
Come, lords, we trifle time away: I long
To have this young one made a Christian.
As I have made ye one, lords, one remain:
250   So I grow stronger, you more honour gain.   *Exeunt*

Act 5 Scene 3   *running scene 14*

*Noise and tumult within: enter Porter [with a broken cudgel] and
his Man*

PORTER   You'll leave your noise anon, ye rascals: *To those*
do you take the court for Paris Garden? Ye rude   *within*
slaves, leave your gaping.
[VOICE] WITHIN   Good master porter, I belong to th'larder.
5   PORTER   Belong to th'gallows, and be hanged, ye rogue! Is
this a place to roar in?— Fetch me a dozen crab-tree staves,
and strong ones: these are but switches to 'em.—   *To his Man*
I'll scratch your heads: you must be seeing   *To those within*
christenings? Do you look for ale and cakes here, you rude
10   rascals?
MAN   Pray, sir, be patient: 'tis as much impossible,
Unless we sweep 'em from the door with cannons,
To scatter 'em, as 'tis to make 'em sleep

---

244 **voice** opinion   246 **shrewd** injurious, vicious   249 **one** united   **5.3** *Location: by a
gate of the royal court, London*   **cudgel** club   **Man** servant   1 **leave** cease   2 **Paris
Garden** bear-baiting arena on London's Bankside, near the Globe theater   **rude** rough,
uncivilized   3 **gaping** shouting   4 **belong to** i.e. work in   6 **crab-tree** i.e. made from the
tough wood of a crab-apple tree   7 **these** i.e. these cudgels   **switches** slim, flexible shoots
cut from a tree   8 **scratch** i.e. beat

On May-day morning, which will never be:
15   We may as well push against Paul's, as stir 'em.

PORTER   How got they in, and be hanged?

MAN   Alas, I know not: how gets the tide in?
As much as one sound cudgel of four foot —
You see the poor remainder — could distribute,   *Holds up the*
20   I made no spare, sir.   *cudgel*

PORTER   You did nothing, sir.

MAN   I am not Samson, nor Sir Guy, nor Colbrand,
To mow 'em down before me: but if I spared any
That had a head to hit, either young or old,
25   He or she, cuckold or cuckold-maker,
Let me ne'er hope to see a chine again,
And that I would not for a cow, God save her!

[VOICE] WITHIN   Do you hear, master porter?

PORTER   I shall be with you presently, good master puppy.—
30   Keep the door close, sirrah.   *To his Man*

MAN   What would you have me do?

PORTER   What should you do, but knock 'em down by
th'dozens? Is this Moorfields to muster in? Or have we some
strange Indian with the great tool come to court, the women
35   so besiege us? Bless me, what a fry of fornication is at door!
On my Christian conscience, this one christening will beget a
thousand: here will be father, godfather, and all together.

MAN   The spoons will be the bigger, sir. There is a fellow
somewhat near the door, he should be a brazier by his face,

14 **May-day morning** traditional day of early rising for dawn festivities   15 **Paul's** St. Paul's Cathedral   16 **and be hanged** an oath   20 **made no spare** didn't hold back (when beating the crowd)   22 **Samson** biblical character possessed of legendary strength   **Sir** . . . **Colbrand** Colbrand was a Danish giant killed by **Sir Guy** of Warwick   25 **cuckold** man with an unfaithful wife   26 **chine** cut of meat from the backbone of an animal (possibly quibbles on the sense of "chink, fissure," i.e. "vagina")   27 **for a cow** a slightly obscure phrase, apparently meaning "for anything," though **cow** may play on the sense of "prostitute"   29 **presently** shortly   **puppy** impertinent young man   30 **close** closed tightly   **sirrah** sir (used to an inferior)   33 **Moorfields** an area of open ground just outside London's city walls, at one point used for training militia   **muster** assemble (soldiers)   34 **strange** foreign   **Indian** native Americans had been known to be exhibited to London's paying public (although "Indian" could also signify a person from the East or West Indies, or the Far East)   **great tool** large penis   35 **fry** seething brood   38 **spoons** spoons given as christening presents/penises   39 **brazier** brass-worker (working in high temperatures)

40   for, o'my conscience twenty of the dog-days now reign in's
nose: all that stand about him are under the line, they need
no other penance: that fire-drake did I hit three times on the
head, and three times was his nose discharged against me:
he stands there like a mortar-piece, to blow us. There was a
45   haberdasher's wife of small wit near him, that railed upon
me till her pinked porringer fell off her head, for kindling
such a combustion in the state. I missed the meteor once,
and hit that woman, who cried out 'Clubs!', when I might see
from far some forty truncheoners draw to her succour,
50   which were the hope o'th'Strand, where she was quartered.
They fell on: I made good my place: at length they came to
th'broomstaff to me: I defied 'em still, when suddenly a file of
boys behind 'em, loose shot, delivered such a shower of
pebbles, that I was fain to draw mine honour in, and let 'em
55   win the work: the devil was amongst 'em, I think, surely.

PORTER   These are the youths that thunder at a playhouse,
and fight for bitten apples, that no audience but the
tribulation of Tower Hill, or the limbs of Limehouse, their
dear brothers, are able to endure. I have some of 'em in *limbo*
60   *patrum*, and there they are like to dance these three days,
besides the running banquet of two beadles that is to come.

Enter Lord Chamberlain

40 dog-days hottest days of the year, associated with the dog-star Sirius   **in's nose** i.e. his
nose is red as if from heat (presumably from drinking)   **41 under the line** at the Equator
42 fire-drake dragon/fiery meteor   **43 discharged** fired off (like a gun)   **44 mortar-piece**
small cannon   **blow us** blow us up/blow his nose all over us   **45 haberdasher** seller of small
items relating to clothing, such as thread and ribbon   **railed upon** ranted at   **46 pinked**
ornamented with small holes or slits   **porringer** hat shaped like a soup dish   **kindling . . .
combustion** provoking such a tumult/lighting such a fire   **47 meteor** i.e. the red-nosed
brazier   **48 'Clubs!'** rallying cry to summon apprentices to a fight   **49 truncheoners** cudgel-
carriers   **succour** aid, assistance   **50 hope o'th'Strand** strapping apprentices from
workshops on the Strand, a London street near the Thames   **was quartered** lodged/lived
51 fell on attacked   **made good** secured, defended   **came . . . me** fought at close quarters
with me (literally, close enough to use broomsticks)   **53 loose shot** marksmen not attached to
a company   **54 fain** obliged   **55 work** earthwork, i.e. fort   **56 youths** i.e. apprentices
58 tribulation troublemakers, rabble   **Tower Hill** site of public executions and a rough
residential area   **limbs** members, residents/fighters, fists   **Limehouse** rough dockyard area
in London's East End (puns on **limb**)   **59 *limbo patrum*** i.e. prison (literally, the name of the
dwelling place for the souls of the unbaptized and of those who had died before Christ's
coming; continues the pun on **limb**)   **60 like** likely   **61 running banquet** i.e. a whipping
through the streets (literally, hasty meal)   **beadles** parish constables

CHAMBERLAIN   Mercy o'me: what a multitude are here!
They grow still, too: from all parts they are coming,
As if we kept a fair here! Where are these porters,
65   These lazy knaves?— You've made a fine hand,
    fellows: *To the Porter and his Man*
There's a trim rabble let in: are all these
Your faithful friends o'th'suburbs? We shall have
Great store of room, no doubt, left for the ladies,
When they pass back from the christening!
70   PORTER   An't please your honour,
We are but men, and what so many may do,
Not being torn a-pieces, we have done:
An army cannot rule 'em.
CHAMBERLAIN   As I live,
75   If the king blame me for't, I'll lay ye all
By th'heels, and suddenly, and on your heads
Clap round fines for neglect: you're lazy knaves,
And here ye lie baiting of bombards, when
Ye should do service. Hark, the trumpets sound: *Trumpet*
80   They're come already from the christening:
Go break among the press, and find a way out
To let the troop pass fairly, or I'll find
A Marshalsea shall hold ye play these two months.
PORTER   Make way there for the princess.
85   MAN   You great fellow,
Stand close up, or I'll make your head ache.
PORTER   You i'th'camlet, get up o'th'rail:
I'll peck you o'er the pales else.   *Exeunt*

---

65 made . . . hand done a fine job (sarcastic)   66 trim fine/smartly dressed (sarcastic)
67 friends plays on the sense of "lovers" (i.e. whores)   o'th'suburbs in the areas outside the
City walls and its jurisdiction, known for lawlessness and prostitution   68 Great . . . room
plenty of space   70 An't if it   73 rule control   75 lay . . . th'heels put you in the stocks or
shackles   76 suddenly straight away   77 round heavy   78 baiting of bombards drinking
from leather jugs/harassing drunkards/giving drinks to drunkards   79 service your job
81 break among push through   press crowd   82 troop christening procession   fairly
easily   83 Marshalsea prison in Southwark   hold ye play keep you from amusement
86 close up i.e. back   87 camlet fabric made from silk and goat hair   o'th'rail off the railing
(possibly the rail around the stage, suggesting that the groundlings in the yard took the part of
the crowd)   88 peck fling   pales railings

Act 5 Scene 4

Enter Trumpets sounding: then two Aldermen, Lord Mayor, Garter,
Cranmer, Duke of Norfolk with his Marshal's staff, Duke of Suffolk,
two Noblemen bearing great standing bowls for the christening gifts:
then four Noblemen bearing a canopy, under which the Duchess of
Norfolk, godmother, bearing the child richly habited in a mantle, etc.,
train borne by a Lady: then follows the Marchioness Dorset, the other
godmother, and Ladies. The troop pass once about the stage, and Garter
speaks

GARTER   Heaven, from thy endless goodness, send prosperous
  life, long, and ever happy, to the high and mighty Princess of
  England, Elizabeth.

Flourish. Enter King [Henry] and Guard

CRANMER   And to your royal grace, and the good
    queen,   *He kneels*

5   My noble partners and myself thus pray
  All comfort, joy, in this most gracious lady,
  Heaven ever laid up to make parents happy,
  May hourly fall upon ye.

KING HENRY VIII   Thank you, good lord archbishop:

10   What is her name?

CRANMER   Elizabeth.

KING HENRY VIII   Stand up, lord.
  With this kiss take my blessing: God protect thee,   *He kisses the*
  Into whose hand I give thy life.   *child*

15   CRANMER   Amen.

KING HENRY VIII   My noble gossips, you've been too prodigal:
  I thank ye heartily: so shall this lady,
  When she has so much English.

CRANMER   Let me speak, sir,

20   For heaven now bids me: and the words I utter

5.4   *Trumpets* trumpeters   *Garter* i.e. Garter King-at-Arms, an important ceremonial post
Marshal's staff the rod of office belonging to the Earl Marshal, a high-ranking state official
standing bowls bowls supported by legs or a base   *habited* clothed   **5 partners** fellow
godparents   **7 laid** stored   **16 gossips** godparents   **prodigal** lavish (with christening gifts)

Let none think flattery, for they'll find 'em truth.
This royal infant — heaven still move about her —
Though in her cradle, yet now promises
Upon this land a thousand thousand blessings,
25 Which time shall bring to ripeness: she shall be —
But few now living can behold that goodness —
A pattern to all princes living with her,
And all that shall succeed: Saba was never
More covetous of wisdom and fair virtue
30 Than this pure soul shall be. All princely graces
That mould up such a mighty piece as this is,
With all the virtues that attend the good,
Shall still be doubled on her. Truth shall nurse her,
Holy and heavenly thoughts still counsel her:
35 She shall be loved and feared. Her own shall bless her:
Her foes shake like a field of beaten corn,
And hang their heads with sorrow: good grows with her.
In her days, every man shall eat in safety
Under his own vine what he plants, and sing
40 The merry songs of peace to all his neighbours.
God shall be truly known, and those about her
From her shall read the perfect ways of honour,
And by those claim their greatness, not by blood.
Nor shall this peace sleep with her: but as when
45 The bird of wonder dies, the maiden phoenix,
Her ashes new create another heir,
As great in admiration as herself.
So shall she leave her blessedness to one,
When heaven shall call her from this cloud of darkness,
50 Who from the sacred ashes of her honour

22 heaven . . . her may God always be at her side   27 pattern exemplary model   28 Saba
the Queen of Sheba, who tested Solomon's wisdom with difficult questions (1 Kings 10:1–10)
31 mould up form, make up   piece masterpiece, work of art   33 still always   35 own own
people   36 beaten (presumably) wind-beaten   41 God i.e. religion   42 read learn
43 greatness power/honor/nobility   blood inheritance   44 sleep i.e. die   45 maiden
phoenix mythical Arabian bird that was consumed by fire every five hundred years, then
resurrected from the ashes; only one existed at a time   47 admiration the inspiring of wonder
48 one i.e. James I, who succeeded Elizabeth in 1603   49 cloud of darkness i.e. earthly life

Shall star-like rise, as great in fame as she was,
And so stand fixed. Peace, plenty, love, truth, terror,
That were the servants to this chosen infant,
Shall then be his, and like a vine grow to him:

55 Wherever the bright sun of heaven shall shine,
His honour and the greatness of his name
Shall be, and make new nations. He shall flourish,
And like a mountain cedar, reach his branches
To all the plains about him: our children's children

60 Shall see this, and bless heaven.

KING HENRY VIII   Thou speakest wonders.

CRANMER   She shall be to the happiness of England
An agèd princess: many days shall see her,
And yet no day without a deed to crown it.

65 Would I had known no more: but she must die,
She must, the saints must have her: yet a virgin,
A most unspotted lily shall she pass
To th'ground, and all the world shall mourn her.

KING HENRY VIII   O lord archbishop,

70 Thou hast made me now a man. Never before
This happy child did I get anything.
This oracle of comfort has so pleased me,
That when I am in heaven I shall desire
To see what this child does, and praise my maker.

75 I thank ye all. To you, my good Lord Mayor,
And your good brethren, I am much beholding:
I have received much honour by your presence,
And ye shall find me thankful. Lead the way, lords:
Ye must all see the queen, and she must thank ye:

80 She will be sick else. This day, no man think
H'as business at his house, for all shall stay:
This little one shall make it holiday.   *Exeunt*

---

52 fixed constant/established/unswayed by varying fortune   **terror** the power to inspire awe
64 deed beneficial action   **65 Would** I wish   **71 get** beget, conceive/gain, achieve
76 beholding indebted   **80 sick** unhappy, hurt   **81 H'as** he has   **stay** remain/cease (work)
82 holiday derived from "Holy-day" (as originally spelled in the Folio), emphasizing the word's
origins as a spiritual as well as celebratory time

The Epilogue

[*Enter Epilogue*]

'Tis ten to one this play can never please
All that are here: some come to take their ease,
And sleep an act or two: but those, we fear,
We've frighted with our trumpets: so 'tis clear,
They'll say 'tis nought. Others to hear the city
Abused extremely, and to cry 'That's witty!'
Which we have not done neither: that, I fear
All the expected good we're like to hear.
For this play at this time, is only in
The merciful construction of good women,
For such a one we showed 'em. If they smile,
And say 'twill do, I know within a while
All the best men are ours, for 'tis ill hap
If they hold when their ladies bid 'em clap.   [*Exit*]

The Epilogue   **5 nought** worthless   **city** London and its citizens   **7 that** so that
10 construction interpretation, judgment, appraisal   **11 such a one** could refer to either
Katherine, Anne, or Elizabeth   **13 ill hap** bad luck   **14 hold** refrain, refuse

TEXTUAL NOTES

F = First Folio text of 1623, the only authority for the play
F2 = a correction introduced in the Second Folio text of 1632
F3 = a correction introduced in the Third Folio text of 1663–64
F4 = a correction introduced in the Fourth Folio text of 1685
Ed = a correction introduced by a later editor
SD = stage direction
SH = speech heading (i.e. speaker's name)

List of parts = Ed

THE . . . EIGHTH *Various contemporary references suggest the play was performed as "All Is True"*
1.1.9 Andres = Ed. F = Andren. Ed = Ardres **10 Guînes** = Ed. F = Guynes **Ardres** = Ed. F = Arde **28 cherubins** = F. Ed = cherubim/cherubims **madams** = F. Ed = mesdames **48–51 All . . . function** F *assigns these lines to Buckingham who states he wasn't present. This edition follows editorial tradition in reassigning them to Norfolk* **54 as you guess** *this edition follows F4's assignation of these words to Buckingham, whereas F places them at the beginning of Norfolk's reply* **72 a** = Ed. F = O **142 venom-mouthed** = Ed. F = venom'd-mouth'd **196 wrenching** = F. Ed = rinsing **213 He privily** = F2. F = Priuily. **255 Montague** *spelled Mountacute in F* **257 Perk** = Ed. F = *Pecke. Emendation is based on Holinshed and Hall's accounts* **chancellor** = Ed. F = Councellour. *The emendation is made in accordance with Holinshed's account* **261 Nicholas** = Ed. F = Michaell. *The emendation is made in accordance with Holinshed's account* **267 lord** = Ed. F = Lords
1.2.75 baseness = F. Ed = business **154 His** = Ed. F = This **165, 166 Hopkins** = Ed. F = Henton. *Henton was the name of Hopkins' monastery* **176 feared** = Ed. F = feare **184 confession's** = Ed. F = Commissions **190 gain** = F4. *Not in F; other suggestions are* win *and* purchase **203 him** = Ed. F = this **216 Bulmer** = Ed. F = *Blumer*
1.3.0 SD *Sands spelled Sandys in F* **13 see** = F. Ed = saw **14 Or** = Ed. F = A **17 SD Enter . . . Lovell** = Ed. *Two lines down in F* **39 oui** = Ed. F = wee. F2 = weare **72 he's** = Ed. F = Ha's. Ed = 'has
1.4.6 first = F. Ed = feast
2.1.26 Perk = Ed. F = *Pecke* **67 SD William** = Ed. F = *Walter. Emendation in accordance with Holinshed* **102 make** = F. Ed = mark

2.2.1 SH CHAMBERLAIN = Ed. *Not in* F **97 one have-at-him** = Ed. F = one;
haue at him

2.3.74 you = Ed. F = you, to you. *Omitted by editors because thought to be a
compositorial error, copied prematurely from the following line* **102 fie, fie,
fie** = F. Ed = fie, fie

2.4.137 SH GRIFFITH = Ed. F = *Gent. Ush.*

3.1.3 SH WOMAN = Ed. F *reads "SONG" instead of using a speech heading, but
the song must be sung by one of the Queen's women* **25 SD** *Campeius* =
F4. F = *Campian* **55 should** = Ed. F = shoul **65 your** = F2. F = our
130 he's = Ed. F = ha's **135 a curse** = F. Ed = accursed

3.2.215 filed = Ed. F = fill'd **402 legative** = F. Ed = legatine, legantine
406 Castles = F. Ed = chattels

4.1.24 SH SECOND GENTLEMAN = F4. F = I, *i.e. First Gentleman*
38 Kimbolton = F3. F = Kymmalton **66 And . . . ones** *some editors
ascribe this line to the First Gentleman, allocating his line to the Second
Gentleman* **67 SH FIRST GENTLEMAN** = Ed. F = 2 SD *and . . . Trumpets
moved from its original position at the end of "The Order of the Coronation"*
121 Stokesley = F4. F = *Stokely* **142 SH FIRST . . . GENTLEMEN** = Ed.
F = *Both*

4.2.8 think = F2. F = thanke **22 convent** = Ed. F = Couent **108 cold** = F. Ed
= colour **114 to** = Ed. F = too. *Some editors retain* F *arguing it means "too
blameworthy"*

5.1.2 SH PAGE = Ed. F = *Boy* **45 time** = F4. F = Lime **138 halidom** *spelled
Holydame in* F **145 good** = F. Ed = ground **163 precipice** = F2. F =
Precepit **164 woo** = Ed. F = woe **184 SH LOVELL** = Ed. F = *Gent.*

5.2.10 piece = F2. F = Peere **16 sound** = F. Ed = found **21 'Mong . . .
lackeys** *some editors direct the pursuivants, pages, footboys and grooms
referred to in the text to enter with Cranmer at the beginning of this scene.
However, it seems perfectly possible that these figures could also be imagined,
hence the need for them to be "pointed out" by Cranmer and Butts*
123 faulty = F2. F = faultly **139, 143 SH CHANCELLOR** = Ed. F = *Cham*
190 base = F. Ed = bare **198 his** = F. F4 = this **243 heart** = F2. F =
hearts

5.3.2 Paris = F4. F = Parish

5.4.42 ways = F4. F = way **76 your** = Ed. F = you

SCENE-BY-SCENE ANALYSIS

PROLOGUE

The prologue tells the audience that they're not going to see a comedy but "Such noble scenes" as may make them weep. Those who "can pity," may "let fall a tear"; others may "find truth." Those who come for amusement will be richly entertained in "two short hours." Only those who have come "to hear a merry, bawdy play" will be disappointed. To present their show in that way would be beneath their intelligence and damage their reputation. Therefore the audience should be serious and imagine they see these characters "great" with many friends and followers and then "in a moment" see how soon they fall: "this mightiness meets misery." If you can laugh at that, the Prologue will say "A man may weep upon his wedding day."

ACT 1 SCENE 1

Lines 1–82: The Dukes of Buckingham and Norfolk discuss the meeting of Henry VIII and the French King François I (at the Field of the Cloth of Gold in June 1520). Buckingham was ill at the time so Norfolk describes the elaborate arrangements and the spectacle in detail. Every day was more splendid than the last as the two kings strove to outdo each other in pomp and magnificence. Buckingham asks who organized it all and Norfolk tells him it was "the right reverend Cardinal of York" (that is Cardinal Wolsey). Buckingham is dismissive of the Cardinal and the way he has "his ambitious finger" in every pie. He wonders why it was anything to do with Wolsey. Norfolk suggests through personal merit, since he's not of noble stock, this merit must be a "gift" from "heaven." Abergavenny says he doesn't know "What heaven hath given him" but he can see his pride, which comes from the devil.

Lines 83–134: They discuss their resentment of Wolsey and his position and influence with the king, asking why he should have had the selection of those to accompany him to France, an expensive enterprise with "little honour." Abergavenny has three relatives whose estates have been crippled. Buckingham knows many who had to sell land to pay for fine clothes and asks what was the point of such "vanity" except to impoverish their heirs. Norfolk doesn't think the peace treaty concluded between England and France was worth it. The terrible storm that followed was an omen that peace wouldn't last. That has now come to pass since the French have seized English merchants' goods at Bordeaux. The ambassador is under house arrest. Buckingham says it's all Wolsey's fault. Norfolk warns him to be careful and advises him that the king/Privy Council know about the mutual hostility between the Cardinal and him, and that he shouldn't underestimate the Cardinal's power. He tells Buckingham to take his advice to heart and have nothing to do with him as the Cardinal approaches in person.

Lines 135–176: As he passes, Wolsey asks his secretary if they have Buckingham's surveyor's statement. They'll examine him in person and when they "know more" Buckingham won't look so proud. Afterward Buckingham complains that Wolsey ("This butcher's cur") has a poisonous tongue but that he doesn't know how to silence him so it's best to let him sleep: a poor scholar's worth more than a noble family nowadays. Norfolk suggests self-control ("temperance") is the only remedy for his anger. Buckingham says he could see Wolsey was talking about him and has some trick to dishonor him. He's convinced he's gone to the king to complain. Norfolk again urges caution and not to let his anger get the better of him. Buckingham is determined, though, to complain to the king about Wolsey's insolence. Norfolk again advises him not to make things so hot for his enemy that he himself gets burned in the process.

Lines 177–229: Buckingham thanks him but says he knows Wolsey to be "corrupt and treasonous." He's convinced that Wolsey set up the whole costly affair (the Field of the Cloth of Gold) in order to show off his own power in France. Wolsey himself drew up the peace treaty but then "Charles the Emperor" (Charles V, King of Spain and Holy Roman Emperor) "came / To whisper Wolsey" under the pretext of visiting his aunt, Katherine of Aragon. Buckingham's charge is that the emperor, fearful of Spain's interest in a league between England and France, bribed Wolsey to change the king's mind and break the treaty. Norfolk says he hopes Buckingham's mistaken but Buckingham assures him that the evidence will prove him right.

Lines 230–267: Brandon and a Sergeant-at-Arms come to arrest Buckingham on a charge of "high treason" and accompany him to the Tower (of London). They also arrest Abergavenny and have warrants for all those connected with Buckingham. Both men accept their fate, saying "the will of heaven be done." Buckingham knows it's pointless to plead his innocence, believing his surveyor has been bribed by Wolsey to lie.

ACT 1 SCENE 2

Lines 1–31: Henry thanks Wolsey for the discovery and prevention of Buckingham's plot. He calls for Buckingham's surveyor to be brought before the court to "justify" his "confessions" and go through Buckingham's "treasons" "point by point." The queen arrives with the Dukes of Norfolk and Suffolk and kneels before the king. As Henry raises her, she says she'll remain kneeling since she's "a suitor" to him. He places her beside him, saying half her suit is granted, since she has half his power, and the other half granted before asked, and tells her to continue. She thanks him and explains that she wishes the king to "love" himself and not forget his "honour" or the "dignity" of his "office." Henry's subjects are grieved by the taxes imposed on them, which are blamed on the Cardinal but that the king himself has not escaped reproach, and there is talk of rebellion.

Lines 32–75: The Duke of Norfolk confirms all this, and explains how the cloth workers have had to lay off those who depend on them for work, who are now starving and desperate. Henry knows nothing of this and asks Wolsey to explain. The Cardinal claims that he's only responsible for "a single part" of state business. Katherine argues that Wolsey is responsible for "fram[ing]" policies. The "exactions" (taxes) the king wishes to know about are an impossible burden to bear. They're said to have been devised by Wolsey but if this is not the case he is blamed unjustly. The king again demands clarification. Katherine apologizes for trying his "patience" and explains that commissions have been set up demanding one sixth of a subject's wealth to be paid immediately, the money supposedly going to pay for the king's wars with France. This is why the people are angry and she wishes he would consider the matter at once, since there's no greater example of dishonorable treatment.

Lines 76–120: Henry exclaims that this is not according to his wishes. The Cardinal explains that his was only a single vote in the Privy Council and that others are just as much responsible. Slander by those who don't know anything about him or his deeds is the price virtue has to suffer. We shouldn't fear to do what's necessary because of those who always complain. Malicious critics often refuse to believe in or censure our best deeds while our worst are praised. If we're too frightened to move in case we're made fun of or criticized, we'll take root and become no more than "state-statues." Henry retorts that "Things done well" and with "care" will not lead to "fear." Things done without a precedent will turn out badly. He asks if Wolsey had any legal precedent. Henry believes not and argues that people must be subject to the law, not the king's will. Taking one sixth of people's income is like hacking at a tree, which may leave it standing but will ultimately lead to its death. Henry orders letters to be sent to all the counties with free pardons. Wolsey tells his secretary to write revoking the tax, adding that he should imply that this has been through his intercession with the king.

Lines 121–244: Buckingham's surveyor enters. Katherine's sorry the duke no longer enjoys the king's favor. Henry's sorry too: the duke's an educated man with great natural gifts but his mind has grown "corrupt." He invites Katherine to listen to the case against him. The Surveyor claims that Buckingham said if the king died without children, he'd seize the throne and revenge himself on the Cardinal. The Surveyor says Buckingham based this on the "vain prophecy of Nicholas Hopkins," a Carthusian monk who was his confessor, that "Neither the king" nor his "heirs" would prosper, and the duke would govern England. Katherine points out that the Surveyor was dismissed because of the tenants' complaints and warns him not to make these charges out of resentment and thus endanger his "nobler soul." The Surveyor claims he'd warned the duke but he took no notice, adding that if the king had died in his last illness, he'd have had Wolsey and Sir Thomas Lovell beheaded. Furthermore, Buckingham planned to assassinate him personally. Wolsey asks if it's safe for Buckingham to remain free. Katherine responds only with the hope that God will put things right: "God mend all." Henry is convinced of Buckingham's guilt and refuses to show him mercy.

ACT 1 SCENE 3

The Lord Chamberlain and Lord Sands are discussing the spellbinding effect of the new fashions brought back from France when Sir Thomas Lovell announces a proclamation against them. They agree that they're glad to see the back of them, English dress and customs are better. All three are going to a great feast later that evening given by Wolsey and praise his generosity.

ACT 1 SCENE 4

Sir Henry Guildford welcomes the ladies to Cardinal Wolsey's feast as the Lord Chamberlain, Sands, and Lovell arrive and seat themselves between the ladies. Their conversation is filled with sexual innuendo. Sands sits next to Anne (Bullen), apologizes for talking "a little wild" and then kisses her. Wolsey arrives and bids all his guests be merry. Sands continues to flirt with Anne. A masque of shepherds (including Henry in disguise) arrive and dance with the ladies. Henry chooses Anne. Wolsey says if there's one among them worthier of the place than he, then he would surrender it with his "love and duty." They confirm that there is but he must guess who. Wolsey chooses Henry, who asks him about Anne. Henry proposes a toast and leads Anne and the others into the next room.

ACT 2 SCENE 1

Lines 1–67: Two Gentlemen discuss Buckingham's trial. He pleaded not guilty and demanded to see his accusers face-to-face. His surveyor, chancellor, and confessor were brought before him, together with the monk, Hopkins, and accused him. He was found guilty. When he came to the bar to hear the judgment, he was initially upset but recovered himself. They blame Wolsey, who had Buckingham's son-in-law made Lord Deputy of Ireland so that he'd be out of the way and not in a position to help his father-in-law. They note that Wolsey sends away anyone the king likes and that everyone hates him while all admire "'bounteous Buckingham / The mirror of all courtesy.'"

Lines 68–153: Buckingham enters with officers of the court and commoners. He addresses those present, proclaiming his innocence and forgiving his enemies. He asks his friends to accompany him and, with their prayers, lift his soul to heaven. Lovell asks forgiveness, which Buckingham gives with "blessings" and his wishes for the king's long life. He relates how his father was betrayed, whereas he at least had a trial, but, like his father, he was betrayed by servants. He warns them to be careful how they choose their friends. He asks for their prayers, then says "Farewell" and "God forgive me" before departing.

Lines 154–194: The two Gentlemen are full of pity. One says he's heard a hint of something even worse—rumor of a separation between "the king and Katherine." The other didn't believe it because Henry commanded the Lord Mayor to stop the rumor. The other replies that "it grows again"; it's believed that the Cardinal or someone near him, "out of malice" to the "good queen" has planted a "scruple" in Henry's head that will "undo" her. Cardinal Campeius, the papal legate, has arrived. They believe that Wolsey is punishing Katherine because her nephew, the Holy Roman Emperor, refused him the archbishopric of Toledo. They conclude that the place is too public and they should continue their conversation in private.

ACT 2 SCENE 2

Lines 1–68: The Lord Chamberlain is reading a letter that describes how his servant was bringing him some horses when one of the Cardinal's men took them, saying "his master would be served before a subject, if not before the king." He reflects that the Cardinal wants to have everything. The Dukes of Norfolk and Suffolk arrive and ask how the king is. The Lord Chamberlain replies that his "conscience" is troubled by his marriage, but Suffolk jokes that Henry's "conscience / Has crept too near another lady." Norfolk agrees and blames the Cardinal. Suffolk says the king will learn the truth one day. Norfolk accuses Wolsey of advising Henry to divorce Katherine who loves him and has been "like a jewel" around his neck for "twenty years" "yet never lost her lustre." Wolsey's plan is for Henry to marry the French king's sister. They should pray for deliverance since he'd turn them all from "princes into pages" and he'll do whatever he wants. Suffolk doesn't care about Wolsey: he'll leave him to the Pope to deal with. They go in to talk to the king.

Lines 69–162: Henry appears sad but he's angry with them for disturbing him. Wolsey and Cardinal Campeius enter. Henry greets them and dismisses Norfolk and Suffolk. Wolsey praises Henry's moral scruples and the justice of his case before introducing Campeius. Henry welcomes him. Campeius says that he and Wolsey will judge the case between him and the queen impartially. Henry wants Katherine to have the best representation and sends for Stephen Gardiner, his new secretary. While Henry and Gardiner speak, Campeius asks Wolsey about Gardiner's predecessor, the virtuous and learned Doctor Pace, saying that Wolsey is blamed for sending him away out of envy and malice. Wolsey replies that he was a fool, whereas Gardiner will do as he asks. Henry says that Blackfriars seems the "most convenient place" to hear the case, lamenting that he must leave Katherine according to his conscience.

ACT 2 SCENE 3

Lines 1–60: Anne is discussing Katherine's situation with an Old Lady. She pities her and respects Katherine's virtue, believing it better to be content to live humbly. She "would not be a queen." The Old Lady disagrees and says she would and so would Anne: she's being hypocritical since she's an attractive woman and hence ambitious. Anne denies it—she wouldn't be a queen "for all the riches under heaven." The Old Lady says she would and asks Anne if she'd like to be a duchess then; Anne says "No." The Old Lady mocks her, saying she's weak, she'll never get anywhere with that attitude.

Lines 61–127: The Lord Chamberlain enters and tells Anne that Henry commends her and has made her Marchioness of Pembroke and given her "A thousand pound a year, annual support." Anne accepts graciously but says she can offer nothing in return but "prayers and wishes." In an aside the Chamberlain confides that the king has been caught by Anne's mixture of "beauty and honour." He hopes she may provide "a gem / To lighten all this isle." On his departure the Old Lady complains that she's "been begging sixteen years in court" but has never had Anne's good fortune. Anne says she doesn't understand and the Old Lady mocks her asking if she's heard the one about the woman who wouldn't be queen for "all the mud in Egypt." Her companion continues to tease her about her good fortune. Anne tells her to think what she pleases. She doesn't know what to think but they should return to comfort the queen. She asks the Old Lady not to repeat what she's heard.

ACT 2 SCENE 4

Lines 1–71: The hearing of the case between the king and Katherine. When Katherine is called she "*makes no answer*" but goes and kneels before Henry. She asks him why he's trying to get rid of her since she has always been "a true and humble wife" to him. Both their fathers were wise men and the validity of their marriage was thoroughly debated beforehand. She asks to be spared till she can be advised by her "friends in Spain." Wolsey says that she has her chosen advocates to represent her so there is no need to wait. Cardinal Campeius agrees.

Lines 72–143: Katherine accuses Wolsey of being her "enemy": it is he who has "blown this coal" between her and Henry, and she refuses him as her judge. Wolsey denies the charge and says everything has been done according to "the whole consistory [formal meeting of Roman Catholic cardinals] of Rome." He cites Henry as witness to the truth of this. Katherine replies that she is not cunning like him: Wolsey appears "meek and humble-mouthed" but his heart is "crammed with arrogancy, spleen and pride." He has been fortunate and enjoyed the king's "favours" but he cares more for worldly honor than spiritual qualities. She again refuses him as her judge, insisting that the Pope alone can judge her case. She curtsies to Henry and starts to leave. Cardinal Campeius accuses Katherine of being stubborn. Henry calls her back but Katherine refuses to listen and vows not to appear in their courts on "this business" in future.

Lines 144–259: After her departure Henry praises Katherine's "rare qualities," her gentleness, piety and nobility: she is "the queen of earthly queens." Wolsey demands his name be cleared, for Henry to admit that he never broached the subject to him. Henry says that is so and that Wolsey has many enemies and it is they who have incensed the queen against him. He goes on to say that on the contrary, Wolsey tried to prevent this. Henry then goes on to explain his reasoning and justify himself. It was the Bishop of Bayonne who first caused him to question his marriage during marriage negotiations between Henry's daughter Mary and the Duke of Orléans, when he demanded assurance that Mary was legitimate given that Henry had married his deceased brother's wife. Henry's conscience was pricked and he asked himself whether this was the reason that all their male children had died. It was then he started to question the legality of his marriage, approaching the Bishop of Lincoln and the Archbishop of Canterbury. Cardinal Campeius says they cannot proceed without the queen's presence. In an aside Henry suspects the Cardinals of deliberate delay, before he breaks up the court.

ACT 3 SCENE 1

Katherine is with her women and asks one of them to sing to "disperse" the "troubles" that make her soul "sad." Griffith enters to say that the "two great cardinals" have come to see her. They ask to speak to her in private but she says she has nothing to hide—"truth loves open dealing." When Wolsey starts to speak in Latin Katherine stops him. He continues in English, assuring her that they come in good faith to give her honest advice and "comforts." She again asks for friends to represent her since no Englishman may go against

Henry's wishes. They tell her to put her trust in "the king's protection." She's angry and says she will put her trust in God alone and warns them to take care that the "burden" of her "sorrows" doesn't fall on them. She has always been loving, faithful, and obedient, and this is her reward, to be cast aside now that she is old. Nothing will make her give up her position as Henry's wife: she is "the most unhappy woman living." They try to persuade her to be patient and accept her situation and not make the king hate her. Katherine tells them to do what they will, apologizing for and excusing her "unmannerly" treatment.

ACT 3 SCENE 2

Lines 1–98: A group of lords have come together to complain about Cardinal Wolsey. The Earl of Surrey (Buckingham's son-in-law) is happy for any opportunity for revenge. Wolsey has no respect for the nobility and passes them all over. The only way to bring him down, though, is to stop him getting to Henry: his "tongue" has "witchcraft" over the king. Norfolk and Suffolk explain that that's no longer the case. By chance Henry has a letter of Wolsey's to the Pope advising him not to grant Henry the annulment of his marriage to Katherine since he's "tangled in affection" with Lady Anne Bullen. Henry sees how Wolsey is playing for time in the matter but it's too late—he's already married Anne and there are orders for her coronation. The lords are all pleased. Cardinal Campeius has now left and they're awaiting the return of Stephen Gardiner, who has consulted all the learned authorities in Europe who agree to Henry's divorce. Katherine is henceforth to be known as "Princess Dowager," "widow to Prince Arthur." Gardiner will be made archbishop as a reward for his services.

Lines 99–172: Cardinal Wolsey enters with Thomas Cromwell. He asks him if the king has received his "packet" and looked over the papers inside. Cromwell says he has and asked Wolsey to attend him this morning. In an aside Wolsey says he wants the king to marry the Duchess of Alençon, the French king's sister, not Anne Bullen. The watching lords comment on how "discontented" Wolsey appears.

Wolsey continues his complaints against Anne and Cranmer. Henry enters, reflecting on the "piles of wealth" Wolsey has "accumulated." He asks the lords if he's arrived. They say he has but seems upset. Henry suggests it may be due to "a mutiny in's mind" and tells them about the inventory in his state papers of all Wolsey's goods. He is disillusioned, having believed that Wolsey's thoughts were on spiritual rather than earthly matters.

Lines 173–250: The king takes his seat and sends Lovell to speak to Wolsey, who greets the king apologetically. Henry says he must have been running over the inventory of his "best graces" which scarcely leaves him time for his "earthly audit." Wolsey says he has time for both. Henry tells him how highly his father valued him and how close Wolsey has been to himself and how well rewarded. Wolsey replies that he has always done all he could for the king and thanks him for his generosity. The king says he has a "loyal breast" and gives him two papers to read, and leaves, frowning at the Cardinal.

Lines 251–412: Wolsey is puzzled, not knowing what has brought about the king's displeasure. He reads the first paper, the inventory of all his wealth, gathered in order "to gain the popedom" and pay his "friends in Rome." He blames himself for his negligence but believes he can explain it away until he finds the letter addressed "To th'Pope" and realizes that it's all over—he can rise no higher and will inevitably fall. The lords reenter and tell him the king orders him to return "the great seal" (of office as Lord Chancellor) and to be confined at Asher House. Wolsey refuses to return it without their "commission"—the king gave it him and only the king can ask for its return. He knows they are motivated by "envy" and "malice." Surrey accuses him of bringing about Buckingham's downfall. Wolsey insults Surrey, saying he has "as little honesty as honour." Surrey is incensed by his "arrogance." They accuse him of hoarding goods and wealth and of treating the king as a servant, signing letters "*Ego et Rex meus*" (I and my king). He did things without the king's knowledge such as taking the "great seal" abroad, making a peace treaty with the Duke of Ferrara (an Italian city-state), and sending money to Rome as bribes for titles and honors. The Lord Chamberlain thinks they've said enough: he feels sorry for Wolsey. Surrey says he "forgive[s] him" and Suffolk adds that he is to "forfeit all [his] goods, lands, tenements, / Castles" and everything else—he is no longer under the king's protection. They leave him saying the king will hear of his refusal to return the great seal.

Lines 413–477: Alone on stage, Wolsey speaks a moving "farewell" soliloquy. He reflects on "the state of man" and the transient nature of earthly glory, which he now turns his back on feeling his "heart new opened." He pities those dependent on "princes' favours" who fall "like Lucifer / Never to hope again." Cromwell enters amazed at the news of Wolsey's downfall but Wolsey reassures him that he feels "A peace above all earthly dignities" of which the king has "cured" him. Cromwell's glad and tells him that "Sir Thomas More" has been chosen to replace him as Lord Chancellor, Cranmer has returned and been made Archbishop of Canterbury, and the Lady Anne, to whom the king has been "in secrecy long married" is now openly acknowledged as queen. All the talk is about her coronation.

Lines 478–533: Wolsey believes that it was the king's marriage to Anne Bullen that finally brought him down. He advises Cromwell to leave him and seek service with the king. He has told him of his loyalty. Cromwell weeps to leave his master. Wolsey confesses that he didn't expect to weep for his miseries but losing Cromwell has made him "play the woman." He hopes that out of his fall Cromwell may rise and advises him to "fling away ambition," to "Love thyself last" and "cherish" his enemies. He should be just and honest and then if he falls, he falls "a blessèd martyr." He tells Cromwell to make an inventory of his goods, all of which belong to the king and bids "Farewell" to the court; his "hopes in heaven do dwell."

ACT 4 SCENE 1

The two Gentlemen meet again, this time to discuss Anne's coronation. The First Gentleman has a list of all the nobles' ceremonial duties. He relates how Katherine is now divorced and ill. The other pities her but then the magnificent coronation procession passes by. They discuss the participants and Anne's beauty. A Third Gentleman joins them and describes the ceremony and the enthusiasm of the crowd for their new queen. Afterward the procession passed on to Whitehall, formerly called York Place before Wolsey's fall. They discuss the rise of Stephen Gardiner, who was the king's secretary and is now Bishop of Winchester, and Thomas Cranmer, now Archbishop of Canterbury, and the enmity between the two men. Thomas Cromwell has been made "Master o'th'Jewel House."

ACT 4 SCENE 2

Lines 1–88: Katherine, now ill, is led between her servants, Griffith and Patience. She sits down and asks about Cardinal Wolsey's death. Griffith explains how after his arrest he became ill and died on his way to London three nights later, "full of repentance, / Continual meditations, tears, and sorrows" and departed in peace. Katherine pities him but offers a harsh analysis of his character. Griffith in reply offers an assessment of his virtues, of his rise, his learning and generosity, and the good death he made. Katherine praises Griffith, wishing no one but "such an honest chronicler" as him to speak about her. She thinks she has not long to live and asks for music while she meditates on "that celestial harmony" she goes to. They sit by her as Katherine sleeps.

Lines 88–192: While she sleeps, Katherine has a vision of heaven in which the six "*personages, clad in white robes*" dance before her and offer her a garland. When she wakes, Katherine calls for the "Spirits of peace" but neither Griffith nor Patience have seen anything. They think she has changed, though, and looks near to death. A messenger arrives with Caputius, an ambassador from her nephew the Spanish Emperor Charles V. He greets her and explains he has been sent by the king to tell her to "take good comfort." She says it's too late for that and asks after the king and wishes him well. She gives Caputius a letter for Henry in which she requests him to take care of their daughter, Mary, and to recompense her faithful servants. She asks to be remembered to the king and retires, asking to be "used with honour" after her death and buried, "although unqueened, yet like / A queen and daughter to a king."

ACT 5 SCENE 1

Lines 1–64: It's late and Stephen Gardiner, Bishop of Winchester, meets Sir Thomas Lovell, who tells him that the new queen is in labor. While the bishop hopes the baby will thrive, he regrets that the situation will not be right while Cranmer, Cromwell, and Anne live. Lovell warns him to be careful: Cranmer is Archbishop of Canterbury and Cromwell has now been made Master of the Rolls, as well as the Jewel House and the king's secretary. Gardiner has told the Privy Council that Cranmer's "A most arch-heretic" and they have spoken to the king. As Gardiner leaves, Henry and Suffolk enter.

Lines 65–183: Henry tells Suffolk he doesn't want to play cards any more and asks Lovell how the queen is. He says she asks him to "pray for her"; her woman says she's suffering greatly. Henry sends Suffolk away and Lord Denny arrives with Cranmer. Henry sends Denny and Lovell away. He tells Cranmer of the complaints made against him that the Privy Council are going to examine in the morning. Cranmer thanks Henry: he knows he has enemies who speak ill of him. Henry is surprised, believing that the archbishop would have demanded to meet with his accusers. Cranmer trusts to his "truth and honesty," without those he is nothing and doesn't care what's said about him. Henry believes in his virtue and gives him a ring to produce at the council if he is in need. Cranmer weeps and Henry sends him away.

Lines 184–207: The Old Lady enters, despite Lovell's protests, to tell Henry the good news. Henry assumes Anne has had a "boy." The Old Lady reassures him that "a girl / Promises boys hereafter" and that she looks like him. He rewards her with a "hundred marks"; as they exit, she's determined to try and get more out of him.

ACT 5 SCENE 2

Lines 1–148: Cranmer arrives to see the Privy Council but finds the door shut against him. The king's physician passes and informs the king. Henry views the scene from above, displeased by this treatment of the archbishop. A table is brought in and the council members take their seats before Cranmer is finally called in. The Lord Chancellor accuses him of teaching "new opinions, / Divers and dangerous, which are heresies." When Cranmer asks to see his accusers face-to-face, he's told that's impossible because of his position as a member of the Privy Council. Gardiner says the king and the council intend to commit him to the Tower where as a "private man again," he may face his accusers. Gardiner is his severest critic, but Cromwell thinks he's "too sharp" and that they should treat the archbishop with respect. The Chancellor calls them to order and all agree that Cranmer should be taken to the Tower as a prisoner until they know the king's wishes.

Lines 149–250: The Guard is called and when Cranmer is assured there is no alternative, he produces Henry's ring, taking his case out of their hands and placing it directly before the king. They recognize the ring and the implication that Cranmer enjoys the king's support and try to blame each other for starting the action against him. Cromwell tells them it serves them right for trying to manufacture a case against Cranmer, whose "honesty" is well known. Henry enters and Gardiner immediately flatters his wisdom and religious sense and tries to win him to their side. Henry, however, tells him he has "a cruel nature" and that he thought better of them than to leave the archbishop waiting outside the door like a servant. He commands them to embrace Cranmer and treat him with respect in future. Henry then asks him to stand as godfather to the new princess before insisting once more that they all embrace Cranmer, starting with Gardiner, who does so. This causes Cranmer to weep, thereby confirming his virtue in Henry's mind. He tells them to hurry to the baby's christening. Now he has made them friends, they must remain so, which will strengthen him and honor them.

ACT 5 SCENE 3

An enthusiastic crowd has gathered outside the gate of the royal court for the christening. The people are noisy and restless and the

Porter and then the Lord Chamberlain try to calm them and make way for the procession.

ACT 5 SCENE 4

A magnificent procession enters for the christening. The Garter King-at-Arms asks heaven to "send prosperous life, long, and ever happy, to the high and mighty Princess of England." Cranmer wishes the king and queen the same and goes on to prophesy that the princess will become "A pattern to all princes." She will be virtuous and learned: "She shall be loved and feared" and bring the nation peace, which will be continued by her successor. He foretells her long life and eventual death, "yet a virgin." Henry is delighted and announces the day shall be a "holiday."

EPILOGUE

The Epilogue fears the play won't have pleased everyone. Those who come to rest and sleep will have been woken by the trumpets, while others who come to hear the city abused will also have been disappointed. So the play must be left to the judgment of good women, since they've shown them one (although her identity is ambiguous). If they smile and judge the play a success, then the men will too, since it's bad luck not to do so when their ladies "bid 'em clap."

HENRY VIII
IN PERFORMANCE:
THE RSC AND BEYOND

FOUR CENTURIES OF *HENRY VIII:* AN OVERVIEW

Shakespeare and Fletcher's late play about the reign of Henry VIII enjoyed great popularity historically and hence has a complete and continuous stage history. Originally designed perhaps to celebrate the marriage of James I's daughter, another Princess Elizabeth, to Frederick V, the Elector Palatine, in the summer of 1613, it has been regularly revived for spectacular royal occasions ever since. Evidence of its early performance and reception exists in several accounts recording the disastrous performance on 29 June 1613, when one of the cannons set the Globe's thatch alight. Sir Henry Wotton's letter of 2 July 1613 offers a detailed account of its staging, as well as voicing his concerns about its manner of representing "greatness" on stage, making it "very familiar, if not ridiculous":

> I will entertain you at the present with what happened this week at the Banks side. The King's players had a new play called All is True, representing some principal pieces of the reign of Henry the Eighth, which set forth with many extraordinary circumstances of pomp and majesty even to the matting of the stage; the knights of the order with their Georges and Garter, the guards with their embroidered coats, and the like: sufficient in truth within awhile to make greatness very familiar, if not ridiculous. Now King Henry making a Masque at the Cardinal Wolsey's house, and certain cannons being shot off at his entry, some of the paper or other stuff, wherewith one of them was stopped, did light on the thatch, where being thought at first but idle smoak, and their eyes more

attentive to the show, it kindled inwardly, and ran round like a train, consuming within less than an hour the whole house to the very ground. This was the fatal period of that virtuous fabrick, wherein yet nothing did perish but wood and straw, and a few forsaken cloaks; only one man had his breeches set on fire, that would perhaps have broyled him, if he had not by the benefit of a provident wit, put it out with a bottle of ale.[64]

Despite this setback, the play remained popular, due to its combination of the treatment of relatively recent history and gorgeous spectacle. It was revived at the rebuilt Globe at the request of George Villiers, Duke of Buckingham, on 29 July 1628.

After the Restoration and reopening of the theaters in 1660, *Henry VIII* was one of the few Shakespearean plays to be regularly staged. Bookseller and actor Thomas Davies records how Thomas Betterton was coached in the part of Henry by William Davenant, a godson of Shakespeare's, who had been instructed by John Lowin, a member of the King's Men. John Downes, Davenant's company bookkeeper records that Betterton was "all new Cloath'd in proper Habits" for the role.[65] According to William Winter, "Betterton's performance was accounted essentially royal, and the example of stalwart predominance, regal dignity, and bluff humour thus set has ever since been followed."[66] He was succeeded in the part by Barton Booth, Charles Macklin, and James Quin, suggesting that Henry was regarded as the star part, although Colley Cibber's Wolsey was noted and praised.

Cibber mounted productions at Drury Lane between 1721 and 1733. His 1727 revival included a notable coronation procession at the beginning of Act 4, designed to coincide with the coronation of George II. David Garrick's 1762 staging for the Theatre Royal, Drury Lane was similarly spectacular, boasting a cast of more than a hundred and thirty for the coronation scene. Emphasis on the pageantry of the play necessitated cuts to the text, a practice that continued as elaborate spectacle came to dominate productions. At the same time, criticism of the play's language and structure were voiced.[67] In a discussion of John Philip Kemble's 1811 production, the *Times*' critic suggests that Shakespeare had been called on to create a piece of hackwork, designed to "palliate . . . adultery," and "obscure" Katherine's memory and Henry's "gross caprices":

> Processions and banquets find their natural place in a work of this kind; and without the occasional display of well-spread tables, well-lighted chandeliers, and well-rouged maids of honour, the audience could not possibly sustain the accumulated *ennui* of *Henry the Eighth*.[68]

The reviewer adds that "The banquet deserved all the praise that can be given to costly elegance. It was the most dazzling stage exhibition that we have ever seen," and goes on to praise the performances of Kemble and his sister, Sarah Siddons: "If Mrs. Siddons and Mr. Kemble desired to show the versatility of their powers, they could not have chosen more suitable parts than Katherine and Wolsey."[69] It became one of Siddons' best-known and loved roles:

> The grandeur of the actress as Queen Katherine, her air of suffering and persecution, enlisted a new order of sympathy, and the well-known denunciation of the Cardinal, like her famous scene in Macbeth, became inseparably associated with *herself*.[70]

Katherine and Wolsey were now seen as the leading roles and the first three acts alone were performed. Edmund Kean's Wolsey was highly praised in his 1822 and 1830 revivals. William Charles Macready played Wolsey from 1823 to 1847 in productions notable for the great actresses who played Katherine, including Helen Faucit, Charlotte Cushman, and Fanny Kemble. For the royal "command" performance of Acts 1–3 at Drury Lane on 10 July 1847, Macready played Wolsey to Charlotte Cushman's Katherine and Samuel Phelps's Henry, in the presence of Queen Victoria and Prince Albert.

Phelps himself played Wolsey in his stagings at Sadler's Wells in 1845 and 1848, after which date he included Act 4: the staging on 16 January 1850 was given to help raise funds for the Great Exhibition of 1851. He revived the play another four times between 1854 and 1862. By far the most successful Victorian production, however, was Charles Kean's 1855 spectacular with himself as Wolsey and his wife, Ellen Tree, as Katherine. The twenty-three-year-old Lewis Carroll recorded in his diary that it was "the greatest theatrical treat I ever had or ever expect to have—I had no idea that anything so superb as the scenery and dresses was ever to be seen on the stage."[71] Kean retained most of the first three acts, "but to allow time for the many processions and tableaux, which included an actual coronation, Acts 4 and 5 contained little else."[72] It was Katherine's vision of Act 4 Scene 2 that seems to have produced the most striking effect:

> But oh, that exquisite vision of Queen Catherine! I almost held my breath to watch; the illusion is perfect, and I felt as if in a dream all the time it lasted. It was like a delicious reverie, or the most beautiful poetry. This is the true end and object of acting—to raise the mind above itself, and out of its petty everyday cares—never shall I forget that wonderful evening, that exquisite vision—sunbeams broke in through the roof and gradually revealed two angelic forms, floating in front of the carved work of the ceiling: the column of sunbeams shone down upon the sleeping queen, and gradually down it floated a troop of angelic forms, transparent, and carrying palm branches in their hands: they waved these over the sleeping queen, with oh! such a sad and solemn grace.— So could I fancy (if the thought be not profane) would real angels seem to our mortal vision . . .[73]

The top angel in the vision was Ellen Terry.[74] Kean's last performance on the London stage was as Wolsey on 29 August 1859. Phelps too made his final appearance in the part in the revival at the Royal Aquarium in 1878 when he "all but collapsed at the end of his final speeches" and had to be "helped off stage when the curtain fell."[75]

In his stage history, George C. D. Odell suggests that Henry Irving's production at the Lyceum in 1892 was "Undoubtedly the greatest—if not the only—Shakespearian 'spectacle' that Irving ever attempted."[76] The richness and accuracy of costumes and sets were much admired, as were the performances of the strong cast. Irving's was an "original conception" of Cardinal Wolsey that "differed radically from that of most of his famous predecessors, and constantly challenged attack and admiration. Certainly it was not the Wolsey of tradition, but forceful intellect was in every fiber of it."[77] Ellen Terry's Katherine was similarly admired: "It had not the somber touch of tragedy that should ennoble it, but it was womanly to the core and thoroughly royal in deportment."[78]

Despite his innovative interpretation, Irving continued the tradition of giving most of the first three acts, but only those parts of the final two that added to the spectacle. Herbert Beerbohm Tree at His Majesty's Theatre was similarly cavalier in his handling of the text, justifying his decision in an essay of 1920: "*Henry VIII* is largely a pageant play. As such it was conceived and written; as such did we endeavour to present it to the public." For this reason, "It was thought desirable to omit almost in their entirety those portions of the play which deal with the Reformation, being as they are practically devoid of dramatic interest and calculated, as they are, to weary an audience."[79] Tree argues this practice was vindicated by the Prologue's reference to "two short hours." Nevertheless reviews make it clear that the drastic cutting of the text did not have the desired effect of speeding the production up:

> Much cut, for Tree removed the whole of the last act and ended at Anne Boleyn's coronation, the play nevertheless occupied four hours: the stage staff of His Majesty's, trained though it was, had to toil frantically to construct Wolsey's ostentatious palace, the hall in Blackfriars where Katherine was tried, and Westminster Abbey itself.[80]

Despite this, Tree's production enjoyed tremendous success, running for a record-breaking 254 performances until 8 April 1911 and earning him this plaudit from *Sporting Life:* "He has achieved that which a few years ago was considered impossible—he has made Shakespeare popular."[81] A twenty-five-minute silent film of this production was made, but all copies were sadly destroyed after six weeks of special cinematic exhibition.

Early-twentieth-century productions continued the tradition of

7. 1910, Herbert Beerbohm Tree production. "[T]he stage staff . . . had to toil frantically to construct Wolsey's ostentatious palace, the hall in Blackfriars where Katherine was tried, and Westminster Abbey itself."

spectacular stagings. Ben Greet's for the tercentenary celebrations of Shakespeare's death at the Stratford Memorial Theatre and the Old Vic was revived two years later in London with Russell Thorndike as Wolsey and Sybil Thorndike as Katherine. Tree had cut the last act completely, moving straight from Katherine's death to Anne's coronation. Such practices were rendered less justified by changing critical perceptions; the work of the eminent scholar E. K. Chambers exposed the subjective nature of the verse tests applied by the "disintegrators" (scholars who held that many of Shakespeare's plays were not written by him but revisions of, or collaborations with, other writers), which argued that Shakespeare was responsible for most of *Henry VIII*. Robert Atkins's 1924 production at the Old Vic, despite staging the complete text, took less time than Tree's four-hour marathon. Atkins was influenced by the ideas of William Poel

and the Elizabethan Stage Society who attempted to recreate Elizabethan staging practices. Use of the complete text rekindled interest
in the role of Henry, evidenced in Tyrone Guthrie's casting of
Charles Laughton in the part in his 1933 production at Sadler's
Wells, with Flora Robson as Katherine.

The play has never enjoyed great popularity in America; it was
first performed in 1799 at New York's Old Park Theater. There was
a production at the same theater in 1811 with George Frederick
Cooke as Henry, and another in 1834 with Charles Kemble as
Wolsey and his daughter Fanny, then twenty-three, as Katherine.
Four years later a production was staged at the National Theater,
Church Street, New York, and another in 1847 at the old Bowery
Theater with Eliza Marian Trewar as Queen Katherine. Many of the
best-known British productions including Kean's, Macready's, and
Irving's were also seen briefly in America. The notable American
actress Charlotte Cushman, whose "Queen Katherine was the con-
summate image of sovereignty and noble womanhood, austere and
yet sweetly patient,"[82] also played the part of Wolsey in 1857.
Edwin Booth played Wolsey in 1876 in a four-act version at the
Arch Street Theater, Philadelphia, and revived it for Booth's Theater, New York, in 1878.

Despite its relative lack of success in America, in 1946 Margaret
Webster inaugurated the American Repertory Theater's first season
at the International Theater with *Henry VIII*, in her attempt to create
"an American Old Vic."[83] Webster's direction received praise as did
David Ffolkes' designs, but the production overall was not a success:
"The fact that a play not seen in New York in this century was used
as an opening guy seemed most hopeful. Indeed the production itself
was a fine one."[84] Webster reduced the play's five acts and sixteen
scenes to two acts and thirteen scenes.[85] The result was "a vivid and
smooth-running production full of colour and pageantry,"[86] but
although it played in repertory throughout the winter, at the end of
the season the American Repertory Theater was forced to close. Theater historian and critic Linda McJ. Micheli argues that "Webster's
Henry VIII stands somewhere between nineteenth-century 'scenic
Shakespeare' and the 'Elizabethan Shakespeare' championed by

William Poel and others in regional and academic theaters since the early 1900s."[87]

Micheli suggests the production is

> illuminated by comparison with Tree's 1910 production, a spectacular culmination of the scenic tradition, and Tyrone Guthrie's Stratford production of 1949, which introduced mainstream audiences to many of the "new ideas" we now take for granted—a thrust stage, an emphasis on continuity and brisk pace, a respect for the full text, a de-emphasizing of spectacle and solemnity.[88]

Webster's production, she concludes, was "[o]n balance . . . closer to Tree's than to Guthrie's."[89]

Guthrie's 1949 Stratford revival is generally regarded as the most significant of the twentieth century, which managed to unify the play by inspired design and directorial decisions. Tanya Moiseiwitsch's set contrived an "excellent compromise between a platform and a picture frame stage . . . with its varied levels, its ample forestage, fifteen feet deep, and its well-thought-out modifications and rearrangements of the gallery and the inner-stage."[90] Reviewers all comment on the "fluidity of movement and the power and the pace thus given to the action":[91]

> the fluid staging which juxtaposed a scene of downfall with one of spectacular rise. The music of the masque . . . is still in our ears when the muffled drums usher in . . . the somber procession of Buckingham on his way to execution. Later, as the fallen Wolsey goes off down the center stairs leading into the orchestra pit, the excitement about Anne's coronation begins on the main stage.[92]

Both Prologue and Epilogue were spoken by the Old Lady (Anne Bullen's friend): a device that divided critics. Guthrie stressed the central role of Henry: "Admirably played by Anthony Quayle . . . Henry dominated the scenes, huge, hot-tempered but human, a mixture of strong-willed sovereign and pouting schoolboy, a pleasure-loving king but a conscientious one, with true Tudor warmth and directness."[93] For Muriel St. Clare Byrne, Diana Wynyard's Katherine "made one feel as if it were being spoken for the first time" while the "test" of Harry Andrews's conception of Wolsey was "that the nearer he came to the audience the better I liked his performance." His Wolsey she thought "just as good as the author meant him to be."[94] Even one of the few critical reviews admits that "Mr. Guthrie made *Henry VIII* a good show" while lamenting "but that is about all he did do; the nuances of character and the play's general conception seemed to have escaped him."[95] Such a negative assessment was very much in the minority though and the play was revived with a new cast at the Old Vic in 1953 to celebrate the coronation of Queen Elizabeth II.

Guthrie was again lauded as "our most flamboyant producer" of a "dazzling production" that

> made full use of the topical humours of the text. The three onlookers at the Coronation of Anne Boleyn, munching Tudor sandwiches and spotting the Earl Marshall, had a contemporary ring, and at the christening of the Princess Elizabeth which ends this play few can have failed to be moved by the sense of occasion.[96]

Public tastes have changed since then and the play has fallen into disfavor, with fewer and fewer revivals and longer periods between them. The most significant from the RSC are discussed below. While Shakespeare's play has become less popular than at any time in its history, the same cannot be said for its main protagonist, Henry VIII. Fascination with Henry, especially his six wives, and with Tudor history in general, has produced new plays as well as numerous films and television programs about the period and its colorful cast.

The 1979 televised version for the BBC TV Shakespeare Collection, directed by Kevin Billington, is widely regarded as one of the most successful in this series. It opted for a "documentary approach"[97] with "a sustained insistence on authenticity of visual impressions and on vocal naturalism."[98] Much of it was shot in "authentic" historical locations, using close-ups and techniques that highlighted the play's intimacy in contrast to the grand pageantry of stage productions: "while traditional staging has exaggerated scenic effects to the disadvantage of the ultimate private and personal issues towards which the play progresses, television can correct the imbalance by its concentration on the individual's inward condition."[99] The strong cast with John Stride as Henry, Timothy West as Wolsey, and Claire Bloom "memorably cast as Queen Katherine"[100] won unanimous praise.

Brian Rintoul successfully paired Shakespeare's play with Robert Bolt's *A Man for All Seasons* about Thomas More, cross-casting the actors playing the king, Cranmer, and Norfolk, in his production for Canada's Stratford, Ontario, Festival in 1986. The juxtaposition illuminated both plays; one reviewer concluded that it drew attention to the ways in which "Shakespeare chooses to sacrifice the extremes of noble idealism and diabolical intrigue."[101]

In his 1991 production of Shakespeare's play for the Chichester Festival, Ian Judge cast Keith Michell, who had played Henry with great success in the BBC television miniseries, *The Six Wives of Henry VIII* (1970) in the title role. It received universally unfavorable reviews with reviewers finding Michell inadequate to the demands of the part on stage:

> the Chichester stage has a rather larger acreage than most television sets, and Shakespeare and Fletcher make greater demands on the voicebox than most screenwriting teams. How does Michell's Henry VIII cope with a challenge he has, as it happens, never faced before? Not much better than anybody else in Ian Judge's lacklustre production.[102]

Mary Zimmerman's production for another festival, the 1997 New York Shakespeare Festival at the Delacorte Theater in Central Park, was more successful and more warmly received. It was significantly the last play in the Public Theater's thirty-six-play Shakespeare Marathon, started by Joseph Papp nine years earlier. Zimmerman's "efficient, often elegant" direction produced a "streamlined staging that's almost miraculous in untangling the convolutions of the story."[103] The period costumes were shown to good effect against a "set of connected archways, shrinking in perspective and painted a lush royal blue . . . lovely in its classic simplicity."[104] The *New York Times'* critic suggested that "the disparate nature of the play" was highlighted by the cast's "varied styles of acting"[105] and speaking. In his view, Jayne Atkinson's Katherine was the outstanding performance, a judgment the elements concurred with on press night:

> The trees in the park seemed to sigh in sympathy as Katherine, played by Jayne Atkinson, presented her case to a less than sympathetic court; the documents in the hands of Katherine's nemesis, the ambitious Cardinal Wolsey (Josef Sommer), threatened to blow away, and as the words of the menaced queen melted from offended dignity into regal anger, there was little question which side the angels were on in this trial.[106]

In 2003 Granada television produced an updated version "without any cod Tudor language" or "ludicrous dancing in pantaloons" which was "partly inspired by *The Sopranos*" and starred Ray Winstone, "one of our seminal screen hard nuts,"[107] as a "gangster king" Henry. There was yet another festival production at Stratford, Ontario, in 2004 directed by Richard Monette described as "another solid offering . . . except for a few gratuitous trappings of self-indulgence including a couple of fruity gentlemen and a dream masque."[108] Seana McKenna's Katherine was again judged the "most attractive figure in the play" and her "powerful and deeply moving" performance conveyed "fierce dignity."[109]

For the 2006 Complete Works Festival of all Shakespeare's plays, the RSC invited AandBC Theatre Company to present their touring production of the play in the historic venue of Stratford's Holy Trinity Church, the same church where the playwright was both baptized and buried. It proved an inspired setting:

> The mellowing evening sun pours in through the stained glass windows on a staging that arranges the audience along the nave like a parliament or congregation in two opposing banks

of raked seating. This leaves a lengthy, narrow acting area . . . though spectators may succumb to Wimbledon Neck as their attention is swivelled from one end to the other. . . . [110]

Director Gregory Thompson exploited the challenge it presented: "The audience's proximity to the acting space serves the play well as audience members are literally drawn into the action by being selected to hold props and serve as members of the jury."[111] Audience members thus enhanced the versatile cast of fifteen. Dressed in period costume, the staging was "lavish" with an emphasis on spectacle:

Fireworks interrupt Wolsey's feast as Henry's disguised revellers swarm into the church. During their entrance, one of the merry company memorably performs a lewd dance with one of the female audience members in the front row.[112]

At the play's center was "Antony Byrne's fine, red-bearded, ambivalent Henry."[113] Corinne Jaber was praised as an "unusually fierce Katherine of Aragon, hurling herself on the floor of the nave in front of the king, [who] dies like a political martyr."[114] Animal metaphors sprang to several critics' minds when describing Anthony O'Donnell as a "toad in red silk"[115] or a "scarlet slug sliding to the top of the pile over the bodies of his victims."[116] The two undoubted stars of the evening, though, were the seven-month-old Alice Wood as Princess Elizabeth—"an alert, silent, lovely child who had the audience spellbound,"[117] and the venue itself, which lent the play "a sombre, melancholy grandeur."[118] Gregory Thompson discusses the production and the challenges he faced in "The Director's Cut" below.

Reviews of the 2010 production at Shakespeare's Globe directed by Mark Rosenblatt all advert to the disastrous fire of the 1613 staging at the original Globe. While several critics still feel the need to apologize for the play, Paul Taylor of the *Independent* describes how Rosenblatt's sophisticated direction managed to

pull off the considerable trick of giving full due to the nostalgic, propagandistic elements in this Shakespeare/Fletcher collaboration, while also highlighting and extending the flickering moments of subversive acknowledgement that there is a much less "official" version of events which cover the contentious birth of the English Reformation. So though the production pulls all the stops out in a blaze of mitres, ivory silk, boy choristers in the gallery, and trumpet acclaim for the culminating baptism and Cranmer's prophecy of future national glory, there turns out to have been a cunning optical illusion here that cuts the sequence down to size.[119]

Dominic Rowan's "trim, darkly handsome and enigmatic"[120] Henry was praised for "wit, energy and sudden enlivening moments of menace,"[121] while Kate Duchêne's Katherine of Aragon as "a foreign-accented outsider" proved "awesomely fiery and confrontational."[122] Miranda Raison's Anne brought "a welcome dash of sex appeal to the fusty proceedings" while Ian McNiece's "grotesque Cardinal Wolsey . . . hisses out his lines like a poisonous snake and slithers across the stage like a disgustingly plump slug."[123] Reviews also picked out

Amanda Lawrence's triple whammy of splendid cameos [which] add up to a brilliant bluff-calling device. A snipe-faced Welsh eccentric, she's the lady-in-waiting who disputes Anne Boleyn's pious disavowal of any yearnings to be queen. She also plays the silent white-faced Fool who, in Rosenblatt's version, shadows the King with a puppet of his deceased son.[124]

AT THE RSC

Politics and Pageantry

The most controversial decision that a director can take in relation to *Henry VIII* seems to be to stage the play at all. Its combination of reportage and pageantry has left critics confused and divided: the terms "whitewash" and "Tudor propaganda" recur constantly. All three RSC productions—Trevor Nunn's in 1969, Howard Davies's in 1983, and Gregory Doran's in 1996—have provoked undisguised hostility from some critics who use its joint authorship (with John Fletcher) and seeming refusal of moral condemnation as sticks with which to beat it:

> *Henry VIII* is an odd play. Why Shakespeare wrote it is a mystery. Whether he wrote it is another. And why Trevor Nunn should have chosen to stage it, in what is without exception the most amazing production I have ever seen at Stratford, is a question which may well vex the scholar in decades to come.[125]

> When he came to write a play dealing with a Tudor monarch in person . . . Shakespeare found himself having to sacrifice all artistic integrity for crude propaganda. . . . Instead of courageously meeting the problem head-on, Shakespeare wrote one of the worst plays ever penned, playing safe by creating a rogueish [*sic*] but loveable King, surrounded by councillors of varying degrees of integrity who pose no real threat to his majesty. . . . There is no earthly reason why anyone should read, see or produce this play.[126]

> Ninety years ago, when Britain still ruled most of the waves, you can imagine Greg Doran's bizarre production of *Henry VIII* would have been acclaimed as a sumptuous celebration of England's Tudor royalty and the glories of the new Protestant supremacy. But to see a Golden Heritage approach seriously adopted in 1996 to this weak chronicle-pageant play, which Shakespeare wrote with John Fletcher, beggars theatrical belief.[127]

Henry VIII is seen then as something of an ideological "problem play." Hugh M. Richmond analyzes what he regards as some of the dilemmas it poses for directors:

> Moral concerns have persisted . . . for every audience of *Henry VIII* since 1613. They constitute the familiar context which attends the play with its sustained dramatic irony: unexpressed but omnipresent in every audience's aware-

ness. . . . Any successful production must communicate this final delicate balance of the sinister and the hopeful, without slipping into a naïve proclamation of one or the other in the last scene. The sustaining of this elusive tone constitutes the unique challenge which the play proposes in production.[128]

Directors have risen to this challenge in a variety of ways in the face of critical hostility. Historically productions had focused on the play's pageantry and the leading roles of King Henry, Katherine of Aragon, and Cardinal Wolsey. Trevor Nunn was reacting against such a conventional approach in his 1969 production, which employed a modern set and production style while locating the play within the context of Shakespeare's other late plays. In his program notes Nunn argued that "They do not idealise the human condition, the beast is there alright, so also is the angel. Man is in search of ripeness or grace or . . . self-knowledge. In the late plays grace is achieved through love."[129] According to John Barber such a context revealed that

> Henry VIII . . . is held together and sustained by the same themes as in the other late works: pity for the unjustly used and hope that a new generation will right ancient wrongs. Thus the newborn Elizabeth is only another Perdita or Miranda.[130]

This reconciliatory conclusion though seemed at odds with a consciously political interpretation, set against the backdrop of 1960s political radicalism and a production style most often described as "Brechtian." It was played within a black box with "a fine, heavy, Elizabethan castle hung against a black backdrop and lit ingeniously to give it varying degrees of depth."[131] Other critics were less complimentary. Irving Wardle referred to the set as "a permanent toytown backdrop of Tudor London."[132] He was one of many to be irritated by the self-conscious "series of newspaper headlines that flash up before every scene."[133] These were subsequently dropped in the London revival.

Wardle speculated that the captions were one of the techniques deployed, "meant to establish a link between modern spectators and

the ordinary citizens who carry so much of the play's narrative."
But, he concluded,

> attitudes to Royalty have changed so much that the link is
> more ironic than direct. Apparently this is not intentional, as
> the production finishes with rapt invocations to peace and
> plenty which are meant in earnest even though they do trans-
> pose the finale from blazing ceremonial into the mood of a gen-
> tle masque.[134]

Various strategies were employed to engage audience participa-
tion. In Act 2 Scene 1 in the discussion between the two Gentlemen,
on the line "We are too open here to argue this" the promptbook
reads "They clock audience." Direct address was used "in the manner of the music-hall"[135] and there was a "splendid football match in
which Emrys Jones's Archbishop Cranmer takes a penalty kick after
the ball has been neatly returned to the stage from the front
stalls."[136] This scene did not, however, impress all the critics with its
splendor:

> in period productions (and this one is no exception) there is
> invariably a varlet whose breeches fall down, supported, for rea-
> sons seldom clear, by quantities of disagreeably self-conscious
> small children. It is nervous work watching Cranmer dribbling
> a woolly ball with these juveniles as he waits ("like a lousy foot-
> boy at chamber door") before his trial; worse is to come when
> the peers in council, routed by the king, line up to pass the
> same ball embarrassedly from hand to hand, as in a number
> rather low down on the bill at the Palladium. Mr. Nunn has
> shown signs before of an alarming weakness for woolly balls,
> but never on such a scale as this.[137]

Ronald Bryden in *The Observer* described the end of the production:
"a sonorous white hippie mass in which actors advance on audience,
chanting Cranmer's wishes for England's prince's 'peace, plenty, love,
truth.'" He regards this as a "triumphant close"[138] to Trevor Nunn's
first season. D.A.N. Jones in *The Listener* was less convinced:

When Cranmer makes his final great speech, that Blake-like vision of a future England of "peace, plenty, love, truth," Nunn uses a modern style for expressing rapture. You know those modish camp-meeting songs, "That's the way God planned it" and "Oh happy day, when Jesus walked," and the mantras of the Hare Krishna group. In this mood, Nunn sets his actors to surge toward the audience chanting the four pleasing words. I think this over-softens a tough play. They have left out the fifth word: "terror."[139]

In retrospect, theater historian Hugh Richmond judged it "one of the most thought-provoking productions of this century."[140]

Nunn's production was seen as radical and modern. Howard Davies's was if possible even more so and again the epithet "Brechtian" crops up repeatedly in discussions of his 1983 production. The play's politics were again emphasized, with the program notes' inclusion of an extract from R. H. Tawney's *Religion and the Rise of Capitalism*. In Davies's view the play "is very much a modern play, dealing with taxes, unemployment and social divisions." His production was clearly glancing at the right-wing politics of Margaret Thatcher's government in the 1980s. The theme of the bureaucratization of a centralizing Tudor state was literalized in the opening scene. Nunn had cut both prologue and epilogue (as well as engaging in considerable textual pruning). Davies's production started with King Henry alone on stage scattering papers and speaking the prologue himself.

Irving Wardle describes the stage as "well and truly alienated. Hayden Griffin's sets consist of enlarged reproductions of Elizabethan street scenes and architectural perspectives, trundled along traverse rails and suspended well above the stage floor."[141] Davies was keen to reveal the reality beneath the surface and like Nunn eschewed traditional pageantry, but "in passages like the masque of Katherine's dream and the staging of the coronation ritual with a group of robed dummies, it supplies something no less visually exciting than conventional pageantry."[142] Katherine's dream was a ghostly dance lit by ethereal blue light. For Anne's coronation Davies incorporated the Folio's detailed stage directions as a dress rehearsal for the real thing. Its pace and energy succeeded as Wardle suggested but it also underlined the insubstantiality of the royal pageant. The Epilogue was delivered by Queen Anne amid more paper being thrown into the air and a whistle blowing "time."

Discussing Davies's 1983 production James Fenton argued, "Truly to shock a modern audience, one would need to go back to that old tradition of pageantry and choristers, historicism and authentic sets."[143] Gregory Doran contrived to do this with his 1996 production explaining the theatrical context for doing so in the program notes:

> Tyrone Guthrie directed a series of energetic productions of the play which re-emphasised the role of Henry. . . . Trevor Nunn's 1969 production by contrast . . . reworked the play in an austere Brechtian frame which foregrounded the play's bleak politics. The most controversial twentieth-century production has been that of Howard Davies at Stratford in 1983 which offered a postmodern resistance to pageantry emphasising the play's profound ambivalence over the slippery concepts of "truth" and "conscience." It is arguably only in the wake of Davies's production and its deliberate resistance to the legacy of splendour that *Henry VIII* can be taken beyond these contrasting and controlling modes, recovered as a Jacobean play, and re-invented for the twenty-first century.[144]

Presumably the term "Jacobean play" implies one that combines spectacle and pageantry (as in the Jacobean masque) and yet is deeply political at the same time. Doran was largely successful. Michael Billington thought the production in the Swan made "good use of the space's opportunity for intimate spectacle."[145] Shaun Usher was alert to both elements:

> We begin with the splendid tableau of a gilded king out-dazzling even the Field of the Cloth of Gold—equal honours here to Robert Jones and Howard Harrison for set and lighting—but like the climactic set-piece of Elizabeth I's christening, the picture lingers only long enough to impress. Then it's on with the power struggles, Henry versus pious Catherine (sic), Cardinal Wolsey versus The Rest.[146]

Billington also describes the way in which politics and spectacle worked together in this production:

> In its last outing in 1983 Howard Davies treated the play as a cynical Brechtian anatomy of power politics: a piece of mocked Tudor. Doran, presumably in a spirit of irony, blazons the play's original title, *All Is True*, across the back-wall and the Stratford programme; the result is not so much to heighten the play's documentary reality as to make you aware how everyone bends the idea of truth to his own purposes. . . . Truth, in short, is a malleable weapon rather than a fixed commodity.
>
> Doran and his designer, Robert Jones, also seek to give the play visual unity by showing Henry periodically emerging from a recessed chamber in golden triumph while brutal realpolitik takes place on the forestage.[147]

Costumes and Music

In *Shakespeare in Performance*, Richmond argues that this is a play that, given its historical specificity, needs to be staged in "historically accurate costume."[148] The designers for all three productions have agreed with him and taken the well-known portraits of the chief protagonists as their inspiration, notably the Holbein portrait of Henry. Both Nunn's and Doran's productions were sumptuously costumed. Deirdre Clancy in Howard Davies's production designed authentic period costumes but in subdued tones of gray and oatmeal suggesting "not Holbein's oils but his drawings."[149]

In his autobiography, Donald Sinden, who played Henry in 1969, recalls the assembled cast at the end singing a magnificent "Gloria."[150] In Doran's production Henry had emerged in his first golden pageant to the magnificent choral singing of "*Exultate, Jubilate*." The masque at the Cardinal's took some by surprise: "Wolsey's priapic house-party staggered some of the audience, but manifestly suggested the Cardinal's vulgarity."[151] It took on demonic overtones as it emerged from and eventually exited via the trapdoor.

The most controversial and original music was by Ilona Sekacs for Davies's 1983 production. Pastiche Kurt Weill, it acted as punctuation between scenes and suggested a parallel with the decadent court of the Weimar Republic: "the music, content sometimes to endorse the pathos, is often sharp and derisive, alerting us to ironies."[152] The dance in the masque at the Cardinal's was a somewhat anachronistic tango in which the fate of women in the play could be read from Henry's brutality in "Haling Anne Bullen to her feet," a fate "not only symbolized but determined in that court dance which whirls women round and throws them away. The men rise and fall, the women are taken and discarded."[153]

"Three Magnificent Acting Parts"[154]

In Sir Henry Wotton's description of the burning down of Shakespeare's Globe when the thatch caught light from a celebratory cannon during a performance of this play, he voiced the objection that its realist dramatic qualities were "sufficient in truth within a while to make greatness very familiar, if not ridiculous."[155] Many critics since have been disconcerted by its "low-key emotions and intimate verbal style"[156] which creates a sense of the ordinariness and realism of the characters, but has subversive potential: "it images directly the contradiction between the sacred royal office and the fallible human individual who holds it, making historical actions intelligible as everyday transactions."[157]

Historical productions of the play focused on pageantry and featured the roles of Katherine and Wolsey as star vehicles. The role of the king has tended to provoke controversy because Shakespeare's Henry is not the monstrous Bluebeard of popular myth. Richmond argues that "At this pivotal point in his career Henry's role must remain as unclear, even incoherent, as it probably seemed to its original audience—and just as bewildering as contemporary politicians often appear to us now, without the advantage of hindsight."[158]

Despite describing the part of Henry as "a stinker,"[159] Donald Sinden was able to utilize his natural charm and charisma in the part in Nunn's production and win over most of the critics. He believed that the play showed "only a veneer of the truth" and found "all the speeches ambiguous."[160] Richmond thought that "This tension between surface characterisation and the latent reality known to the

audience by hindsight is what lent memorable force to Sinden's performance."[161] Many critics commented on the paleness of his make-
up (and all commented on half his beard coming off during the trial
scene on the opening night). K. E. B. of the *Nottingham Evening Post*
found Sinden "a Henry of distinction and, praise be not over-padded.
His gradual accession of authority from the time that Wolsey dominated and deceived him until he emerged as the ruler in fact as well
as in name, bluff but not blustering, was a delight to watch."[162]

Nunn had dispensed with Prologue and Epilogue. This is Sinden's
own description of the ending:

> At the end of the play . . . the assembled characters sang a
> magnificent "Gloria" and then left the stage in stately proces-
> sion. Only Henry remained in a spotlight, holding the infant
> Elizabeth who had just been christened. Here I tried to do a most
> difficult thing. The end of the play is a cry for peace in the time
> of the future Elizabeth I and in a few brief seconds I, as Henry
> with no lines, looked into the future, saw the horror that was to
> come, questioned why, realised the failure of the hope, crashed
> into the twentieth century and pleaded silently that where the
> sixteenth century had failed, those of the future may succeed.
> Many people told me it was a most moving moment.[163]

Richard Griffiths, who played the part in Davies's 1983 production, is on record as calling *Henry VIII* "a belting good play,"[164] and
was proudly proclaimed as the only actor to play the part without
padding. He played Henry in a deliberately naturalistic way, in keeping with the downplaying of the pageantry. Ned Chaillot thought he
made him "a likeable rogue,"[165] while J. C. Trewin suggested, "There
will probably be argument about Henry, as Richard Griffiths presents
him; but it is a pleasure to have a King who is not simply an angry
boomer behind a Holbein mask."[166] Sheridan Morley, however, complained that he "never inspires the remotest terror or authority."[167]

Paul Jesson in Doran's production, which played up the pageantry,
attempted more bluffness while at the same time making Henry
human. As Benedict Nightingale saw it, Paul "Jesson's splendidly

bluff, blunt King learns to see through fake and value honesty," and he goes on to blame Shakespeare for Henry's lack of villainy, complaining that "The principals are all relentlessly goodmouthed."[168] Shaun Usher found it an impressive performance:

> Jesson has the presence to fulfil that wide-as-he-is-tall image from the school history books, and the skill to convey arrogant yet sentimental sensibility with deep veins of deviousness and humbug. Previously, Henrys have been upstaged by Catherine of Aragon, or dwarfed in surrounding pageantry; Jesson is never in danger of being deposed.[169]

Queen Katherine

Queen Katherine was played in the past by theatrical legends such as Sarah Siddons, Ellen Terry, Sybil Thorndike, and Edith Evans. The part requires intelligence, spirit, dignity, and pathos: a part "Dame Peggy Ashcroft seemed born to play."[170] She brought great personal commitment to the role and, according to Trevor Nunn, felt the play did less than justice to Katherine's historical dilemma and hence attempted to incorporate extra material from the transcript of the trial, which he vetoed. Ashcroft, by common consent, triumphed. John Barber singled hers out as "the one outstanding performance of the night," describing how,

> When besotted with Anne Bullen, the King spurns his Queen; she reacts first with fire then with melancholy, at last with a pitiful pride. The actress finally came to resemble a Rembrandt portrait of a shrivelled old lady. She speaks always like a queen and even when dying and desolate can hang a word on the air like a jewel.[171]

Keith Brace was also struck by her final scene:

> Dame Peggy more or less created her own play in the death of Katherine, where the emotions aroused were out of proportion

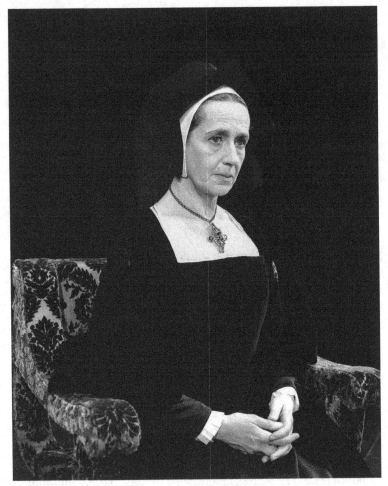

8. 1969, Trevor Nunn production. Peggy Ashcroft as Katherine who reacted "first with fire then with melancholy, at last with pitiful pride. The actress finally came to resemble a Rembrandt portrait of a shrivelled old lady."

to the actual emotional content of the words spoken. She carried the scene at her own slow, but never wearying pace. It was, ironically, more Brechtian as a statement about death rather than a re-enactment of death than all those silly headlines.[172]

Gemma Jones, too, in Davies's 1983 production made a fine Katherine, intelligent and dignified in standing up for the rights of the people in council, committed to her husband. Davies offered a fuller staging of her celestial vision and, maintaining her dignity, she became a figure of pathos in her death.

Jane Lapotaire played Katherine in 1996, emphasizing her status as an outsider by employing a soft Spanish accent and having her ladies sing and dance sevillanas to a flamenco guitar at the beginning of Act 3. Her Katherine was very human, vulnerable, and angry. Benedict Nightingale thought her "a fine Katherine of Aragon . . . who brings patience, dignity and, in her final encounter with Cardinal Wolsey, a moving mix of queenly outrage and simple pain."[173] The celestial vision was simply represented by a shining light playing across her, bathing her sleeping figure: "Hers is the pathos of the evening."[174]

Cardinal Wolsey

The chosen part of Kemble, Irving, and Gielgud; it was played in Nunn's production by Brewster Mason, a huge, intimidating figure and an RSC stalwart. Gordon Parsons thought he played the part "as a benign, scarlet slug of a man,"[175] but Charles Landstone thought him "too coarse as Wolsey, bringing sarcasm in place of pathos to his famous dying speech."[176]

John Thaw, fresh from his TV success in *The Sweeney*, played the part in Davies's production. His performance was not to everyone's taste: "John Thaw played Wolsey much in the role of a shopkeeper. Even in the lines where his downfall causes him to reject worldly ambition, you feel it wouldn't take much for him to open his shop elsewhere."[177] Ned Chaillot, however, argued that, "With Mr. Griffiths going lightly from strength to strength, there is room for a touch of the tragic in the characters of Wolsey and Katherine, and John Thaw's Wolsey achieves the tragic in realizing how ill he has served his God."[178]

Ian Hogg, Wolsey in Doran's production, discussed the play in an interview with the *Birmingham Post*:

On the rare occasions [the play] is done it tends to be very highly dressed up, because people doubt the power of the text.

9. 1983, Howard Davies production. John Thaw as Cardinal Wolsey "achieves the tragic in realizing how ill he has served his God."

But Greg Doran, who is directing this production, has relied a lot on the speed of the words, which moves it at a great lick. If you weigh it down with big scene changes you lose that momentum.[179]

Michael Billington saw him as "a chunky Ipswich over-achiever with a cottage-loaf face who undergoes genuine repentance,"[180] and Naomi Koppel in the *Evening Standard* thought that "Ian Hogg steals the show as Cardinal Wolsey, charting the rise and fall of the butcher's son from Ipswich who cannot quite rid himself of his accent."[181]

In all three productions, the three leads were strongly played and well-balanced. Each production also featured outstanding performances in lesser roles.

Richard Pascoe played Buckingham in 1969. Philip Hope-Wallace argued that he delivered his "great speech of farewell to life . . . as well as I have heard it."[182] Emrys Jones's Cranmer in the same production brought "a hang-dog charm to the part of Cranmer—his hectic football game with the boys while awaiting questioning by the council is a masterstroke."[183]

Queen Anne is a small part without a great deal of scope but in 1969, "Janet Key made Anne Bullen radiantly beautiful, which is about all the part allows."[184] Davies had given the prologue to Henry to deliver and to balance out the proceedings, gave Sarah Berger as Anne the Epilogue. He also made the "Old Lady" younger and added a bevy of other young women in Act 2 Scene 3. Claire Marchionne in Doran's production made her seem less than demure in the masque at Wolsey's and brought her on at the end, where she put her hand to her neck, presumably to serve as a visual reminder of her ultimate fate. Cherry Morris's Old Lady in 1996 was Welsh (as one reviewer commented, there were a lot of accents in this production) and her performance was singled out for its vitality:

> as the Old Lady, Cherry Morris is brimful of sheer human essence. By some strange fluke, Shakespeare is at his best in the few lines he gives to this minor character. Listening to her, we are keenly alive in the moment as nowhere else in the play.[185]

The Chamberlain does not generally get a mention, but Guy Henry's performance in 1996 was picked out by a number of critics for the sophistication and clarity he brought to the part: "There is plenty of wry humour, particularly in Guy Henry's Lord Chamberlain, and also in Cherry Morris's down-to-earth Welsh lady-in-waiting."[186] Perhaps in recognition of their presence onstage as assets, Doran used Guy Henry to speak the Prologue and Morris in place of the Third Gentleman, enlivening the scene while commenting on events such as Anne's coronation.

Conclusion

Originating perhaps as an occasional play for the wedding celebrations of James I's daughter Elizabeth, *Henry VIII* was immensely popular, especially for the celebration of royal occasions, until the twentieth century, when, rather than being played on its intrinsic dramatic merit, it seems frequently to have been relegated to the status of a "festival play" and revived out of a sense of duty. All three RSC productions, though, have proved successful, if controversial, demonstrating that in the right hands it's still a play with real theatrical virtues:

> Truth to life is at once the problem and the fascination of *Henry VIII*. This play is a controlled and possibly cynical experiment. It may not be artistically great, but it is artistically interesting. Its structure and resolution may be "flawed" by ambivalence, divorce, and disjunction, but . . . these "flaws" are patterned and full of meaning, controlled and deliberate. They comment on human truth and art, explaining how literally, objectively true to life great art can be.[187]

THE DIRECTOR'S CUT: INTERVIEWS WITH GREGORY DORAN AND GREGORY THOMPSON

Gregory Doran, born in 1958, studied at Bristol University and the Bristol Old Vic theater school. He began his career as an actor, before becoming associate director at the Nottingham Playhouse. He played some minor roles in the RSC ensemble before directing for the company, first as a freelance, then as associate and subsequently chief associate director. His productions, several of which have starred his partner Antony Sher, are characterized by extreme intelligence and lucidity. He has made a particular mark with several of Shakespeare's lesser-known plays, including *Henry VIII* in the Swan Theatre in 1996, which he's discussing here, and *King John* in 2001, as well as highly acclaimed revivals of works by other contemporary Elizabethan and Jacobean writers.

Gregory Thompson was born in Sheffield and studied mathematics and philosophy at the London School of Economics, before training at Sheffield Youth theater, the National Theatre Studio and Theatre de Complicite. In 1998 he founded AandBC Theatre Company to create touring productions of classical and new drama. These included many productions for Lincoln's Inn Fields and Somerset House in London. Other productions include *Mahabharata, The Winter's Tale, The Rape of Lucrece,* and *The Tale That Wags the Dog* (a storytelling show about the relationships between men and women). He won a Young Vic's Jerwood Director's Award in 2006 and was named Best Director at the 2006 Critics' Awards for Theatre in Scotland for his production of Brian Friel's *Molly Sweeney* at Glasgow Citizens' Theatre. From 2006 to 2007 Gregory was director of Glasgow's Tron theater. Here he's discussing AandBC's production of *Henry VIII,* commissioned by the RSC as part of the 2006 Complete Works Festival and performed in the iconic setting of Holy Trinity Church, Stratford-upon-Avon.

Henry VIII was seen traditionally as a great patriotic celebration and was often staged on the occasion of royal coronations; do you think perceptions of the play have changed and might that account for its relative lack of popularity today?

Doran: Howard Davies tells a story about when he directed the play [in 1983]. There was a meeting in which all the plays were being divvied up for the following year and he went out to the toilet. When he came back he discovered that he was directing *Henry VIII!* When Adrian Noble offered it to me in 1996 various people suggested that it was a poisoned chalice and that it was the one Shakespeare play that doesn't work. I knew that it had been an excuse for a lot of pageantry, that there had been great productions which had staged not only the execution of the Duke of Buckingham but also his journey to the tower by barge, with whole streets of cheering crowds following the coronation of Queen Anne, and spectacular flights of angels for the dream of Queen Katherine.

When you do plays at Stratford you are always aware of previous productions. I had seen that Howard Davies production with Richard Griffiths (Henry), John Thaw (Wolsey), and Gemma Jones (Katherine) and was fascinated by how they had eschewed that pageantry. I remember that the coronation of Queen Anne was a sort of rehearsal: they had dummies dressed up as the various people and they read the stage directions out loud as dialogue. I shared their sense that pageantry had swamped previous productions of the play. It was my first Shakespeare for the RSC and it was a play and a period that I researched a lot. A very significant point about the pageantry is that it is political propaganda. Right at the beginning of the play the Duke of Norfolk describes the Field of the Cloth of Gold: how the French were "All clinquant, all in gold" and what a spectacular affair it was. But as Buckingham says, it's "like a glass, / Did break i'th'wrenching": in other words they had spent an awful lot of money on a Tudor policy of magnificence, and that magnificence was deliberately designed to display wealth and power.

That first scene seems to suggest that the point of the play is in part to demonstrate the hollowness of that policy of propaganda. I began to look at the play from a political perspective in overall terms, but also and particularly at how the pageantry was part of a policy

10. 1996, Gregory Doran production. "[T]he pageantry was part of a policy of magnificence. The play also sweeps from the epic to the intimate in a very specific way."

of magnificence. The play also sweeps from the epic to the intimate in a very specific way. My designer, Rob Jones, and I both realized quite quickly that the Swan Theatre itself was going to help us to solve this problem, in that we could present some spectacular pageantry but then lock it away and become intimate.

Thompson: I think one of the problems with the play is that it is seen as a great patriotic celebration and without care the pageantry can obscure what story there is. The play deals with a tricky piece of our history: Henry VIII was a ruthless tyrant and, in the last fifteen years of his reign, an unstable capricious despot. In many ways the play is about how dangerous it is to be in the court of a tyrant.

Much of the impact of the play has been lost, of course, because for the most part the modern audience no longer has sufficient knowledge of Tudor politics to be aware of the absences and omissions of people and events. Even so, we still recognize today that in the play there is only a hint of Henry's desperation for an heir; no real debate about the legality of his marriage to Katherine; no mention of him becoming Supreme Head of the English Church; four of his wives are missing and no wives are beheaded.

I think the relative lack of popularity of the play is due to its episodic nature and lack of narrative drive. It's not *Hamlet*. Henry has only a few decisions to make: to judge the veracity of Buckingham's surveyor, to remove Wolsey for feathering his own nest, to legitimize his attraction for Anne Bullen and to select and protect Cranmer. None of them are particularly difficult.

Unsurprisingly for a play written when the divine right of kings was a hot issue there is little criticism of the king in the text, saving a hint that his interest in Anne Bullen is merely sexual, but for a play regarded by some as a great patriotic celebration there isn't much praise for Henry either. The play illustrates the trick used by rulers and governments for centuries: pageantry disguises that it's dangerous at court.

Early performances seem to have used the subtitle *All Is True*; were you tempted by this strategy and would it make a difference to perceptions about the play?

Doran: I am entirely convinced that the play is called *All Is True*. Henry Wotton's letter about the burning down of the Globe says that the King's Men were performing a play called *All Is True*, so it seems to me to be the proper title. But it also hints at those rather enigmatic Shakespearean titles like *All's Well That Ends Well*, *As You Like It*, or *What You Will*. It struck me that the title is a bit like a comedian saying, "this is an absolutely true story": the more the comedian emphasizes the truth of his tale, the more you question its veracity. I think the title comes with suspicion attached to it, in the same way that *All's Well That Ends Well* always seems to me to require a question mark at the end of the title.

We took it a stage further and had in the designer Rob Jones's set two huge doors, which opened to reveal the Field of the Cloth of Gold at the beginning. When they closed at the end of that piece of pageantry, you saw emblazoned in gold letters across these doors the words "All Is True." It kept in mind a sense that there was an agenda attached to this dramatization. Was it all true? Can you be true? What is the historical fact? Is there a whitewash job going on? Is this a political gesture to rehabilitate Katherine of Aragon?

One has to remember that Shakespeare had already treated this subject, or at least been part of a collaboration on this very period of history, when he wrote *Thomas More*. The manuscript of that play suggests it's in five different hands and it may therefore be that he was only one collaborator of many in that play, but in the reign of Queen Elizabeth that was an extremely subversive subject to discuss, a regular hot potato. In a way *Thomas More* canonizes the man who had refused the right of Henry to divorce Katherine, and therefore the right of the present Queen—the daughter of Anne Bullen—to reign. To write a play about that and put it on the stage during Elizabeth's reign was an extraordinary thing to do. Coming back to that same period in history at the end of his career suggests that there was business Shakespeare felt he had left unattended. We blazoned "All Is True" on the walls to suggest to the audience that they had to keep a question mark in their minds.

Thompson: The RSC used *Henry VIII*, which is a sensible marketing decision as it is how the play is known. *All Is True* is a great title, though, as one of the driving ideas in the play is that in the court all is true. "All Is true" in the court in the sense that whatever is the current appearance, fashion or policy is taken to be the true and eternal will of the king. Of course, when there is a change in appearance, fashion, or policy then the new situation becomes the true and eternal will of the king. We see Anne shift from lady-in-waiting to heaven-sent queen and then go missing. We know that she becomes the whore that bewitched a king.

When all is true, words cannot be trusted. The members of the court survive and thrive through favor and position as all the power is concentrated in and flows through the king. Words are used to curry favor and maintain position and, as so often with strong government, the first casualty is the truth.

Speaking truth to power is, of course, a Shakespearean theme and the play begs the question: who will speak the truth to the king? The play opens with Norfolk and Buckingham complaining about Wolsey's ambitious schemes and Norfolk warns Buckingham to be careful about telling Henry the truth. Wolsey sees to it that Buckingham doesn't live long enough to influence Henry.

It is a rare person who speaks truth to power. Even the Lady who brings news of the birth of Elizabeth initially tells Henry that the baby is a boy. Katherine uses her position as queen to expose Wolsey's tax gathering and to question the reliability of Buckingham's surveyor as a witness against Buckingham. Cranmer is the only one who fears nothing that can be said against him when pressed by the king.

In Act 3 Scene 1 Katherine refuses to accept Wolsey's scheme for a divorce: she holds fast to the truth, particularly the truth that she is lawfully married to Henry. In Act 3 Scene 2 Wolsey's corruption is exposed and he tells Cromwell to fling away ambition. These two juxtaposed scenes, one where someone holds fast to what she believes to be true and one where someone discards all that is false, were what attracted me to the play.

There are more occurrences (twenty-one) of the word "truth" in *Henry VIII* than in any other Shakespeare play. (*All's Well That Ends Well* has eighteen; *Henry IV Part Two* has sixteen.) The Chorus immediately muddies the water though:

. . . Such as give
Their money out of hope they may believe,
May here find truth too.

Hope and belief are not usual signs of truth. The Chorus goes on to make clear that what is being shown has been selected and is a partial view:

. . . For, gentle hearers, know
To rank our chosen truth with such a show
As fool and fight is, beside forfeiting
Our own brains, and the opinion that we bring
To make that only true we now intend,
Will leave us never an understanding friend.

There has been much criticism of the episodic nature of the plot; was it a problem to find a narrative line or did you detect a more subtle shaping of material in the play in the way it juxtaposes contrasting scenes, moods, and characters?

Doran: I deliberately did not try to solve all the problems of the play before we went into rehearsal, but to see how the play unfurled itself during that process. It inevitably has an episodic quality, but then so does history. To begin with I thought that the potential downfall of Cranmer was one episode too many and felt that I should cut Cranmer from the story. But as we rehearsed and grew to know the play, it seemed to me that it is a learning process for Henry himself: he learns how to trust and who to trust. He trusts Wolsey and then the lords gang up against Wolsey, conspire against him, and bring about his downfall. The lords also conspire against Cranmer, and yet this time Henry, knowing Cranmer to be a good man, gives him his support and his blessing. There is an arc to the story in terms of Henry VIII himself learning how to deal with the people around him. The structure of the play emerged by us allowing it to emerge.

Thompson: The narrative line isn't obvious and there are some delicious juxtapositions. The theater is all about juxtaposition and this play delivers, including: a celebration followed by an execution; the elevation of a lady-in-waiting followed by the trial of a queen; a man of lies followed by a woman of truth; and the coronation of a new queen followed by the death of an old one.

However, there are always two questions to begin with when directing a play: what kind of play is it? And what's the story?

Henry VIII is clearly a history play. One might call it a docudrama. It deals with events over twenty or so years in the middle of Henry's reign from the Field of the Cloth of Gold in 1520 to the birth of Elizabeth in 1533 and Cranmer's political struggles in 1535.

It shows both the public and private lives of the court and we took a decision to have Henry in various states of dress and undress: from his golden and white state outfits recognizable from the iconography to having him entering court in his hunting dress and struggling with his conscience in his nightgown.

The trickier question with this play is: what's the story? The first four acts deal with exits: the trial and death of Buckingham, the fall of Wolsey, the divorce and death of Katherine, and the disappearance of Anne Bullen after the coronation. These leavings are balanced with the wooing and elevation of Anne Bullen to Queen of England, the identification, promotion, and protection of Cranmer, the birth of Elizabeth and the prophecy of her great reign and the one who will come after.

Perhaps the real story is in the departures of Buckingham, Wolsey, and Katherine, and the disappearance of Anne Bullen?

We made a great deal of the exits: using the architecture of the church to give Buckingham, Wolsey, and Katherine long walks down the nave to a glorious exit beyond the audience and the crossing to the altar. A countertenor sang an ethereal tune and the lighting was suitably dramatic. A ghostly nightgowned Anne watched the christening of Elizabeth from the altar.

The story of the play might be that the only way out of the Tudor court is by death.

Another way of answering the "what's the story?" question is to look at the journey of the main character. What happens to Henry VIII? Henry shifts from trusting the ambitious Wolsey who sowed division to trusting the pious Cranmer and ordering the factions to unite behind him. Henry leaves the barren Katherine and ends, by way of the fecund Anne Bullen, holding the new hope Elizabeth. So the kingdom moves from barren corruption to fertile prosperity. Our sympathies, though, are with Wolsey and Katherine.

There is a contemporary political parallel too. Wolsey was a ruthless and powerful political servant who operated as the power of the throne. He is shown in the play to serve his own interests as well as those of the state. The feared Robert Cecil, who had straddled the reigns of both Elizabeth and James, had been seen in some quarters as another Wolsey. Cecil had died in 1612 and *Henry VIII* was first performed in 1613. After Wolsey's fall a new man arrives: Cranmer. Cranmer serves both God and the king and is incorruptible. It's as if Shakespeare is asking, what kind of man do you want in government? Interestingly, James I's solution to the problem of having so much power in one position was to leave the office of Secretary of State vacant until 1614.

The divisions rift by Henry's madness were still causing tensions in James's reign and so the choice of which parts of the story Shakespeare would tell was politically sensitive. The Jacobean audience would have been acutely aware of one absent character. There is just one reference in the play to Mary Tudor. Just before her death, Katherine reveals that she has commended her daughter to Henry and asked for her protection. Henry had only one real job: to provide an heir. Three of his children ruled: Edward, Mary, and Elizabeth. Edward was born after the play ends. Elizabeth is celebrated. Where is Mary? Her absence is part of the story too.

The 1762 Drury Lane production boasted 130 figures in the coronation procession in Act 4, including "The Queen's herbwoman, strewing flowers" and "six Beef-Eaters"; does that sort of lavish spectacle attract you and how did you create your own coronation procession?

Doran: I tried to set up the glory of the spectacle, which has a theatrical impact, at the same time as saying that the narrative is going to end as everybody knew: in Anne Bullen's head being chopped off. We tried to place those pieces of spectacle not just as excuses for a lot of nice costumes and some music, but as something that you could see had a political agenda.

Thompson: Spectacle is an important part of theater and I, like many people attracted to theater, love the lavish and we indulged in spectacle where mentioned in the text: fireworks were visible through the west window for the entry of the goat men for example. However, if we had the resources to create the sort of extravaganzas seen in Drury Lane in the eighteenth century I suspect I would have preferred to double the actors' wages before spending anything on herbwomen strewing flowers or Beef-Eaters for the coronation.

Our coronation procession was about raising Anne as Henry had done. She was pushed down the nave above head height on a wheeled platform. Her eyes were focused on the horizon and her arms outstretched. She was a kind of sacrifice and is not seen again in the play.

The questions I was asking in rehearsal were: what does the spectacle do? What is the coronation scene about in terms of the play as a whole? What does it add to our understanding? Why are the gentlemen discussing who is who and where they are in the procession? Why does one gentleman recognize some people but not all?

I think that with the passage of time we have lost some of the significance. Shakespeare is showing us—or reminding the Jacobean audience—who had influence in the Tudor court after the removal of Katherine of Aragon. The contemporary audience will also have a sense of who was missing from the coronation. The marriage to Anne Bullen split the country. Thomas More's friends bought him a gown to wear at the coronation. He kept the gown but did not attend. It is akin to the much-commented absence of past Prime Ministers Tony Blair and Gordon Brown from the wedding of Prince William to Kate Middleton. Or the position of the Leader of the Opposition, Ed Miliband, tucked away in the third row, when President Obama addressed Parliament recently. The absences and positions are lost on many but significant for those in the know. I am not sure whether we successfully communicated this or not but I do think that the scene is about more than spectacle and makes a dramatic comment

11. 2006, Gregory Thompson production. Aoife McMahon as Anne Bullen. "Our coronation procession was about raising Anne as Henry had done. She was pushed down the nave above head height on a wheeled platform. Her eyes were focused on the horizon and her arms outstretched. She was a kind of sacrifice and is not seen again in the play."

on the rise and fall of members of the court. Again the play hints that the Tudor court was a dangerous place to be.

Although the play is called *Henry VIII*, there's a stage history of Wolsey and Katherine being seen as the leading roles; how did you manage the balance between these three characters in dramatic terms?

Doran: Adrian Noble gave me very good advice in making sure that the casting was the best I could possibly get, and in securing Jane Lapotaire (Katherine), Ian Hogg (Wolsey), and Paul Jesson (Henry) to play those three roles I didn't have to do that balancing; it sorted itself out. Wolsey is a great starring role. It was one of Irving's roles and is an amazingly good part even though he disappears halfway through. I think maybe if you put all your eggs into that basket and have a star actor playing Wolsey to the detriment of the other characters, then once he has left the stage the audience is left wondering when he's going to come back on.

Katherine of Aragon is a wonderful part but I remember Jane Lapotaire describing it, after many performances, as a lonely part. There are four of what we described as "seasonal" scenes. She has her spring, her summer, her great moment in her autumn and then her decline into winter, but she doesn't spend a lot of the time interacting and that was difficult. But it's a spectacular role for an older actress.

Thompson: The play does the balancing act. I didn't want to interfere with the dynamics of the play as written but to bring them out. I thought the best way was to be as physically close to the characters as possible.

Our Henry was as powerful and capricious as we could make him. We wanted to show the man and the monarch and consciously imitated the known portraits and popular images of Henry. Antony Byrne is a powerful, intelligent, and leonine actor with an RSC pedigree and I knew would give us a look of Henry in his prime. The play does not cover Henry's decline into illness and obesity and so I wanted a younger stronger Henry than has been cast in the past.

Similarly, Anthony O'Donnell is an award-winning actor with a history with the RSC and enjoys the same physical stature as Wolsey. He is a rich comic actor and is more usually considered for lighter roles. I had a hunch that he would capture the tragedy of Wolsey's loss.

For Katherine, the common choice is for a British actress to play Spanish. I was attracted to the authenticity of hearing a foreigner trying to speak English beautifully. I remembered Corinne Jaber from Peter Brook's *Mahabharata*. The sense of the queen as both an insider and outsider in the court, both at home and far from home, was a given as soon as she spoke.

Having made the casting decisions the next step is to set up a framework so that all three characters are as powerful as can be. Actors gain power in the theater by going on a journey so we needed to play the forcefulness of Wolsey where his look could silence even the aristocrats of court and he's second only to the king; the potency of Katherine as she marches into Henry's court to fight her case; the vitality of Henry as he never tires but runs from hunting to court to party and dance and then show how Wolsey, the man who has lost all he has strived for, seeks to preserve some dignity; how Katherine's fierce energy even at her last breath affords her a spiritual awakening; and how Henry despairs of providing an heir and is desperate to find a courtier he can trust and rely on. I believe the balance in dramatic terms is achieved by playing the twists and turns of fortune to the maximum so that the joy is joyous and the tragedy terrible.

Shakespeare is kinder to Henry than history has been—he doesn't blame or criticize his actions; did you play up the image of him as "bluff King Hal," Bluebeard in a fatsuit, or did you see him as growing in stature as king in your production?

Doran: Henry is at this stage in his vigorous youth; not the fat old man of the later Holbein image. He has vigor and he grows throughout the role. There are some potentially subversive moments within the play. I learnt a very important lesson: it is possible to over-produce these plays. It tends to be done either by changing scenery between scenes or by putting musical cues between scenes. It's very common practice but you can miss extra elements of the writing by doing it. You can do the same if you put an interval in the wrong place. At the end of Act 2 Scene 2, just before the first entrance of Anne Bullen, Henry is debating what he's going to do about Queen Katherine. Finally he says that he must leave her: "O, my lord, / Would it not grieve an able man to leave / So sweet a bedfellow? But, conscience, conscience: / O, 'tis a tender place, and I must leave her." The end of that scene seems to suggest that Henry VIII is basing his decision to divorce Katherine entirely upon his conscience. The next scene begins with Anne Bullen talking to the Old Lady character: her first line is "Not for that neither: here's the pang that pinches." It's in the middle of a conversation they are already having. If you run the two scenes together, it's as if Anne is answering the last line of the previous scene, saying it's nothing to do with conscience—which of course is what many of the people in the audience are thinking. That is a rather subversive thing to do, but it allowed us to keep questioning the "All Is True" nature of the piece, and try to see what the perspective of the writers to the material was: what their attitude was in suggesting to the audience to keep questioning the historical "facts."

Thompson: I think that it may not be Shakespeare who was being kind to Henry but that our perception of "bluff King Hal" came from the Victorian era and their view of history as the history of great men. No doubt this image was redoubled in the popular imagination of the last century by the gargantuan Henry of Charles Laughton in *The Private Life of Henry VIII* (1933) stalking the corridors to get to Anne Bullen and even Sid James in *Carry on Henry* (1971) as "a great guy with his chopper." We can thank David Starkey and his ilk for our subtler understanding of Henry's tyranny.

Even in the reign of James I, it would have been dangerous for Shakespeare to portray the tyranny of the late Queen's father. It was a balancing act for Shakespeare: how to bring true praise to the king and censure the tyranny. It is significant that the play ends before Henry begins the madness of beheading his wives. In the second half of the play Henry is "rescued" by the arrival of Cranmer and Elizabeth. I prefer to think that Shakespeare is being as critical as he could be in the circumstances. The play is saying that the court of Henry VIII is a very dangerous place to be and even now it would be dangerous to present much beyond the birth of Elizabeth.

The part of Katherine is powerfully drawn and immensely sympathetic—Shakespeare strengthens her character notably in relation to the accounts in the chronicle sources he used; how did you capitalize on this?

Doran: The other element that my research threw up was that, in 1613, with a potential Catholic marriage for King James's son, Prince Henry, on the cards, there was a political agenda to putting on the play in the first place. In the rather Augustan policy that James had of trying to reconcile England with Spain post-Armada, one of the things that a play might do was to tackle the issue of the Spanish Queen, Katherine of Aragon, and what had happened to her. The play virtually canonizes Katherine of Aragon and that seemed to me to be an intensely political gesture.

I read a piece of research by Professor Glynne Wickham that it was possible that the play had been staged at Blackfriars theater (we know the play was also staged at the Globe because it was during a production of it that the Globe burnt down), in which case the scene of Katherine's trial would have played in the very room in which the trial had actually happened (before it was converted into a theater). That must have been an intensely political act in itself.

Thompson: I'm afraid I didn't refer to the historical sources in relation to Katherine but directed from the play. The sources are useful when they give you something not in the play rather than when they give you less. You can only play what's written, of course.

Interestingly, Shakespeare weakens the drama of the masque. In George Cavendish's *Thomas Wolsey, Late Cardinall, His Lyffe And Deathe*, when asked to identify which of the disguised masquers is the king, Wolsey chooses the wrong man: Sir Edward Neville. Neville was a great sportsman, the David Beckham of his day, and Henry's jousting champion. Like the Chechen leader, Ramzan Kadyrov, inviting superstars from the world of football to play against a Chechen team including himself as center-forward, Henry would joust with Sir Edward Neville on his team.

Henry was delighted that Wolsey was deceived into choosing the disguised Neville and burst into laughter. Why did Shakespeare dilute the drama of the scene so that Wolsey found out the king straightway? Perhaps many in his audience would have known this mistaking and it would have added to the idea that "All Is True." Perhaps some even remembered that Edward Neville, like Buckingham before him, was beheaded by Henry VIII on the testimony of another. There was danger even in friendship with Henry.

Shakespeare's other late plays (*Cymbeline, The Winter's Tale, The Tempest*) rely on magic for their resolution but *Henry VIII* is resolutely earthbound apart from Katherine's vision in Act 4 Scene 2. Many modern productions cut this scene; how and why did you stage it?

Doran: We tried various things. I referred earlier to the canonization of Katherine because it seems to me that she learns within that scene some of the lessons that will allow her into heaven. At Kimbolton, where she is in her declining years, her steward Griffith has given her an account of Wolsey's death and she becomes vicious about Wolsey, whom she counts her enemy. Griffith, rather astonishingly, points out what a good man Wolsey was, the institutions that he patronized and funded, and says one of the wonderful lines in the play: "Men's evil manners live in brass, their virtues / We write in water." Having counted Cardinal Wolsey's good points, Katherine responds, "After my death I wish no other herald, / No other speaker of my living actions, / To keep mine honour from corruption, / But such an honest chronicler as Griffith." It's as if she has learned both patience and tolerance, and those two lessons allow her out of purgatory and into heaven. Her waiting maid is even called Patience.

In the staging of that scene we decided ultimately that, in a stage the size of the Swan space, Jane Lapotaire's expression alone could create a greater vision than I could summon up. We put a shaft of light onto her as she opened her eyes, saw her vision and then woke up and told us what she had seen. In the context of the production we were doing that seemed sufficient.

Thompson: I staged it as Katherine's vision. She is near death and she sees angels. Our angels gained height from the reverse of the platform used in Anne's coronation: as Anne was raised up to be queen so Katherine could ascend to heaven.

Why would it be cut? Making a Catholic Queen the emotional center of a play is a political act on Shakespeare's part. Her vision reinforces both her religion and her special nature. It is the Catholic that is welcomed to eternal happiness by spirits of peace. Katherine is the spiritual heart of the play. She refuses to do anything that is not the truth. This makes her a powerful figure. Like Hermione, like Innogen, she holds fast to the truth; and, like Hermione and Thaisa, she dies. For Katherine there is no resurrection, of course, only loss. That a Spanish Queen and the mother of Mary Tudor was being honored in this way on the Jacobean stage is remarkable.

The spiritual nature of the scene is not normally found in a history play but it does connect *Henry VIII* to *Cymbeline*, *The Winter's Tale*, *The Tempest*, and *Pericles*. There is a criticism of *Henry VIII* that on the one hand it's not enough like *Henry V* to be a proper history, and on the other that it is a pity that it is not more of a romance like *The Winter's Tale*. It is what it is and the romance elements are fascinating.

Like the later plays there is a lost mother, sinned against but pure; a ruler, blind to sin, who learns to trust truth; and a new daughter who provides hope for a glorious future.

There is a curious amalgam of Leontes and Camillo, the reformed man and the wise counselor, in Wolsey and Cranmer. I toyed with the idea of doubling the roles and casting one actor in both parts. At the end of the third act Wolsey bids farewell to the hopes of court and vows to rely upon his integrity to heaven. In the fifth act a new man arrives, Cranmer. He is to be housed in the Tower on the testimony of others. Cranmer welcomes the trial and relies on his truth and honesty to see him through. Fortunately for Cranmer, of course, Henry favors him and gives him his token for protection. In terms of the late plays the Leontes journey from sin to humility is taken by Wolsey/Cranmer.

The play offers a running commentary on events through various anonymous characters such as the "Gentlemen," "Old Lady," and so on; how important are they and what do you think they're supposed to represent?

Doran: The Old Lady in particular is very important in providing a cynical note. There's an extraordinary moment where she tells Henry VIII that Anne Bullen has given birth, and she so wants to impress the King and to gain from the King's opinion of her that she says, "Ay, ay, my liege, / And of a lovely boy." Henry in our production gave whoops of joy and started dancing around, and then the Old Lady says "'Tis a girl / Promises boys hereafter." The sense that the character has a cynical edge was great fun to play. I had the late Cherry Morris in that role and she managed to catch that wry edge which is a very important element within the play.

Thompson: They are very important and they represent the truth: the reality. They puncture the glamour of the court and say what's really going on. The Lady fingers Anne's ambition despite the denials and is smart enough to both lie to Henry about the sex of his baby and tell him the truth. The Gentlemen have seen the comings and goings of court, the rises and falls. Their gossip is more real in some ways than the politicking of the court.

The play ends on the high point of the christening of the baby princess, the future Queen Elizabeth, in general peace and reconciliation; how are we supposed to understand and respond to the contradictory events we've witnessed—with a cynical shrug, feel-good patriotic fervor, or something more complex?

Doran: The final speech is absurd if you think of it in literal terms: there is Cranmer taking the baby Elizabeth, who will become Queen Elizabeth I, and projecting not only her future but also her death and the fact that King James will rise out of it. Also, in 1613, if this play was being performed around the wedding of James's daughter, also called Elizabeth, then he might have been projecting a future for her too. It's a difficult speech to get the tone of. You also have to remember the context for which it was written. It would be wrong to somehow try and subvert it by making it a fanatical aria, because at root it's a plea for the security of the state.

Henry VIII is only one monarch away from the *Henry VI/ Richard III* sequence of history plays. In that tetralogy you have all the horror and instability of the Wars of the Roses, ending in the coronation of the new King Henry VII hoping to bring peace to the land. If you see *Henry VIII* as the last beat of that story—as the very next king (after Richmond becomes Henry VII)—then you understand the context in which he is determined that he will provide an heir for the country and stability for his kingdom. That helps you understand that final speech in the context of a desire to bring stability to a country that had been wracked by civil war for so long. If I get round to doing the *Henry VI/Richard III* plays I think it would be very interesting to play *Henry VIII* at the end of that cycle.

There is a heritage element with the Tudors, which you have to resist but you also have to be aware of, because by and large the audience does know the story. It's a story that we are told many times and has been very popular on film and television. At the very end of our production, as Anne's baby was being celebrated, Anne appeared at the back just before the lights went and she put her hand to her neck. It used to get gasps from the audience. It allowed the aspirational quality of Cranmer's speech to exist, but then added a health warning at the end of the play.

Thompson: I think it's something more complex. Cranmer actually gives highest praise to the one who comes after Elizabeth: Shakespeare's current king, James I. Henry's great failing is that he did not produce a healthy male heir and Cranmer is legitimizing Henry's legacy by making Elizabeth a sufficient heir.

It is significant that the play ends before the great terror and fervor of the Reformation—before the monasteries were dissolved and the churches whitewashed. Like the order from the Taliban to destroy the Buddhas of Bamiyan, the word went out to destroy the icons of England, and much of our religious heritage was obliterated with no less force than the dynamite of Afghanistan. And there was more cruelty and martyrdom to come, all in the name of the living God. Edward's Reformation, the Catholic Restoration under Mary and Elizabethan Settlement were reinforced with executions and imprisonments. In 1613 it was still in living memory.

Shakespeare grew up in a world shaped by those who had experienced the terror that had begun eighty years before. There were people still alive who were born in Henry's reign. The memory of the recession of the thirties still informs our political discourse today and someone born in 1964 came into a world shaped by the political resolution of the Second World War and benefited from the Welfare State, a response to the economic suffering of the depression. So Shakespeare, born in 1564, came into a world shaped by the Elizabethan Settlement and with a dread of civil strife.

The Jacobean audience would have known what came next: whether or not they regarded her as a Bird of Wonder, they would certainly remember that she was loved and feared.

We had a real baby stand in for Elizabeth. It humanized Henry and brought a remarkable focus from the audience. It was our own way of using the principle that "Pageantry causes you to forget that it's dangerous at court." However successful or otherwise the production had been, the wonder of a real baby brought generous applause.

SHAKESPEARE'S CAREER IN THE THEATER

BEGINNINGS

William Shakespeare was an extraordinarily intelligent man who was born and died in an ordinary market town in the English Midlands. He lived an uneventful life in an eventful age. Born in April 1564, he was the eldest son of John Shakespeare, a glove maker who was prominent on the town council until he fell into financial difficulties. Young William was educated at the local grammar in Stratford-upon-Avon, Warwickshire, where he gained a thorough grounding in the Latin language, the art of rhetoric, and classical poetry. He married Ann Hathaway and had three children (Susanna, then the twins Hamnet and Judith) before his twenty-first birthday: an exceptionally young age for the period. We do not know how he supported his family in the mid-1580s.

Like many clever country boys, he moved to the city in order to make his way in the world. Like many creative people, he found a career in the entertainment business. Public playhouses and professional full-time acting companies reliant on the market for their income were born in Shakespeare's childhood. When he arrived in London as a man, sometime in the late 1580s, a new phenomenon was in the making: the actor who is so successful that he becomes a "star." The word did not exist in its modern sense, but the pattern is recognizable: audiences went to the theater not so much to see a particular show as to witness the comedian Richard Tarlton or the dramatic actor Edward Alleyn.

Shakespeare was an actor before he was a writer. It appears not to have been long before he realized that he was never going to grow into a great comedian like Tarlton or a great tragedian like Alleyn. Instead, he found a role within his company as the man who patched up old plays, breathing new life, new dramatic twists, into tired repertory pieces. He paid close attention to the work of the university-educated dramatists who were writing history plays and tragedies for the public stage in a style more ambitious, sweeping, and poetically grand than anything that had been seen before. But he may also have noted that what his friend and rival Ben Jonson would call "Marlowe's mighty line" sometimes faltered in the mode of comedy. Going to university, as Christopher Marlowe did, was all well and good for honing the arts of rhetorical elaboration and classical allusion, but it could lead to a loss of the common touch. To stay close to a large segment of the potential audience for public theater, it was necessary to write for clowns as well as kings and to intersperse the flights of poetry with the humor of the tavern, the privy, and the brothel: Shakespeare was the first to establish himself early in his career as an equal master of tragedy, comedy, and history. He realized that theater could be the medium to make the national past available to a wider audience than the elite who could afford to read large history books: his signature early works include not only the classical tragedy *Titus Andronicus* but also the sequence of English historical plays on the Wars of the Roses.

He also invented a new role for himself, that of in-house company dramatist. Where his peers and predecessors had to sell their plays to the theater managers on a poorly paid piecework basis, Shakespeare took a percentage of the box-office income. The Lord Chamberlain's Men constituted themselves in 1594 as a joint stock company, with the profits being distributed among the core actors who had invested as sharers. Shakespeare acted himself—he appears in the cast lists of some of Ben Jonson's plays as well as the list of actors' names at the beginning of his own collected works—but his principal duty was to write two or three plays a year for the company. By holding shares, he was effectively earning himself a royalty on his work, something no author had ever done before in England. When the Lord Chamberlain's Men collected their fee for performance at court in the Christmas season of 1594, three of them went along to the Treasurer of the Chamber: not just Richard Burbage the tragedian and Will Kempe the clown, but also Shakespeare the scriptwriter. That was something new.

The next four years were the golden period in Shakespeare's

career, though overshadowed by the death of his only son, Hamnet, age eleven, in 1596. In his early thirties and in full command of both his poetic and his theatrical medium, he perfected his art of comedy, while also developing his tragic and historical writing in new ways. In 1598, Francis Meres, a Cambridge University graduate with his finger on the pulse of the London literary world, praised Shakespeare for his excellence across the genres:

> As Plautus and Seneca are accounted the best for comedy and tragedy among the Latins, so Shakespeare among the English is the most excellent in both kinds for the stage; for comedy, witness his *Gentlemen of Verona*, his *Errors*, his *Love Labours Lost*, his *Love Labours Won*, his *Midsummer Night Dream* and his *Merchant of Venice*: for tragedy his *Richard the 2*, *Richard the 3*, *Henry the 4*, *King John*, *Titus Andronicus* and his *Romeo and Juliet*.

For Meres, as for the many writers who praised the "honey-flowing vein" of *Venus and Adonis* and *Lucrece*, narrative poems written when the theaters were closed due to plague in 1593–94, Shakespeare was marked above all by his linguistic skill, by the gift of turning elegant poetic phrases.

PLAYHOUSES

Elizabethan playhouses were "thrust" or "one-room" theaters. To understand Shakespeare's original theatrical life, we have to forget about the indoor theater of later times, with its proscenium arch and curtain that would be opened at the beginning and closed at the end of each act. In the proscenium arch theater, stage and auditorium are effectively two separate rooms: the audience looks from one world into another as if through the imaginary "fourth wall" framed by the proscenium. The picture-frame stage, together with the elaborate scenic effects and backdrops beyond it, created the illusion of a self-contained world—especially once nineteenth-century developments in the control of artificial lighting meant that the auditorium could be darkened and the spectators made to focus on the lighted stage. Shakespeare, by contrast, wrote for a bare platform stage with a standing audience gathered around it in a courtyard in full daylight. The audience were always conscious of themselves and their fellow spectators, and they shared the same "room" as the actors. A sense of immediate presence and the creation of rapport with the audience were all-important. The actor could not afford to imagine he was in a closed world, with silent witnesses dutifully observing him from the darkness.

Shakespeare's theatrical career began at the Rose Theatre in Southwark. The stage was wide and shallow, trapezoid in shape, like a lozenge. This design had a great deal of potential for the theatrical equivalent of cinematic split-screen effects, whereby one group of characters would enter at the door at one end of the tiring-house wall at the back of the stage and another group through the door at the other end, thus creating two rival tableaux. Many of the battle-heavy and faction-filled plays that premiered at the Rose have scenes of just this sort.

At the rear of the Rose stage, there were three capacious exits, each over ten feet wide. Unfortunately, the very limited excavation of a fragmentary portion of the original Globe site, in 1989, revealed nothing about the stage. The first Globe was built in 1599 with similar proportions to those of another theater, the Fortune, albeit that the former was polygonal and looked circular, whereas the latter was rectangular. The building contract for the Fortune survives and allows us to infer that the stage of the Globe was probably substantially wider than it was deep (perhaps forty-three feet wide and twenty-seven feet deep). It may well have been tapered at the front, like that of the Rose.

The capacity of the Globe was said to have been enormous, perhaps in excess of three thousand. It has been conjectured that about eight hundred people may have stood in the yard, with two thousand or more in the three layers of covered galleries. The other "public" playhouses were also of large capacity, whereas the indoor Blackfriars theater that Shakespeare's company began using in 1608—the former refectory of a monastery—had overall internal dimensions of a mere forty-six by sixty feet. It would have made for a much more intimate theatrical experience and had a much smaller capacity, probably of about six hundred people. Since they paid at least six-pence a head, the Blackfriars attracted a more select or "private" audience. The atmosphere would have been closer to that of an indoor performance before the court in the Whitehall Palace or at Richmond. That Shakespeare always wrote for indoor production at court as well as outdoor performance in the public theater should make us cautious about inferring, as some scholars have, that the opportunity provided by the intimacy of the Blackfriars led to a sig-nificant change toward a "chamber" style in his last plays—which, besides, were performed at both the Globe and the Blackfriars. After the occupation of the Blackfriars a five-act structure seems to have become more important to Shakespeare. That was because of artifi-cial lighting: there were musical interludes between the acts, while the candles were trimmed and replaced. Again, though, something similar must have been necessary for indoor court performances throughout his career.

Front of house there were the "gatherers" who collected the money from audience members: a penny to stand in the open-air yard, another penny for a place in the covered galleries, sixpence for the prominent "lord's rooms" to the side of the stage. In the indoor "private" theaters, gallants from the audience who fancied making themselves part of the spectacle sat on stools on the edge of the stage itself. Scholars debate as to how widespread this practice was in the public theaters such as the Globe. Once the audience were in place and the money counted, the gatherers were available to be extras on-stage. That is one reason why battles and crowd scenes often come later rather than early in Shakespeare's plays. There was no formal prohibition upon performance by women, and there certainly were women among the gatherers, so it is not beyond the bounds of possi-bility that female crowd members were played by females.

The play began at two o'clock in the afternoon and the theater had to be cleared by five. After the main show, there would be a jig—which consisted not only of dancing but also of knockabout comedy (it is the origin of the farcical "afterpiece" in the eighteenth-century theater). So the time available for a Shakespeare play was about two and a half hours, somewhere between the "two hours' traffic" men-tioned in the prologue to *Romeo and Juliet* and the "three hours' spectacle" referred to in the preface to the 1647 Folio of Beaumont and Fletcher's plays. The prologue to a play by Thomas Middleton refers to a thousand lines as "one hour's words," so the likelihood is that about two and a half thousand, or a maximum of three thousand lines made up the performed text. This is indeed the length of most of Shakespeare's comedies, whereas many of his tragedies and histories are much longer, raising the possibility that he wrote full scripts, possibly with eventual publication in mind, in the full knowledge that the stage version would be heavily cut. The short Quarto texts published in his lifetime—they used to be called "Bad" Quartos—provide fascinating evidence as to the kind of cutting that probably took place. So, for instance, the First Quarto of *Hamlet* neatly merges two occasions when Hamlet is overheard, the "Fishmonger" and the "nunnery" scenes.

The social composition of the audience was mixed. The poet Sir John Davies wrote of "A thousand townsmen, gentlemen and whores, / Porters and servingmen" who would "together throng" at the public playhouses. Though moralists associated female playgoing with adultery and the sex trade, many perfectly respectable citizens' wives were regular attendees. Some, no doubt, resembled the modern groupie: a story attested in two different sources has one citizen's wife making a postshow assignation with Richard Burbage and ending up in bed with Shakespeare—supposedly eliciting from the latter the quip that William the Conqueror was before Richard III. Defenders of theater liked to say that by witnessing the comeuppance of villains on the stage, audience members would repent of their own wrongdoings, but the reality is that most people went to the theater then, as they do now, for entertainment more than moral edification. Besides, it would be foolish to suppose that audiences behaved in a homogeneous way: a pamphlet of the 1630s tells of how two men went to see *Pericles* and one of them laughed while the other wept. Bishop John Hall complained that people went to church for the same reasons that they went to the theater: "for company, for custom, for recreation . . . to feed his eyes or his ears . . . or perhaps for sleep."

Men-about-town and clever young lawyers went to be seen as much as to see. In the modern popular imagination, shaped not least by *Shakespeare in Love* and the opening sequence of Laurence Olivier's *Henry V* film, the penny-paying groundlings stand in the yard hurling abuse or encouragement and hazelnuts or orange peel at the actors, while the sophisticates in the covered galleries appreciate Shakespeare's soaring poetry. The reality was probably the other way around. A "groundling" was a kind of fish, so the nickname suggests the penny audience standing below the level of the stage and gazing in silent open-mouthed wonder at the spectacle unfolding above them. The more difficult audience members, who kept up a running commentary of clever remarks on the performance and who occasionally got into quarrels with players, were the gallants. Like Hollywood movies in modern times, Elizabethan and Jacobean plays exercised a powerful influence on the fashion and behavior of the young. John Marston mocks the lawyers who would open their lips, perhaps to court a girl, and out would "flow / Naught but pure Juliet and Romeo."

THE ENSEMBLE AT WORK

In the absence of typewriters and photocopying machines, reading aloud would have been the means by which the company got to know a new play. The tradition of the playwright reading his complete script to the assembled company endured for generations. A copy would then have been taken to the Master of the Revels for licensing. The theater book-holder or prompter would then have copied the parts for distribution to the actors. A partbook consisted of the character's lines, with each speech preceded by the last three or four words of the speech before, the so-called cue. These would have been taken away and studied or "conned." During this period of learning the parts, an actor might have had some one-to-one instruction, perhaps from the dramatist, perhaps from a senior actor who had played the same part before, and, in the case of an apprentice, from his master. A high percentage of Desdemona's lines occur in dialogue with Othello, of Lady Macbeth's with Macbeth, Cleopatra's with Antony, and Volumnia's with Coriolanus. The roles would almost certainly have been taken by the apprentice of the lead actor, usually Burbage, who delivers the majority of the cues. Given that

12. Hypothetical reconstruction of the interior of an Elizabethan playhouse during a performance.

apprentices lodged with their masters, there would have been ample opportunity for personal instruction, which may be what made it possible for young men to play such demanding parts.

After the parts were learned, there may have been no more than a single rehearsal before the first performance. With six different plays to be put on every week, there was no time for more. Actors, then, would go into a show with a very limited sense of the whole. The notion of a collective rehearsal process that is itself a process of discovery for the actors is wholly modern and would have been incomprehensible to Shakespeare and his original ensemble. Given the number of parts an actor had to hold in his memory, the forgetting of lines was probably more frequent than in the modern theater. The book-holder was on hand to prompt.

Backstage personnel included the property man, the tire-man who oversaw the costumes, call boys, attendants, and the musicians, who might play at various times from the main stage, the rooms above, and within the tiring-house. Scriptwriters sometimes made a nuisance of themselves backstage. There was often tension between the acting companies and the freelance playwrights from whom they purchased scripts: it was a smart move on the part of Shakespeare and the Lord Chamberlain's Men to bring the writing process in-house.

Scenery was limited, though sometimes set pieces were brought on (a bank of flowers, a bed, the mouth of hell). The trapdoor from below, the gallery stage above, and the curtained discovery-space at the back allowed for an array of special effects: the rising of ghosts and apparitions, the descent of gods, dialogue between a character at a window and another at ground level, the revelation of a statue or a pair of lovers playing at chess. Ingenious use could be made of props, as with the ass's head in *A Midsummer Night's Dream*. In a theater that does not clutter the stage with the material paraphernalia of everyday life, those objects that are deployed may take on powerful symbolic weight, as when Shylock bears his weighing scales in one hand and knife in the other, thus becoming a parody of the figure of Justice who traditionally bears a sword and a balance. Among the more significant items in the property cupboard of Shakespeare's company, there would have been a throne (the "chair of state"), joint stools, books, bottles, coins, purses, letters (which are brought onstage, read, or referred to on about eighty occasions in the complete works), maps, gloves, a set of stocks (in which Kent is put in *King Lear*), rings, rapiers, daggers, broadswords, staves, pistols, masks and vizards, heads and skulls, torches and tapers and lanterns, which served to signal night scenes on the daylit stage, a buck's head, an ass's head, animal costumes. Live animals also put in appearances, most notably the dog Crab in *The Two Gentlemen of Verona* and possibly a young polar bear in *The Winter's Tale*.

The costumes were the most important visual dimension of the play. Playwrights were paid between £2 and £6 per script, whereas Alleyn was not averse to paying £20 for "a black velvet cloak with sleeves embroidered all with silver and gold." No matter the period of the play, actors always wore contemporary costume. The excitement for the audience came not from any impression of historical accuracy, but from the richness of the attire and perhaps the transgressive thrill of the knowledge that here were commoners like themselves strutting in the costumes of courtiers in effective defiance of the strict sumptuary laws whereby in real life people had to wear the clothes that befitted their social station.

To an even greater degree than props, costumes could carry symbolic importance. Racial characteristics could be suggested: a breastplate and helmet for a Roman soldier, a turban for a Turk, long robes for exotic characters such as Moors, a gabardine for a Jew. The figure of Time, as in *The Winter's Tale*, would be equipped with hourglass, scythe, and wings; Rumour, who speaks the prologue of *2 Henry IV*, wore a costume adorned with a thousand tongues. The wardrobe in the tiring-house of the Globe would have contained much of the same stock as that of rival manager Philip Henslowe at the Rose: green gowns for outlaws and foresters, black for melancholy men such as Jaques and people in mourning such as the Countess in *All's Well That Ends Well* (at the beginning of *Hamlet*, the prince is still in mourning black when everyone else is in festive garb for the wedding of the new king), a gown and hood for a friar (or a feigned friar like the duke in *Measure for Measure*), blue coats and tawny to distinguish the followers of rival factions, a leather apron and ruler for a carpenter (as in the opening scene of *Julius Caesar*—and in *A Midsummer Night's Dream*, where this is the only sign that Peter Quince is a carpenter), a cockle hat with staff and a pair of sandals for a pilgrim or palmer (the disguise assumed by Helen in *All's Well*), bodices and kirtles with farthingales beneath for the boys who are to be dressed as girls. A gender switch such as that of Rosalind or Jessica seems to have taken between fifty and eighty lines of dialogue—Viola does not resume her "maiden weeds," but remains in her boy's costume to the end of *Twelfth Night* because a change would have slowed down the action at just the moment it was speeding to a climax. Henslowe's inventory also included "a robe for to go invisible": Oberon, Puck, and Ariel must have had something similar.

As the costumes appealed to the eyes, so there was music for the ears. Comedies included many songs. Desdemona's willow song, perhaps a late addition to the text, is a rare and thus exceptionally poignant example from tragedy. Trumpets and tuckets sounded for ceremonial entrances, drums denoted an army on the march. Background music could create atmosphere, as at the beginning of *Twelfth Night*, during the lovers' dialogue near the end of *The Mer-*

chant of Venice, when the statue seemingly comes to life in *The Winter's Tale,* and for the revival of Pericles and of Lear (in the Quarto text, but not the Folio). The haunting sound of the hautboy suggested a realm beyond the human, as when the god Hercules is imagined deserting Mark Antony. Dances symbolized the harmony of the end of a comedy—though in Shakespeare's world of mingled joy and sorrow, someone is usually left out of the circle.

The most important resource was, of course, the actors themselves. They needed many skills: in the words of one contemporary commentator, "dancing, activity, music, song, elocution, ability of body, memory, skill of weapon, pregnancy of wit." Their bodies were as significant as their voices. Hamlet tells the player to "suit the action to the word, the word to the action": moments of strong emotion, known as "passions," relied on a repertoire of dramatic gestures as well as a modulation of the voice. When Titus Andronicus has had his hand chopped off, he asks "How can I grace my talk, / Wanting a hand to give it action?" A pen portrait of "The Character of an Excellent Actor" by the dramatist John Webster is almost certainly based on his impression of Shakespeare's leading man, Richard Burbage: "By a full and significant action of body, he charms our attention: sit in a full theatre, and you will think you see so many lines drawn from the circumference of so many ears, whiles the actor is the centre. . . ."

Though Burbage was admired above all others, praise was also heaped upon the apprentice players whose alto voices fitted them for the parts of women. A spectator at Oxford in 1610 records how the audience were reduced to tears by the pathos of Desdemona's death. The puritans who fumed about the biblical prohibition upon cross-dressing and the encouragement to sodomy constituted by the sight of an adult male kissing a teenage boy onstage were a small minority. Little is known, however, about the characteristics of the leading apprentices in Shakespeare's company. It may perhaps be inferred that one was a lot taller than the other, since Shakespeare often wrote for a pair of female friends, one tall and fair, the other short and dark (Helena and Hermia, Rosalind and Celia, Beatrice and Hero).

We know little about Shakespeare's own acting roles—an early allusion indicates that he often took royal parts, and a venerable tradition gives him old Adam in *As You Like It* and the ghost of old King Hamlet. Save for Burbage's lead roles and the generic part of the clown, all such castings are mere speculation. We do not even know for sure whether the original Falstaff was Will Kempe or another actor who specialized in comic roles, Thomas Pope.

Kempe left the company in early 1599. Tradition has it that he fell out with Shakespeare over the matter of excessive improvisation. He was replaced by Robert Armin, who was less of a clown and more of a cerebral wit: this explains the difference between such parts as Lancelet Gobbo and Dogberry, which were written for Kempe, and the more verbally sophisticated Feste and Lear's Fool, which were written for Armin.

One thing that is clear from surviving "plots" or storyboards of plays from the period is that a degree of doubling was necessary. *2 Henry VI* has over sixty speaking parts, but more than half of the characters appear only in a single scene and most scenes have only six to eight speakers. At a stretch, the play could be performed by thirteen actors. When Thomas Platter saw *Julius Caesar* at the Globe in 1599, he noted that there were about fifteen. Why doesn't Paris go to the Capulet ball in *Romeo and Juliet*? Perhaps because he was doubled with Mercutio, who does. In *The Winter's Tale*, Mamillius might have come back as Perdita and Antigonus been doubled by Camillo, making the partnership with Paulina at the end a very neat touch. Titania and Oberon are often played by the same pair as Hippolyta and Theseus, suggesting a symbolic matching of the rulers of the worlds of night and day, but it is questionable whether there would have been time for the necessary costume changes. As so often, one is left in a realm of tantalizing speculation.

THE KING'S MAN

On Queen Elizabeth's death in 1603, the new king, James I, who had held the Scottish throne as James VI since he had been an infant, immediately took the Lord Chamberlain's Men under his direct patronage. Henceforth they would be the King's Men, and for the rest of Shakespeare's career they were favored with far more court performances than any of their rivals. There even seem to have been rumors early in the reign that Shakespeare and Burbage were being considered for knighthoods, an unprecedented honor for mere actors—and one that in the event was not accorded to a member of the profession for nearly three hundred years, when the title was bestowed upon Henry Irving, the leading Shakespearean actor of Queen Victoria's reign.

Shakespeare's productivity rate slowed in the Jacobean years, not because of age or some personal trauma, but because there were frequent outbreaks of plague, causing the theaters to be closed for long periods. The King's Men were forced to spend many months on the road. Between November 1603 and 1608, they were to be found at various towns in the south and Midlands, though Shakespeare probably did not tour with them by this time. He had bought a large house back home in Stratford and was accumulating other property. He may indeed have stopped acting soon after the new king took the throne. With the London theaters closed so much of the time and a large repertoire on the stocks, Shakespeare seems to have focused his energies on writing a few long and complex tragedies that could have been played on demand at court: *Othello, King Lear, Antony and Cleopatra, Coriolanus,* and *Cymbeline* are among his longest and poetically grandest plays. *Macbeth* survives only in a shorter text, which shows signs of adaptation after Shakespeare's death. The bitterly satirical *Timon of Athens,* apparently a collaboration with Thomas Middleton that may have failed on the stage, also belongs to this period. In comedy, too, he wrote longer and morally darker works than in the Elizabethan period, pushing at the very bounds of the form in *Measure for Measure* and *All's Well That Ends Well.*

From 1608 onward, when the King's Men began occupying the indoor Blackfriars playhouse (as a winter house, meaning that they only used the outdoor Globe in summer?), Shakespeare turned to a more romantic style. His company had a great success with a revived and altered version of an old pastoral play called *Mucedorus.* It even featured a bear. The younger dramatist John Fletcher, meanwhile, sometimes working in collaboration with Francis Beaumont, was pioneering a new style of tragicomedy, a mix of romance and royalism laced with intrigue and pastoral excursions. Shakespeare experimented with this idiom in *Cymbeline,* and it was presumably with his blessing that Fletcher eventually took over as the King's Men's company dramatist. The two writers apparently collaborated on three plays in the years 1612–14: a lost romance called *Cardenio* (based on the love-madness of a character in Cervantes's *Don Quixote*), *Henry VIII* (originally staged with the title "All Is True"), and *The Two Noble Kinsmen*, a dramatization of Chaucer's "Knight's Tale." These were written after Shakespeare's two final solo-authored plays, *The Winter's Tale*, a self-consciously old-fashioned work dramatizing the pastoral romance of his old enemy Robert Greene, and *The Tempest*, which at one and the same time drew together multiple theatrical traditions, diverse reading, and contemporary interest in the fate of a ship that had been wrecked on the way to the New World.

The collaborations with Fletcher suggest that Shakespeare's career ended with a slow fade rather than the sudden retirement supposed by the nineteenth-century Romantic critics who read Prospero's epilogue to *The Tempest* as Shakespeare's personal farewell to his art. In the last few years of his life Shakespeare certainly spent more of his time in Stratford-upon-Avon, where he became further involved in property dealing and litigation. But his London life also continued. In 1613 he made his first major London property purchase: a freehold house in the Blackfriars district, close to his company's indoor theater. *The Two Noble Kinsmen* may have been written as late as 1614, and Shakespeare was in London on business a little over a year before he died of an unknown cause at home in Stratford-upon-Avon in 1616, probably on his fifty-second birthday.

About half the sum of his works were published in his lifetime, in texts of variable quality. A few years after his death, his fellow actors began putting together an authorized edition of his complete *Comedies, Histories and Tragedies*. It appeared in 1623, in large "Folio" format. This collection of thirty-six plays gave Shakespeare his immortality. In the words of his fellow dramatist Ben Jonson, who contributed two poems of praise at the start of the Folio, the body of his work made him "a monument without a tomb":

And art alive still while thy book doth live
And we have wits to read and praise to give . . .
He was not of an age, but for all time!

SHAKESPEARE'S WORKS:
A CHRONOLOGY

1589–91	*? Arden of Faversham* (possible part authorship)
1589–92	*The Taming of the Shrew*
1589–92	*? Edward the Third* (possible part authorship)
1591	*The Second Part of Henry the Sixth*, originally called *The First Part of the Contention Betwixt the Two Famous Houses of York and Lancaster* (element of coauthorship possible)
1591	*The Third Part of Henry the Sixth*, originally called *The True Tragedy of Richard Duke of York* (element of co-authorship probable)
1591–92	*The Two Gentlemen of Verona*
1591–92; perhaps revised 1594	*The Lamentable Tragedy of Titus Andronicus* (probably cowritten with, or revising an earlier version by, George Peele)
1592	*The First Part of Henry the Sixth*, probably with Thomas Nashe and others
1592/94	*King Richard the Third*
1593	*Venus and Adonis* (poem)
1593–94	*The Rape of Lucrece* (poem)
1593–1608	*Sonnets* (154 poems, published 1609 with *A Lover's Complaint*, a poem of disputed authorship)
1592–94/ 1600–03	*Sir Thomas More* (a single scene for a play originally by Anthony Munday, with other revisions by Henry Chettle, Thomas Dekker, and Thomas Heywood)
1594	*The Comedy of Errors*
1595	*Love's Labour's Lost*

1595–97	*Love's Labour's Won* (a lost play, unless the original title for another comedy)
1595–96	*A Midsummer Night's Dream*
1595–96	*The Tragedy of Romeo and Juliet*
1595–96	*King Richard the Second*
1595–97	*The Life and Death of King John* (possibly earlier)
1596–97	*The Merchant of Venice*
1596–97	*The First Part of Henry the Fourth*
1597–98	*The Second Part of Henry the Fourth*
1598	*Much Ado About Nothing*
1598–99	*The Passionate Pilgrim* (20 poems, some not by Shakespeare)
1599	*The Life of Henry the Fifth*
1599	"To the Queen" (epilogue for a court performance)
1599	*As You Like It*
1599	*The Tragedy of Julius Caesar*
1600–01	*The Tragedy of Hamlet, Prince of Denmark* (perhaps revising an earlier version)
1600–01	*The Merry Wives of Windsor* (perhaps revising version of 1597–99)
1601	"Let the Bird of Loudest Lay" (poem, known since 1807 as "The Phoenix and Turtle" [turtledove])
1601	*Twelfth Night, or What You Will*
1601–02	*The Tragedy of Troilus and Cressida*
1604	*The Tragedy of Othello, the Moor of Venice*
1604	*Measure for Measure*
1605	*All's Well That Ends Well*
1605	*The Life of Timon of Athens*, with Thomas Middleton
1605–06	*The Tragedy of King Lear*
1605–08	? contribution to *The Four Plays in One* (lost, except for *A Yorkshire Tragedy*, mostly by Thomas Middleton)

1606	*The Tragedy of Macbeth* (surviving text has additional scenes by Thomas Middleton)
1606–07	*The Tragedy of Antony and Cleopatra*
1608	*The Tragedy of Coriolanus*
1608	*Pericles, Prince of Tyre*, with George Wilkins
1610	*The Tragedy of Cymbeline*
1611	*The Winter's Tale*
1611	*The Tempest*
1612–13	*Cardenio*, with John Fletcher (survives only in later adaptation called *Double Falsehood* by Lewis Theobald)
1613	*Henry VIII (All Is True)*, with John Fletcher
1613–14	*The Two Noble Kinsmen*, with John Fletcher

KINGS AND QUEENS OF ENGLAND: FROM THE HISTORY PLAYS TO SHAKESPEARE'S LIFETIME

	Life Span	*Reign*
Angevins:		
Henry II	1133–1189	1154–1189
Richard I	1157–1199	1189–1199
John	1166–1216	1199–1216
Henry III	1207–1272	1216–1272
Edward I	1239–1307	1272–1307
Edward II	1284–1327	1307–1327 deposed
Edward III	1312–1377	1327–1377
Richard II	1367–1400	1377–1399 deposed
Lancastrians:		
Henry IV	1367–1413	1399–1413
Henry V	1387–1422	1413–1422
Henry VI	1421–1471	1422–1461 and 1470–1471
Yorkists:		
Edward IV	1442–1483	1461–1470 and 1471–1483
Edward V	1470–1483	1483 not crowned: deposed and assassinated
Richard III	1452–1485	1483–1485
Tudors:		
Henry VII	1457–1509	1485–1509
Henry VIII	1491–1547	1509–1547
Edward VI	1537–1553	1547–1553

	Life Span	*Reign*
Jane	1537–1554	1553 not crowned: deposed and executed
Mary I	1516–1558	1553–1558
Philip of Spain	1527–1598	1554–1558 co-regent with Mary
Elizabeth I	1533–1603	1558–1603
Stuart:		
James I	1566–1625	1603–1625 James VI of Scotland (1567–1625)

KING JOHN FAMILY TREE

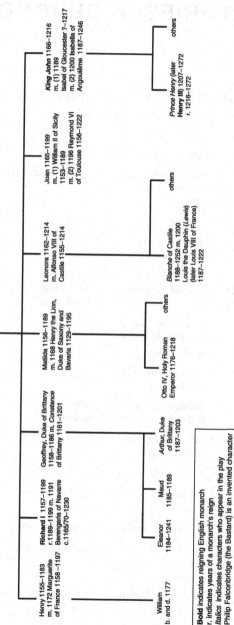

Henry II (1133–1189 r. 1154–1189) = m. Eleanor of Aquitaine (*Queen Elinor*) (1122–1204)

Bold indicates reigning English monarch
r. indicates years of a monarch's reign
Italics indicates characters who appear in the play
Philip Falconbridge (the Bastard) is an invented character

William
b. and d. 1177

Henry 1155–1183
m. 1172 Marguerite
of France 1158–1197

Richard I 1157–1199
r.1189–1199 m. 1191
Berengaria of Navarre
c.1165?70–1230

Eleanor
1184–1241

Maud
1185–1189

Geoffrey, Duke of Brittany
1158–1186 m. *Constance*
of Brittany 1161–1201

Arthur, Duke
of Brittany
1187–1203

Matilda 1156–1189
m. 1168 Henry the Lion,
Duke of Saxony and
Bavaria 1129–1195

Otto IV, Holy Roman
Emperor 1176–1218

others

Leonora 1162–1214
m. Alfonso VIII of
Castile 1155–1214

Blanche of Castile
1188–1252 m. 1200
Louis the Dauphin (*Lewis*)
(later Louis VIII of France)
1187–1222

others

Joan 1165–1199
m. (1) William II of Sicily
1153–1189
m. (2) 1196 Raymond VI
of Toulouse 1156–1222

King John 1166–1216
m. (1) 1189
Isabel of Gloucester ?–1217
m. (2) 1200 Isabella of
Angoulême 1187–1246

Prince Henry (later
Henry III) 1207–1272
r. 1216–1272

others

THE HISTORY BEHIND THE HISTORIES: A CHRONOLOGY

Square brackets indicate events that happen just outside a play's timescale but are mentioned in the play.

Date	Event	Location	Play
22 May 1200	Truce between King John and Philip Augustus	Le Goulet, Normandy	*King John*
Apr 1203	Death of Arthur	Rouen	*King John*
1209	Pope Innocent III excommunicates King John		*King John*
18/19 Oct 1216	Death of King John	Swineshead, Lincolnshire	*King John*
Apr–Sep 1398	Quarrel, duel, and exile of Bullingbrook and Mowbray	Coventry	*Richard II*
3 Feb 1399	Death of John of Gaunt	Leicester	*Richard II*
Jul 1399	Bullingbrook lands in England	Ravenspur, Yorkshire	*Richard II*
Aug 1399	Richard II captured by Bullingbrook	Wales	*Richard II*
30 Sep 1399	Richard II abdicates	London	*Richard II*
13 Oct 1399	Coronation of Henry IV	London	*Richard II*
Jan–Feb 1400	Death of Richard II	Pontefract Castle	*Richard II*
22 Jun 1402	Owen Glendower captures Edmund Mortimer	Bryn Glas, Wales	*1 Henry IV*
14 Sep 1402	Henry Percy defeats Scottish army	Homildon Hill, Yorkshire	*1 Henry IV*

Date	Event	Location	Play
21 Jul 1403	Battle of Shrewsbury; death of Henry Percy (Hotspur)	Battlefield, near Shrewsbury, Shropshire	*1 & 2 Henry IV*
Feb 1405	Tripartite Indenture between Owen Glendower, Edmund Mortimer, and Northumberland (Henry Percy)	Bangor	*1 Henry IV*
May–Jun 1405	Rebellion of Archbishop of York (Richard Scroop), Earl of Norfolk (Thomas Mowbray), and Lord Bardolph	Yorkshire	*2 Henry IV*
8 Jun 1405	Trial and execution of Archbishop of York and Earl of Norfolk	York	*2 Henry IV*
20 Mar 1413	Death of Henry IV	Westminster Abbey	*2 Henry IV*
9 Apr 1413	Coronation of Henry V	Westminster Abbey	*2 Henry IV*
c.1415–16?	Death of Owen Glendower	Wales?	*2 Henry IV*
Early Aug 1415	Execution of Earl of Cambridge, Lord Scroop, and Sir Thomas Grey	Southampton	*Henry V*
14 Aug–22 Sep 1415	Siege of Harfleur	Harfleur, Normandy	*Henry V*
25 Oct 1415	Battle of Agincourt	Agincourt, Pas de Calais	*Henry V*
31 Aug 1422	Death of Henry V	Bois de Vincennes, near Paris	*1 Henry VI*
18 Jan 1425	Death of Edmund Mortimer	Ireland	*1 Henry VI*
Oct 1428–May 1429	Siege of Orléans	Orléans	*1 Henry VI*
17 Oct 1428	Death of Lord Salisbury	Orléans	*1 Henry VI*

Date	Event	Location	Play
18 Jun 1429	Capture of Lord Talbot at battle of Patay	Patay, near Orléans	*1 Henry VI*
18 Jul 1429	Coronation of Charles VII	Rheims Cathedral	*1 Henry VI*
6 Nov 1429	Coronation of Henry VI as King of England	Westminster Abbey	[*1 Henry VI*]
23 May 1430	Capture of Joan of Arc	Compiègne, near Soissons	*1 Henry VI*
30 May 1431	Execution of Joan of Arc	Saint-Ouen, near Paris	*1 Henry VI*
16 Dec 1431	Coronation of Henry VI as King of France	Notre Dame Cathedral, Paris	*1 Henry VI*
14 Sep 1435	Death of Duke of Bedford	Rouen	*1 Henry VI*
Summer–Autumn 1441	Arrest and trial of Eleanor Cobham and accomplices	London	*2 Henry VI*
20 May 1442	Lord Talbot created Earl of Shrewsbury	Paris	*1 Henry VI*
23 Apr 1445	Marriage of Henry VI and Margaret of Anjou	Titchfield, Hampshire	*2 Henry VI*
23 Feb 1447	Death of Humphrey, Duke of Gloucester	Bury St. Edmunds	*2 Henry VI*
11 Apr 1447	Death of Cardinal Beaufort	Winchester	*2 Henry VI*
2 May 1450	Death of Earl of Suffolk	English Channel	*2 Henry VI*
Jun–Jul 1450	Rebellion of Jack Cade	Kent and London	*2 Henry VI*
Spring 1452	Richard, Duke of York, marches on London	London	*2 Henry VI*
17 Jul 1453	Death of Lord Talbot at battle of Cantillon	Cantillon, Gascony	*1 Henry VI*
22 May 1455	First battle of St. Albans	St. Albans, Hertfordshire	*2 Henry VI*

Date	Event	Location	Play
10 Jul 1460	Battle of Northampton	Northampton	[*3 Henry VI*]
Oct 1460	Richard, Duke of York, holds Parliament	London	*3 Henry VI*
30 Dec 1460	Battle of Wakefield	Wakefield, Yorkshire	*3 Henry VI*
2 Feb 1461	Battle of Mortimer's Cross	Near Wigmore, Herefordshire	*3 Henry VI*
29 Mar 1461	Battle of Towton	Near Tadcaster, Yorkshire	*3 Henry VI*
28 Jun 1461	Coronation of Edward IV	Westminster Abbey	*3 Henry VI*
1 May 1464	Marriage of Edward IV and Elizabeth Woodville	Northamptonshire	*3 Henry VI*
Jul 1465	Henry VI captured	Lancashire	*3 Henry VI*
26 Jul 1469	Battle of Edgecote Moor	Near Banbury, Oxfordshire	*3 Henry VI*
Oct 1470–Apr/May 1471	Readeption (restoration) of Henry VI	London	*3 Henry VI*
14 Apr 1471	Battle of Barnet; death of Warwick	Barnet, near London	*3 Henry VI*
4 May 1471	Battle of Tewkesbury; death of Edward, Prince of Wales	Tewkesbury, Gloucestershire	*3 Henry VI*
21 May 1471	Death of Henry VI	Tower of London	*3 Henry VI*
12 Jul 1472	Marriage of Richard, Duke of Gloucester, to Anne	Westminster Abbey	*Richard III*
18 Feb 1478	Death of Duke of Clarence	Tower of London	*Richard III*
9 Apr 1483	Death of Edward IV	Westminster	*Richard III*
Jun 1483	Death of Lord Hastings	Tower of London	*Richard III*

Date	Event	Location	Play
6 Jul 1483	Coronation of Richard III	Westminster Abbey	*Richard III*
2 Nov 1483	Death of Duke of Buckingham	Salisbury	*Richard III*
16 Mar 1485	Death of Queen Anne	Westminster	*Richard III*
22 Aug 1485	Battle of Bosworth Field	Leicestershire	*Richard III*
30 Oct 1485	Coronation of Henry VII	Westminster Abbey	[*Richard III*]
18 Jan 1486	Marriage of Henry VII and Elizabeth of York	Westminster Abbey	[*Richard III*]
Jun 1520	Meeting of Henry VIII and Francis I	"Field of the Cloth of Gold," near Calais, France	[*Henry VIII*]
17 May 1521	Death of Duke of Buckingham	Tower Hill, London	*Henry VIII*
29 Nov 1530	Death of Wolsey	Leicester	*Henry VIII*
25 Jan 1533	Marriage of Henry VIII and Anne Bullen (Boleyn)	Whitehall	*Henry VIII*
1 Jun 1533	Coronation of Anne Bullen (Boleyn)	Westminster Abbey	*Henry VIII*
7 Sep 1533	Birth of Princess Elizabeth	Greenwich Palace	*Henry VIII*
10 Sep 1533	Christening of Princess Elizabeth	Greenwich Palace	*Henry VIII*

FURTHER READING
AND VIEWING

KING JOHN

Critical Approaches

Campbell, Lily B., *Shakespeare's "Histories": Mirrors of Elizabethan Policy* (1947). Still relevant examination of the plays in their historical context: chapter XII, "The Troublesome Reign of King John," offers interesting parallels with Henry VIII and Elizabeth I.

Candido, Joseph, ed., *Shakespeare: The Critical Tradition: King John* (1996). Valuable collection of early critical essays and performance reviews from 1790 to 1919.

Chernaik, Warren, *The Cambridge Introduction to Shakespeare's History Plays* (2007). Contains short, useful overviews: chapter 5, "Gain, Be My Lord: *King John*" (pp. 70–90).

Curren-Aquino, Deborah T., ed., *King John: New Perspectives* (1989). Thoughtful, varied collection of twentieth-century critical essays.

Howard, Jean E., and Phyllis Rackin, *Engendering a Nation: A Feminist Account of Shakespeare's English Histories* (1997). Introductory chapters focus on gender as an issue in Shakespeare's history plays: chapter 9, on *King John*, explores the centrality of women, maternity, and the "ideological faultlines" that the play explores (pp. 119–36); reprinted in *Shakespeare's Histories*, ed. Emma Smith (2004), pp. 182–95.

Jones, Robert C., *These Valiant Dead: Renewing the Past in Shakespeare's Histories* (1991). Examines Shakespeare's understanding of history as expressed by characters within the plays; chapter 4 on *King John*, "'Perfect Richard' versus 'This Old World,'" considers the role of the Bastard as a central character and critical commentator.

Piesse, A. J., "King John: Changing Perspective," in *The Cambridge Companion to Shakespeare's History Plays*, ed. M. Hattaway (2002).

Examines the textual relationship between Shakespeare's play, the anonymous *The Troublesome Reign of King John of England*, and John Bale's *King Johan*, considering the relationship between the legitimacy of the historical play text and the illegitimate character of the Bastard.

Shirley, Frances A., ed., *King John and Henry VIII: Critical Essays* (1988). Comprehensive selection of important critical essays that examine all aspects of the plays from language, structure, and historical context to performance—*King John* (pp. 3–205).

THE PLAY IN PERFORMANCE

Hodgdon, Barbara, *The End Crowns All: Closure and Contradiction in Shakespeare's History* (1991). Focuses on the plays' endings, moving between textual meanings and theatrical representation in significant C20 productions; chapter 2, "Fashioning Obedience: King John's 'True Inheritors,' " examines *King John* (pp. 22–43).

Jackson, Russell, and Robert Smallwood, eds., *Players of Shakespeare 3* (1993). Actors give details of their roles and performances; Nicholas Woodeson talks about his performance as *King John* in Deborah Warner's 1988 production (pp. 87–98).

Shattuck, Charles A., *William Charles Macready's King John* (1962). Includes details of performance, illustrations, and a facsimile promptbook of this famous, historical production.

Smallwood, Robert, ed., *Players of Shakespeare 6* (2004). Guy Henry, Kelly Hunter, and Jo Stone-Fewings discuss playing Henry, Constance, and the Bastard, respectively, in Gregory Doran's 2002 production (pp. 22–36, 37–49, 50–67).

Tardiff, Joseph C., ed., *Shakespearean Criticism* 24 (1994). Good stage history overview with reviews and retrospective accounts of selected productions.

AVAILABLE ON DVD

King John directed by William Kennedy, Laurie Dickson, and Walter Fieffer Dando (1899). A three-minute silent short of Herbert Beerbohm Tree's historic production was made: available on YouTube.

King John directed by David Giles for the BBC Shakespeare Series (1984, DVD 2004). Highly praised production with Leonard Rossiter, John Thaw, and Claire Bloom.

HENRY VIII

Critical Approaches

Baillie, William M., "*Henry VIII:* A Jacobean History," in *Shakespeare Studies* 12 (1979), pp. 247–66. Detailed analysis, setting the play within its historical context.

Berry, Edward I., "Henry VIII and the Dynamics of Spectacle," *Shakespeare Studies* 12 (1979), pp. 229–46. Persuasive essay that argues for the play's value as a blend of history, tragedy, masque, and romance.

Chernaik, Warren, *The Cambridge Introduction to Shakespeare's History Plays* (2007). Chapter 9 on *Henry VIII* offers a short introductory overview with some references to the play in performance (pp. 168–78).

Dean, Paul, "Dramatic Mode and Historical Vision in *Henry VIII*," in *Shakespeare Quarterly* 37(2) (Summer 1986), pp. 175–89. Examines the play's romance structure in relation to its chronicle sources.

Glimp, David, "Staging Government: Shakespeare's Life of *King Henry the Eighth* and the Government of Generations," in *Criticism* 41(1) (Winter 1999), pp. 41–69. Discusses problematics of the interaction between political authority and anxieties regarding theatrical representation in the Elizabethan/Jacobean period.

Hattaway, Michael, ed., *Cambridge Companion to Shakespeare's History Plays* (2002). Excellent introduction and overview to subject; there's no specific chapter on *Henry VIII*, but there are numerous references in passing, especially in chapter 3 by David M. Bergeron, "Pageants, Masques and History" (pp. 41–56), and chapter 13 by R. A. Foakes, "Shakespeare's Other Historical Plays" (pp. 214–28), discusses *Henry VIII* (pp. 223–28).

Kamps, Ivo, "Possible Pasts: Historiography and Legitimation in *Henry VIII*" in *College English*, Vol. 58, No. 2, Feb. 1996, pp.

192–215. Sees the play as a Jacobean response to developments in sixteenth- and seventeenth-century historiographical discourses, marking a break with Tudor thinking about history and a unique Jacobean response.

Magnusson, A. Lynne, "The Rhetoric of Politeness and Henry VIII" in *Shakespeare Quarterly*, Vol. 43, No. 4, Winter 1992, pp. 391–409. A detailed linguistic analysis, focusing on class and gender.

Noll, Mark A., "The Reformation and Shakespeare: Focus on *Henry VIII*" in *Shakespeare and the Christian Tradition*, ed. Beatrice Batson (1994). Sees Shakespeare's play as an exploration of the English Reformation and ally of historians in their search for its "human meaning."

Ornstein, Robert, *A Kingdom for a Stage* (1972). Discusses *Henry VIII* in terms of the play's opacity and ambiguity, calling it an "extended double-entendre," and arguing that Shakespeare found it easier to adapt to Fletcher's "courtly manner" than Fletcher to "imitate his way with history," pp. 203–220.

Shirley, Frances A., ed., *King John and Henry VIII: Critical Essays* (1988). Comprehensive selection of important critical essays that examine all aspects of the plays from language, structure, and historical context to performance—*Henry VIII*, pp. 209–378.

Wilson Knight, G. "Henry VIII and the Poetry of Conversion" in *The Crown of Life: Essays in Interpretation of Shakespeare's Final Plays*, pp. 256–336. Influential, now classic essay, which argues Shakespeare's final plays are centrally concerned with the nature of art.

THE PLAY IN PERFORMANCE

Richmond, Hugh, *Shakespeare in Performance: Henry VIII* (1994). Wide-ranging, detailed stage history overview with chapters on performance issues and important productions up to 1983.

Shrimpton, Nicholas, "Shakespeare Performances in Stratford-upon-Avon and London, 1982–3," *Shakespeare Survey* 37, 1984, pp. 163–73. Includes perceptive, detailed account of Howard Davies's 1983 RSC production of *Henry VIII*.

Smallwood, Robert, ed., *Players of Shakespeare 4* (1998). Features actors discussing their roles and performances in detail; Paul Jesson talks about playing Henry in Gregory Doran's 1996 production (pp. 114–31), and Jane Lapotaire talks about playing Katherine in the same production (pp. 132–51).

AVAILABLE ON DVD

The Famous History of the Life of King Henry the Eighth directed by Kevin Billington for the BBC Television Shakespeare Series (1979, DVD 2005). Excellent, televisually sophisticated version with John Stride, Claire Bloom, and Ronald Pickup: one of the best in this series.

REFERENCES: *KING JOHN* AND *HENRY VIII*

KING JOHN

1. Francis Meres, *Palladis Tamia. Wits Treasury* (1598).
2. Anthony Munday, *Death of Robert, Earl of Huntingdon* (1601), ed. John C. Meagher (1965).
3. Emmett L. Avery, "Cibber, King John, and the Students of the Law," *Modern Language Notes* 53, 1938, pp. 272–75.
4. Stanley Wells, ed., *Nineteenth-Century Shakespeare Burlesques* (1977).
5. Thomas Davies, *Memoirs of the Life of David Garrick* (1784).
6. Francis Gentleman, *The Dramatic Censor* (1770).
7. Davies, *Memoirs of the Life of David Garrick* I, pp. 55–56.
8. Thomas Campbell, *Life of Mrs Siddons* (1834), pp. 112–14.
9. *The Times* (London), 25 October 1842.
10. Hazlitt, *London Magazine*, 1820; quoted in Jonathan Bate, "The Romantic Stage," in Jonathan Bate and Russell Jackson, eds., *Shakespeare: An Illustrated Stage History* (1996).
11. Bate, "The Romantic Stage."
12. Henry N. Coleridge, ed., *Specimens of the Table Talk of Samuel Taylor Coleridge* (1836). Extract reprinted in Jonathan Bate, ed., *The Romantics on Shakespeare* (1992), p. 160.
13. Alan S. Downer, *The Eminent Tragedian William Charles Macready* (1966), p. 69.
14. Downer, *The Eminent Tragedian William Charles Macready*, p. 80.
15. A. B. Walkley, "Review of *King John*," *The Speaker*, 30 September 1899. Reprinted in H. H. Furness, ed., *The New Variorum Edition of King John* (1919), p. 689.
16. See Campbell's biography of Mrs. Siddons (Campbell, *Life of Mrs Siddons*, particularly pp. 117–18).
17. *Daily Telegraph*, 17 April 1957.
18. Geraldine Cousin, *King John* (Shakespeare in Performance Series) (1994).
19. *The Times* (London), 4 May 1989.
20. Charles Spencer, "Second-Rate Shakespeare," *Daily Telegraph*, 9 March 2001.

21. Kate Bassett, "Three Rattling Nights Out With a Loutish King, One Trollop and a Paedophile," *Independent on Sunday*, 11 March 2001.

22. *Stratford-upon-Avon Herald*, 19 April 1957.

23. Bate, "The Romantic Stage," p. 107.

24. Michael R. Booth, *Victorian Spectacular Theatre, 1850–1910* (1981); Martin Meisel, *Realizations: Narrative, Pictorial, and Theatrical Arts in Nineteenth-Century England* (1983).

25. Meisel, *Realizations*, p. 38.

26. James Robinson Planché, *The Recollections and Reflections of J.R. Planché (Somerset Herald): A Professional Autobiography* (1872), pp. 56–57.

27. Charles H. Shattuck, *William Charles Macready's King John* (1962).

28. Ibid.

29. Ibid.

30. All of these features of Tree's production may be gleaned from a contemporary review by Max Beerbohm, Tree's half-brother: Max Beerbohm, "Review of King John," *Saturday Review*, 30 September 1899, reprinted in Max Beerbohm, *More Theatres, 1898–1903* (1969), pp. 191–93.

31. Antony Davies, "From the Old Vic to Gielgud and Olivier," in Bate and Jackson, *Shakespeare: An Illustrated Stage History*, pp. 139–59.

32. Clause 39 states that "no free man shall be . . . imprisoned or dispossessed . . . except by the lawful judgement of his peers or by the law of the land."

33. John Palmer, *Political Characters of Shakespeare* (1945), p. 322.

34. Malcolm A. Nelson, *The Robin Hood Tradition in the English Renaissance* (1973).

35. F. J. Child, ed., *English and Scottish Popular Ballads*, five vols. (1882–98) (reprinted 1965); R. B. Dobson and J. Taylor, eds., *Rymes of Robin Hode: An Introduction to the English Outlaw* (1976).

36. See for example Kenneth McClellan, *Whatever Happened to Shakespeare?* (1978); Cousin, *King John*.

37. See for example Jonathan Bate, *Shakespearean Constitutions: Politics, Theatre, Criticism* (1989); A. R. Braunmuller, ed., *The Oxford Shakespeare Edition of King John* (1989).

38. *Spectator*, 12 June 1970.

39. *New Statesman*, 19 June 1970; quoted in Cousin, *King John*, p. 63.

40. Peter Thomson, "A Necessary Theatre: The Royal Shakespeare Season 1970 Reviewed," *Shakespeare Survey* 24, 1971, pp. 117–26.

41. *Observer*, 24 March 1974.

42. R. L. Smallwood, "Shakespeare Unbalanced: The Royal Shakespeare Company's *King John*, 1974–75," *Deutsche Shakespeare-Gesellschaft West Jahrbuch*, 1976, pp. 79–99.

43. Peter Thomson, "The Smallest Season: The Royal Shakespeare Company at Stratford in 1974," *Shakespeare Survey* 28, 1975, pp. 137–48.

44. Cousin, *King John*, p. 101.

45. *Daily Telegraph*, 30 May 1988.

46. *Observer*, 15 May 1988.

47. Cousin, *King John*, p. 116.

48. *The Times*, 4 May 1989.

49. *Daily Telegraph*, 30 May 1988.

50. *Independent*, 12 May 1988.

51. *Financial Times*, 12 May 1988.

52. Ibid.

53. Michael Billington, "Bold Return for Shakespeare's Orphan," *Guardian*, 8 March 2001.

54. Charles Spencer "Laying Bare the Dark Heart of the Political Process," *Daily Telegraph*, 30 March 2001.

55. Billington, "Bold Return for Shakespeare's Orphan."

56. Adrien Bonjour, "The Road to Swinstead Abbey: A Study of the Sense and Structure of King John," *ELH*, Vol. 18, No. 4, December 1951, pp. 253–74.

57. *The Times* (London), 25 October 1842; quoted in Shattuck, *William Charles Macready's King John*, p. 49.

58. Kate Bassett, "Ullo John, Got a Zippy Satirical and Welcome New Staging?" *Independent on Sunday*, 1 April 2001.

59. John Peter, *Sunday Times* (London), 1 April 2001.

60. Michael Billington, "A Kingly Klutz in Stratford," *Guardian*, 30 March 2001.

61. *Independent*, 8 August 2006.

62. *Independent*, 8 August 2006.

63. *Daily Telegraph*, 7 August 2006.

HENRY VIII

64. Sir Henry Wotton, letter dated 2 July 1613, in Logan Pearsall Smith, ed., *The Life and Letters of Sir Henry Wotton* (1970); also available at: www.globe-theatre.org.uk/globe-theatre-fire.htm.

65. John Downes, *Roscius Anglicanus* (1708).

66. William Winter, "*King Henry VIII*—Historical Comment," in *Shakespeare on the Stage* (1911), pp. 516–64.

67. *The Times* (London), 21 October 1811.

68. Ibid.

69. Ibid.

70. Percy Fitzgerald, "Kemble Manager," *The Kembles*, Vol. I (1871), pp. 276–97.

71. Lewis Carroll, diary entry for 22 June 1855, *The Diaries of Lewis Carroll*, Vol. I, ed. Roger Lancelyn Green (1953), pp. 53–54.

72. C. B. Young, "The Stage History of 'Henry VIII,'" in *Henry the Eighth* (1962), pp. xxxviii–l.

73. Carroll, *The Diaries of Lewis Carroll*, Vol. I.

74. Young, "The Stage History of 'Henry VIII.'"

75. Ibid.

76. George C. D. Odell, "Scenery and Stage Decoration: Irving's 'Henry VIII' 1892," *Shakespeare: From Betterton to Irving* (1920, reprinted 1963), pp. 444–46.

77. John Rankin Towse, "Henry Irving and Ellen Terry," *Sixty Years of the Theatre: An Old Critic's Memories* (1916), pp. 286–317.

78. Ibid.

79. Herbert Beerbohm Tree, *Henry VIII and His Court* (1910).

80. J. C. Trewin, "End of an Era: 1906–1913," *Shakespeare on the English Stage, 1900–1964: A Survey of Productions* (1964), pp. 38–50.

81. *Sporting Life*, 26 January 1911.

82. Winter, "*King Henry VIII*—Historical Comment."

83. Margaret Webster, *Don't Put Your Daughter on the Stage* (1972).

84. "International News," *Shakespeare Survey* 1, 1948, pp. 112–17.

85. George Jean Nathan, *The Theatre Book of the Year, 1946 & 1947*, pp. 156–58.

86. "International News," *Shakespeare Survey* 1, 1948.

87. Linda McJ. Micheli, "Margaret Webster's 'Henry VIII': The Survival of 'Scenic Shakespeare' in America," *Theatre Research International*, Vol. II, No. 3, Autumn 1986, pp. 213–22.

88. Ibid.

89. Ibid.

90. Muriel St. Clare Byrne, *Shakespeare Survey* 3, 1950, pp. 120–29.

91. Ibid.

92. Alice Venezky, "The 1950 Season at Stratford-upon-Avon—A Memorable Achievement in Stage History," *Shakespeare Quarterly* II, 1951, pp. 73–77.

93. Ibid.

94. Muriel St. Clare Byrne, *Shakespeare Survey* 3.

95. Robert Herring, *Life and Letters and The London Mercury*, Vol. 62, July–September 1949, pp. 217–18.

96. Audrey Williamson, "Coronation Fanfare," *Contemporary Theatre: 1953–1956* (1956), pp. 1–21.

97. Hugh M. Richmond, *Shakespeare in Performance: King Henry VIII* (1994), p. 111.

98. Richmond, *King Henry VIII*, p. 109.

99. Richmond, *King Henry VIII*, p. 119.

100. Richmond, *King Henry VIII*, p. 109.

101. Herbert S. Weil Jr, *Shakespeare Quarterly* 38, Summer 1987, p. 238.

102. Benedict Nightingale, *The Times* (London), 24 May 1991.

103. Greg Evans, *Variety*, Vol. 367, No. 9, 30 June 1997, p. 72.

104. Evans, *Variety*.

105. Ben Brantley, *New York Times*, 27 June 1997, p. C3.

106. Brantley, *New York Times*, 27 June 1997.

107. James Rampton, *Independent*, 8 October 2003.

108. Rob Reid, *Record*, 24 August 2004, p. B4.

109. Reid, *Record*, 24 August 2004.

110. Paul Taylor, *Independent*, 30 August 2006.

111. Liisa Spink, *Cahiers Elisabéthain*, Complete Works Festival Special Issue (2007), p. 51.

112. Spink, *Cahiers Elisabéthain*, Complete Works Festival Special Issue.

113. Michael Billington, *Guardian*, 26 August 2006.

114. Ibid.

115. Charles Spencer, *Daily Telegraph*, 26 August 2006.

116. *Morning Star*, 30 August 2006.

117. Taylor, *Independent*, 30 August 2006.

118. Billington, *Guardian*, 26 August 2006.

119. Paul Taylor, *Independent*, 27 May 2010.

120. Ibid.

121. Charles Spencer, *Telegraph*, 25 May 2010.

122. Taylor, *Independent*, 27 May 2010.

123. Spencer, *Telegraph*, 25 May 2010.

124. Taylor, *Independent*, 27 May 2010.

125. Hilary Spurling, *Spectator*, 18 October 1969.

126. Misha Glenny, *Tribune*, 8 July 1983.

127. Nicholas de Jongh, *Evening Standard*, 27 November 1996.

128. Richmond, *Shakespeare in Performance: Henry VIII*, p. 16.

129. Trevor Nunn, *Henry VIII* RSC programme notes, 1969.

130. *Daily Telegraph*, 10 October 1969.

131. B. A. Young, *Financial Times*, 10 October 1969.

132. Irving Wardle, *The Times* (London), 11 October 1969.

133. Ibid.

134. Ibid.

135. Young, *Financial Times*, 10 October 1969.

136. Harold Hobson, *Sunday Times* (London), 12 October 1969.

137. Spurling, *Spectator*, 18 October 1969.

138. Ronald Bryden, *Observer*, 12 October 1969.

139. D.A.N. Jones, *The Listener*, 16 October 1969.

140. Richmond, *Shakespeare in Performance: King Henry VIII* , p. 17.

141. Irving Wardle, *The Times* (London), 16 June 1983.

142. Ibid.

143. James Fenton, *Sunday Times* (London), 19 June 1983.

144. Gregory Doran, RSC programme notes, 1996.

145. Michael Billington, *Guardian*, 28 November 1996.

146. Shaun Usher, *Daily Mail*, 29 November 1996.

147. Billington, *Guardian*, 28 November 1996.

148. Richmond, *Shakespeare in Performance: King Henry VIII*, p. 145.

149. Giles Gordon, *Spectator*, 22 November 1983.

150. Donald Sinden, *Laughter in the Second Act* (1985), p. 267.

151. Paul Lapworth, *Stratford Herald*, 28 November 1996.

152. Philip Brockbank, *Times Literary Supplement*, 24 June 1983.

153. Brockbank, *Times Literary Supplement*, 24 June 1983.

154. John Barber, *Daily Telegraph*, 10 October 1969.

155. Wotton, letter dated 2 July 1613.

156. Richmond, *Shakespeare in Performance: King Henry VIII*, p. 3.

157. Margot Heinemann, *Cambridge Companion to English Renaissance Drama*, ed. A. R. Braunmuller and Michael Hattaway (1990), p. 179.

158. Richmond, *Shakespeare in Performance: King Henry VIII*, p. 24.

159. Sinden, *Laughter in the Second Act*, pp. 199–200.

160. Ibid.

161. Richmond, *Shakespeare in Performance: King Henry VIII*, p. 25.

162. K.E.B., *Nottingham Evening Post*, 10 October 1969.

163. Sinden, *Laughter in the Second Act*, p. 267.

164. Richard Griffiths, in an interview for the *Guardian*, 14 June 1983.

165. Ned Chaillot, *Wall Street Journal*, 1 July 1983.

166. J. C. Trewin, *The Lady*, 30 June 1983.

167. Sheridan Morley, *Punch*, 22 June 1983.

168. Benedict Nightingale, *The Times* (London), 28 November 1996.
169. Shaun Usher, *Daily Mail*, 29 November 1996.
170. Keith Brace, *Birmingham Post*, 10 October 1969.
171. John Barber, *Daily Telegraph*, 10 October 1969.
172. Brace, *Birmingham Post*, 10 October 1969.
173. Nightingale, *The Times*, 28 November 1996.
174. Paul Lapworth, *Stratford Herald*, 28 November 1996.
175. Gordon Parsons, *Morning Star*, 11 October 1969.
176. Charles Landstone, *Jewish Chronicle*, 16 October 1969.
177. Betty Smith, *Stratford Herald*, 24 June 1983.
178. Ned Chaillot, *Wall Street Journal*, 1 July 1983.
179. Ian Hogg, in an interview with Terry Grierley for the *Birmingham Post*, 26 November 1996.
180. Billington, *Guardian*, 28 November 1996.
181. Naomi Koppel, *Evening Standard*, 29 November 1996.
182. Philip Hope-Wallace, *Arts Guardian*, 10 October 1969.
183. Parsons, *Morning Star*, 11 October 1969.
184. Young, *Financial Times*, 10 October 1969.
185. Alastair Macaulay, *Financial Times*, 28 November 1996.
186. Macaulay, *Financial Times*, 28 November 1996.
187. Judith H. Anderson, *Biographical Truth: The Representation of Historical Persons in Tudor-Stuart Writing* (1984), p. 13.

ACKNOWLEDGMENTS
AND PICTURE CREDITS

Preparation of "*King John* in Performance" and "*Henry VIII* in Performance" was assisted by a generous grant from the CAPITAL Centre (Creativity and Performance in Teaching and Learning) of the University of Warwick for research in the RSC archive at the Shakespeare Birthplace Trust.

Thanks as always to our indefatigable and eagle-eyed copy editor, Tracey Dando, and to Ray Addicott for overseeing the production process with rigor and calmness.

Picture research by Michelle Morton. Grateful acknowledgment is made to the Shakespeare Birthplace Trust for assistance with picture research (special thanks to Helen Hargest) and reproduction fees.

Images of RSC productions are supplied by the Shakespeare Centre Library and Archive, Stratford-upon-Avon. This Library, maintained by the Shakespeare Birthplace Trust, holds the most important collection of Shakespeare material in the UK, including the Royal Shakespeare Company's official archive. It is open to the public free of charge.

For more information see www.shakespeare.org.uk.

1. Directed by Douglas Seale (1957). Tom Holte © Shakespeare Birthplace Trust
2. Directed by Herbert Beerbohm Tree (1899). Reproduced by permission of the Shakespeare Birthplace Trust
3. Directed by Buzz Goodbody (1970). Joe Cocks Studio Collection © Shakespeare Birthplace Trust
4. Directed by Deborah Warner (1988). Joe Cocks Studio Collection © Shakespeare Birthplace Trust

5. Directed by Josie Rourke (2006). Stewart Hemley © Royal Shakespeare Company
6. Directed by Gregory Doran (2001). Malcolm Davies © Shakespeare Birthplace Trust
7. Directed by Herbert Beerbohm Tree (1910). Reproduced by permission of the Shakespeare Birthplace Trust
8. Directed by Trevor Nunn (1969). Tom Holte © Shakespeare Birthplace Trust
9. Directed by Howard Davies (1983). Joe Cocks Studio Collection © Shakespeare Birthplace Trust
10. Directed by Gregory Doran (1996). Malcolm Davies © Shakespeare Birthplace Trust
11. Directed by Gregory Thompson (2006). Ellie Kurttz © Royal Shakespeare Company
12. Reconstructed Elizabethan Playhouse © Charcoalblue

MODERN LIBRARY IS ONLINE AT
WWW.MODERNLIBRARY.COM

MODERN LIBRARY ONLINE IS YOUR GUIDE TO CLASSIC LITERATURE ON THE WEB

THE MODERN LIBRARY E-NEWSLETTER

Our free e-mail newsletter is sent to subscribers, and features sample chapters, interviews with and essays by our authors, upcoming books, special promotions, announcements, and news. To subscribe to the Modern Library e-newsletter, visit **www.modernlibrary.com**.

THE MODERN LIBRARY WEBSITE

Check out the Modern Library website at
www.modernlibrary.com for:

- The Modern Library e-newsletter
- A list of our current and upcoming titles and series
- Reading Group Guides and exclusive author spotlights
- Special features with information on the classics and
  other paperback series
- Excerpts from new releases and other titles
- A list of our e-books and information on where to buy them
- The Modern Library Editorial Board's 100 Best Novels and
  100 Best Nonfiction Books of the Twentieth Century written in
  the English language
- News and announcements

Questions? E-mail us at **modernlibrary@randomhouse.com**.
For questions about examination or desk copies, please visit
the Random House Academic Resources site at
www.randomhouse.com/academic.

Printed in the United States
by Baker & Taylor Publisher Services